A Devil and Her Love Song

Story & Art by
Miyoshi Tomori

Volume 6

A Devil and Her Love Song

Volume 6
CONTENTS

Song 34................5

Song 35................31

Song 36................57

Song 37................85

Song 38................110

Song 39................145

Song 40................171

The devil makes me LOVELY!!!

STORY THUS FAR

After the choral competition, Maria finds herself surrounded by new friends, but that's not the only change in her life. Not only has she started falling for Shin, but she's also reconnected with Anna Mouri, her only friend from St. Katria!

Anna has been visiting Maria and her friends at Totsuka High every day, but now she's told Maria that she's in love with Shin too...and worse, that being with Maria was a painful experience for her...

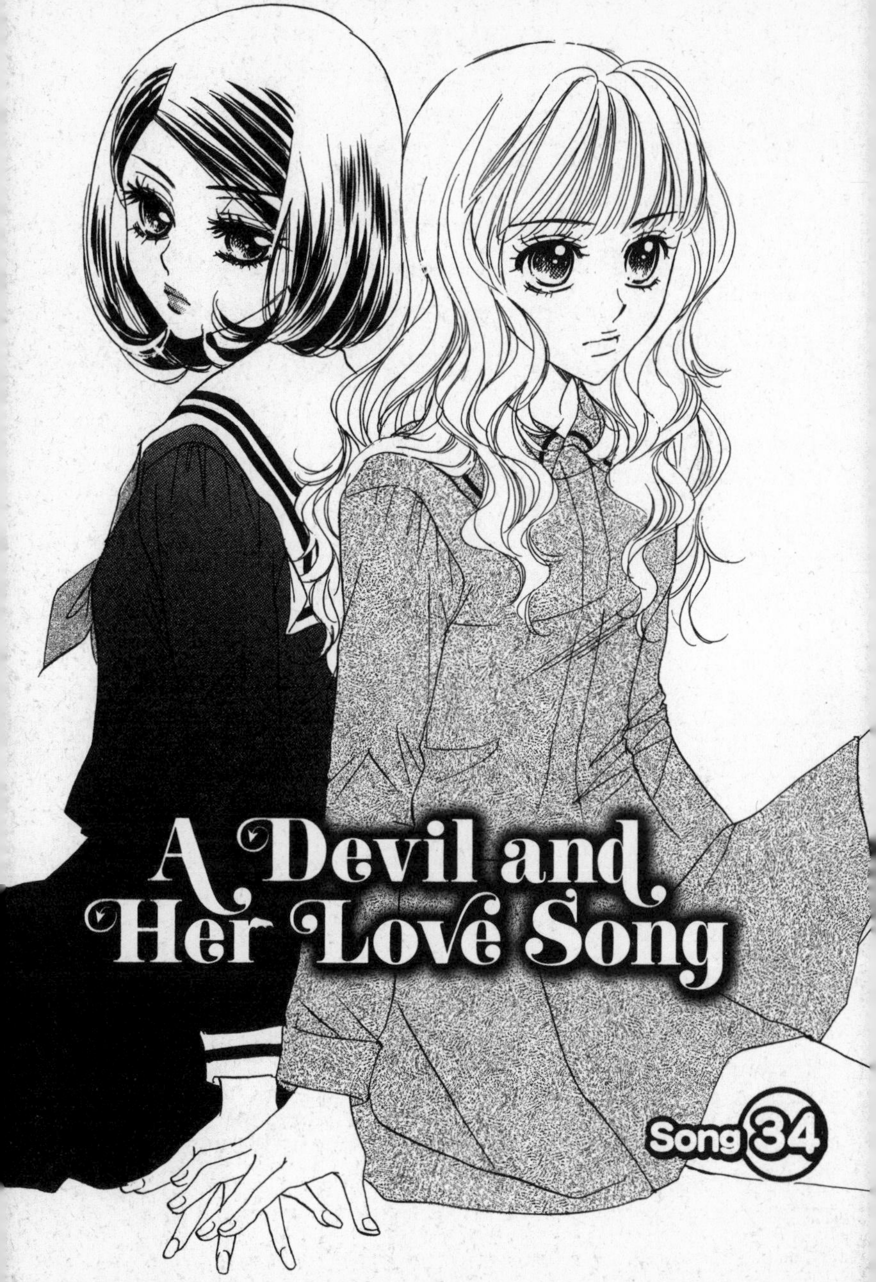
A Devil and Her Love Song
Song 34

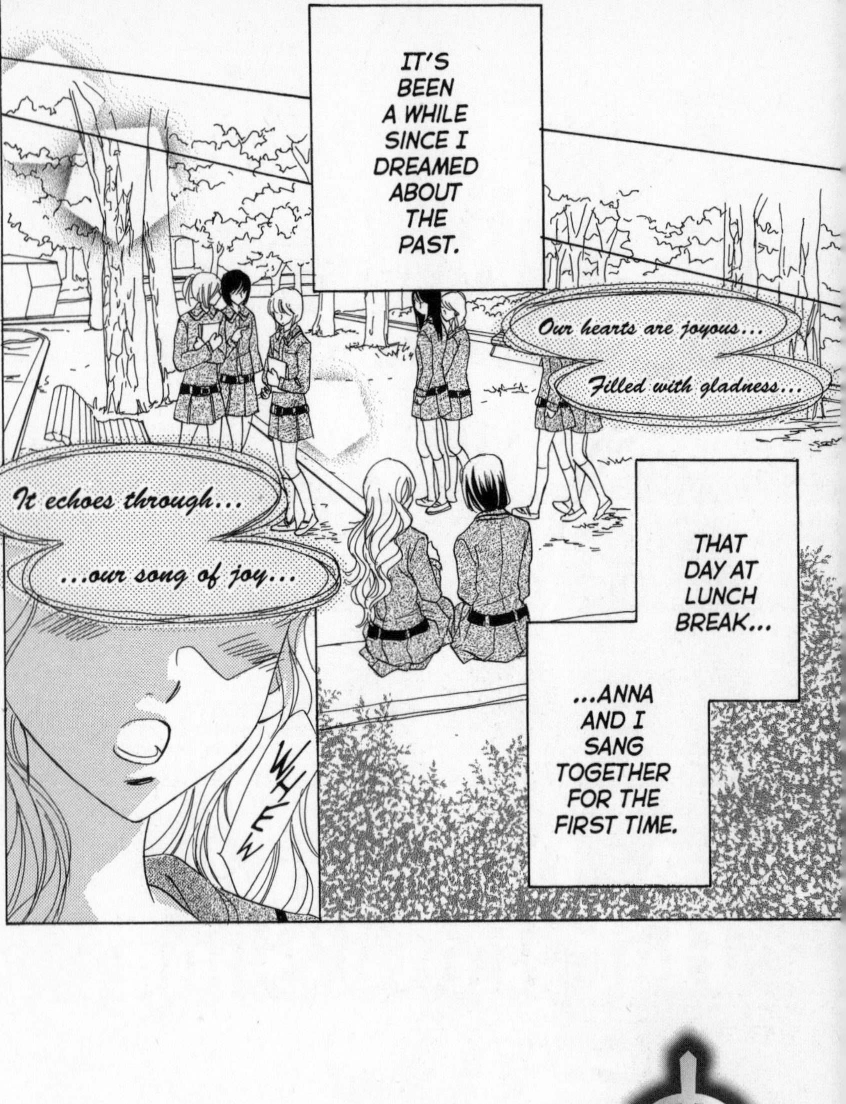
IT'S BEEN A WHILE SINCE I DREAMED ABOUT THE PAST.
Our hearts are joyous...
Filled with gladness...
It echoes through...
...our song of joy...
THAT DAY AT LUNCH BREAK...
...ANNA AND I SANG TOGETHER FOR THE FIRST TIME.
WHEW

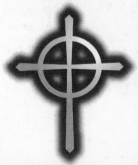

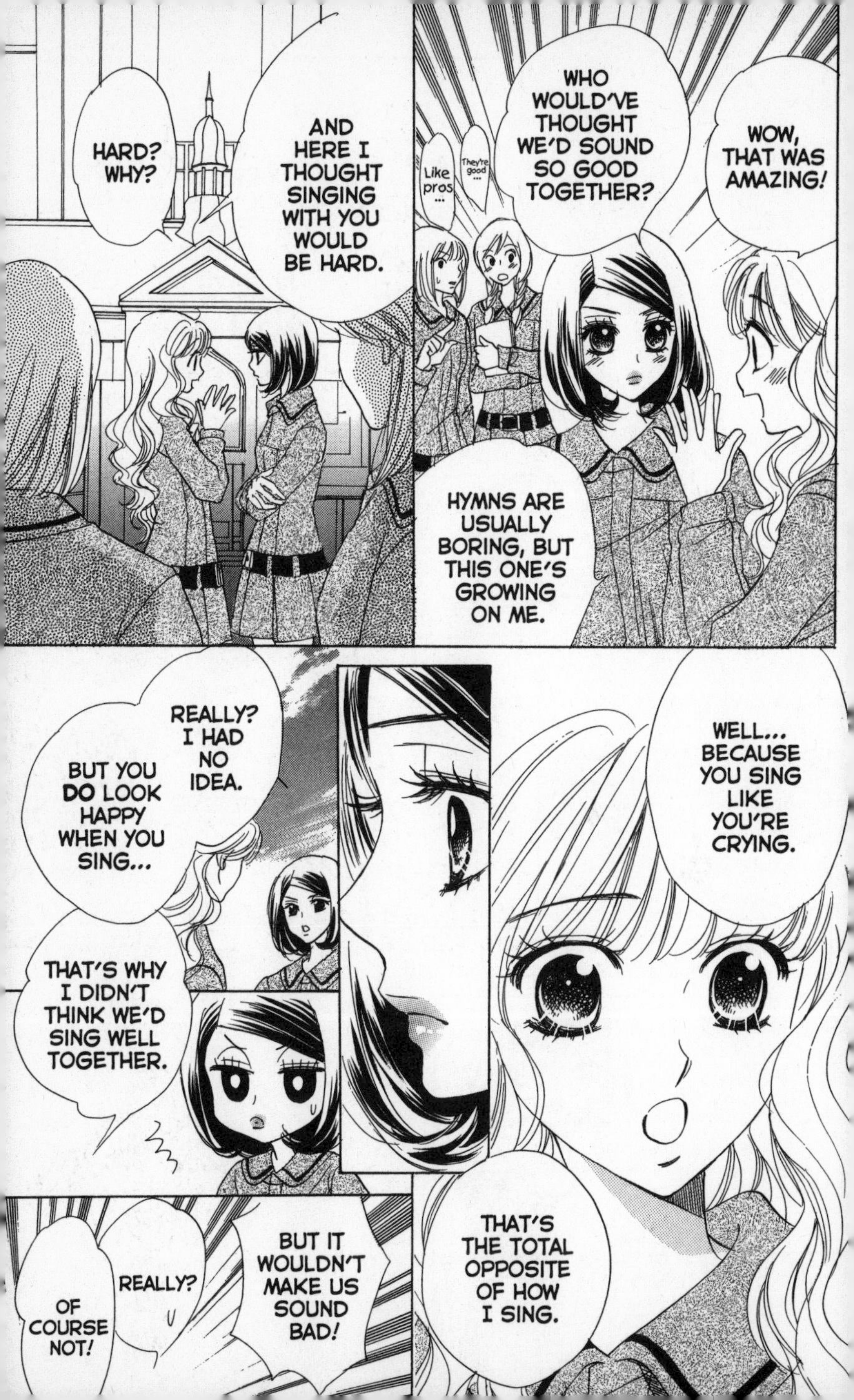
WOW, THAT WAS AMAZING!
WHO WOULD'VE THOUGHT WE'D SOUND SO GOOD TOGETHER?
They're good...
Like pros...
HYMNS ARE USUALLY BORING, BUT THIS ONE'S GROWING ON ME.
AND HERE I THOUGHT SINGING WITH YOU WOULD BE HARD.
HARD? WHY?
WELL... BECAUSE YOU SING LIKE YOU'RE CRYING.
THAT'S THE TOTAL OPPOSITE OF HOW I SING.
REALLY? I HAD NO IDEA.
BUT YOU DO LOOK HAPPY WHEN YOU SING...
THAT'S WHY I DIDN'T THINK WE'D SING WELL TOGETHER.
BUT IT WOULDN'T MAKE US SOUND BAD!
REALLY?
OF COURSE NOT!

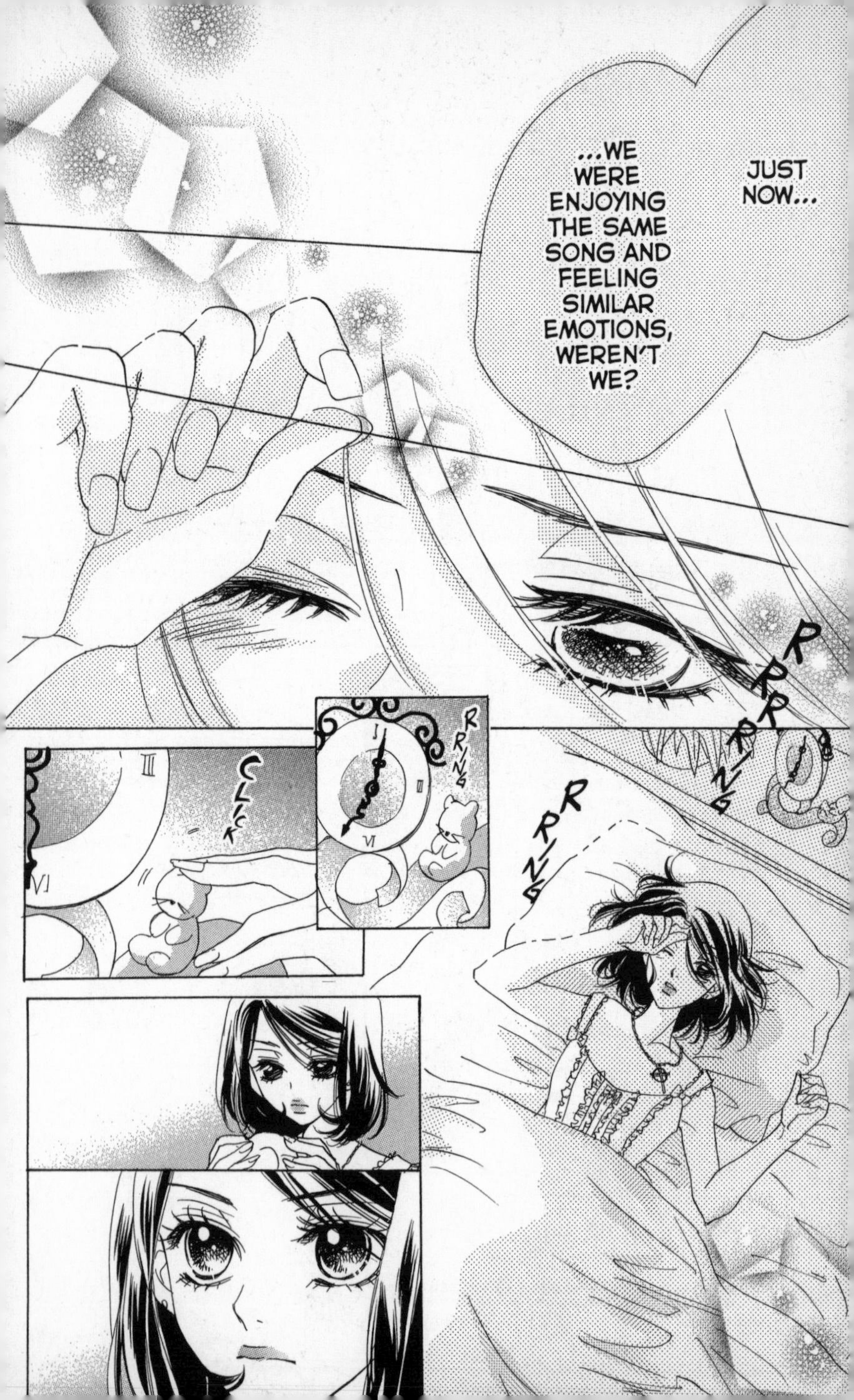
JUST NOW...
...WE WERE ENJOYING THE SAME SONG AND FEELING SIMILAR EMOTIONS, WEREN'T WE?
RRRRING
RRING
RRING
CLICK

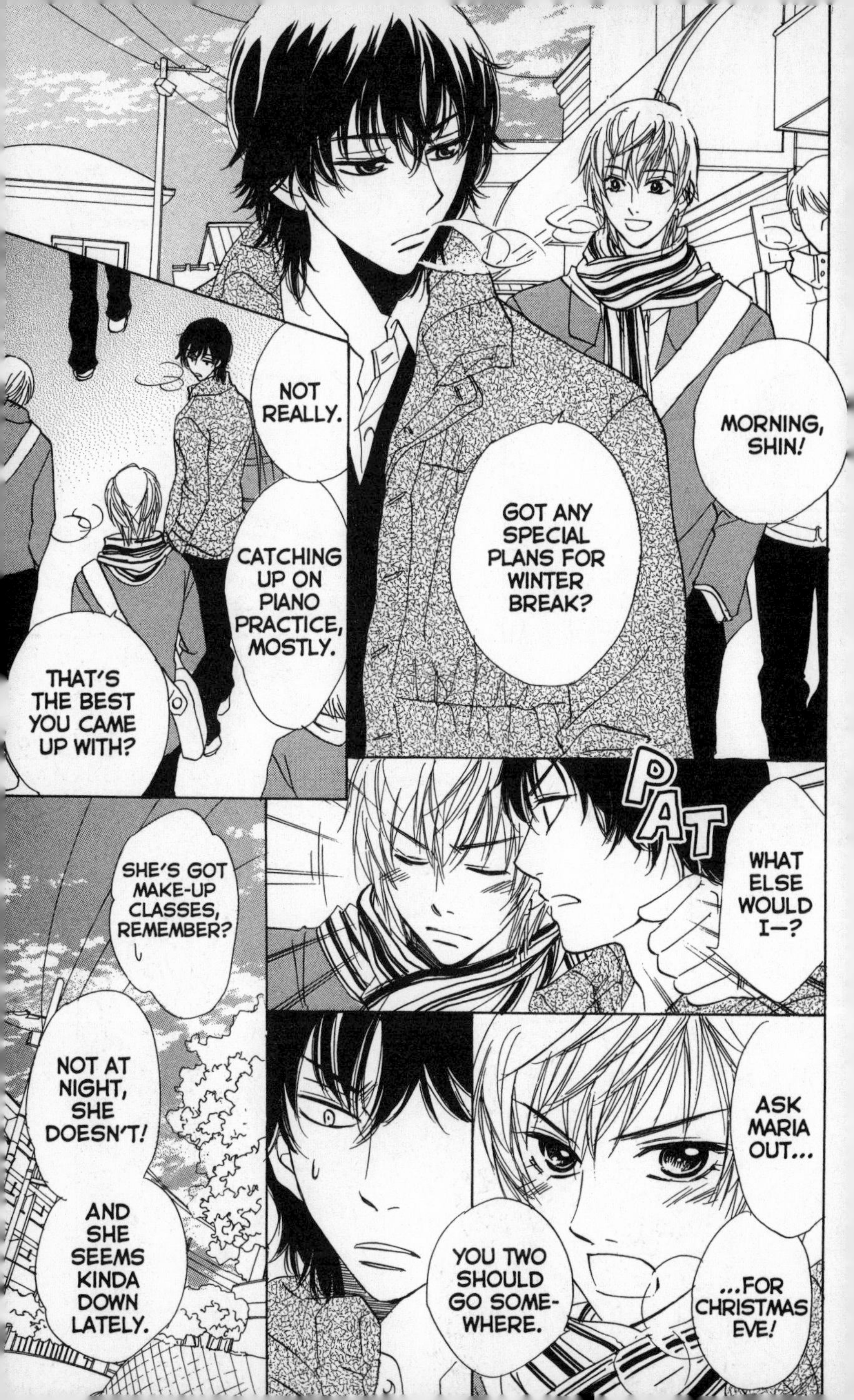
MORNING, SHIN!
GOT ANY SPECIAL PLANS FOR WINTER BREAK?
NOT REALLY.
CATCHING UP ON PIANO PRACTICE, MOSTLY.
THAT'S THE BEST YOU CAME UP WITH?
PAT
WHAT ELSE WOULD I—?
ASK MARIA OUT...
...FOR CHRISTMAS EVE!
YOU TWO SHOULD GO SOME-WHERE.
SHE'S GOT MAKE-UP CLASSES, REMEMBER?
NOT AT NIGHT, SHE DOESN'T!
AND SHE SEEMS KINDA DOWN LATELY.

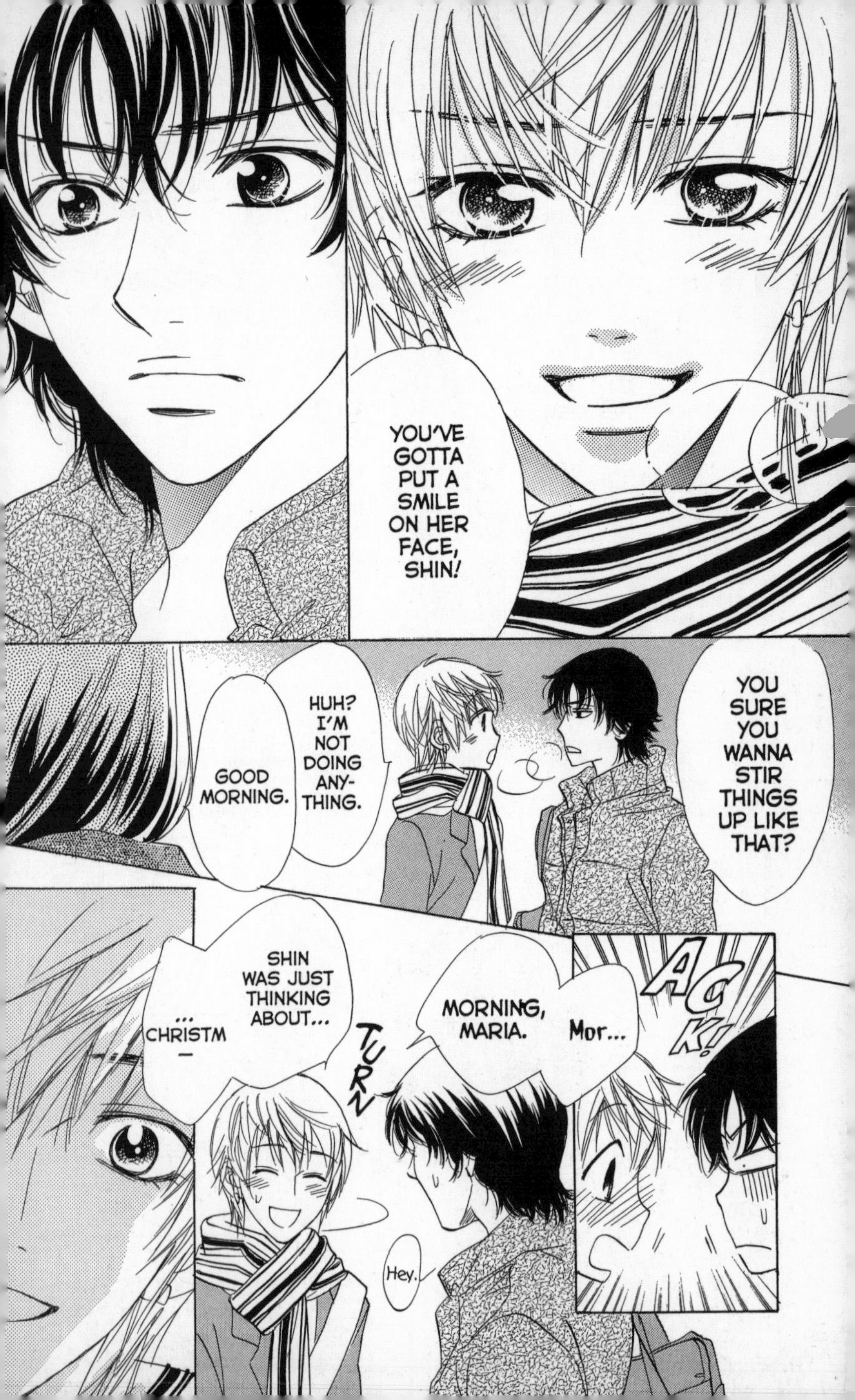
YOU'VE GOTTA PUT A SMILE ON HER FACE, SHIN!
YOU SURE YOU WANNA STIR THINGS UP LIKE THAT?
HUH? I'M NOT DOING ANYTHING.
GOOD MORNING.
ACK!
Mor...
MORNING, MARIA.
TURN
Hey.
SHIN WAS JUST THINKING ABOUT...
...CHRISTM—

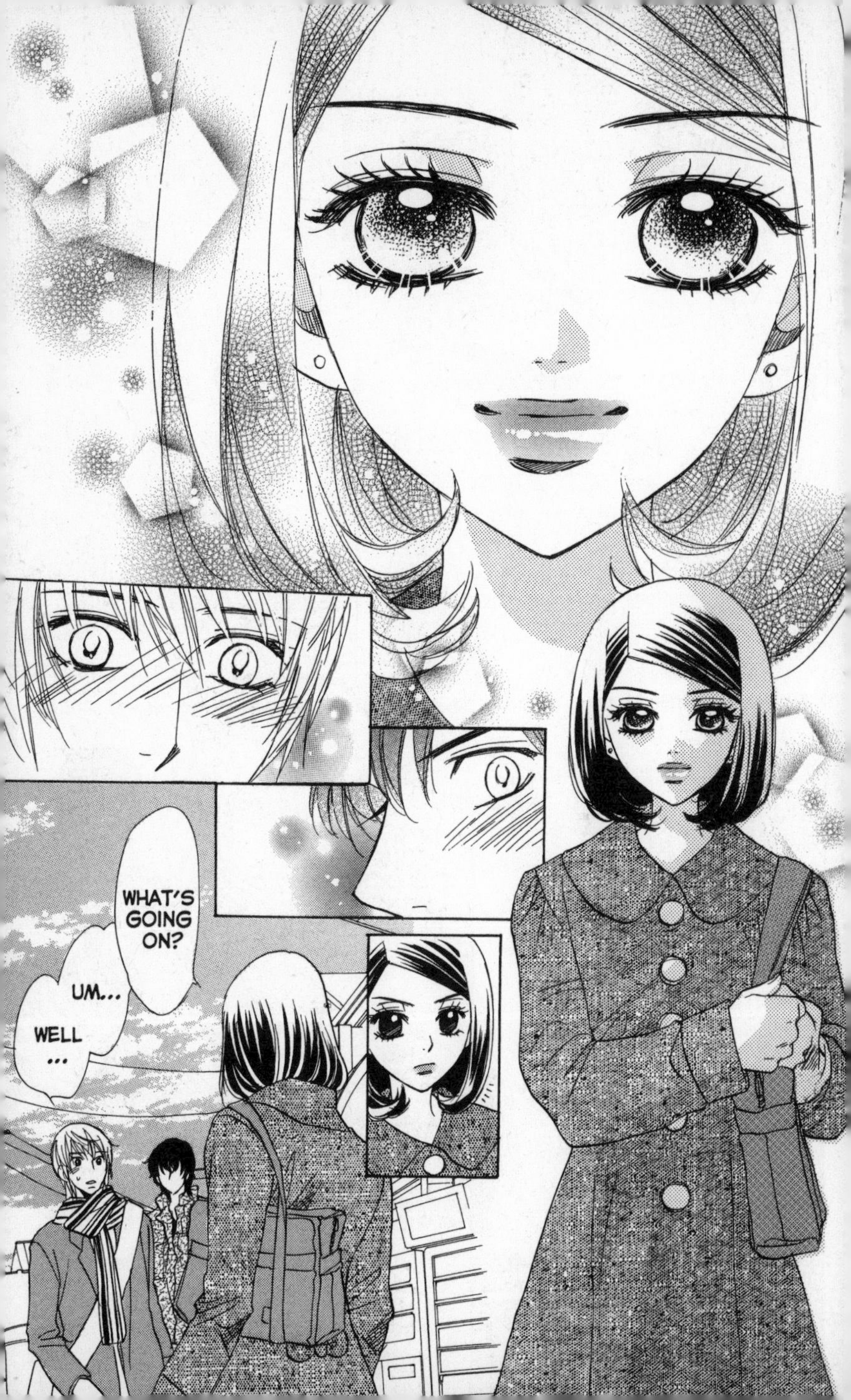
WHAT'S GOING ON?
UM...
WELL ...

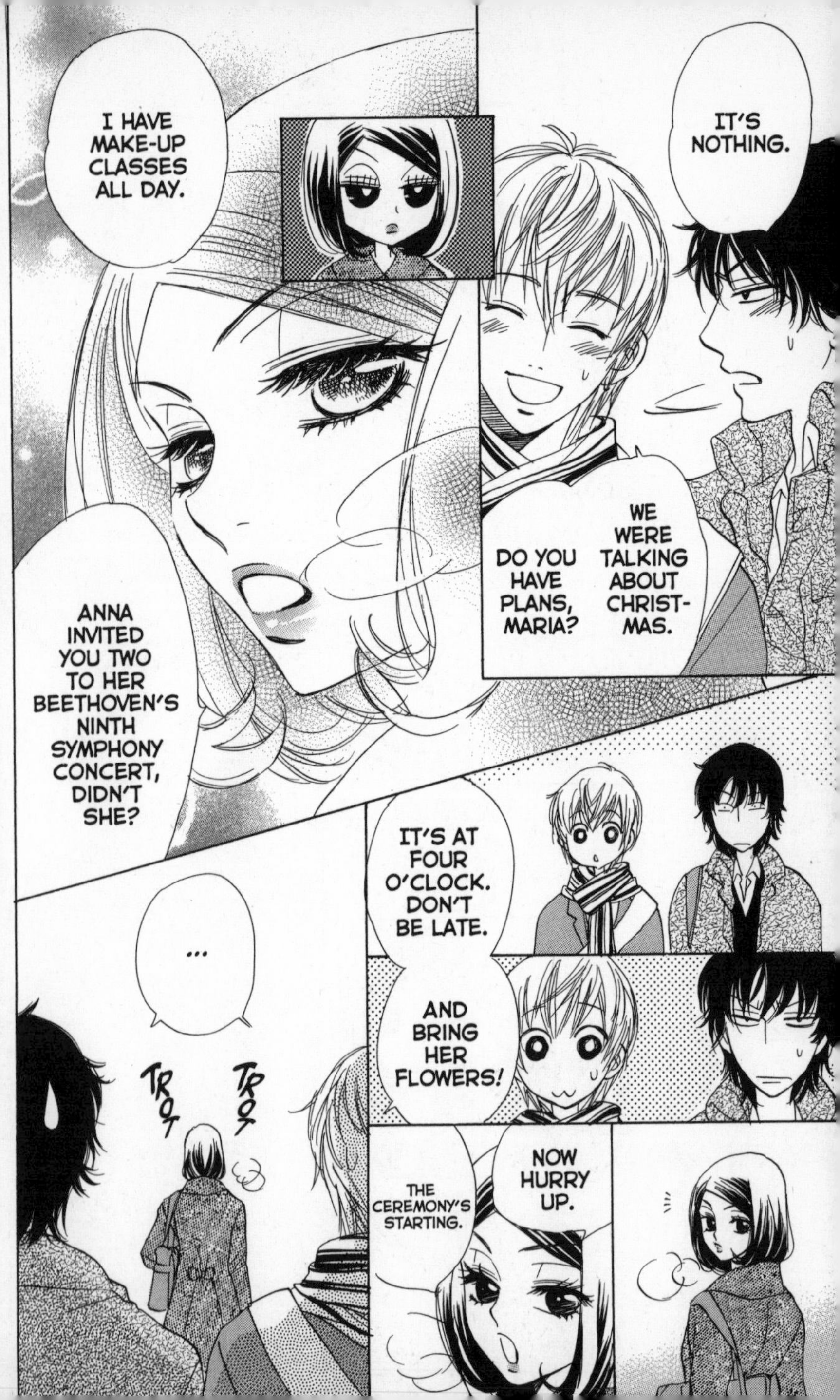
IT'S NOTHING.
WE WERE TALKING ABOUT CHRIST-MAS.
DO YOU HAVE PLANS, MARIA?
I HAVE MAKE-UP CLASSES ALL DAY.
ANNA INVITED YOU TWO TO HER BEETHOVEN'S NINTH SYMPHONY CONCERT, DIDN'T SHE?
IT'S AT FOUR O'CLOCK. DON'T BE LATE.
AND BRING HER FLOWERS!
NOW HURRY UP.
THE CEREMONY'S STARTING.
...
TROT TROT

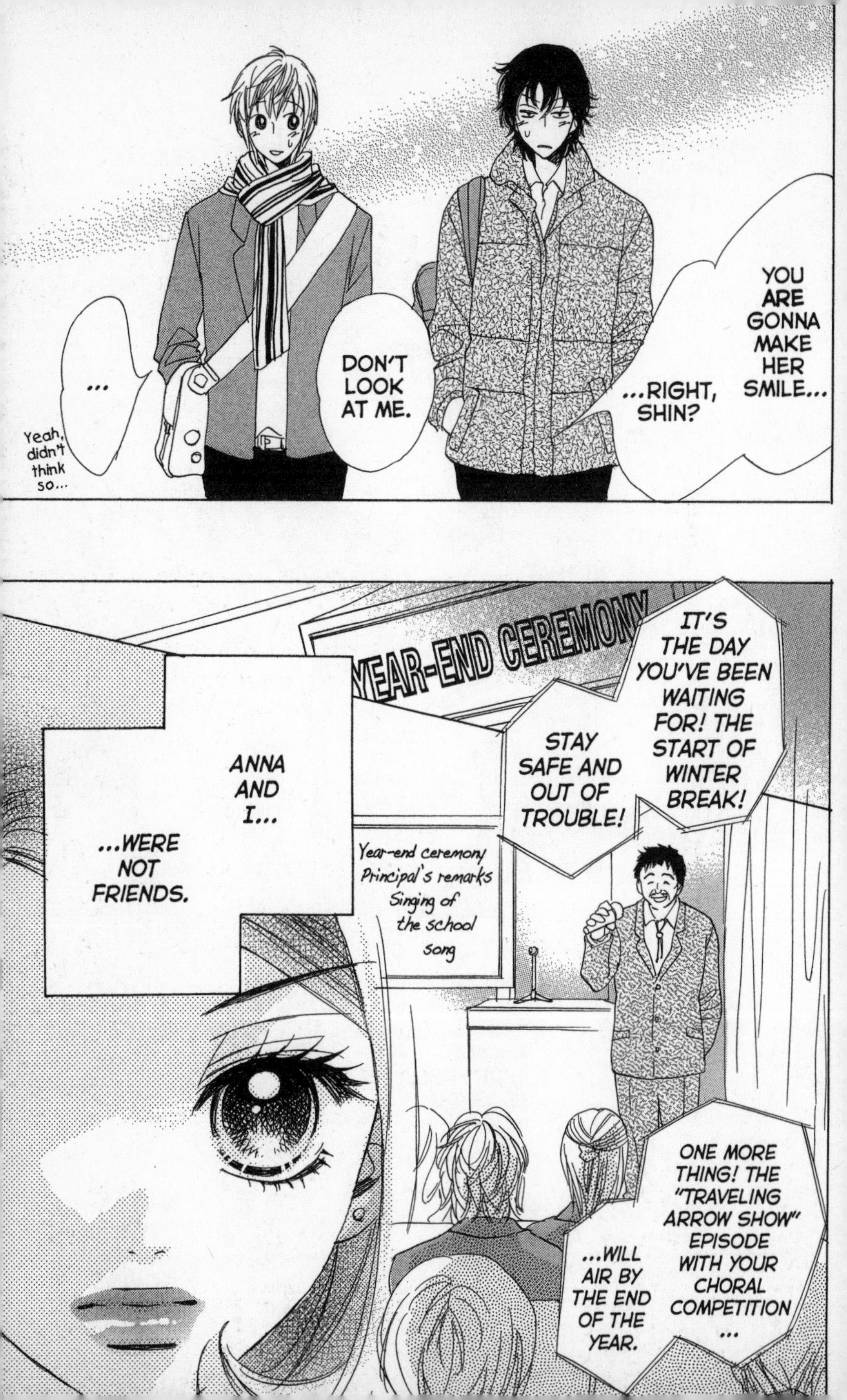
YOU ARE GONNA MAKE HER SMILE...
...RIGHT, SHIN?
DON'T LOOK AT ME.
...
Yeah, didn't think so...
YEAR-END CEREMONY
IT'S THE DAY YOU'VE BEEN WAITING FOR! THE START OF WINTER BREAK!
STAY SAFE AND OUT OF TROUBLE!
Year-end ceremony Principal's remarks Singing of the school song
ANNA AND I...
...WERE NOT FRIENDS.
ONE MORE THING! THE "TRAVELING ARROW SHOW" EPISODE WITH YOUR CHORAL COMPETITION ...
...WILL AIR BY THE END OF THE YEAR.

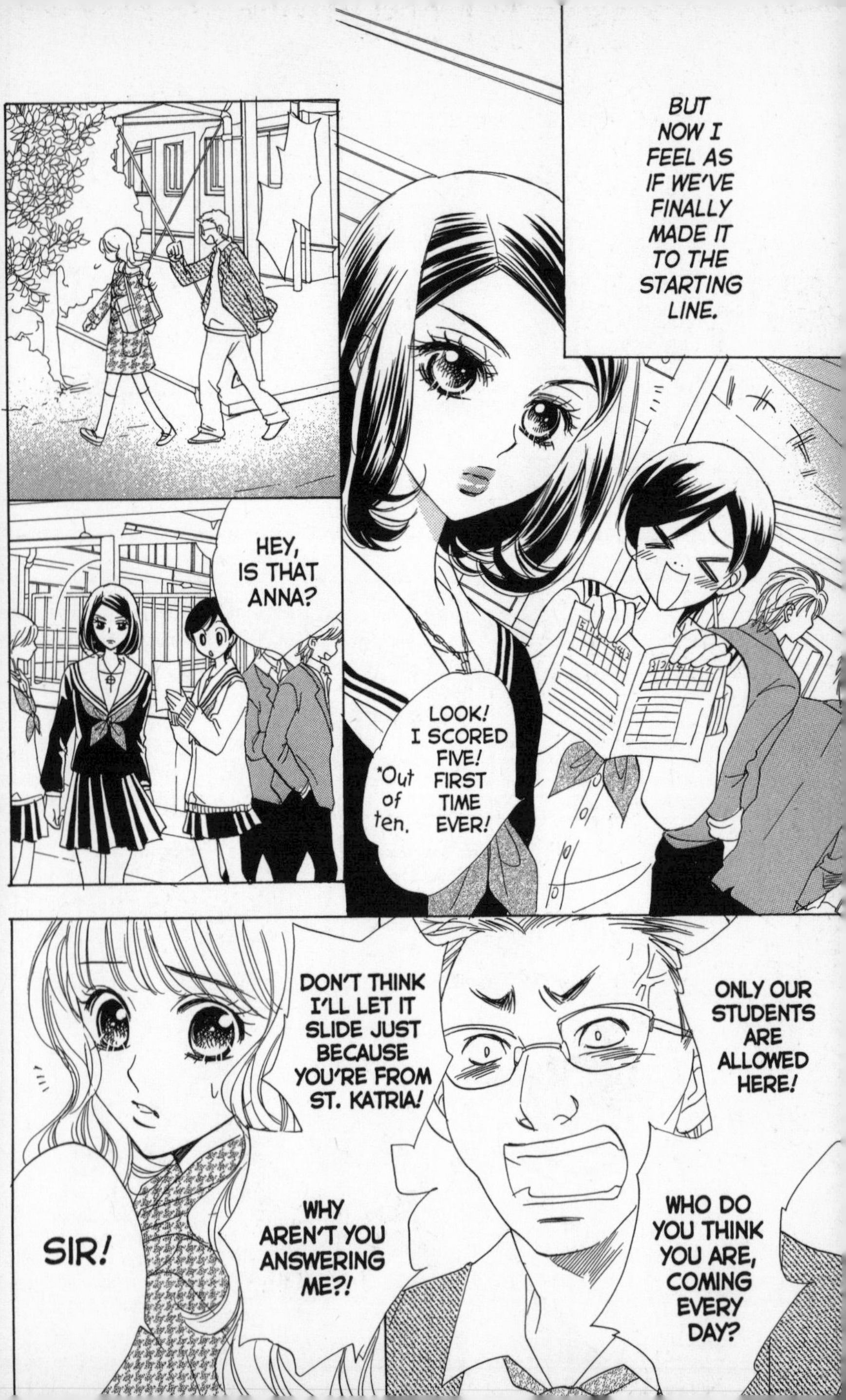
BUT NOW I FEEL AS IF WE'VE FINALLY MADE IT TO THE STARTING LINE.
LOOK! I SCORED FIVE! FIRST TIME EVER!
*Out of ten.
HEY, IS THAT ANNA?
ONLY OUR STUDENTS ARE ALLOWED HERE!
DON'T THINK I'LL LET IT SLIDE JUST BECAUSE YOU'RE FROM ST. KATRIA!
WHO DO YOU THINK YOU ARE, COMING EVERY DAY?
WHY AREN'T YOU ANSWERING ME?!
SIR!

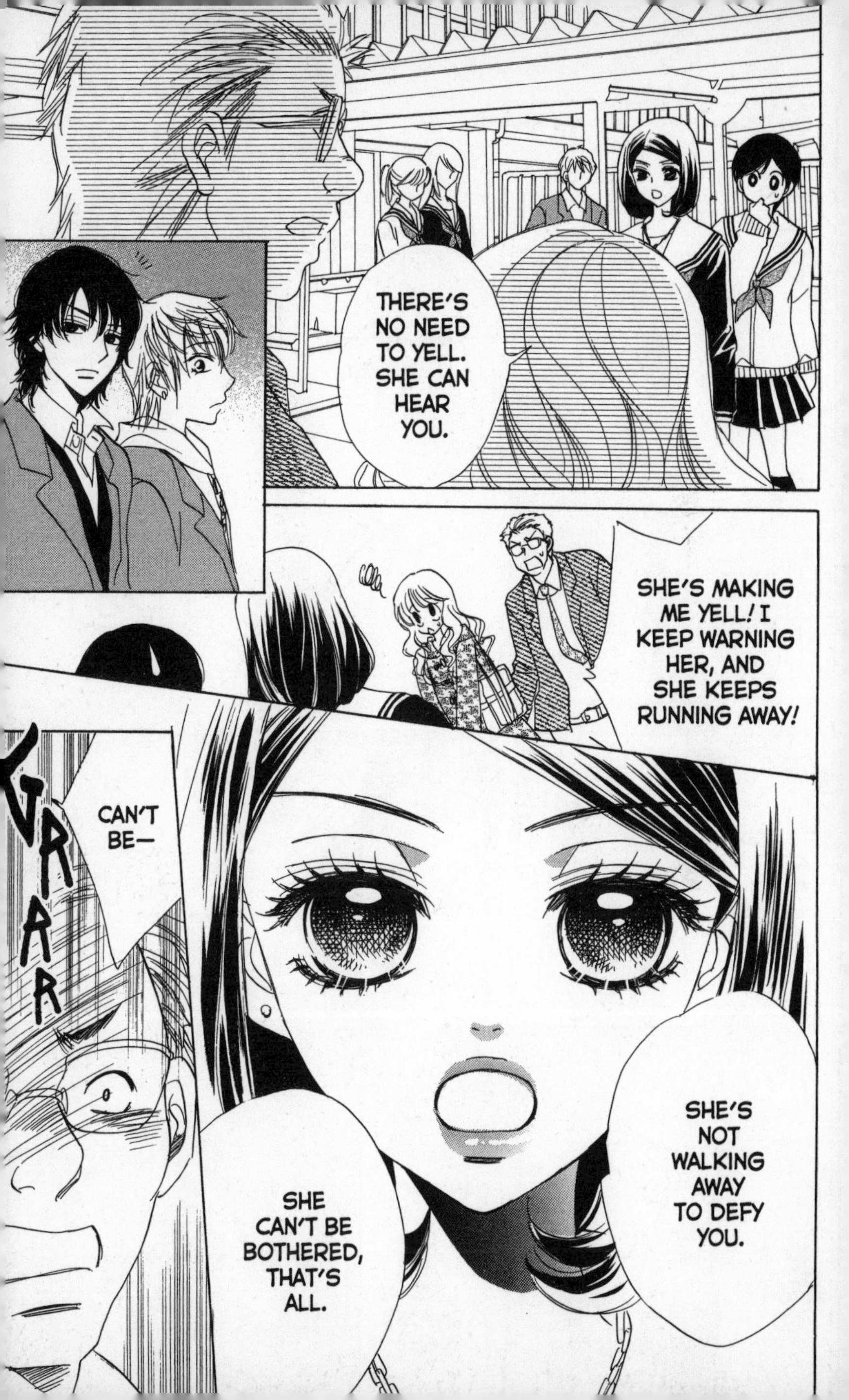
THERE'S NO NEED TO YELL. SHE CAN HEAR YOU.
SHE'S MAKING ME YELL! I KEEP WARNING HER, AND SHE KEEPS RUNNING AWAY!
SHE'S NOT WALKING AWAY TO DEFY YOU.
SHE CAN'T BE BOTHERED, THAT'S ALL.
CAN'T BE—
GRAR

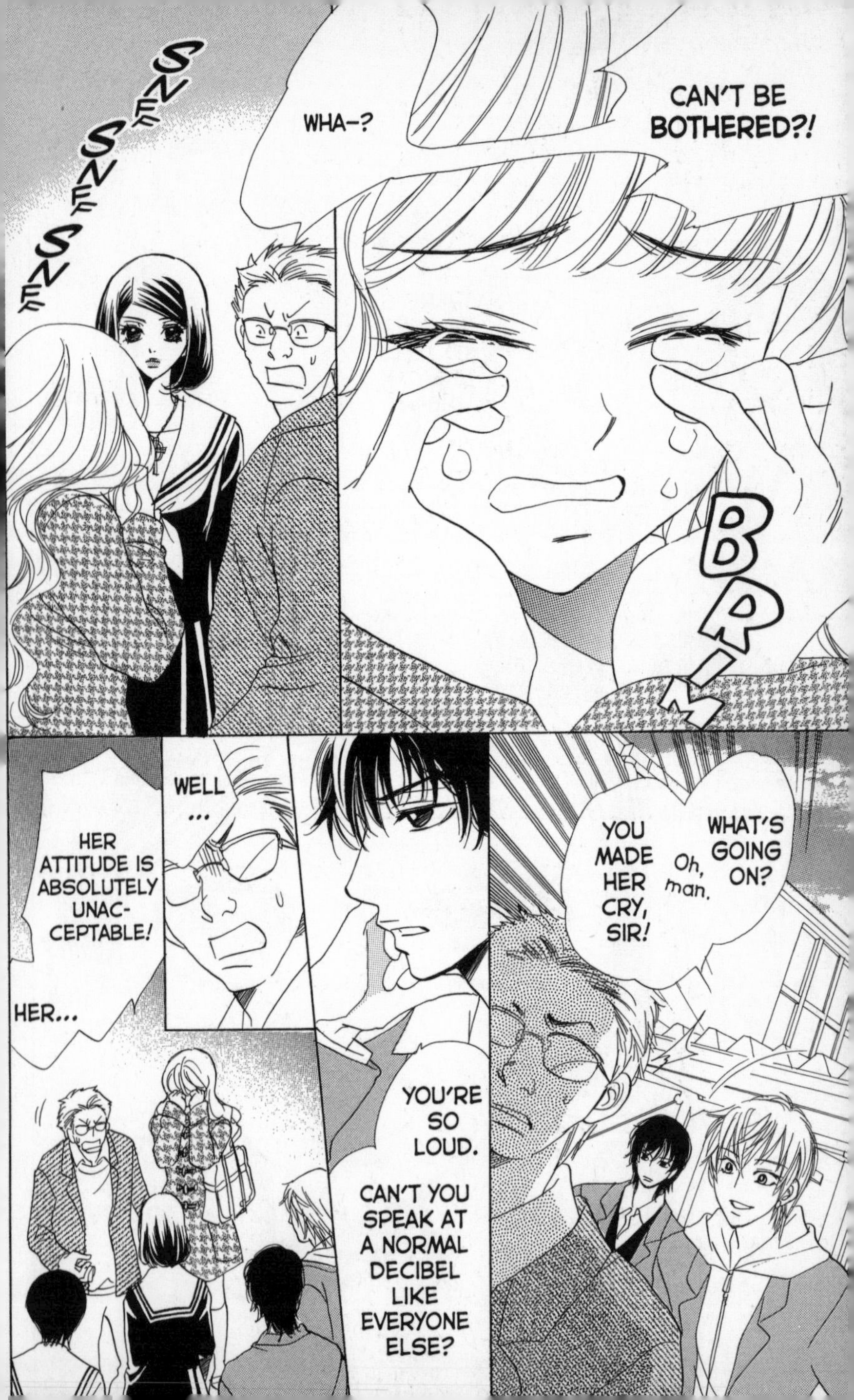

CAN'T BE BOTHERED?!
BRIM
WHA-?
SNFF SNFF SNFF
WHAT'S GOING ON?
Oh, man.
YOU MADE HER CRY, SIR!
YOU'RE SO LOUD.
CAN'T YOU SPEAK AT A NORMAL DECIBEL LIKE EVERYONE ELSE?
WELL ...
HER ATTITUDE IS ABSOLUTELY UNAC-CEPTABLE!
HER...

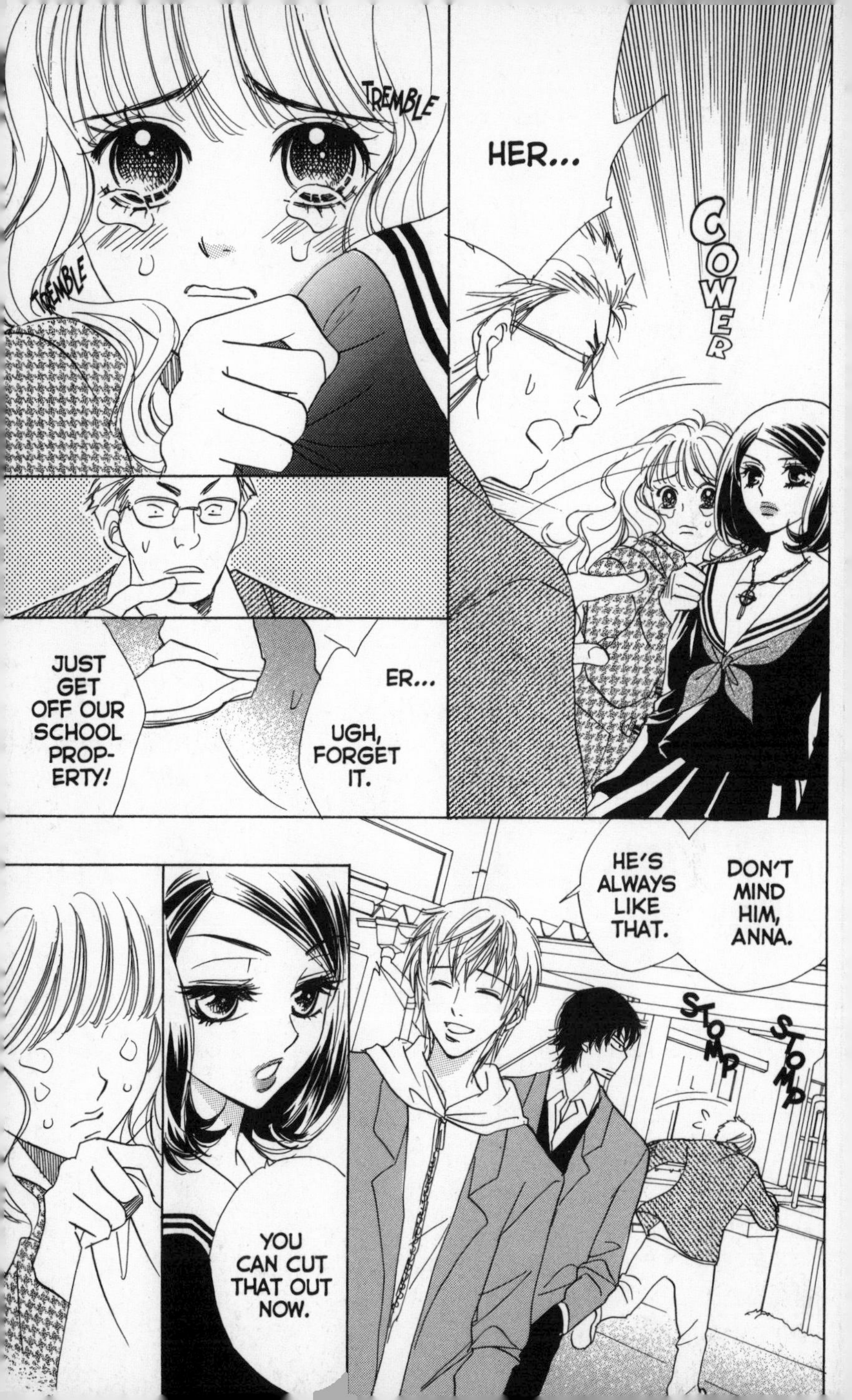
HER...
COWER
TREMBLE
TREMBLE
ER...
UGH, FORGET IT.
JUST GET OFF OUR SCHOOL PROP-ERTY!
DON'T MIND HIM, ANNA.
HE'S ALWAYS LIKE THAT.
STOMP
STOMP
YOU CAN CUT THAT OUT NOW.

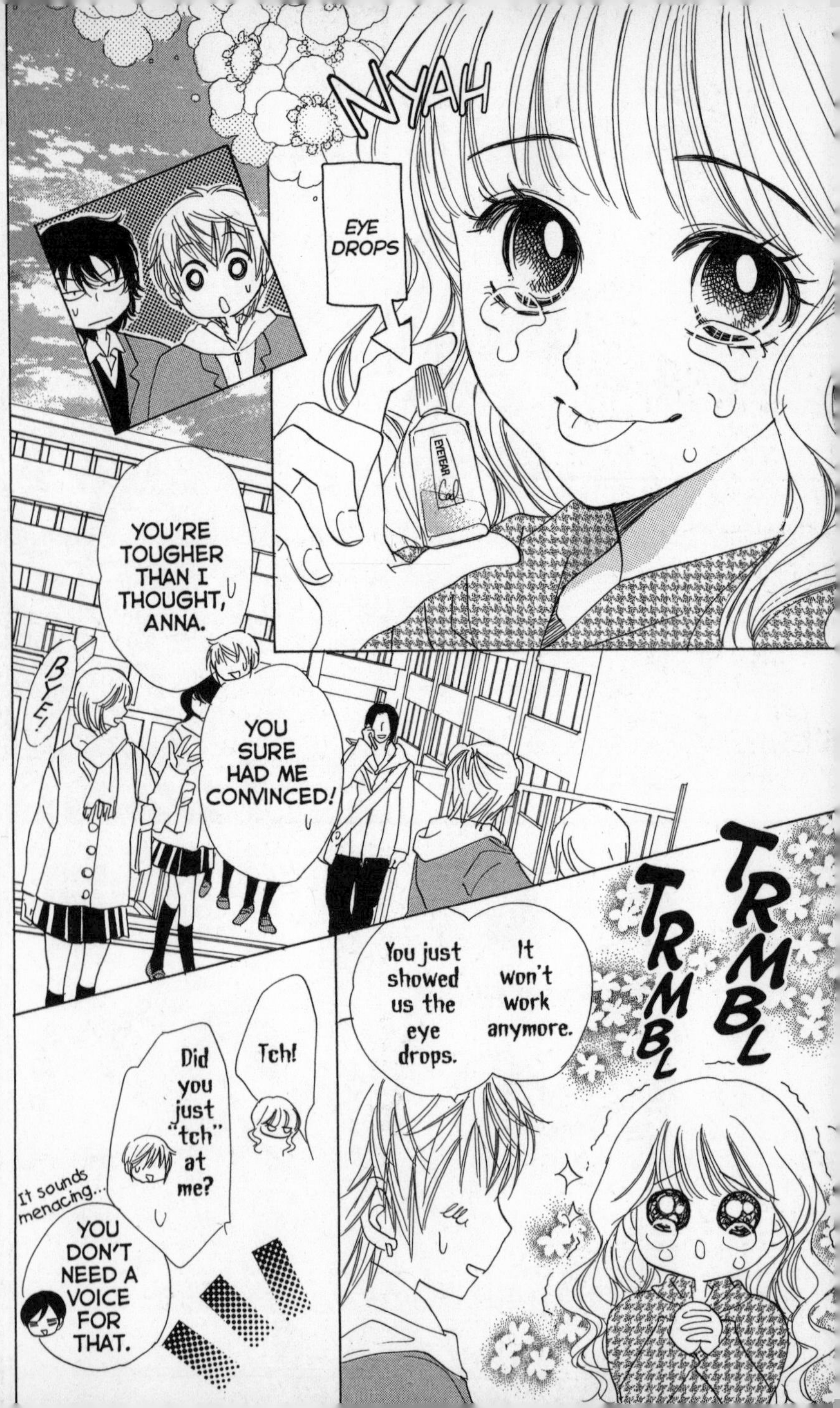
NYAH
EYE DROPS
EYETEAR Cool
YOU'RE TOUGHER THAN I THOUGHT, ANNA.
BYE!
YOU SURE HAD ME CONVINCED!
TRMBL TRMBL
You just showed us the eye drops. It won't work anymore.
Tch!
Did you just "tch" at me?
It sounds menacing...
YOU DON'T NEED A VOICE FOR THAT.

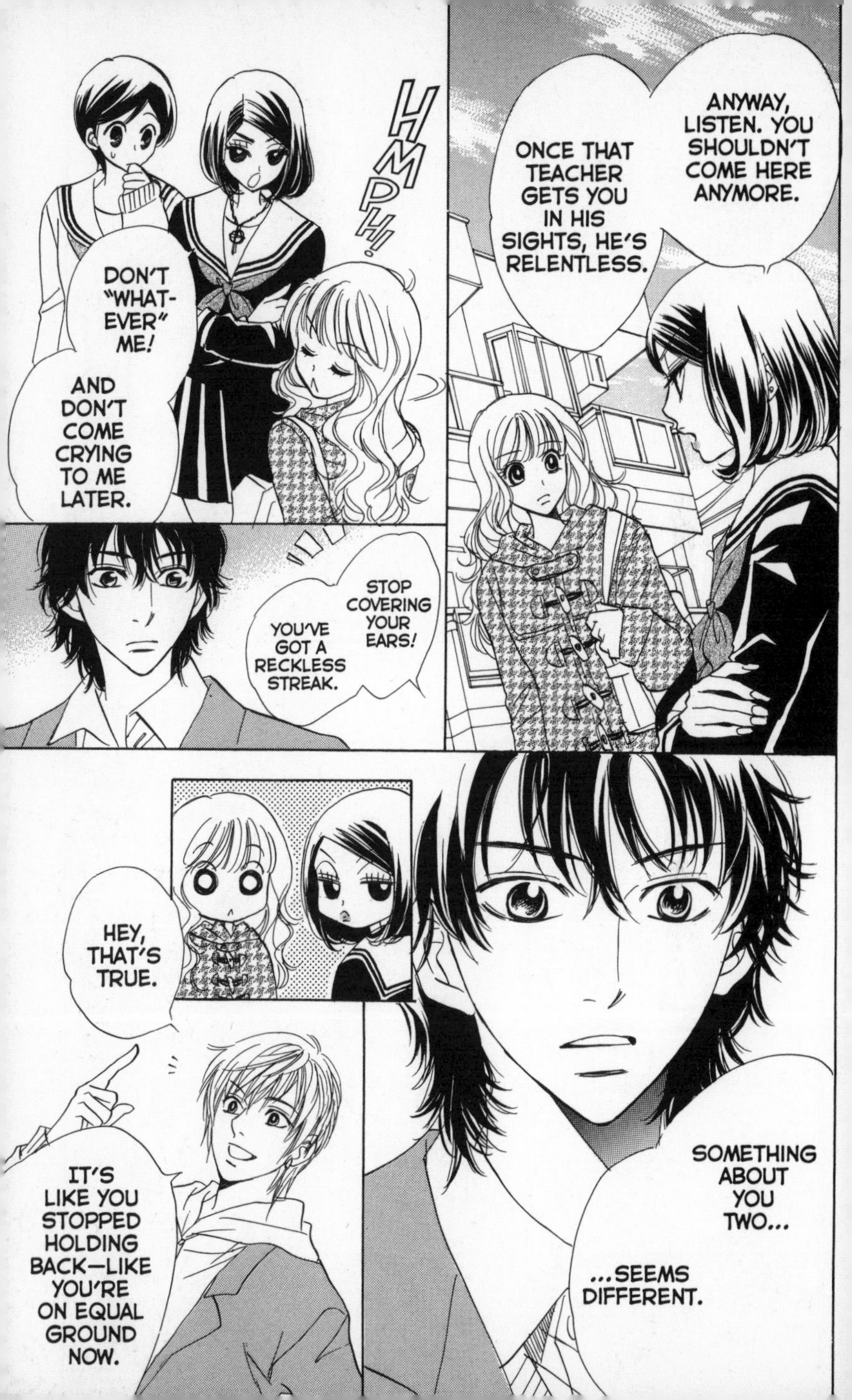

ANYWAY, LISTEN. YOU SHOULDN'T COME HERE ANYMORE.
ONCE THAT TEACHER GETS YOU IN HIS SIGHTS, HE'S RELENTLESS.
HMPH!
DON'T "WHAT-EVER" ME!
AND DON'T COME CRYING TO ME LATER.
STOP COVERING YOUR EARS!
YOU'VE GOT A RECKLESS STREAK.
SOMETHING ABOUT YOU TWO...
...SEEMS DIFFERENT.
HEY, THAT'S TRUE.
IT'S LIKE YOU STOPPED HOLDING BACK—LIKE YOU'RE ON EQUAL GROUND NOW.

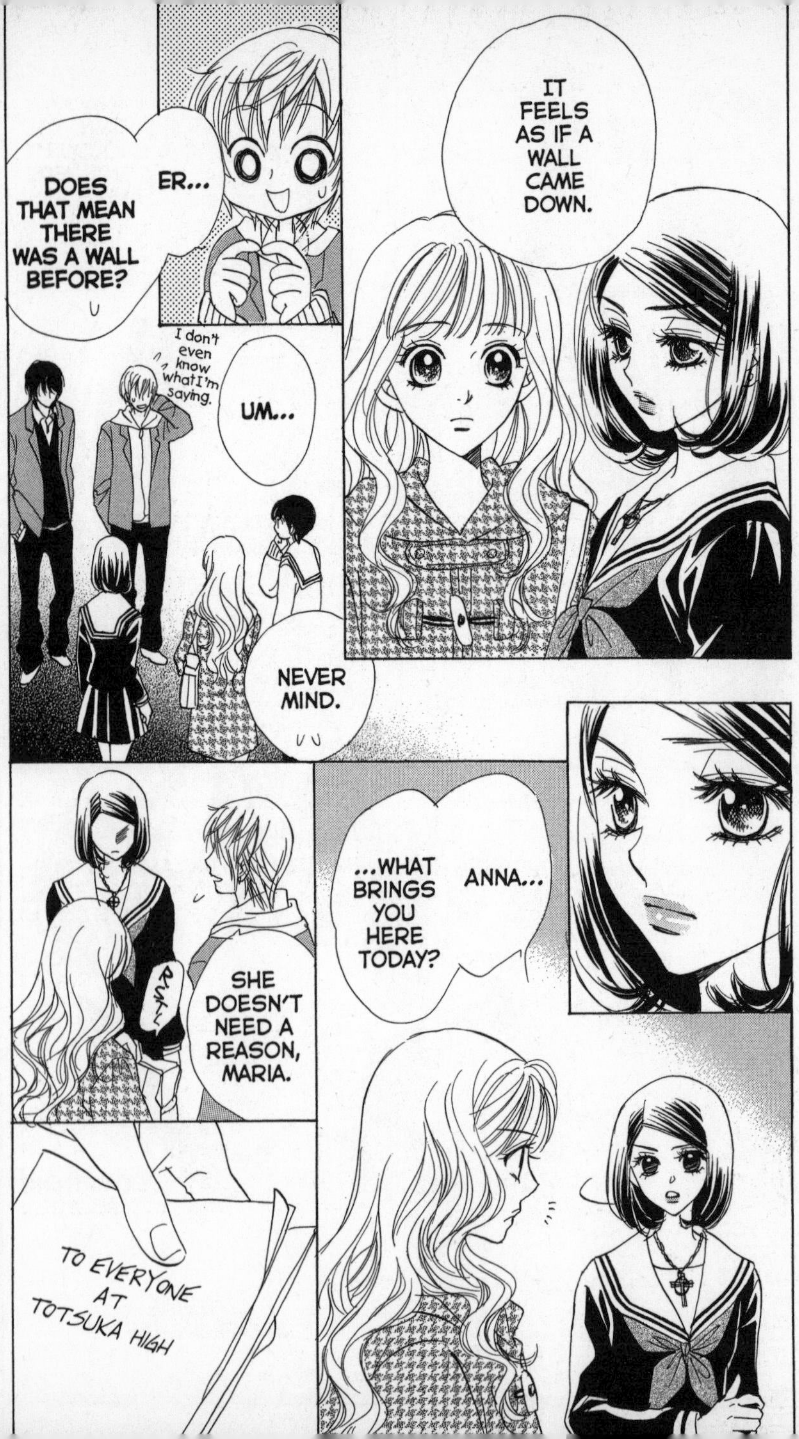
IT FEELS AS IF A WALL CAME DOWN.
ER...
DOES THAT MEAN THERE WAS A WALL BEFORE?
UM...
I don't even know what I'm saying.
NEVER MIND.
ANNA...
...WHAT BRINGS YOU HERE TODAY?
SHE DOESN'T NEED A REASON, MARIA.
RSTL
TO EVERYONE AT TOTSUKA HIGH

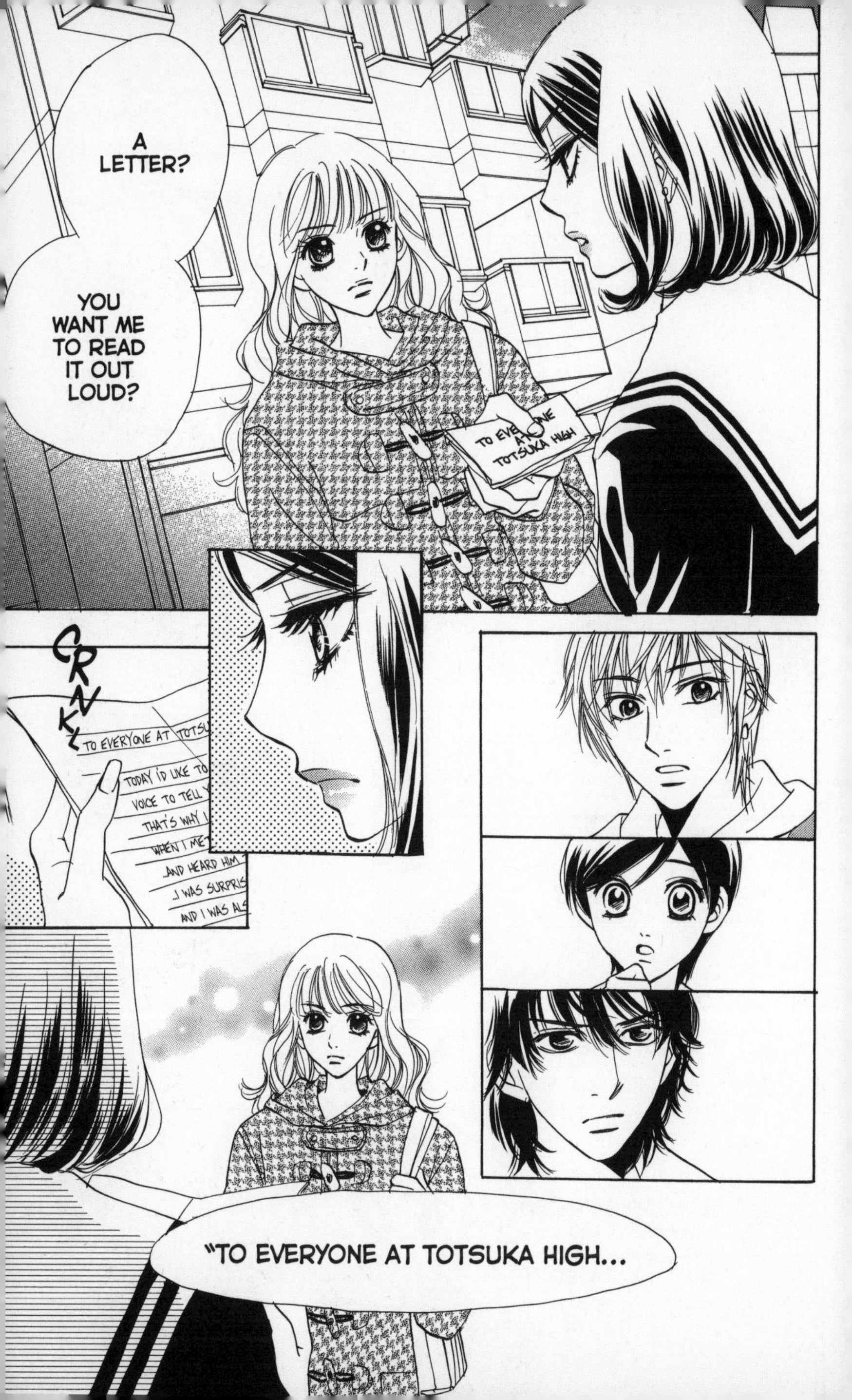

A LETTER?
YOU WANT ME TO READ IT OUT LOUD?
TO EVERYONE AT TOTSUKA HIGH
CRNKL
TO EVERYONE AT TOTSU
TODAY I'D LIKE TO
VOICE TO TELL
THAT'S WHY I
WHEN I ME
...AND HEARD HIM
...I WAS SURPRIS
AND I WAS AL
"TO EVERYONE AT TOTSUKA HIGH...

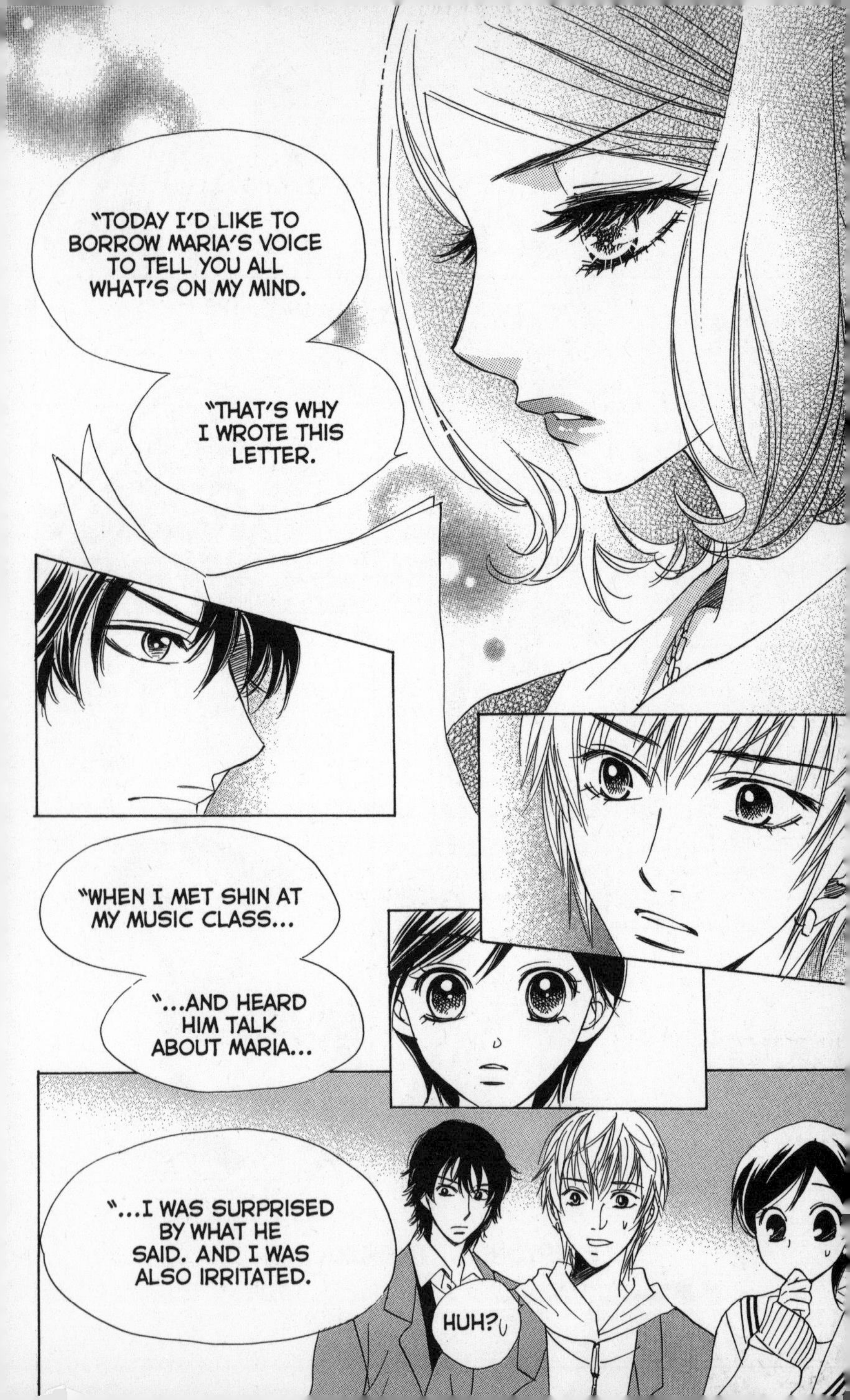
"TODAY I'D LIKE TO BORROW MARIA'S VOICE TO TELL YOU ALL WHAT'S ON MY MIND.
"THAT'S WHY I WROTE THIS LETTER.
"WHEN I MET SHIN AT MY MUSIC CLASS...
"...AND HEARD HIM TALK ABOUT MARIA...
"...I WAS SURPRISED BY WHAT HE SAID. AND I WAS ALSO IRRITATED.
HUH?

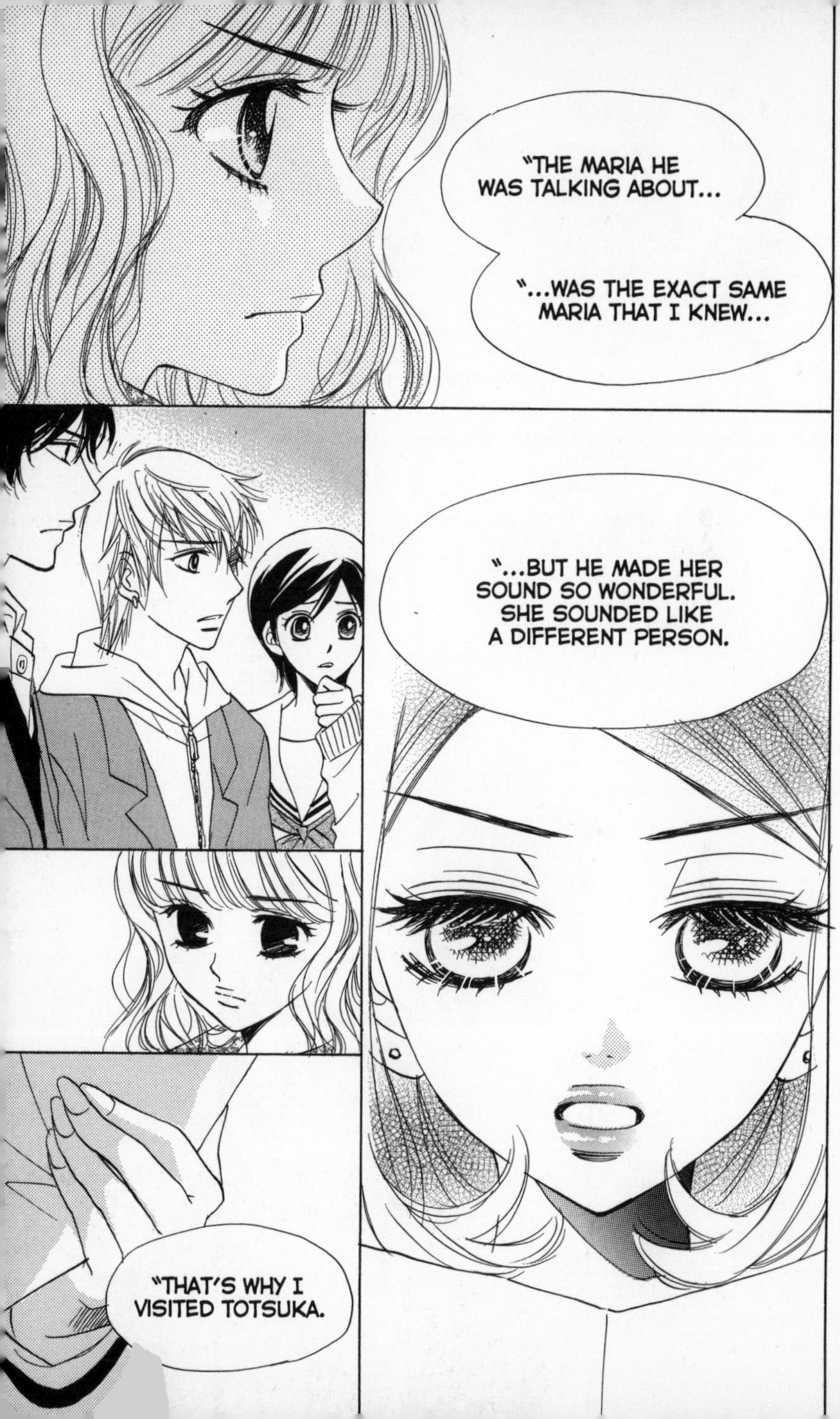
"THE MARIA HE WAS TALKING ABOUT...
"...WAS THE EXACT SAME MARIA THAT I KNEW...
"...BUT HE MADE HER SOUND SO WONDERFUL. SHE SOUNDED LIKE A DIFFERENT PERSON.
"THAT'S WHY I VISITED TOTSUKA.

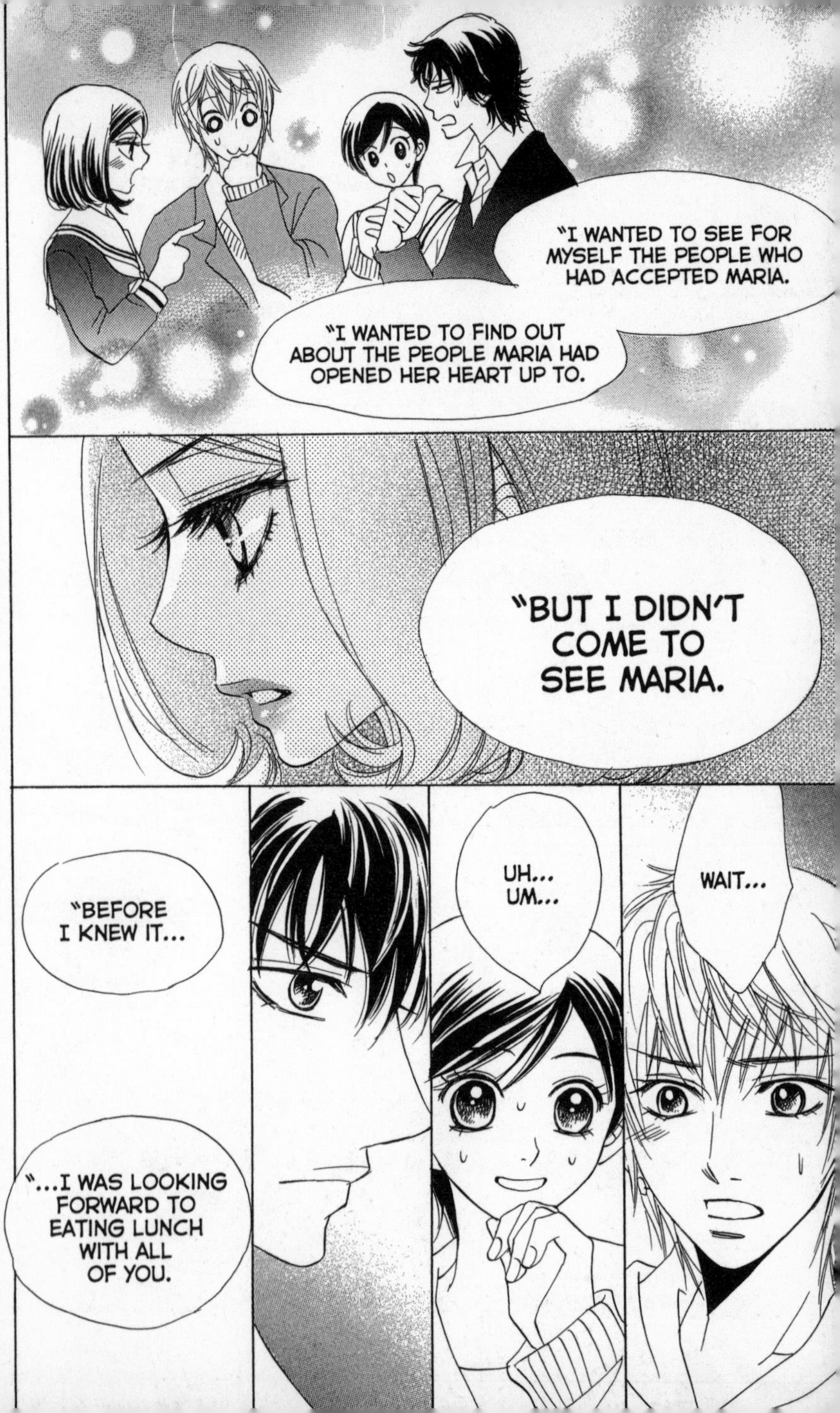
“I WANTED TO SEE FOR MYSELF THE PEOPLE WHO HAD ACCEPTED MARIA.
“I WANTED TO FIND OUT ABOUT THE PEOPLE MARIA HAD OPENED HER HEART UP TO.
“BUT I DIDN'T COME TO SEE MARIA.
WAIT...
UH... UM...
“BEFORE I KNEW IT...
“...I WAS LOOKING FORWARD TO EATING LUNCH WITH ALL OF YOU.

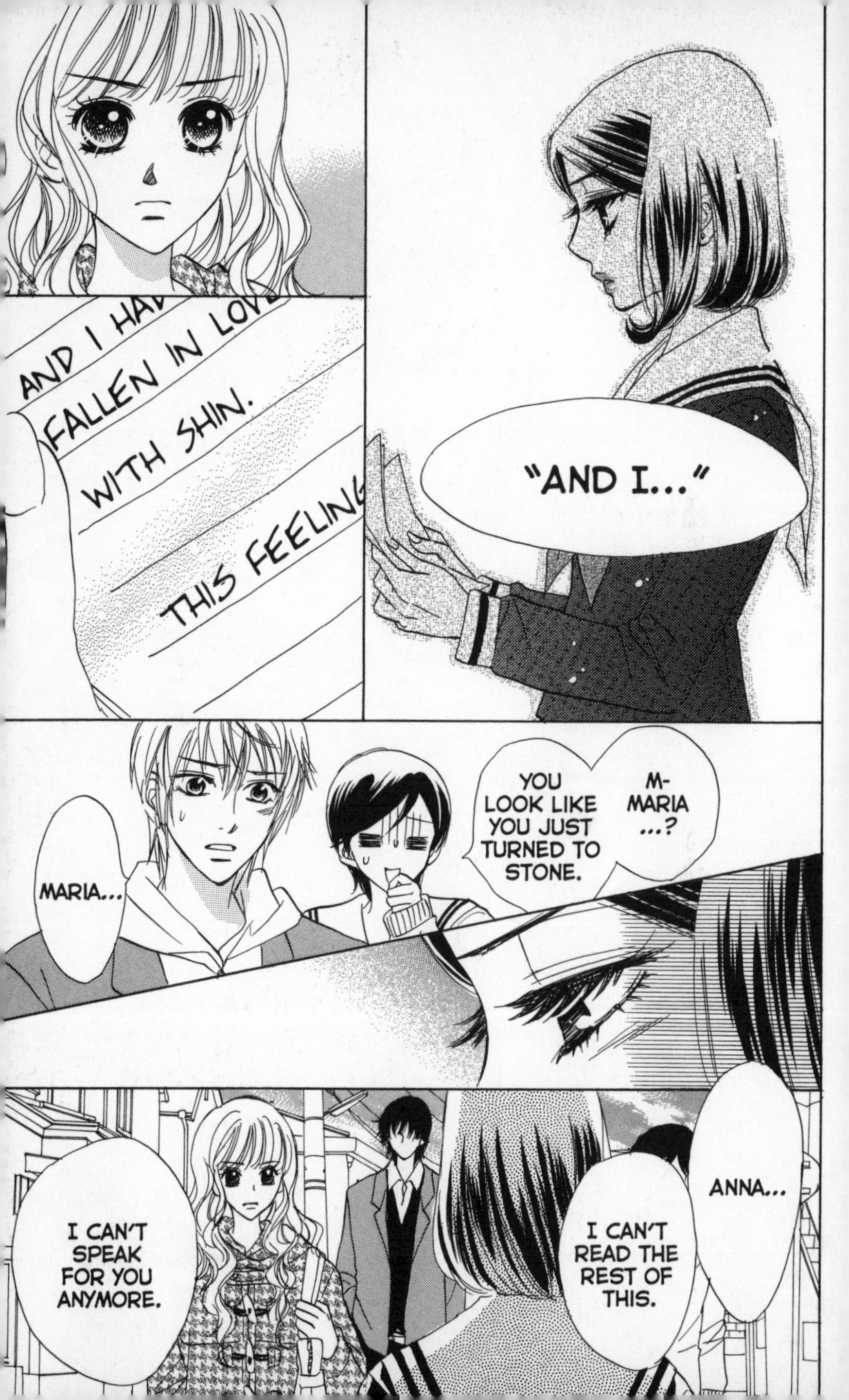
"AND I..."
AND I HA
FALLEN IN LOV
WITH SHIN.
THIS FEELING
M-MARIA ...?
YOU LOOK LIKE YOU JUST TURNED TO STONE.
MARIA...
ANNA...
I CAN'T READ THE REST OF THIS.
I CAN'T SPEAK FOR YOU ANYMORE.

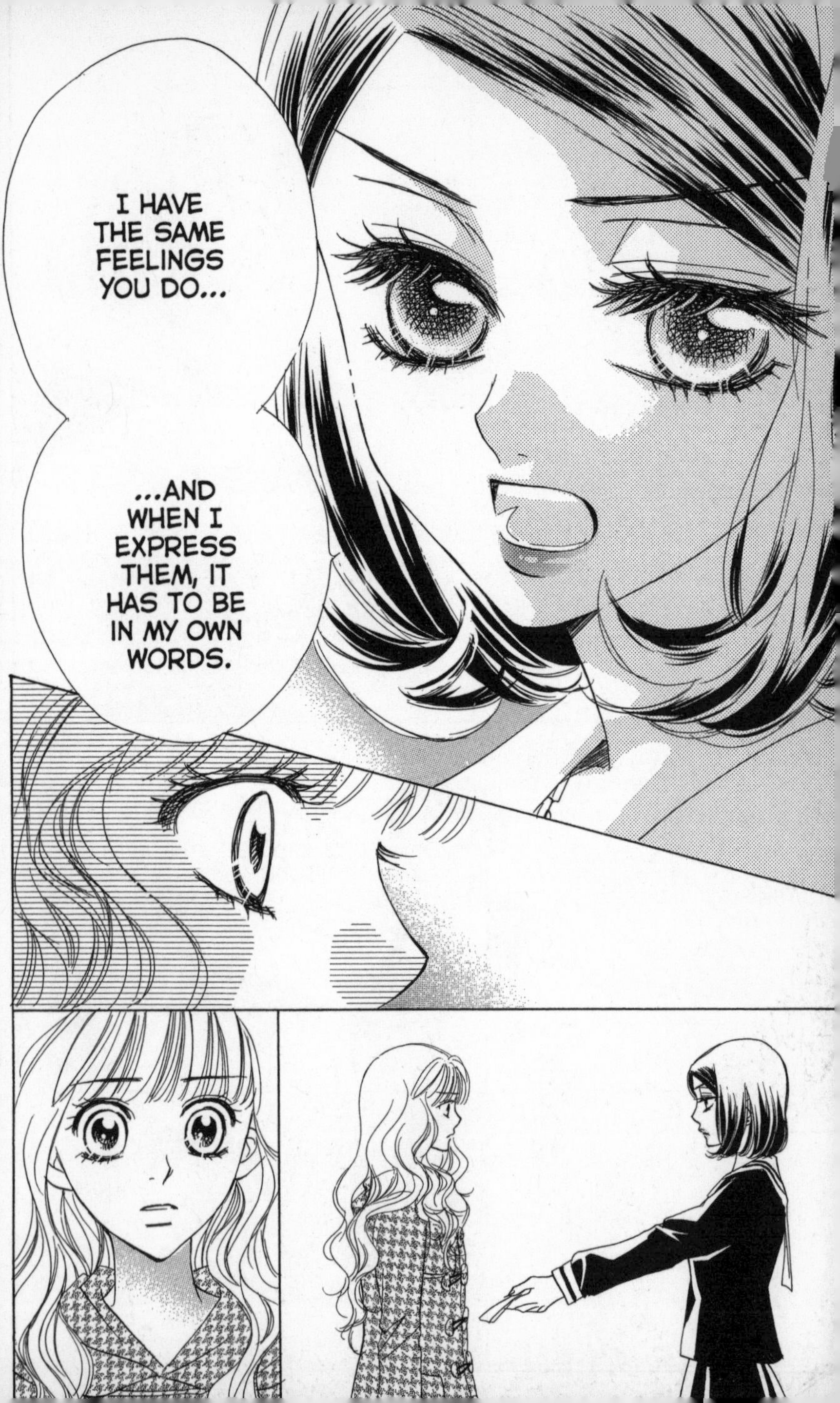
I HAVE THE SAME FEELINGS YOU DO...
...AND WHEN I EXPRESS THEM, IT HAS TO BE IN MY OWN WORDS.

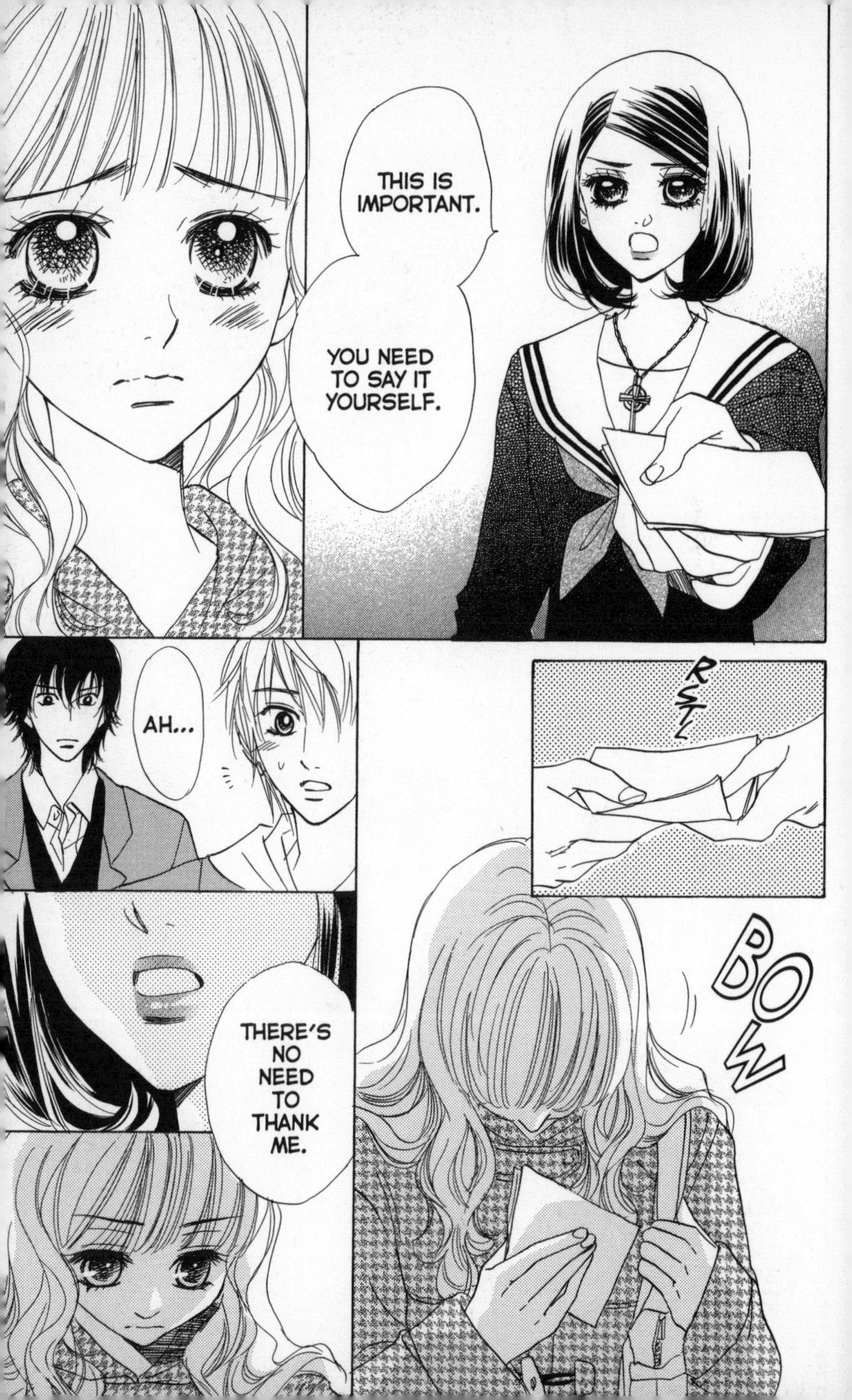
THIS IS IMPORTANT.
YOU NEED TO SAY IT YOURSELF.
RSTL
AH...
BOW
THERE'S NO NEED TO THANK ME.

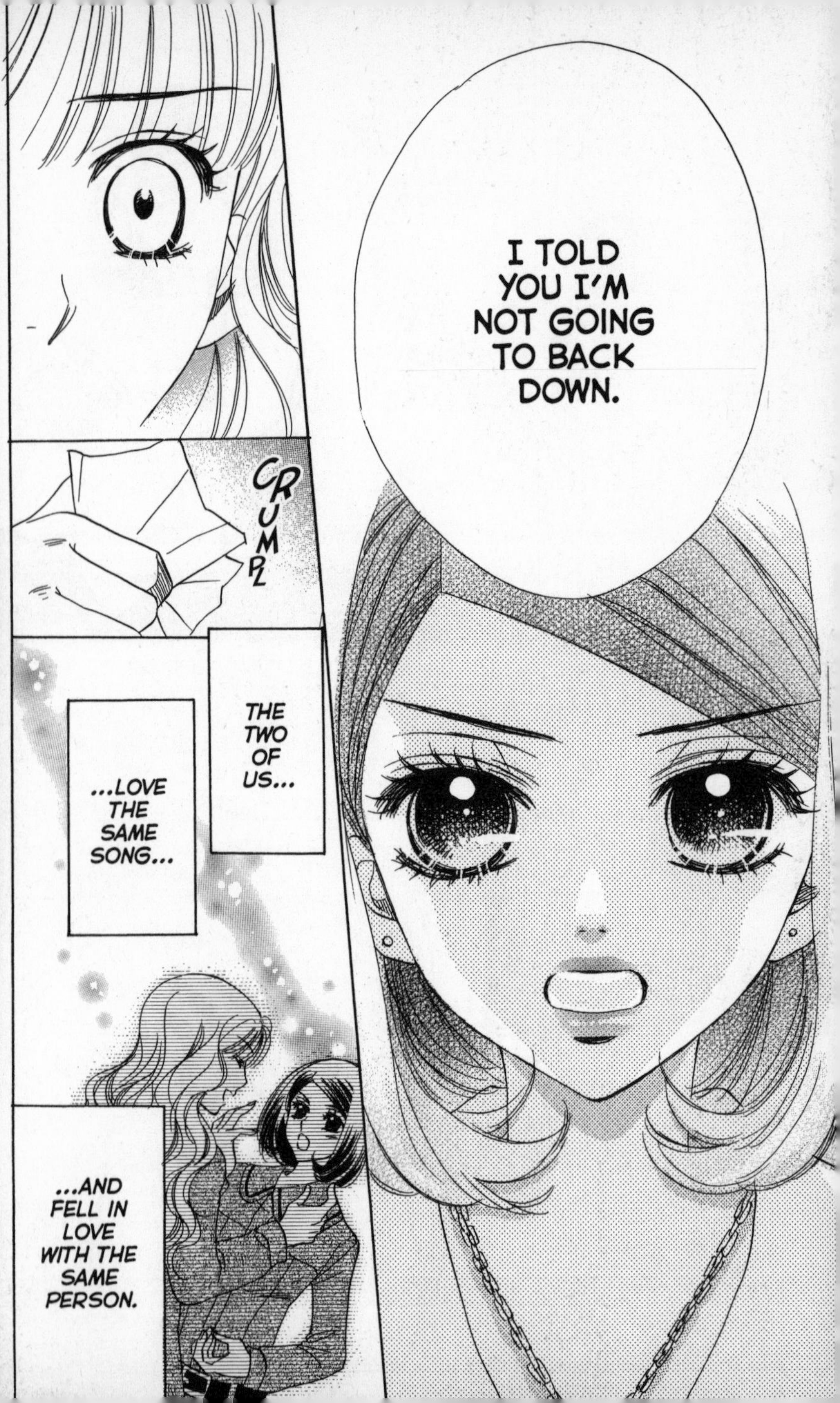

I TOLD YOU I'M NOT GOING TO BACK DOWN.
CRUMPL
THE TWO OF US...
...LOVE THE SAME SONG...
...AND FELL IN LOVE WITH THE SAME PERSON.

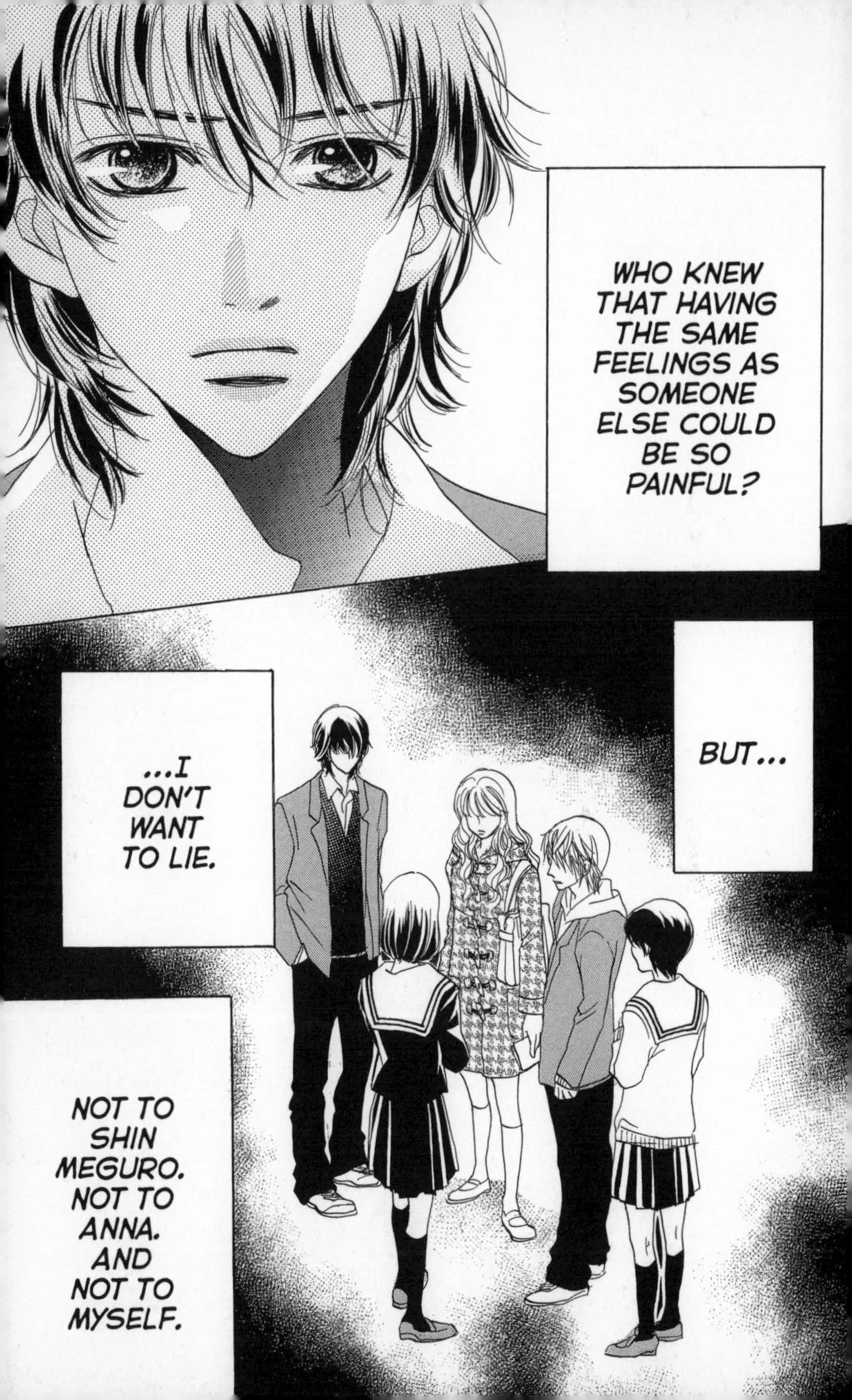
WHO KNEW THAT HAVING THE SAME FEELINGS AS SOMEONE ELSE COULD BE SO PAINFUL?
BUT...
...I DON'T WANT TO LIE.
NOT TO SHIN MEGURO. NOT TO ANNA. AND NOT TO MYSELF.

A Devil and Her Love Song

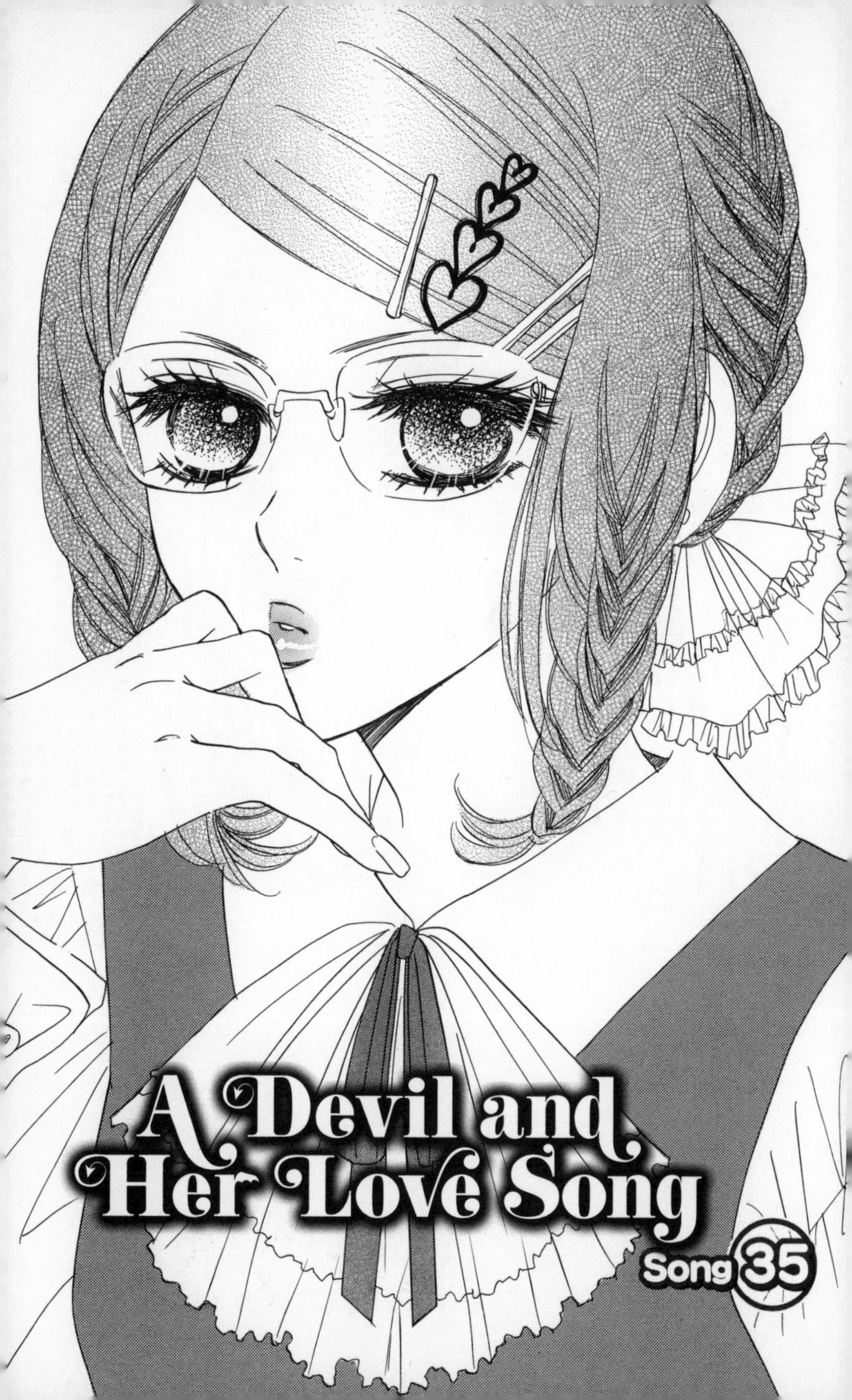
A Devil and Her Love Song
Song 35

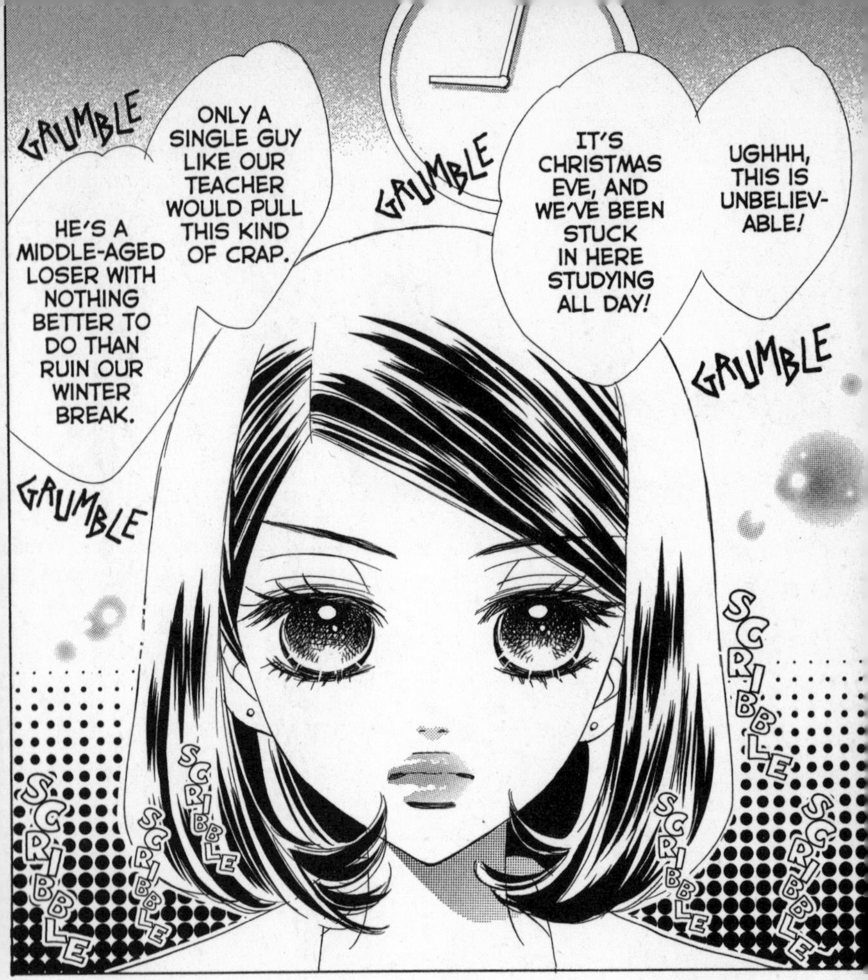
UGHHH, THIS IS UNBELIEV-ABLE!
GRUMBLE
IT'S CHRISTMAS EVE, AND WE'VE BEEN STUCK IN HERE STUDYING ALL DAY!
GRUMBLE
ONLY A SINGLE GUY LIKE OUR TEACHER WOULD PULL THIS KIND OF CRAP.
GRUMBLE
HE'S A MIDDLE-AGED LOSER WITH NOTHING BETTER TO DO THAN RUIN OUR WINTER BREAK.
GRUMBLE
SCRIBBLE
SCRIBBLE
SCRIBBLE
SCRIBBLE
SCRIBBLE
SCRIBBLE

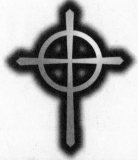

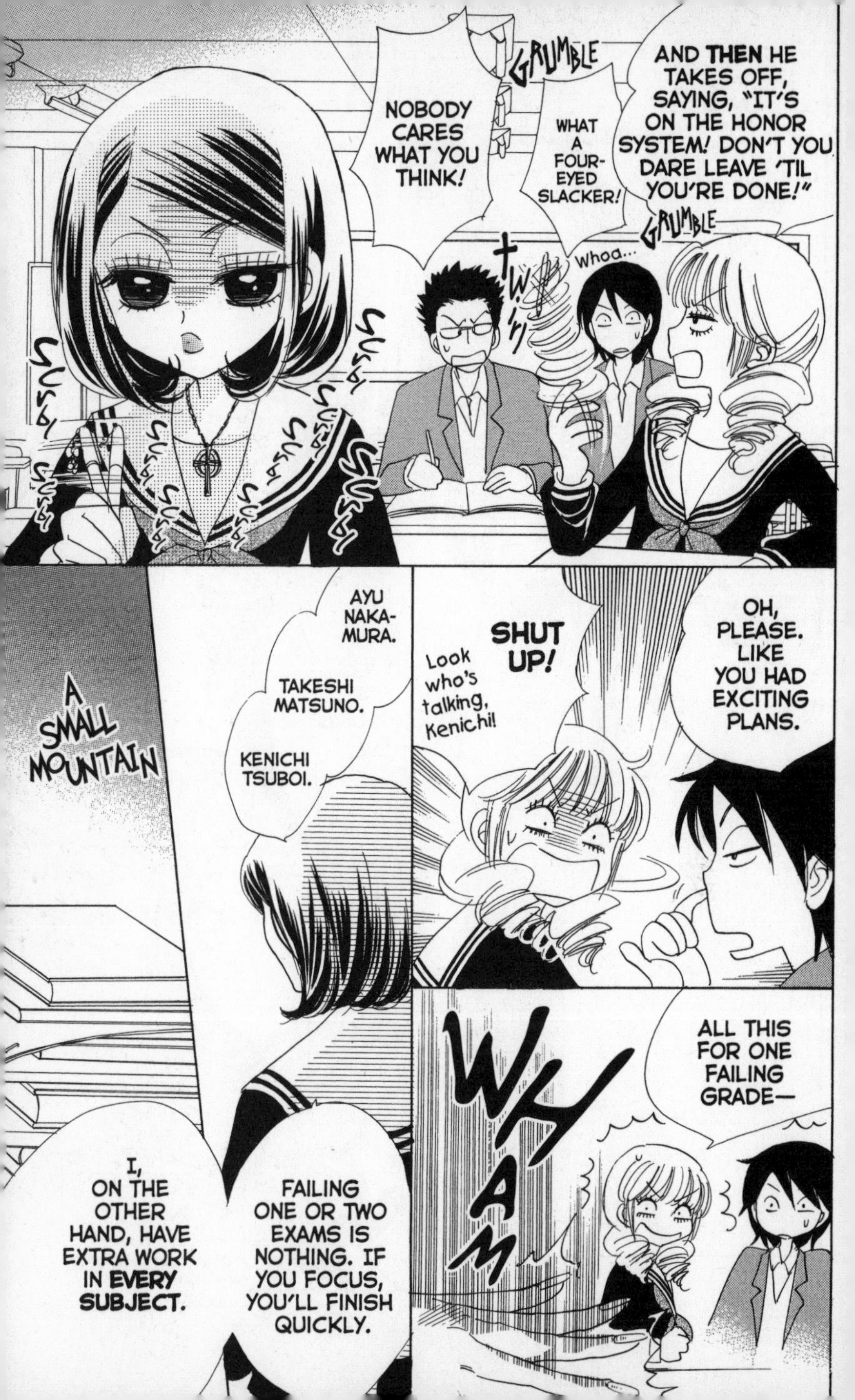
AND THEN HE TAKES OFF, SAYING, "IT'S ON THE HONOR SYSTEM! DON'T YOU DARE LEAVE 'TIL YOU'RE DONE!"
GRUMBLE
WHAT A FOUR-EYED SLACKER!
GRUMBLE
NOBODY CARES WHAT YOU THINK!
Whoa...
OH, PLEASE. LIKE YOU HAD EXCITING PLANS.
SHUT UP!
Look who's talking, Kenichi!
ALL THIS FOR ONE FAILING GRADE—
WHAM
AYU NAKAMURA.
TAKESHI MATSUNO.
KENICHI TSUBOI.
A SMALL MOUNTAIN
FAILING ONE OR TWO EXAMS IS NOTHING. IF YOU FOCUS, YOU'LL FINISH QUICKLY.
I, ON THE OTHER HAND, HAVE EXTRA WORK IN EVERY SUBJECT.

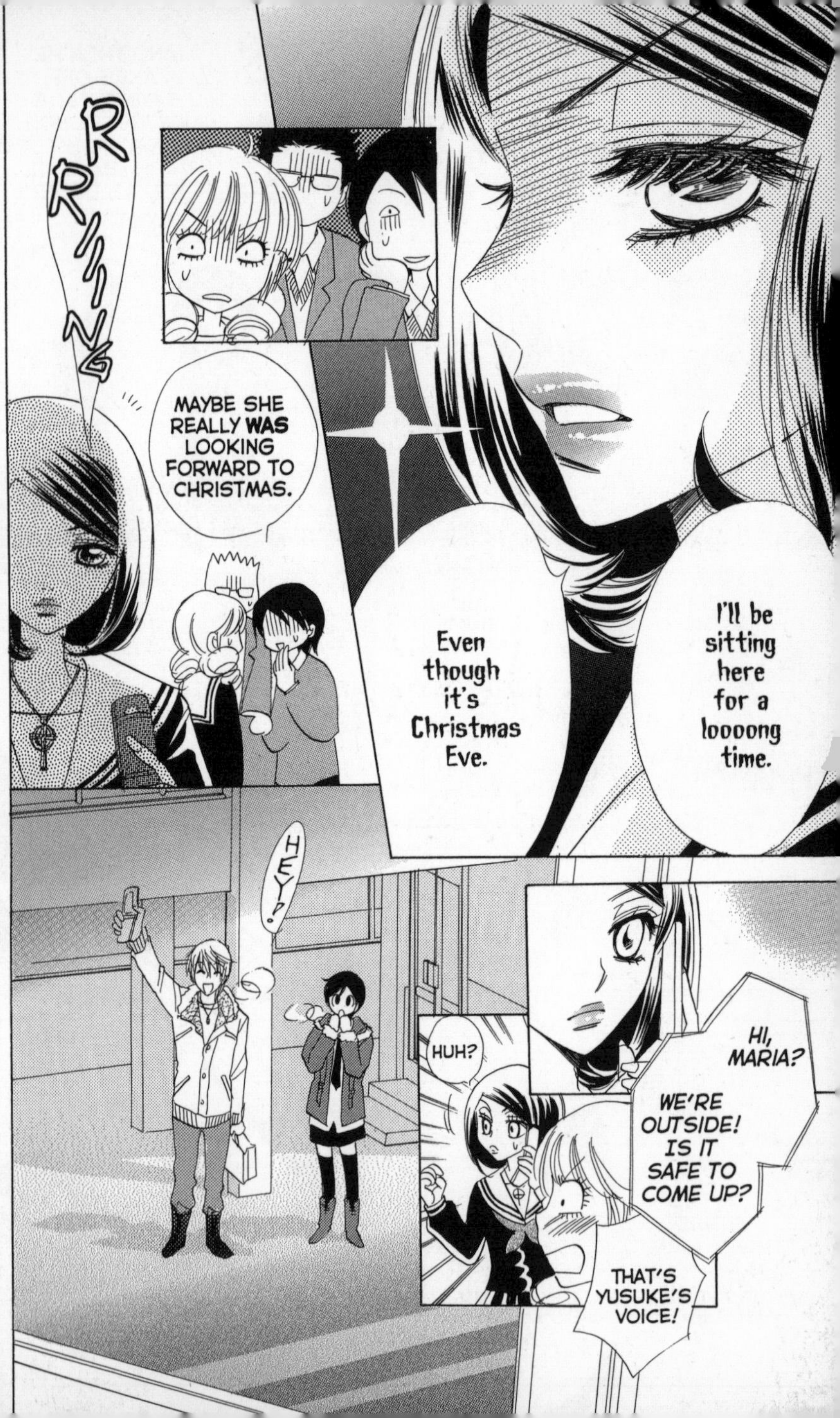
I'll be sitting here for a looooong time.
Even though it's Christmas Eve.
RRIIING
MAYBE SHE REALLY **WAS** LOOKING FORWARD TO CHRISTMAS.
HI, MARIA?
WE'RE OUTSIDE! IS IT SAFE TO COME UP?
HUH?
THAT'S YUSUKE'S VOICE!
HEY!

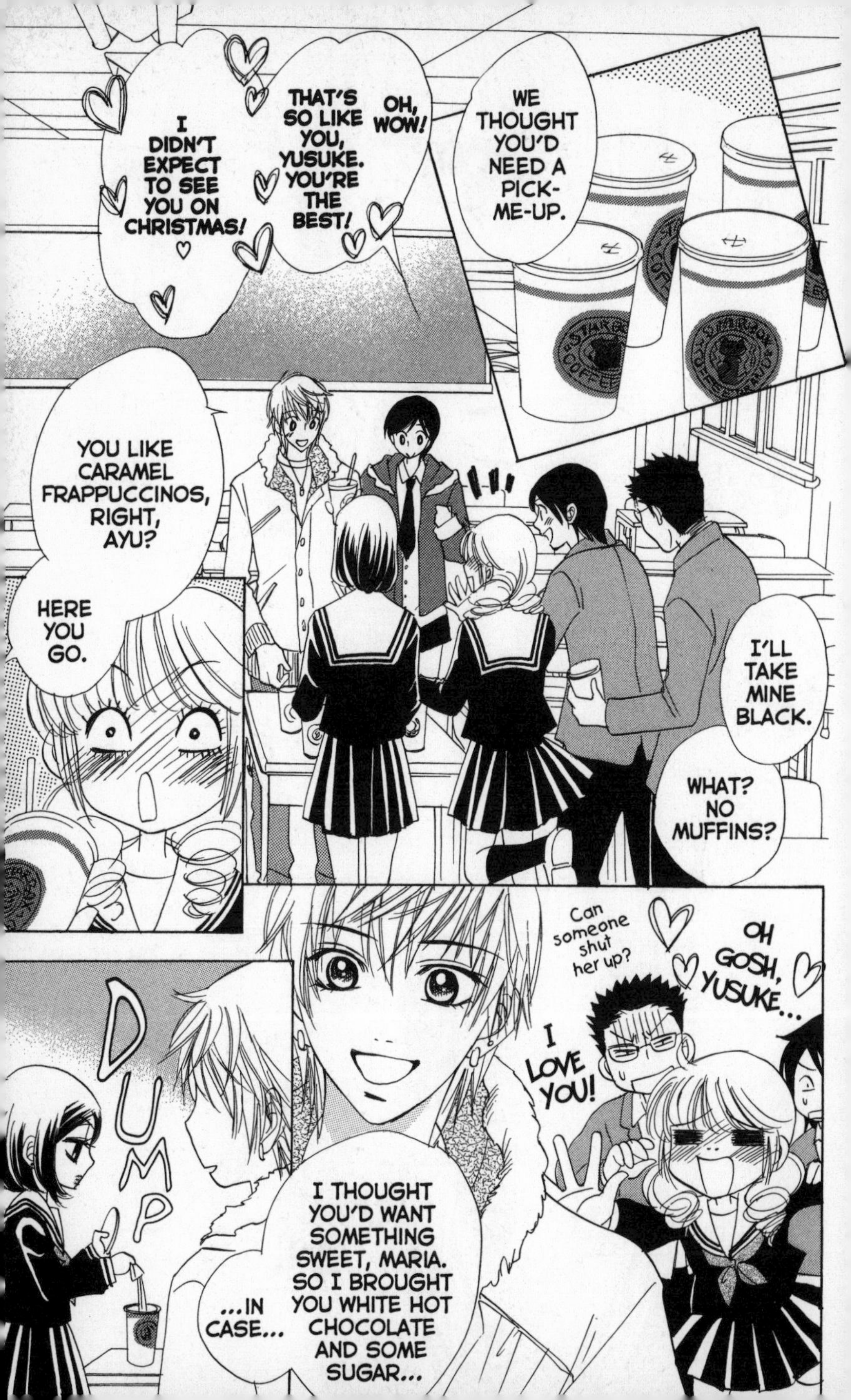
WE THOUGHT YOU'D NEED A PICK-ME-UP.
OH, WOW!
THAT'S SO LIKE YOU, YUSUKE. YOU'RE THE BEST!
I DIDN'T EXPECT TO SEE YOU ON CHRISTMAS!
I'LL TAKE MINE BLACK.
WHAT? NO MUFFINS?
YOU LIKE CARAMEL FRAPPUCCINOS, RIGHT, AYU?
HERE YOU GO.
OH GOSH, YUSUKE...
I LOVE YOU!
Can someone shut her up?
I THOUGHT YOU'D WANT SOMETHING SWEET, MARIA. SO I BROUGHT YOU WHITE HOT CHOCOLATE AND SOME SUGAR...
...IN CASE...
DUMP

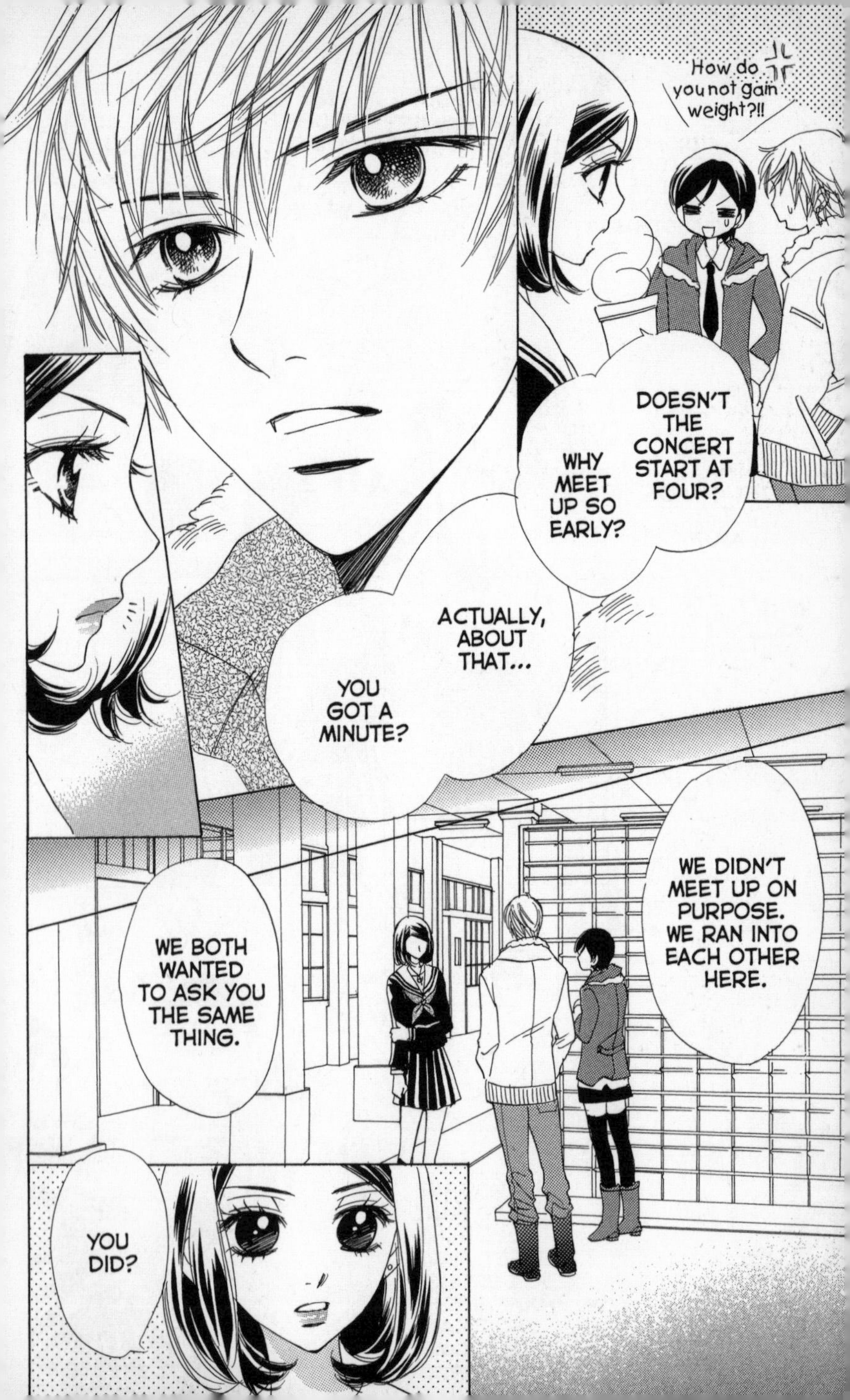
How do you not gain weight?!!
DOESN'T THE CONCERT START AT FOUR?
WHY MEET UP SO EARLY?
ACTUALLY, ABOUT THAT...
YOU GOT A MINUTE?
WE DIDN'T MEET UP ON PURPOSE. WE RAN INTO EACH OTHER HERE.
WE BOTH WANTED TO ASK YOU THE SAME THING.
YOU DID?

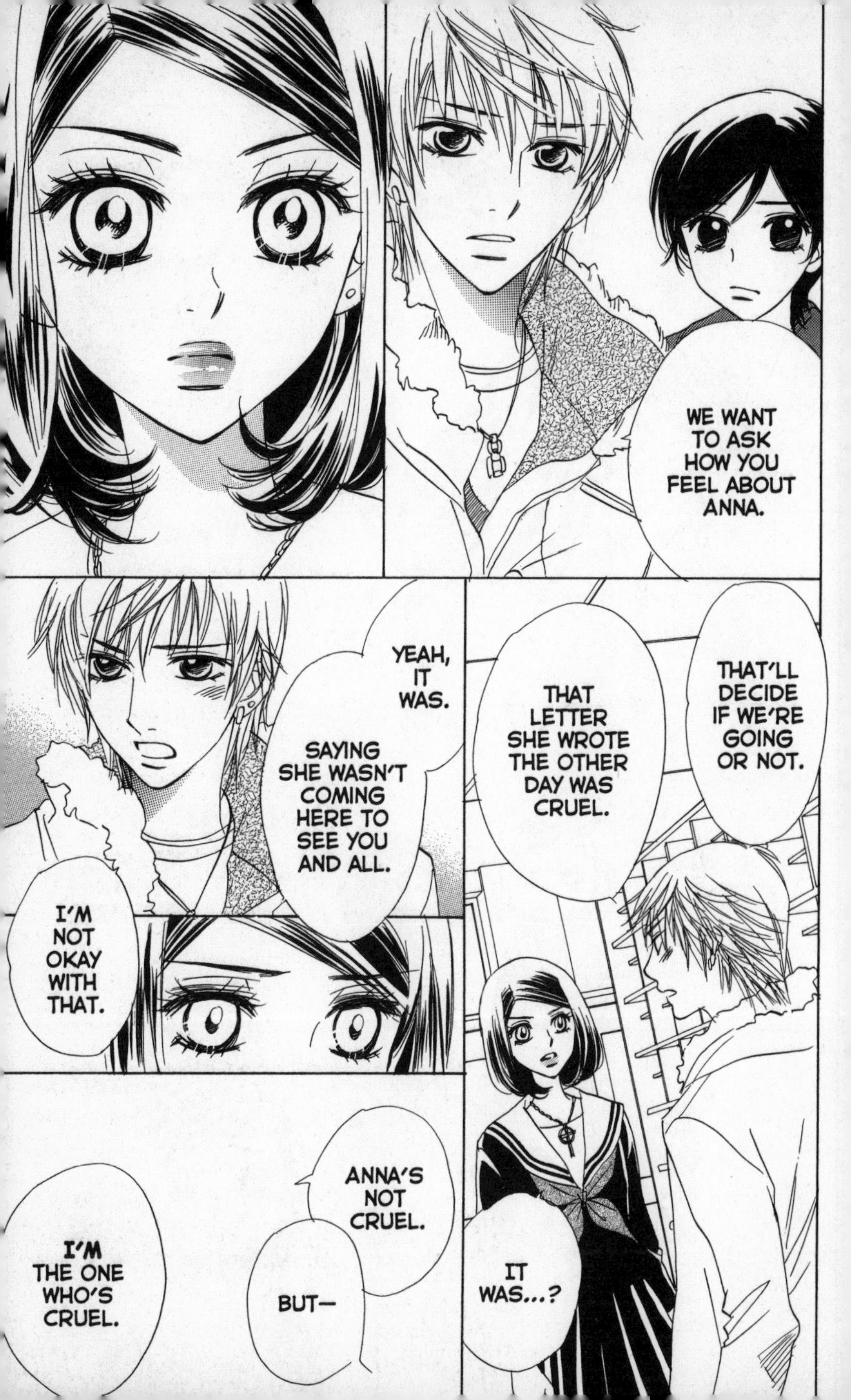
WE WANT TO ASK HOW YOU FEEL ABOUT ANNA.
THAT'LL DECIDE IF WE'RE GOING OR NOT.
THAT LETTER SHE WROTE THE OTHER DAY WAS CRUEL.
IT WAS...?
YEAH, IT WAS.
SAYING SHE WASN'T COMING HERE TO SEE YOU AND ALL.
I'M NOT OKAY WITH THAT.
ANNA'S NOT CRUEL.
BUT—
I'M THE ONE WHO'S CRUEL.

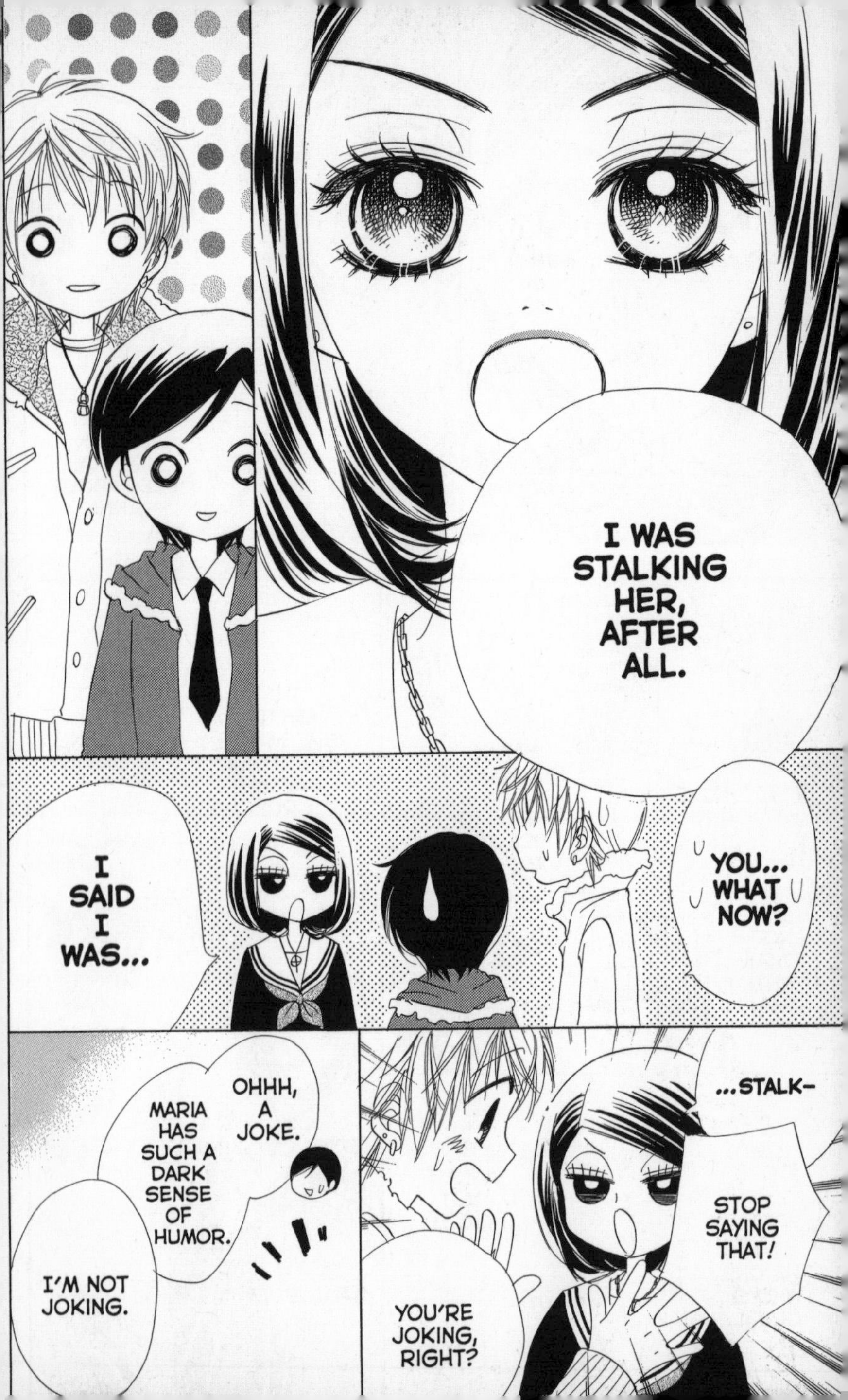
I WAS STALKING HER, AFTER ALL.
YOU... WHAT NOW?
I SAID I WAS...
...STALK-
STOP SAYING THAT!
YOU'RE JOKING, RIGHT?
OHHH, A JOKE.
MARIA HAS SUCH A DARK SENSE OF HUMOR.
I'M NOT JOKING.

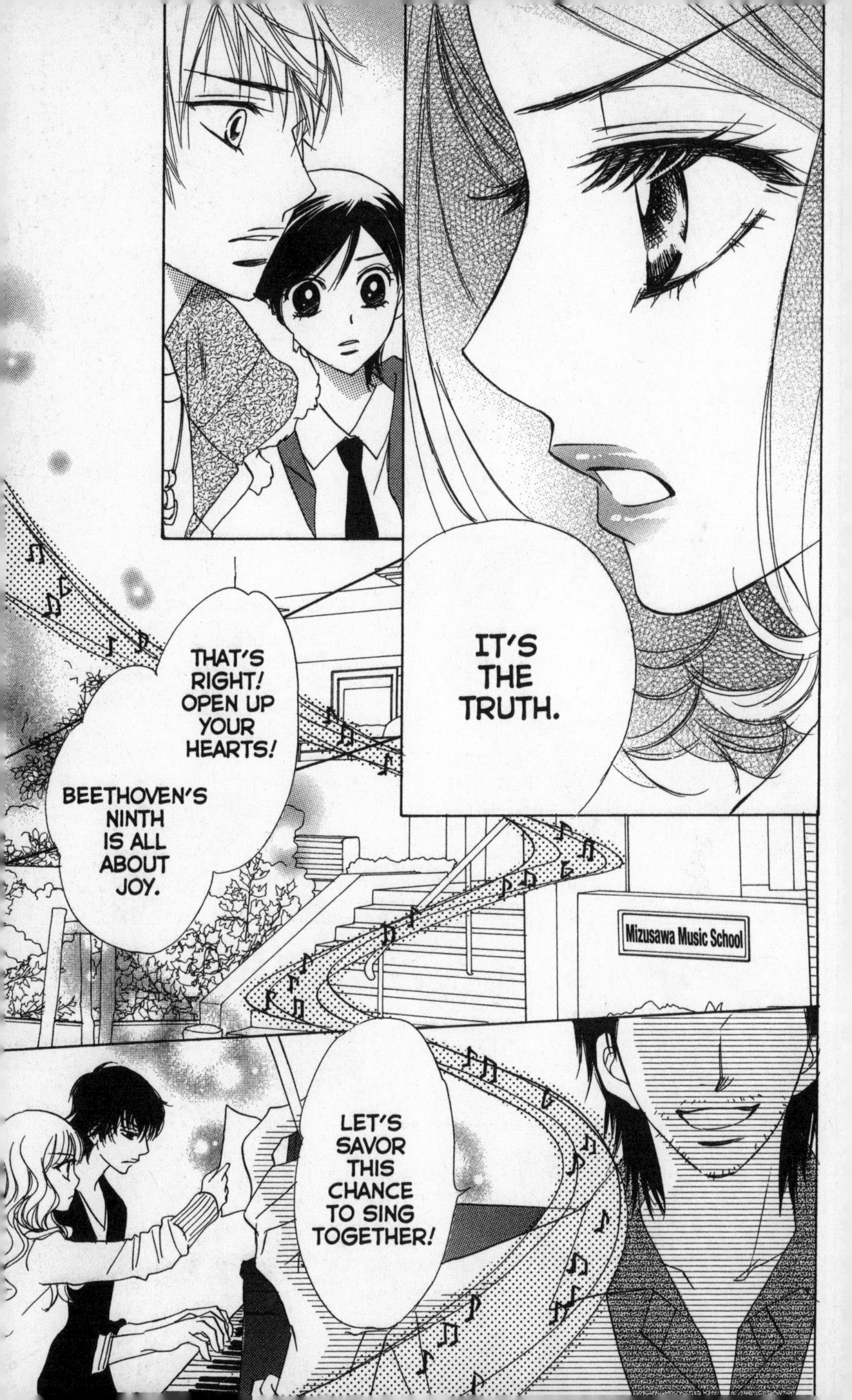
IT'S THE TRUTH.
THAT'S RIGHT! OPEN UP YOUR HEARTS!
BEETHOVEN'S NINTH IS ALL ABOUT JOY.
Mizusawa Music School
LET'S SAVOR THIS CHANCE TO SING TOGETHER!

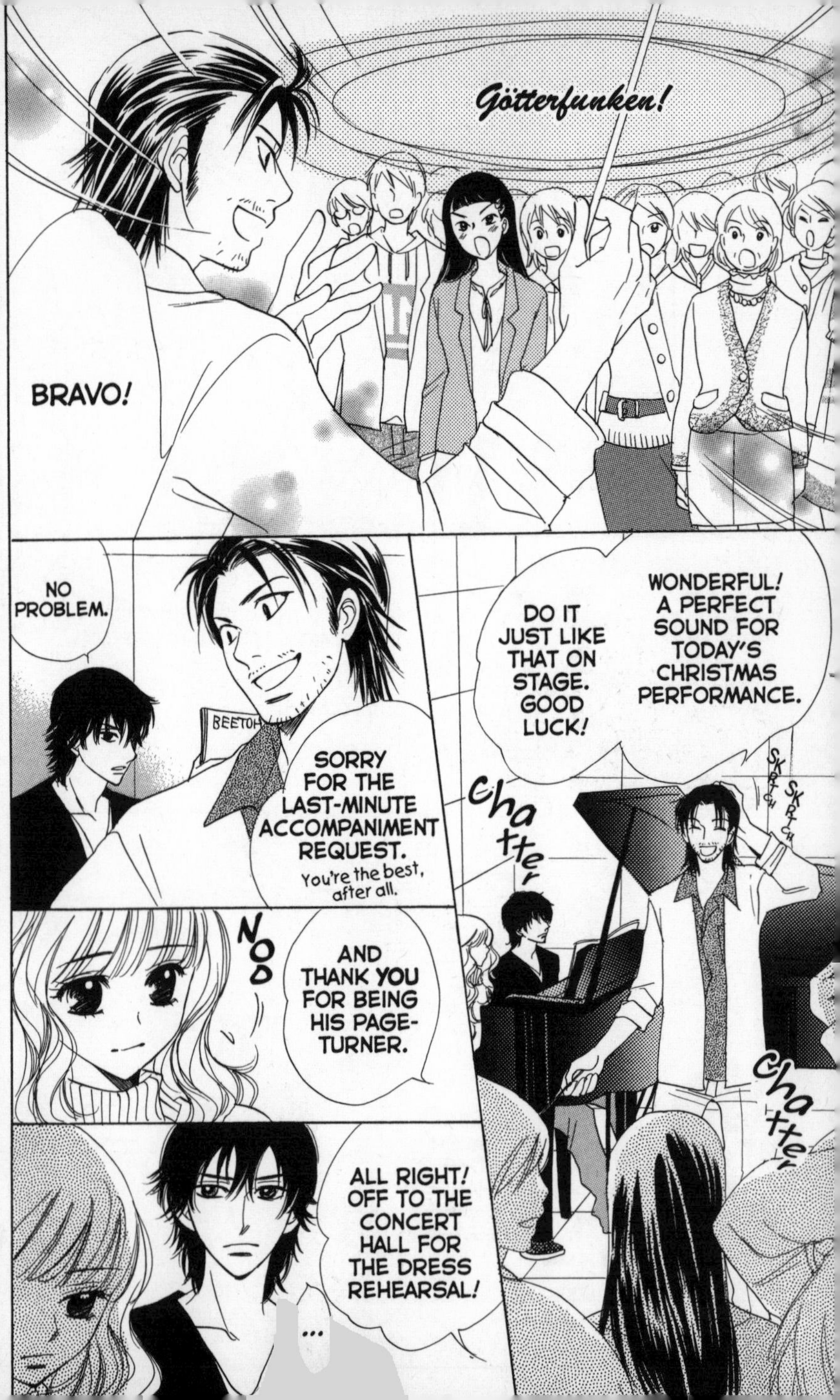
Götterfunken!
BRAVO!
WONDERFUL! A PERFECT SOUND FOR TODAY'S CHRISTMAS PERFORMANCE.
DO IT JUST LIKE THAT ON STAGE. GOOD LUCK!
SKRITCH SKRITCH
Chatter
Chatter
SORRY FOR THE LAST-MINUTE ACCOMPANIMENT REQUEST.
You're the best, after all.
NO PROBLEM.
BEETOH
AND THANK YOU FOR BEING HIS PAGE-TURNER.
NOD
ALL RIGHT! OFF TO THE CONCERT HALL FOR THE DRESS REHEARSAL!
...

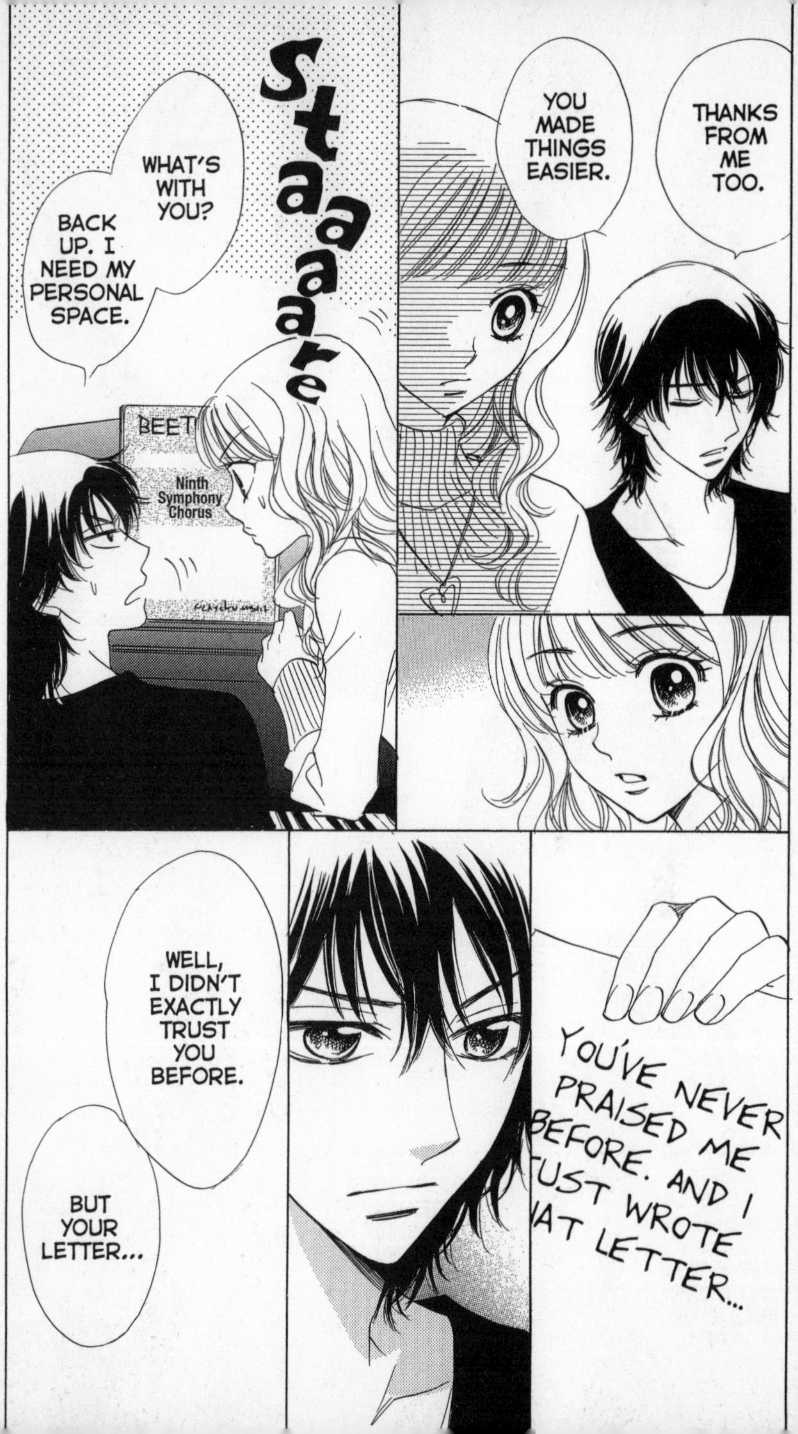
THANKS FROM ME TOO.
YOU MADE THINGS EASIER.
STAAAAARE
WHAT'S WITH YOU?
BACK UP. I NEED MY PERSONAL SPACE.
BEET
Ninth Symphony Chorus
YOU'VE NEVER PRAISED ME BEFORE. AND I UST WROTE AT LETTER...
WELL, I DIDN'T EXACTLY TRUST YOU BEFORE.
BUT YOUR LETTER...

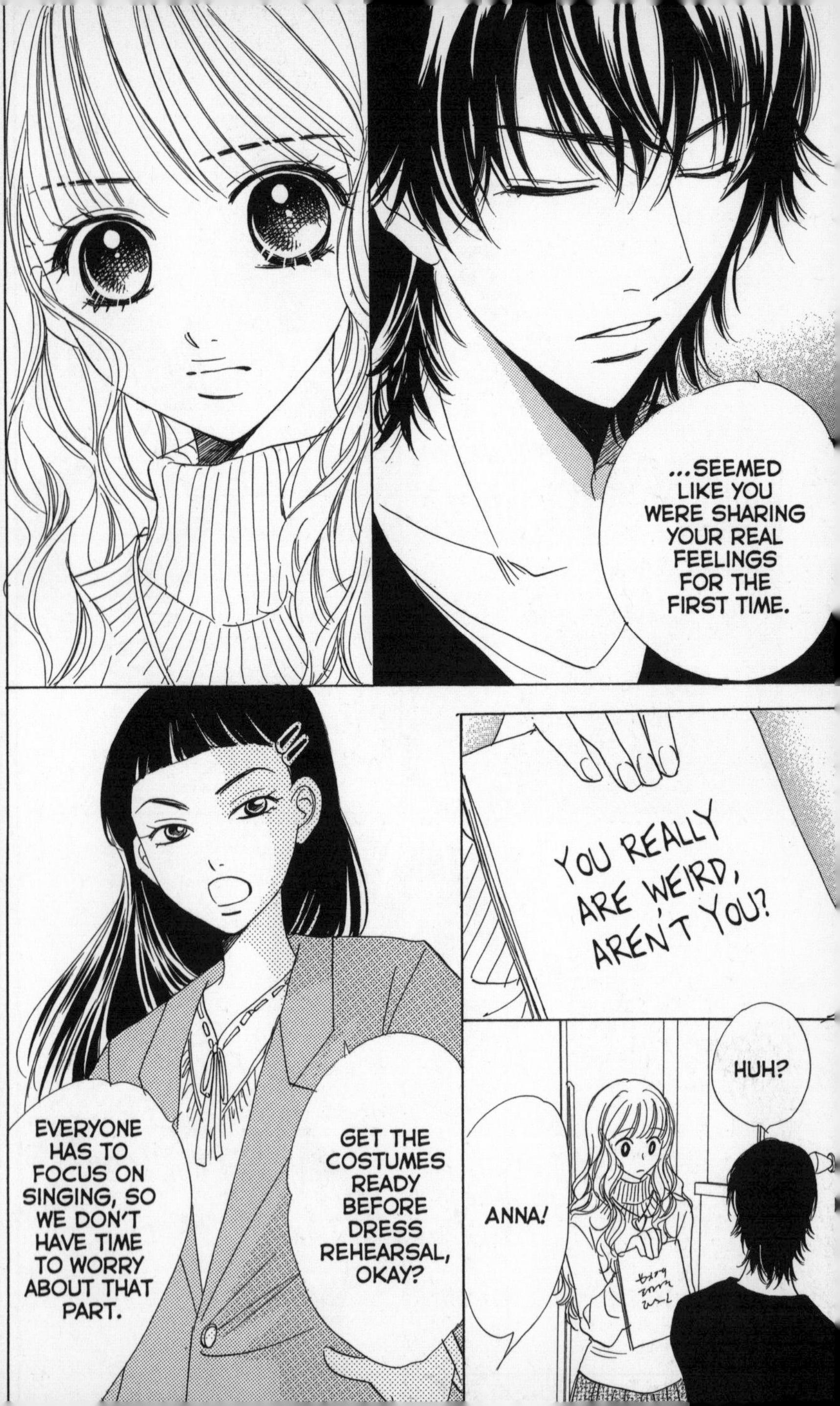
...SEEMED LIKE YOU WERE SHARING YOUR REAL FEELINGS FOR THE FIRST TIME.
YOU REALLY ARE WEIRD, AREN'T YOU?
HUH?
ANNA!
GET THE COSTUMES READY BEFORE DRESS REHEARSAL, OKAY?
EVERYONE HAS TO FOCUS ON SINGING, SO WE DON'T HAVE TIME TO WORRY ABOUT THAT PART.

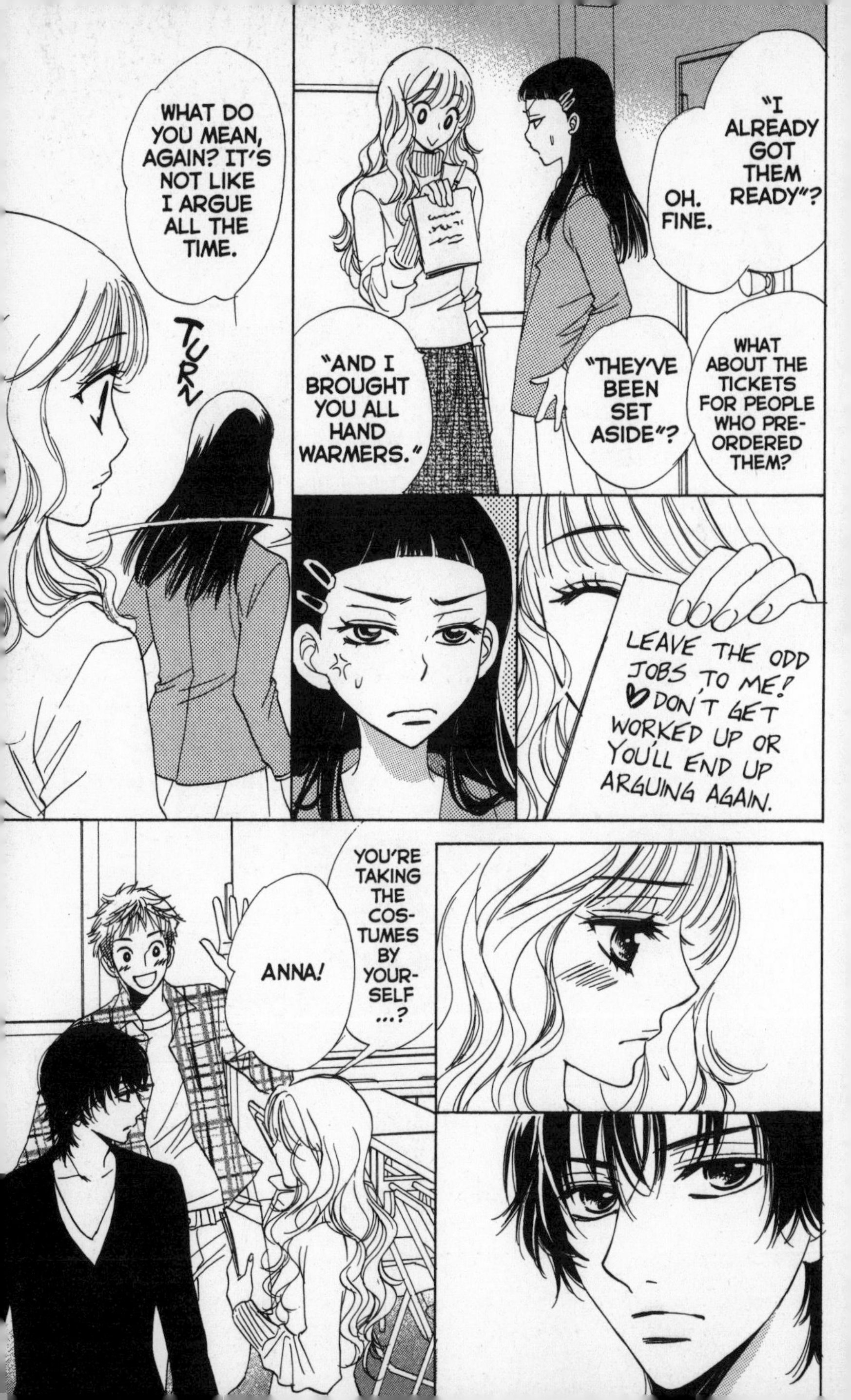

"I ALREADY GOT THEM READY"?
OH. FINE.
WHAT ABOUT THE TICKETS FOR PEOPLE WHO PRE-ORDERED THEM?
"THEY'VE BEEN SET ASIDE"?
"AND I BROUGHT YOU ALL HAND WARMERS."
LEAVE THE ODD JOBS TO ME! ♥ DON'T GET WORKED UP OR YOU'LL END UP ARGUING AGAIN.
WHAT DO YOU MEAN, AGAIN? IT'S NOT LIKE I ARGUE ALL THE TIME.
TURN
YOU'RE TAKING THE COS-TUMES BY YOUR-SELF ...?
ANNA!

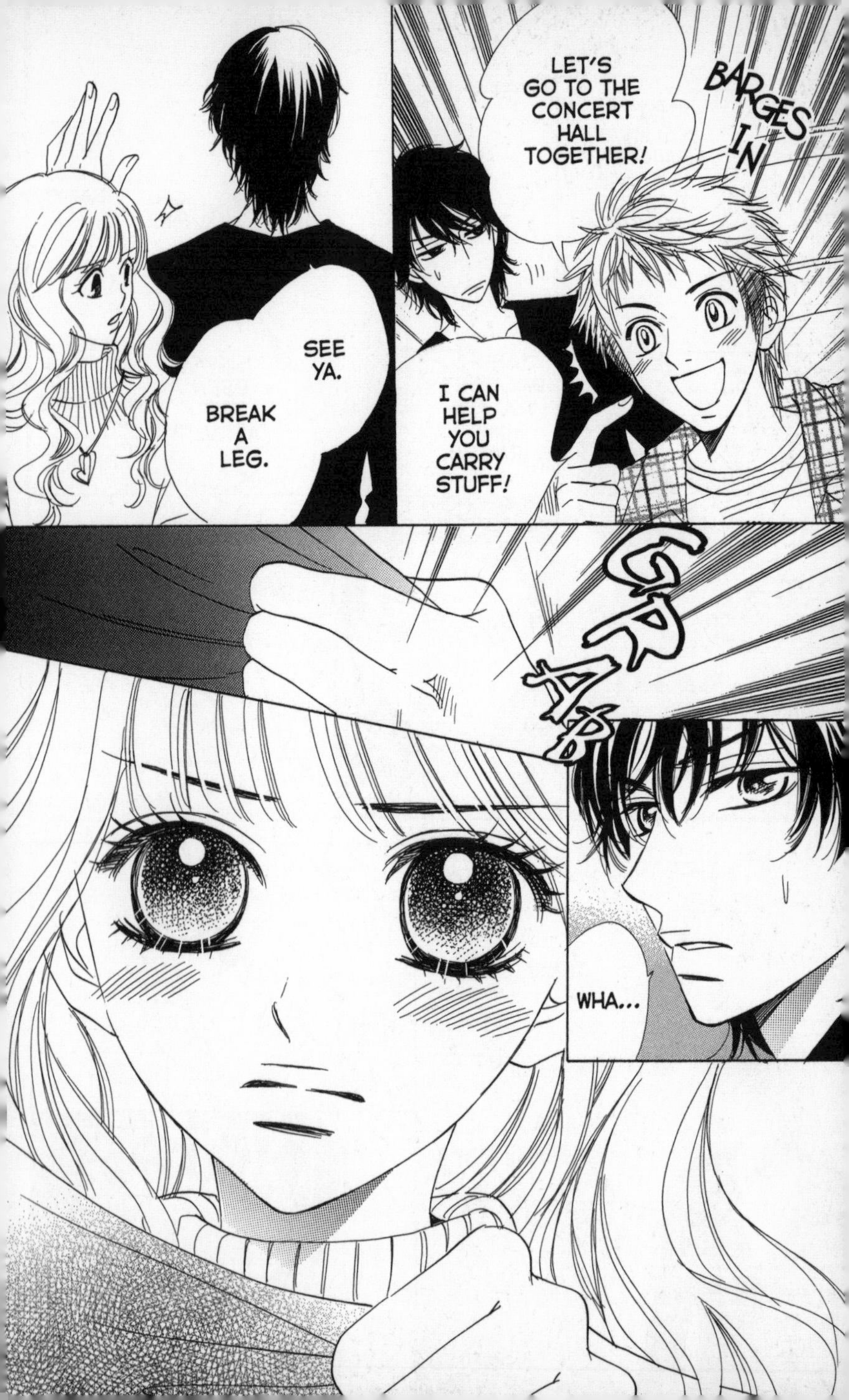
LET'S GO TO THE CONCERT HALL TOGETHER!
BARGES IN
I CAN HELP YOU CARRY STUFF!
SEE YA.
BREAK A LEG.
GRAB
WHA...

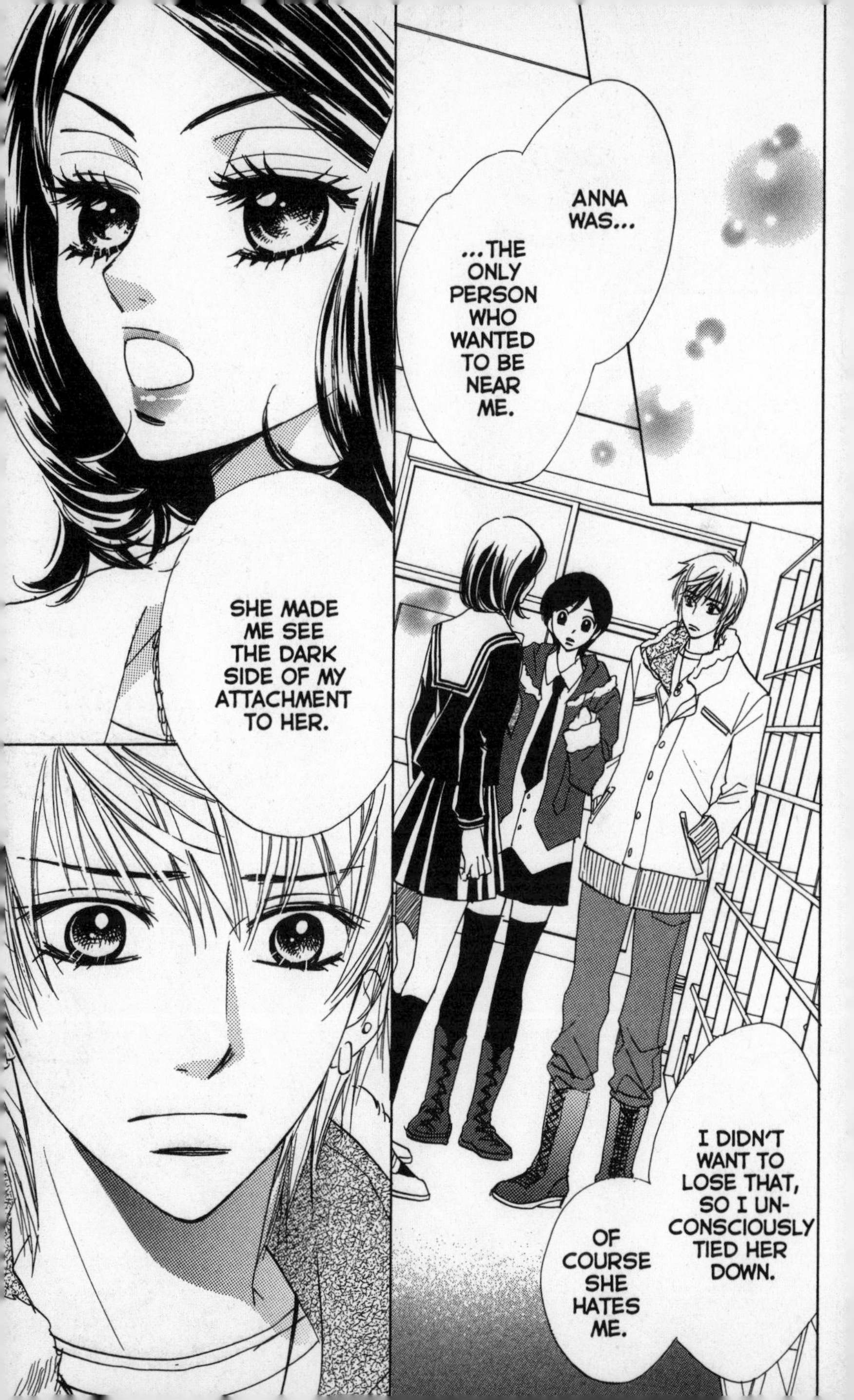
ANNA WAS...
...THE ONLY PERSON WHO WANTED TO BE NEAR ME.
I DIDN'T WANT TO LOSE THAT, SO I UN-CONSCIOUSLY TIED HER DOWN.
OF COURSE SHE HATES ME.
SHE MADE ME SEE THE DARK SIDE OF MY ATTACHMENT TO HER.

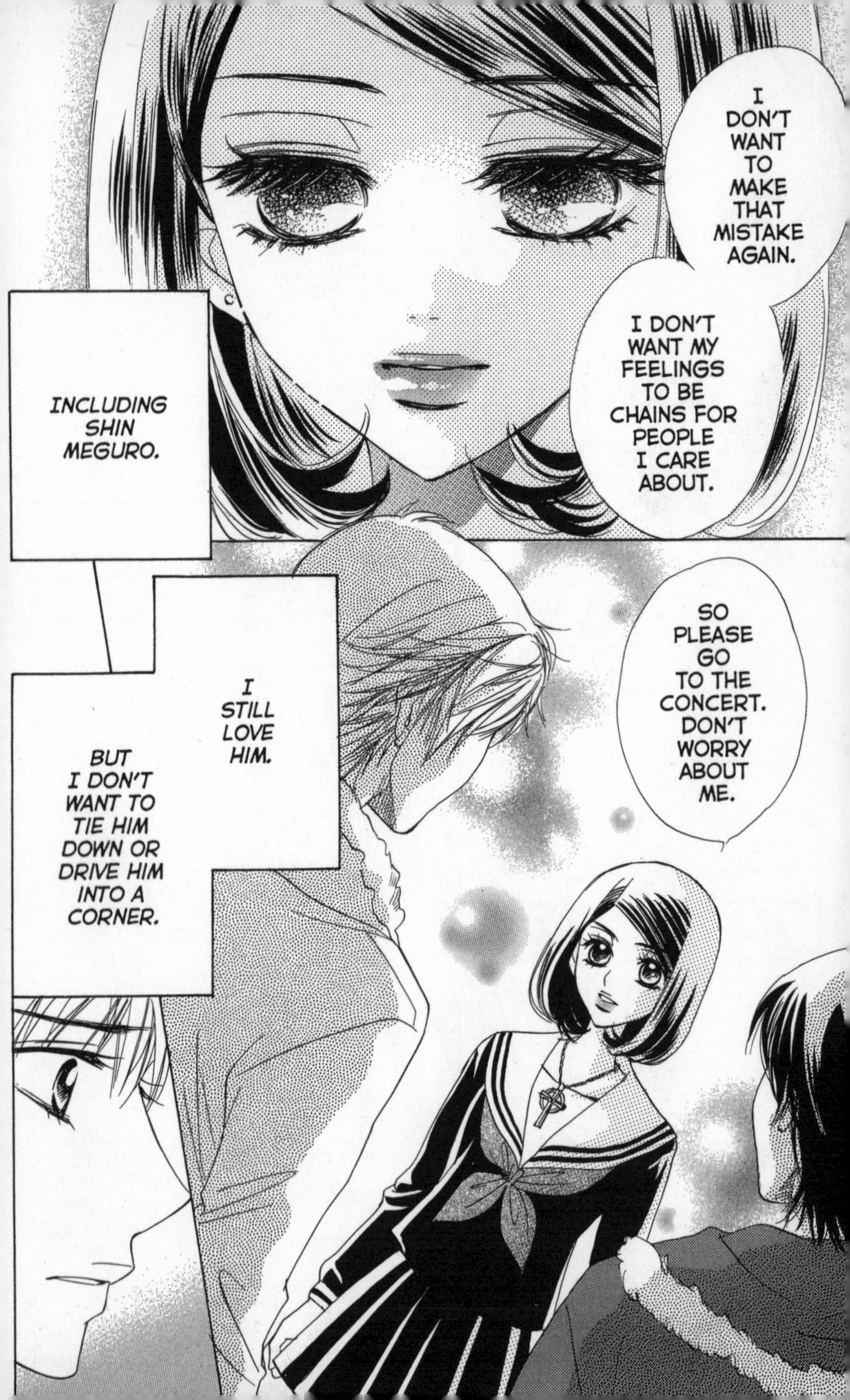
I DON'T WANT TO MAKE THAT MISTAKE AGAIN.
I DON'T WANT MY FEELINGS TO BE CHAINS FOR PEOPLE I CARE ABOUT.
INCLUDING SHIN MEGURO.
SO PLEASE GO TO THE CONCERT. DON'T WORRY ABOUT ME.
I STILL LOVE HIM.
BUT I DON'T WANT TO TIE HIM DOWN OR DRIVE HIM INTO A CORNER.

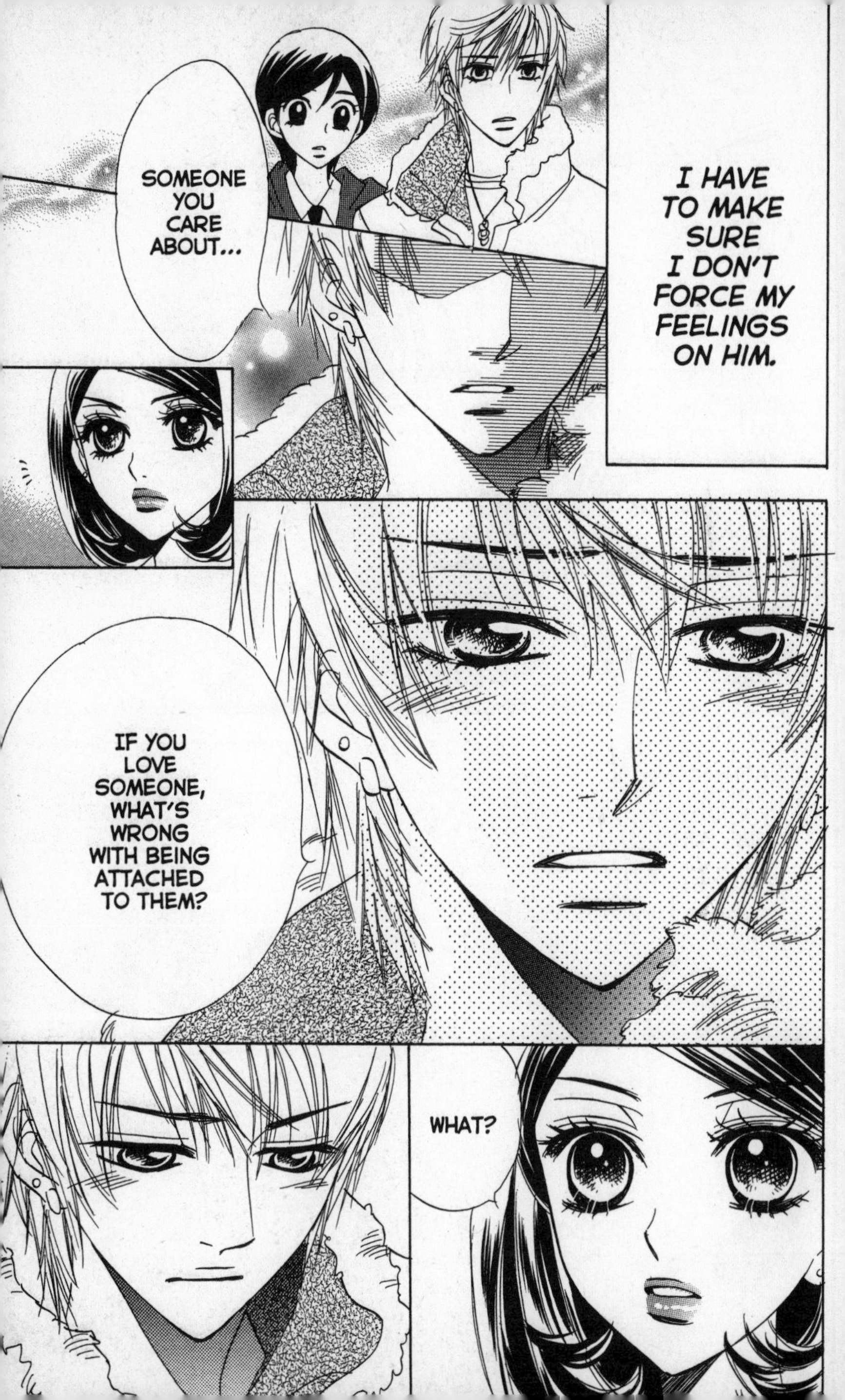
I HAVE TO MAKE SURE I DON'T FORCE MY FEELINGS ON HIM.
SOMEONE YOU CARE ABOUT...
IF YOU LOVE SOMEONE, WHAT'S WRONG WITH BEING ATTACHED TO THEM?
WHAT?

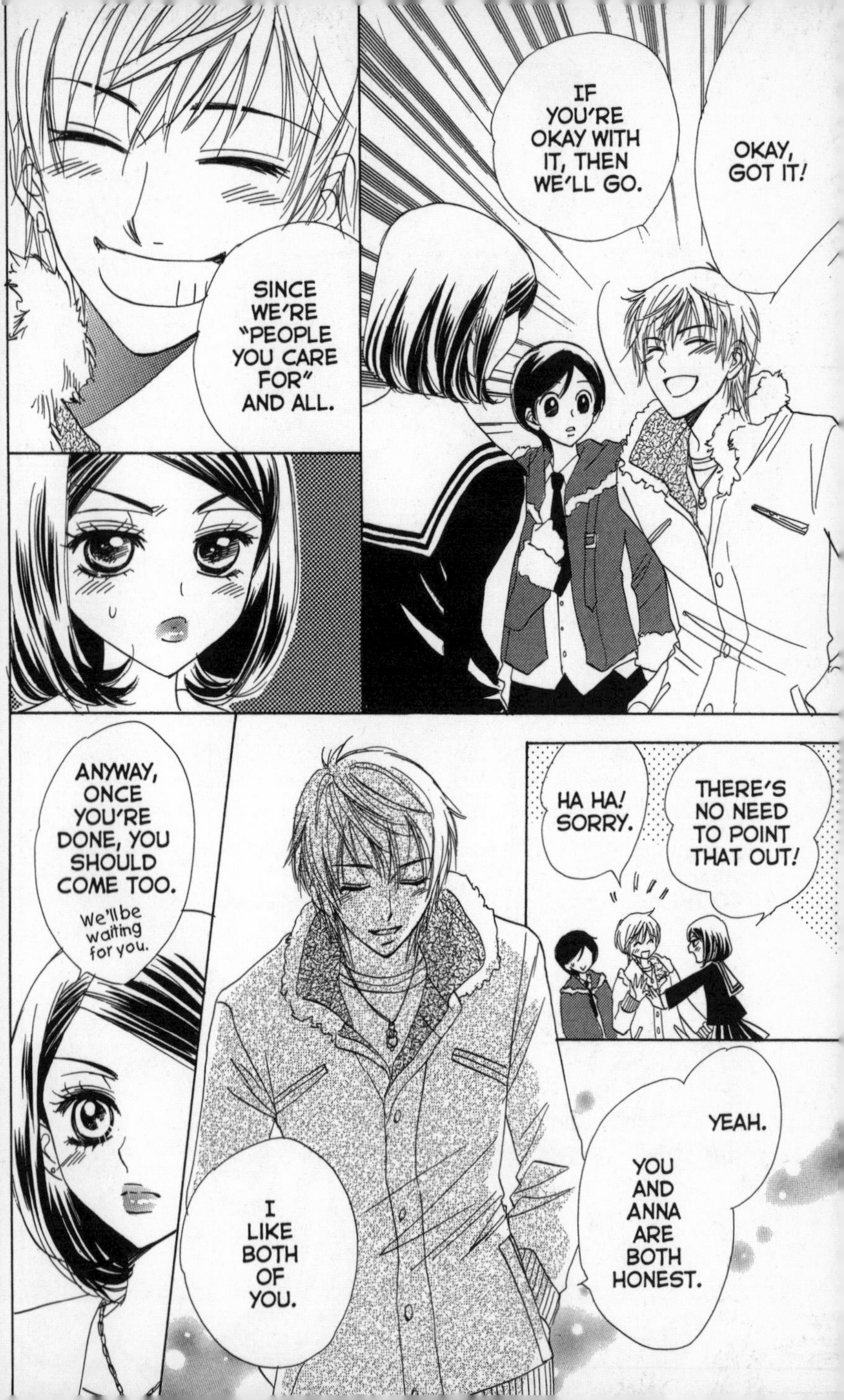
IF YOU'RE OKAY WITH IT, THEN WE'LL GO.
OKAY, GOT IT!
SINCE WE'RE "PEOPLE YOU CARE FOR" AND ALL.
THERE'S NO NEED TO POINT THAT OUT!
HA HA! SORRY.
YEAH.
YOU AND ANNA ARE BOTH HONEST.
I LIKE BOTH OF YOU.
ANYWAY, ONCE YOU'RE DONE, YOU SHOULD COME TOO.
We'll be waiting for you.

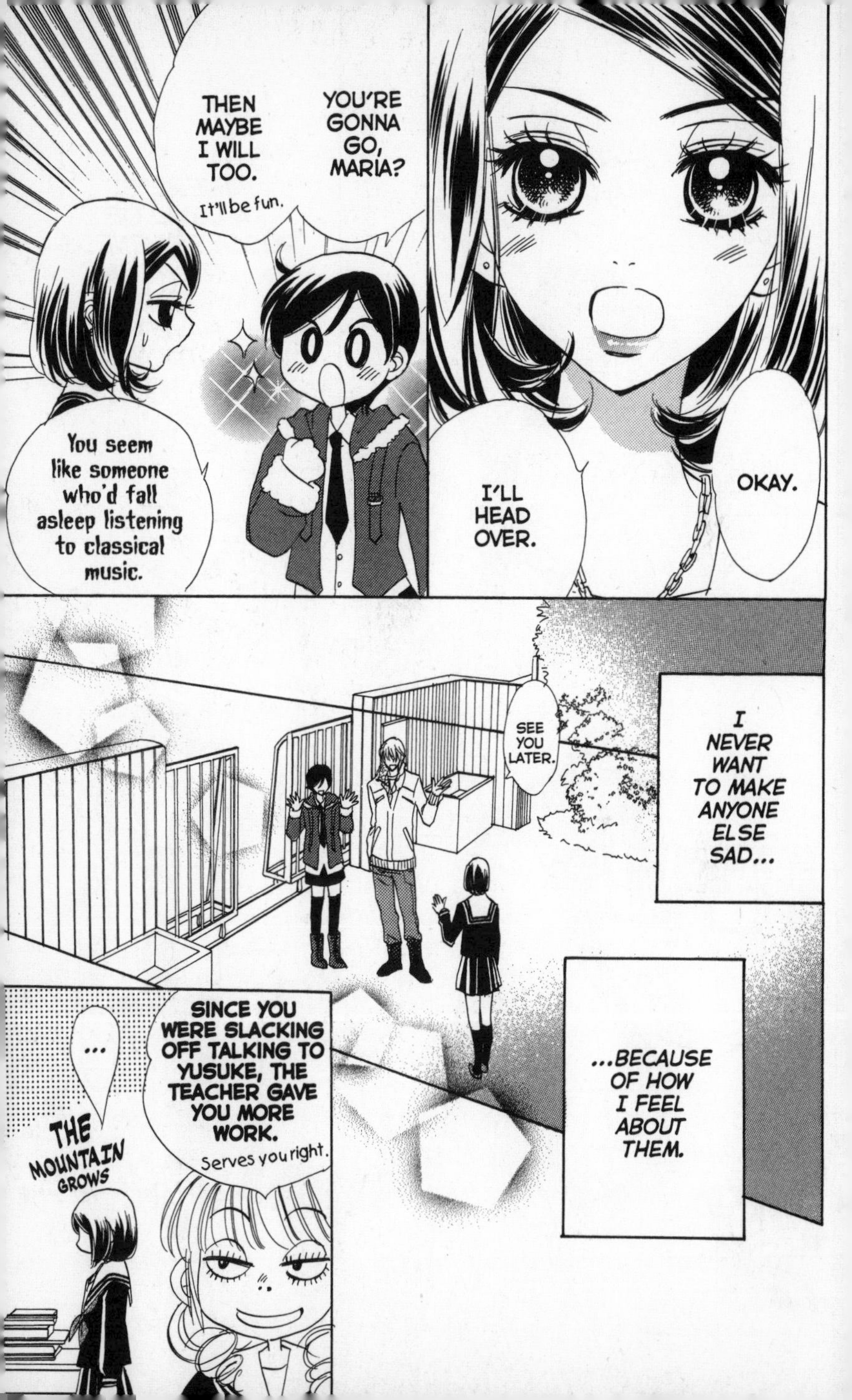
OKAY.
I'LL HEAD OVER.
YOU'RE GONNA GO, MARIA?
THEN MAYBE I WILL TOO.
It'll be fun.
You seem like someone who'd fall asleep listening to classical music.
I NEVER WANT TO MAKE ANYONE ELSE SAD...
SEE YOU LATER.
...BECAUSE OF HOW I FEEL ABOUT THEM.
SINCE YOU WERE SLACKING OFF TALKING TO YUSUKE, THE TEACHER GAVE YOU MORE WORK.
Serves you right.
...
THE MOUNTAIN GROWS

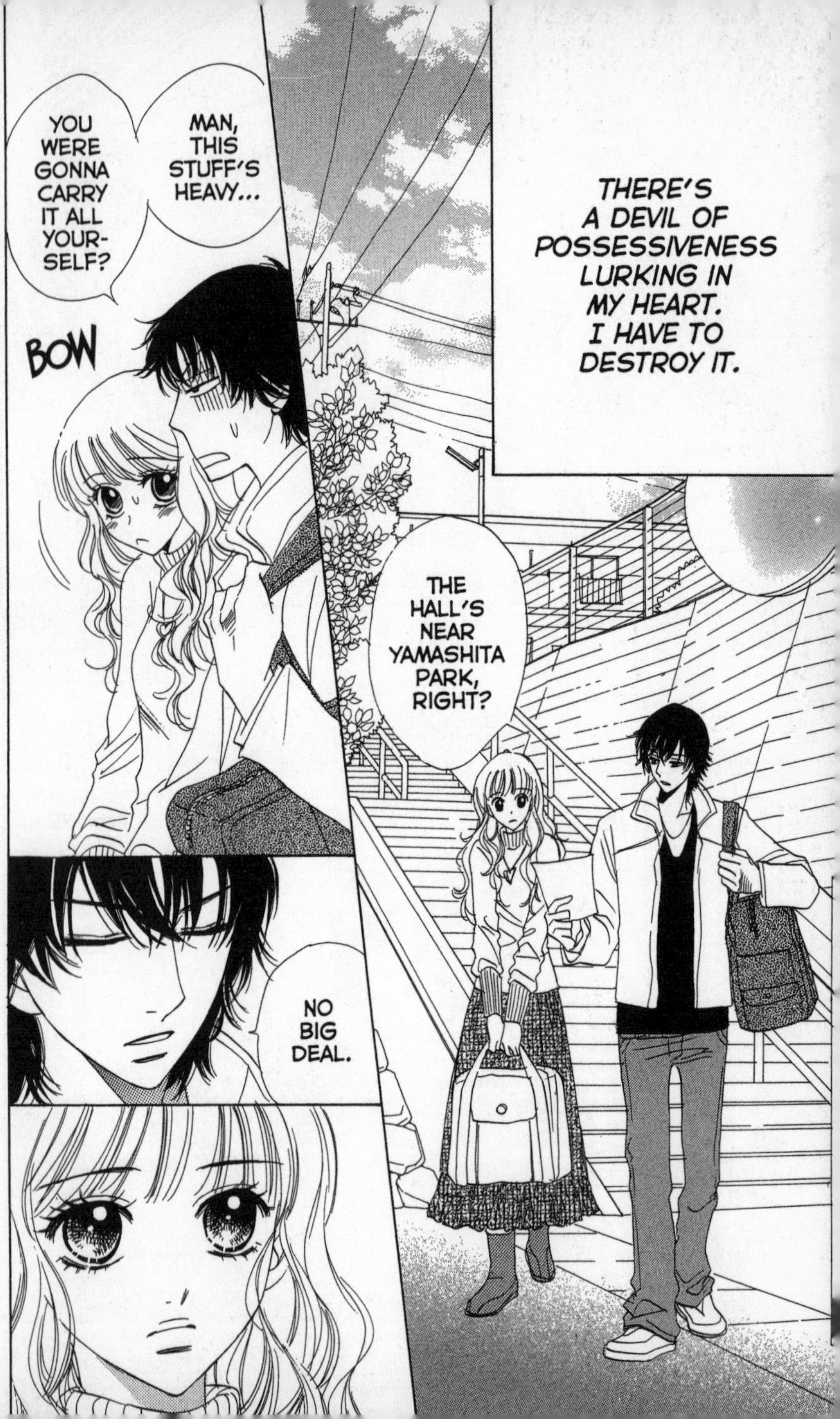
THERE'S A DEVIL OF POSSESSIVENESS LURKING IN MY HEART. I HAVE TO DESTROY IT.
THE HALL'S NEAR YAMASHITA PARK, RIGHT?
MAN, THIS STUFF'S HEAVY...
YOU WERE GONNA CARRY IT ALL YOUR-SELF?
BOW
NO BIG DEAL.

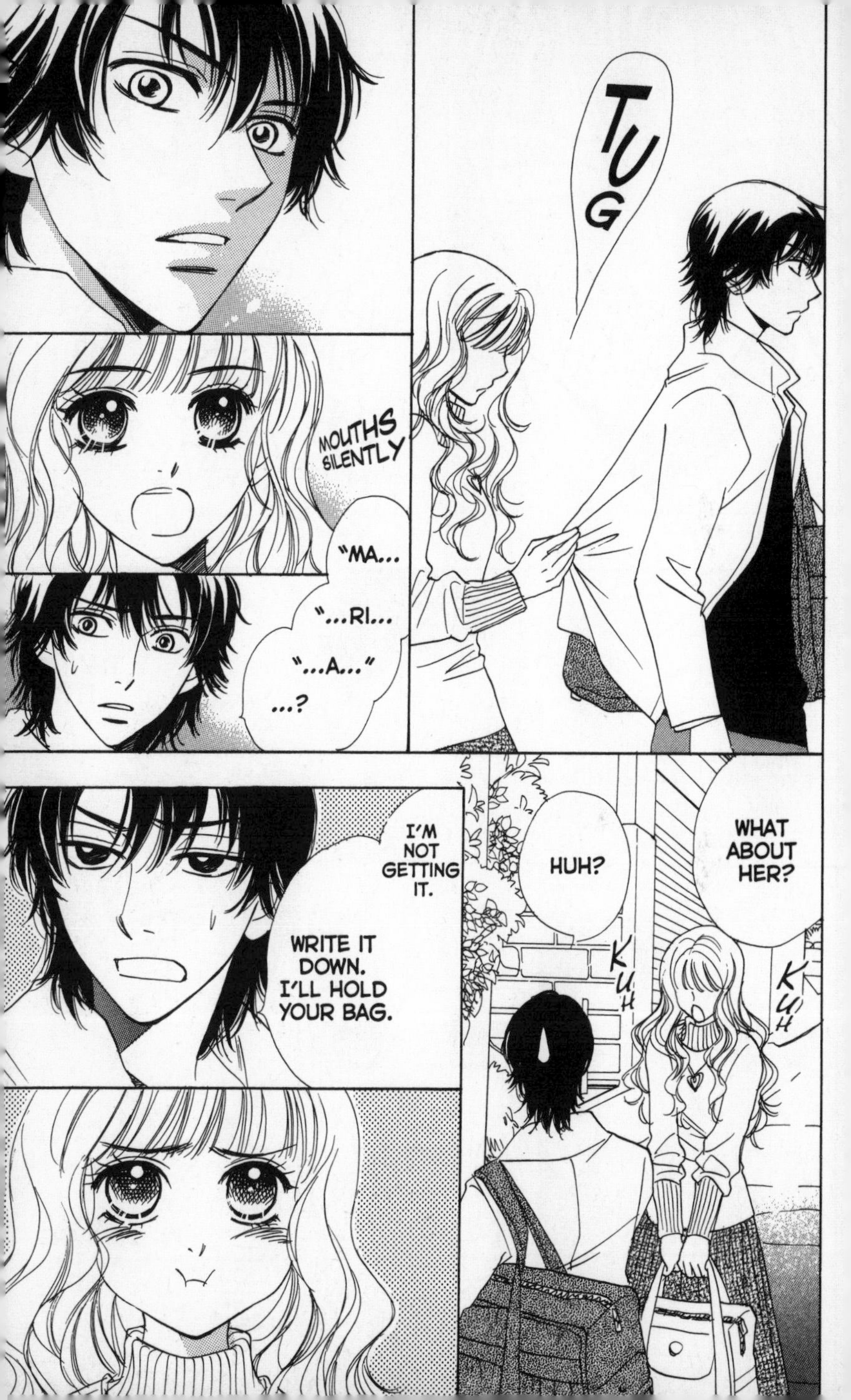
TUG
MOUTHS SILENTLY
"MA...
"...RI...
"...A..."
...?
WHAT ABOUT HER?
KUH
HUH?
KUH
I'M NOT GETTING IT.
WRITE IT DOWN. I'LL HOLD YOUR BAG.

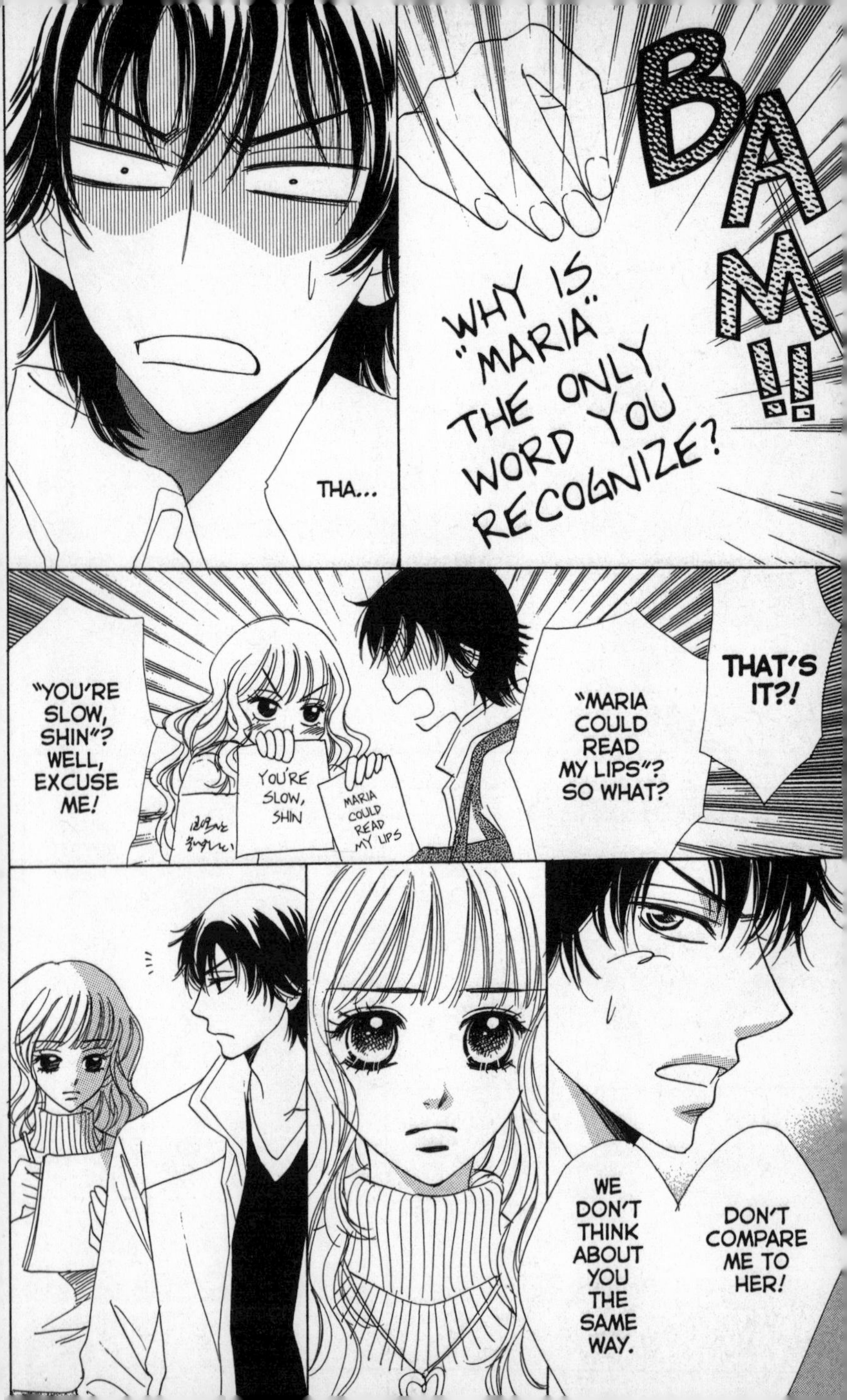
BAM!!
WHY IS "MARIA" THE ONLY WORD YOU RECOGNIZE?
THA...
THAT'S IT?!
"MARIA COULD READ MY LIPS"? SO WHAT?
MARIA COULD READ MY LIPS
YOU'RE SLOW, SHIN
"YOU'RE SLOW, SHIN"? WELL, EXCUSE ME!
DON'T COMPARE ME TO HER!
WE DON'T THINK ABOUT YOU THE SAME WAY.

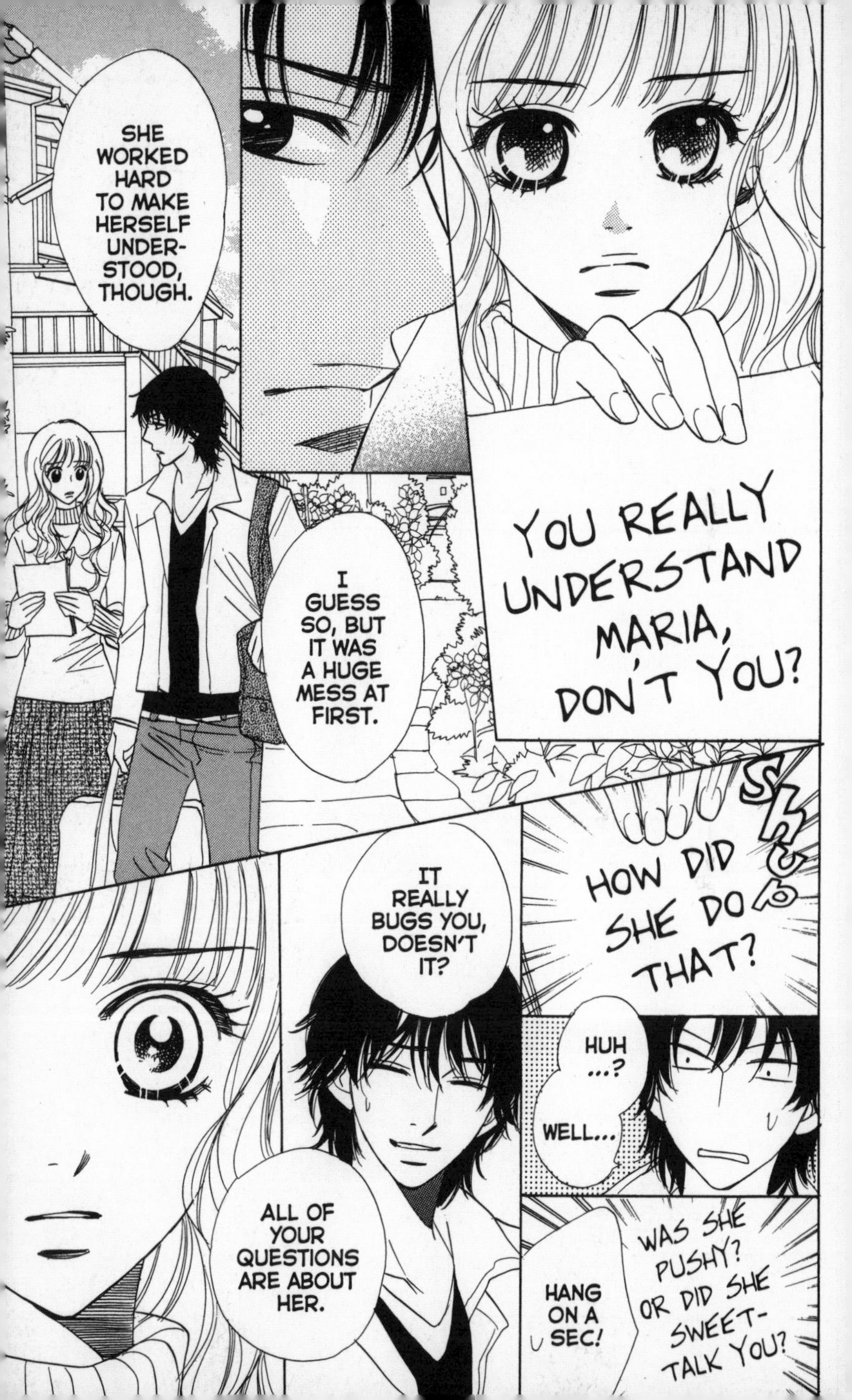
YOU REALLY UNDERSTAND MARIA, DON'T YOU?
I GUESS SO, BUT IT WAS A HUGE MESS AT FIRST.
SHE WORKED HARD TO MAKE HERSELF UNDER-STOOD, THOUGH.
SHUP
HOW DID SHE DO THAT?
HUH ...?
WELL...
WAS SHE PUSHY? OR DID SHE SWEET-TALK YOU?
HANG ON A SEC!
IT REALLY BUGS YOU, DOESN'T IT?
ALL OF YOUR QUESTIONS ARE ABOUT HER.

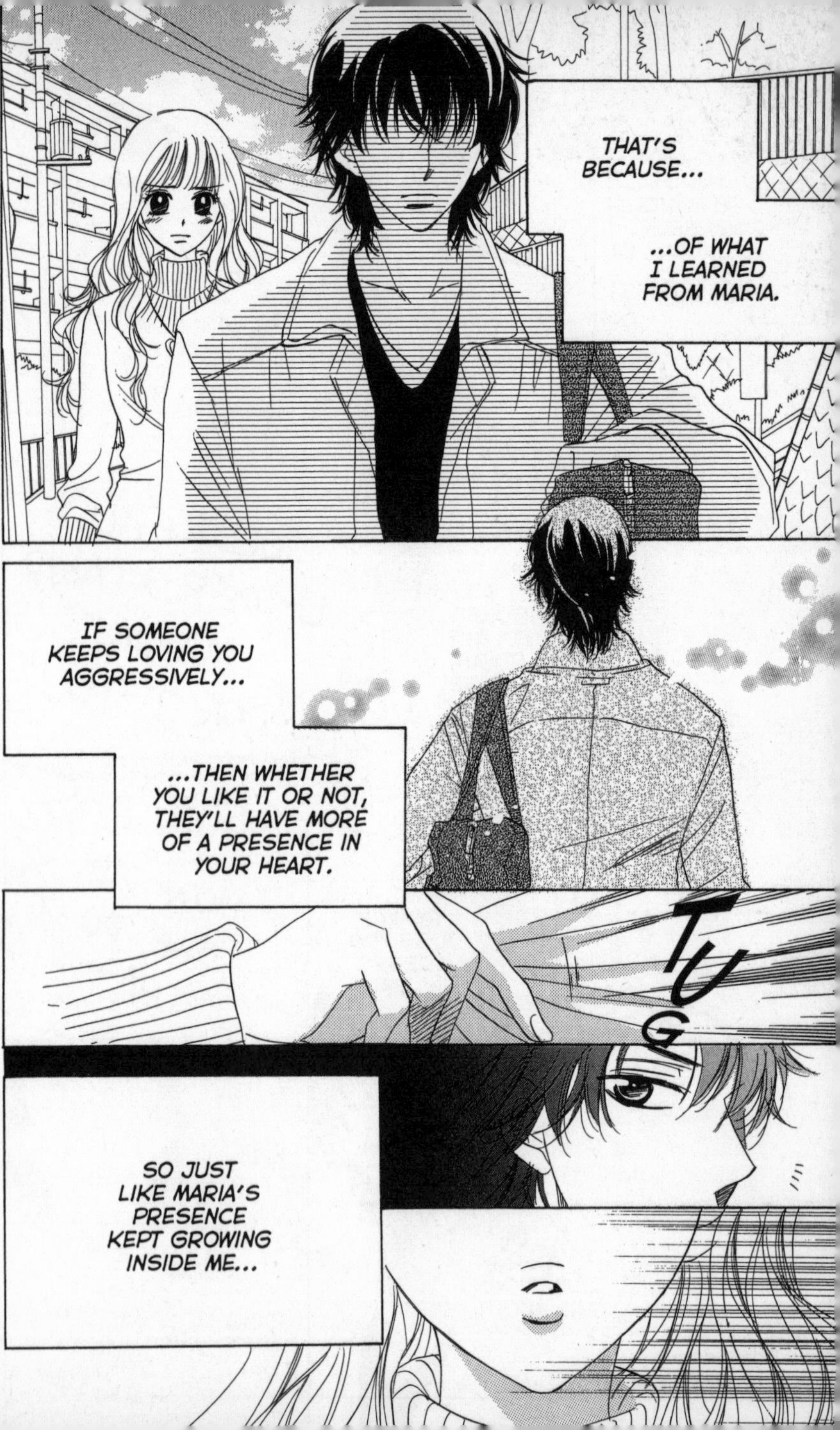
THAT'S BECAUSE...
...OF WHAT I LEARNED FROM MARIA.
IF SOMEONE KEEPS LOVING YOU AGGRESSIVELY...
...THEN WHETHER YOU LIKE IT OR NOT, THEY'LL HAVE MORE OF A PRESENCE IN YOUR HEART.
TUG
SO JUST LIKE MARIA'S PRESENCE KEPT GROWING INSIDE ME...

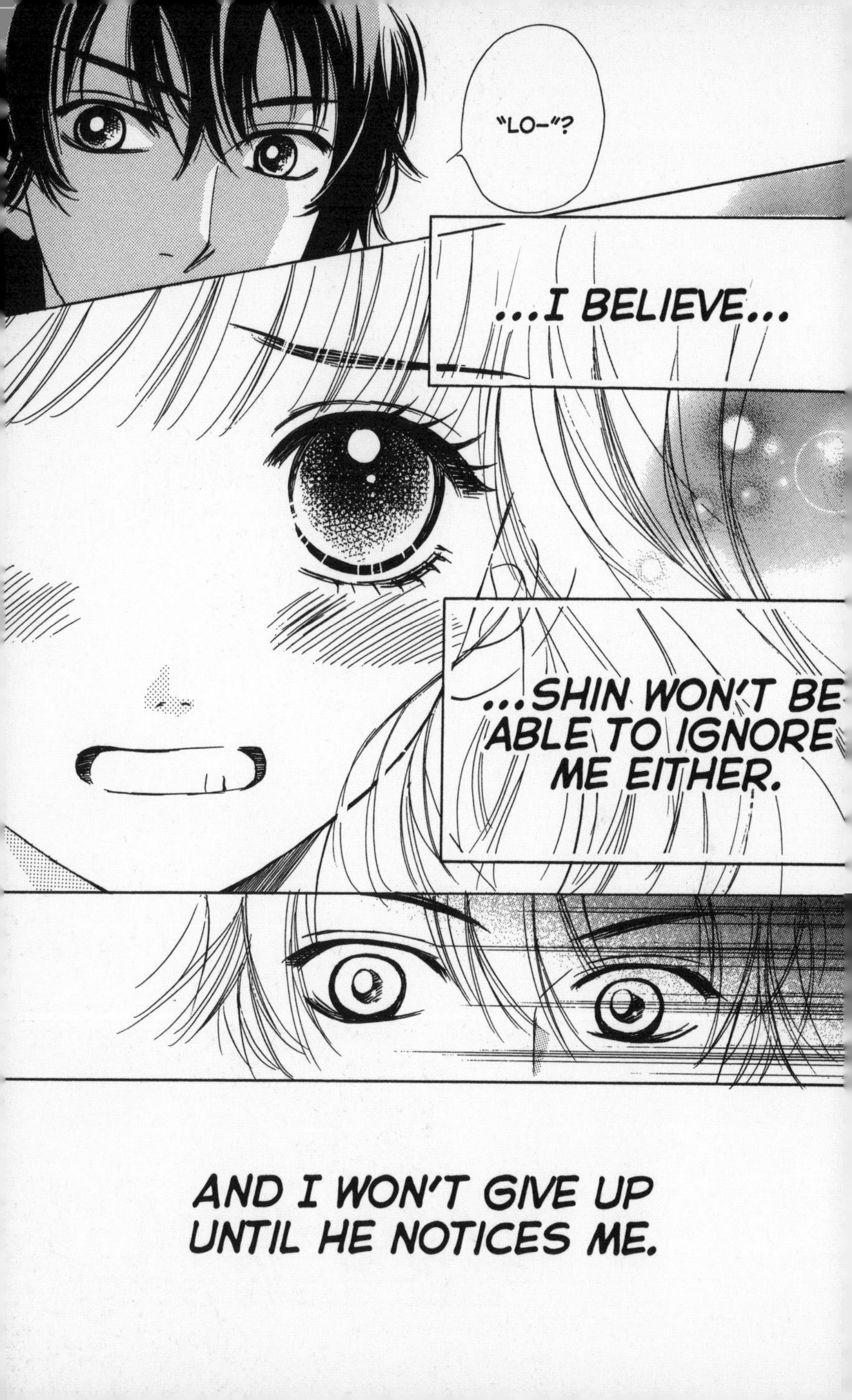
"LO-"?
...I BELIEVE...
...SHIN WON'T BE ABLE TO IGNORE ME EITHER.
AND I WON'T GIVE UP UNTIL HE NOTICES ME.

A Devil and Her Love Song

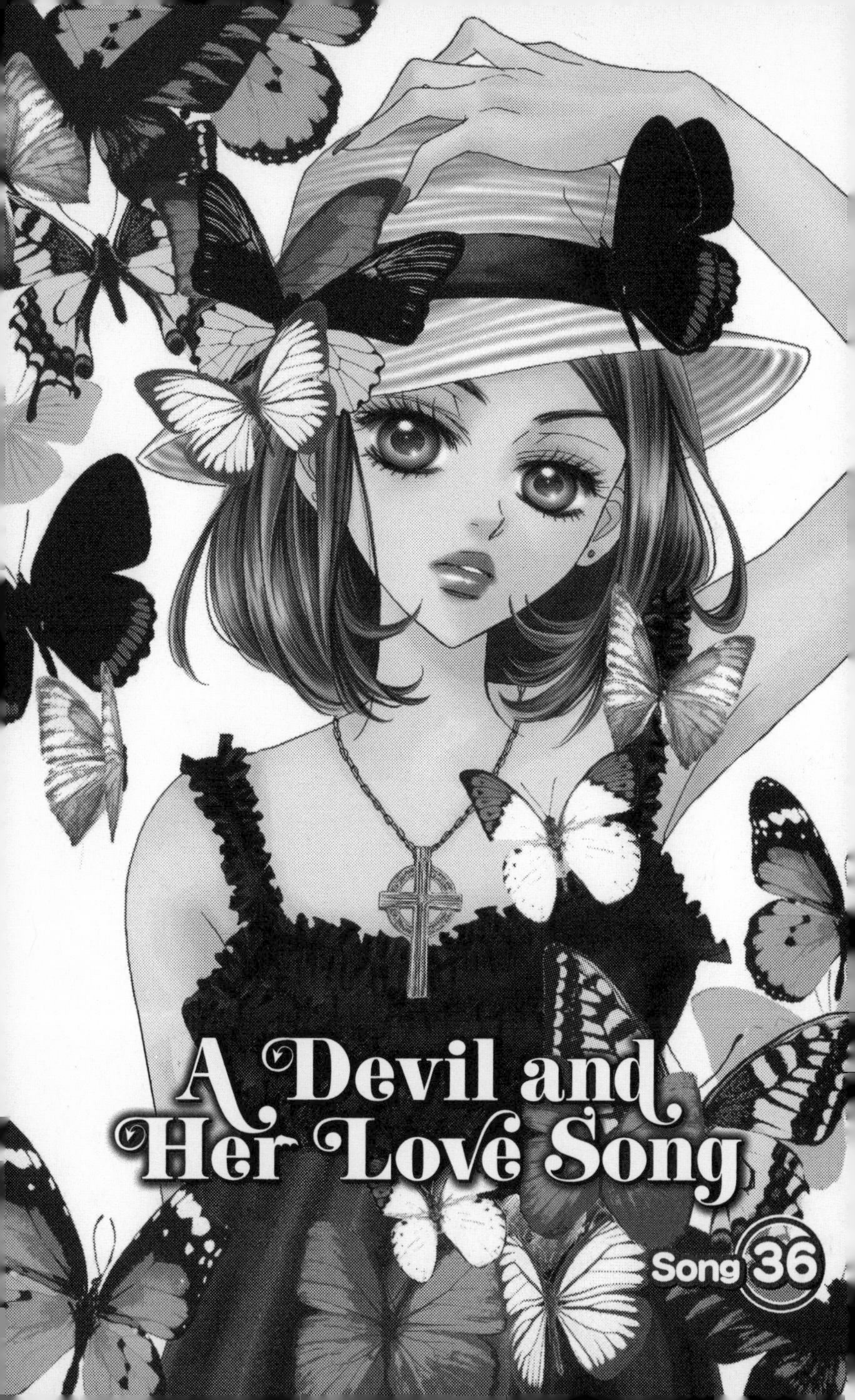
A Devil and
Her Love Song
Song 36

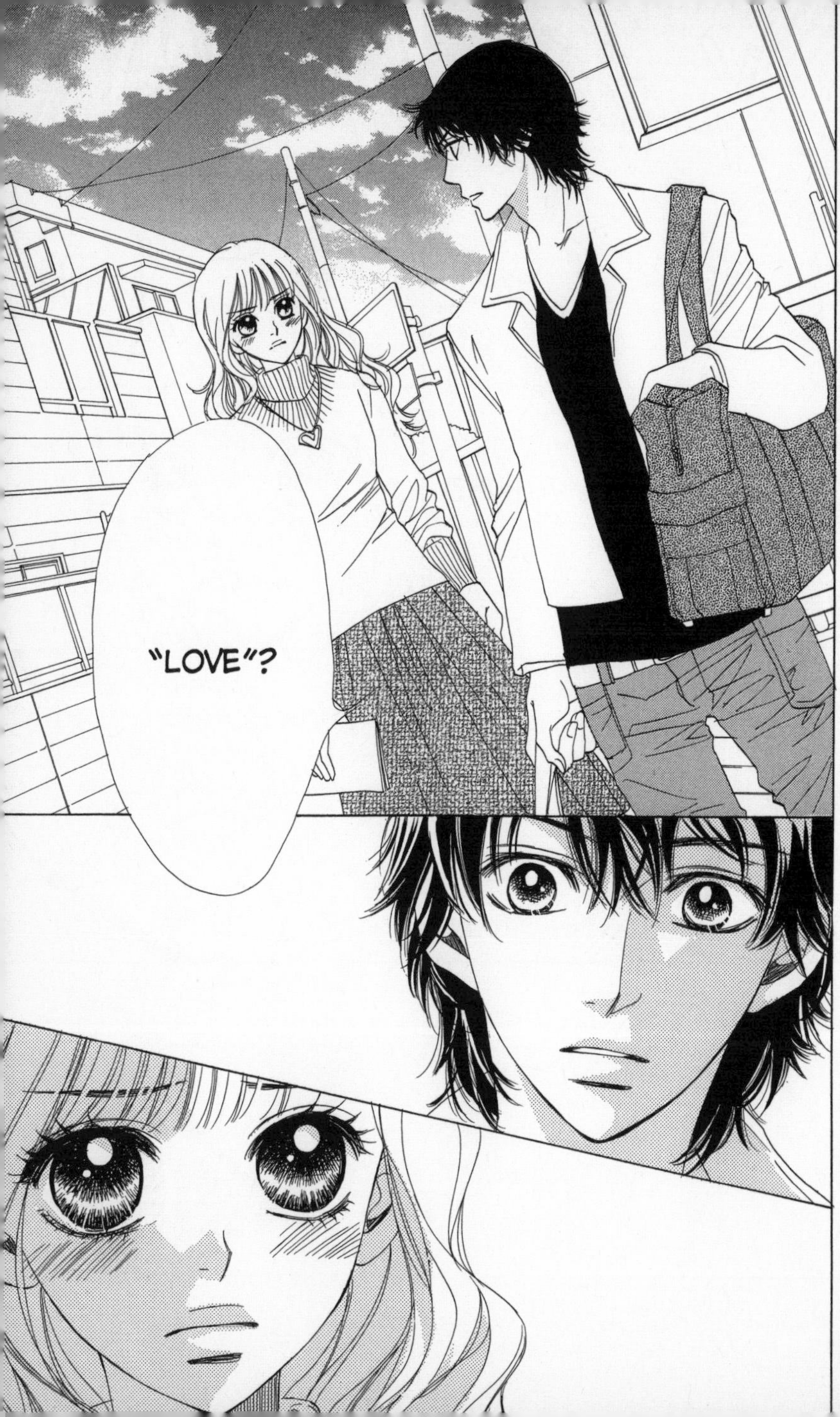
"LOVE"?

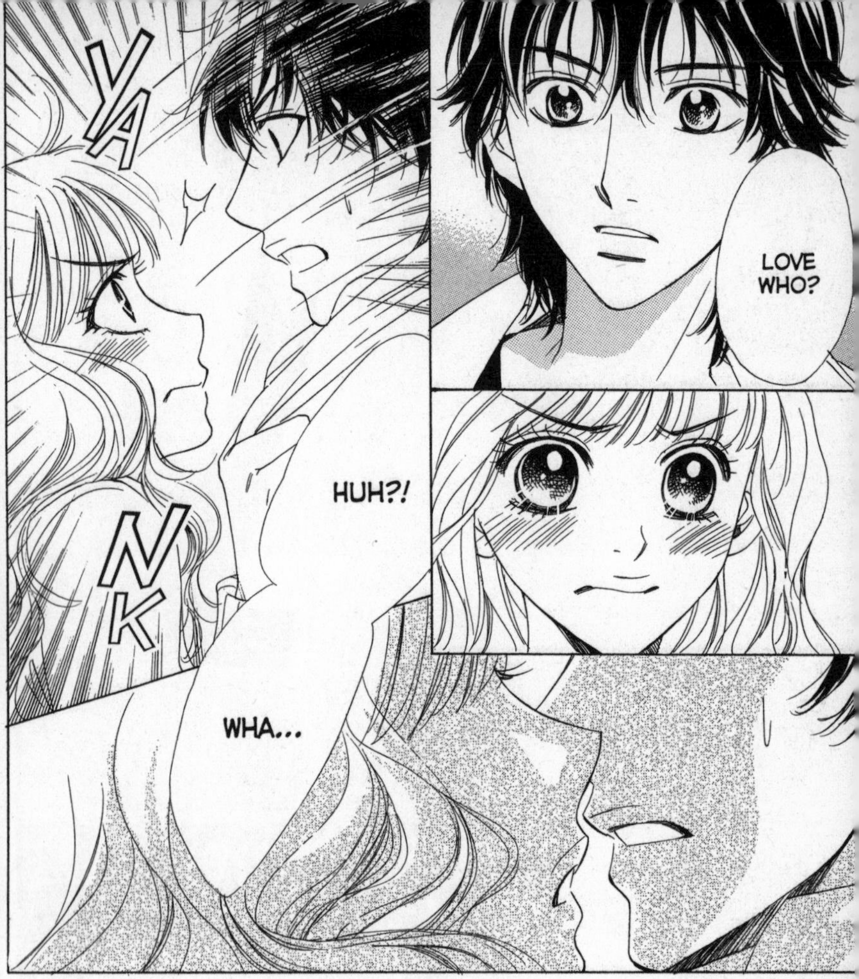
LOVE WHO?
YANK
HUH?!
WHA...

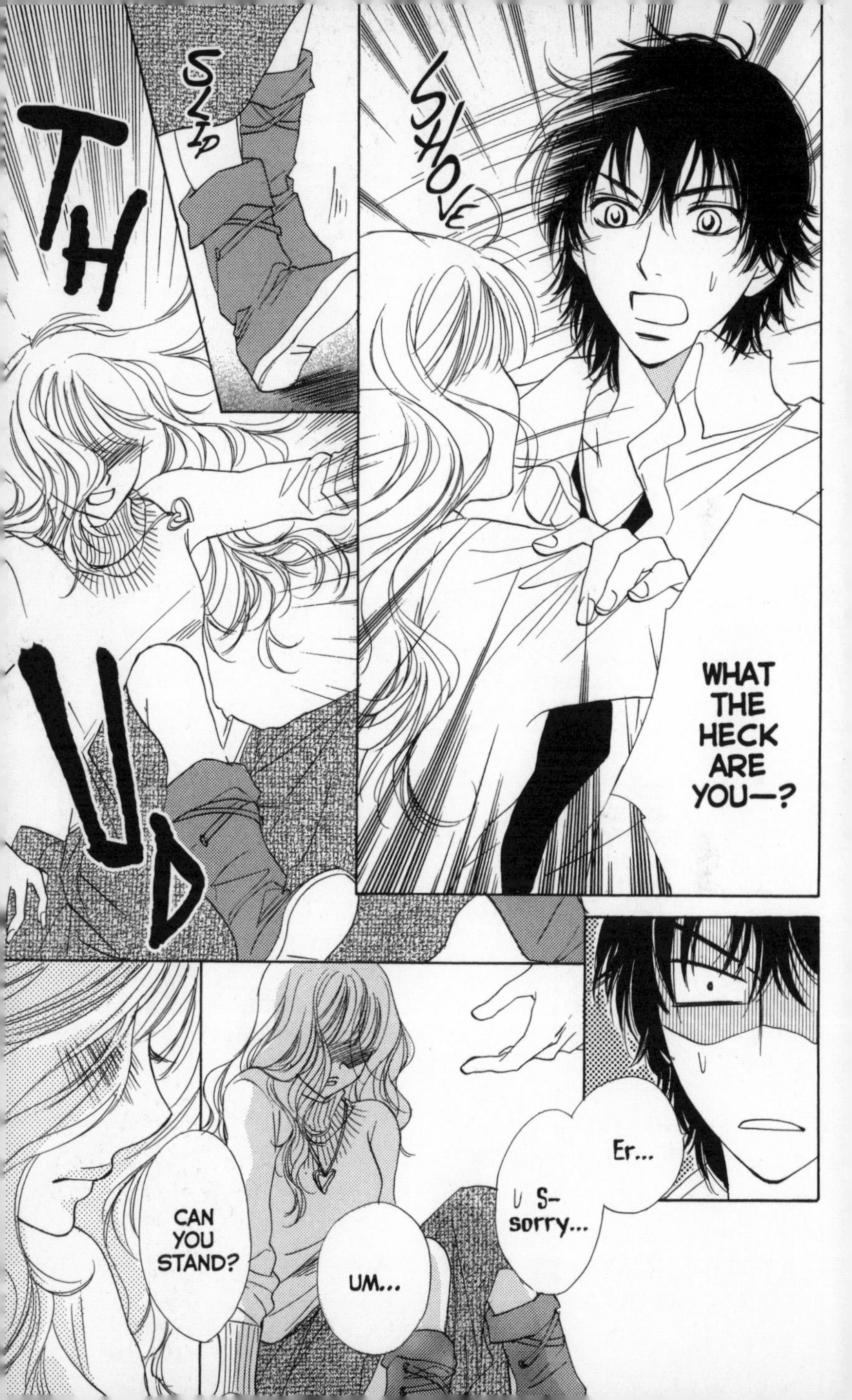
SHOVE
WHAT THE HECK ARE YOU—?
SLIP
THUD
Er...
S-sorry...
UM...
CAN YOU STAND?

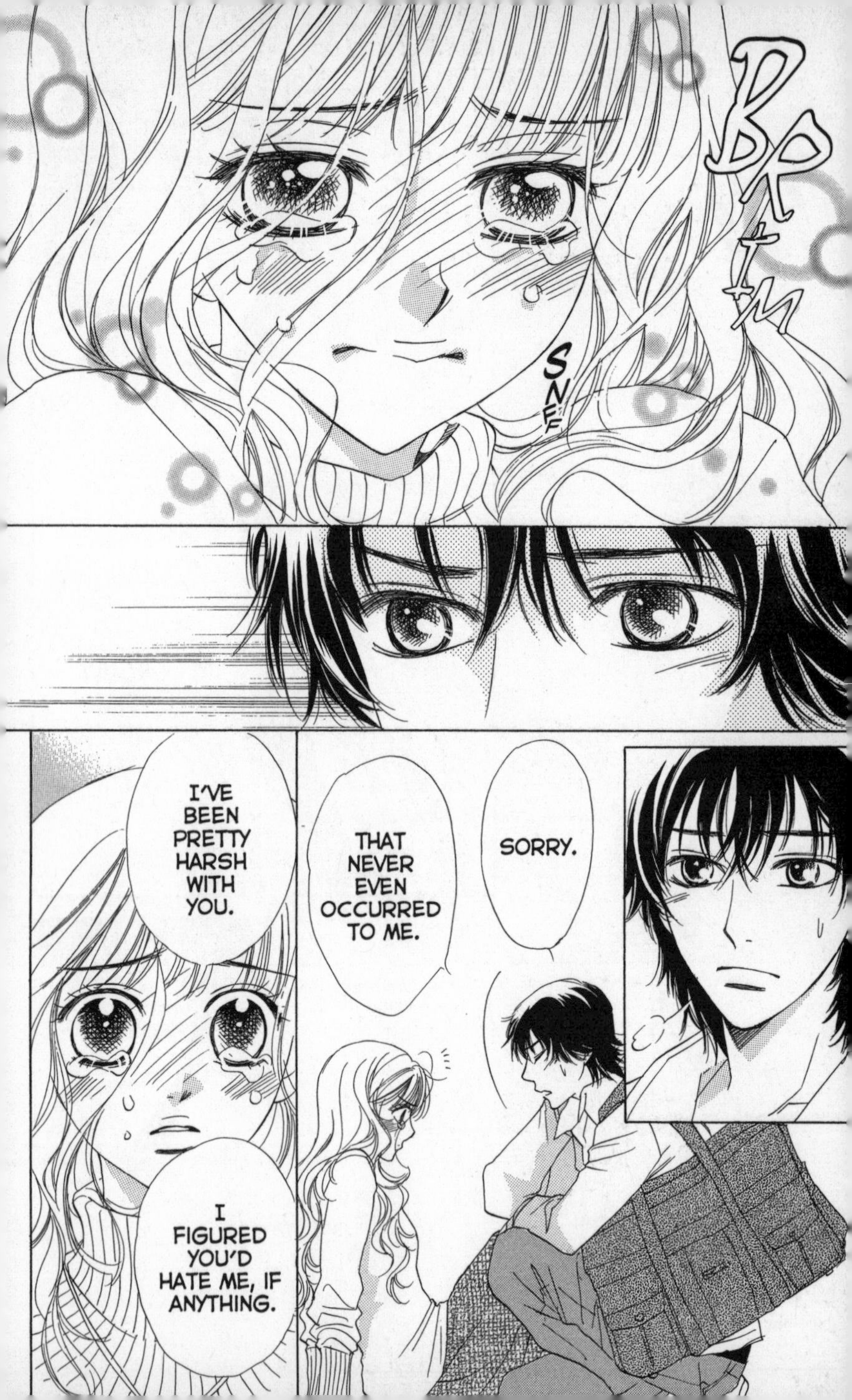
BRIM
SNFF
SORRY.
THAT NEVER EVEN OCCURRED TO ME.
I'VE BEEN PRETTY HARSH WITH YOU.
I FIGURED YOU'D HATE ME, IF ANYTHING.

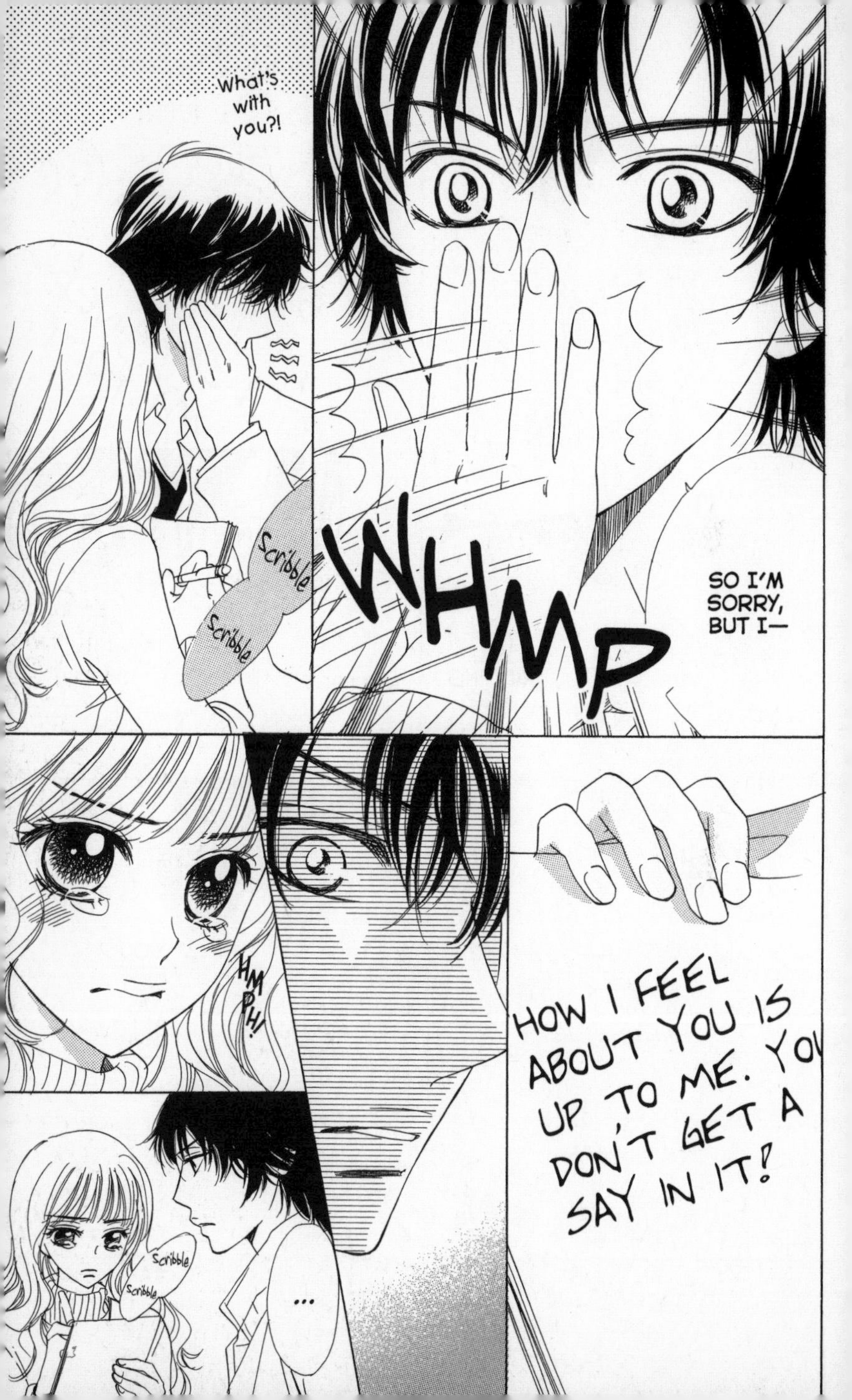
SO I'M SORRY, BUT I—
WHMP
What's with you?!
Scribble Scribble
HOW I FEEL ABOUT YOU IS UP TO ME. YO DON'T GET A SAY IN IT!
HMPH!
Scribble Scribble
...

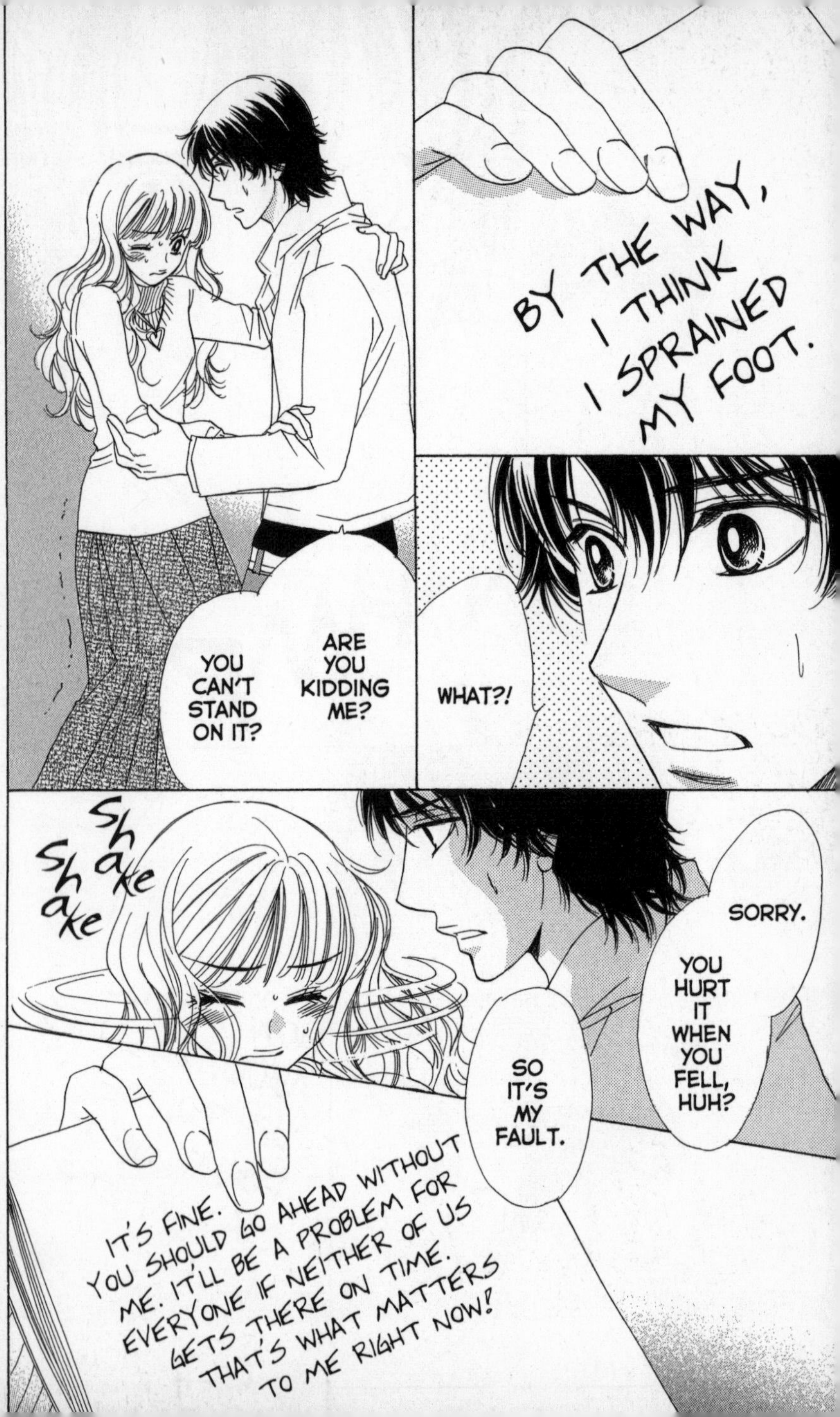
BY THE WAY, I THINK I SPRAINED MY FOOT.
WHAT?!
ARE YOU KIDDING ME?
YOU CAN'T STAND ON IT?
SORRY.
YOU HURT IT WHEN YOU FELL, HUH?
SO IT'S MY FAULT.
Shake Shake
IT'S FINE. YOU SHOULD GO AHEAD WITHOUT ME. IT'LL BE A PROBLEM FOR EVERYONE IF NEITHER OF US GETS THERE ON TIME. THAT'S WHAT MATTERS TO ME RIGHT NOW!

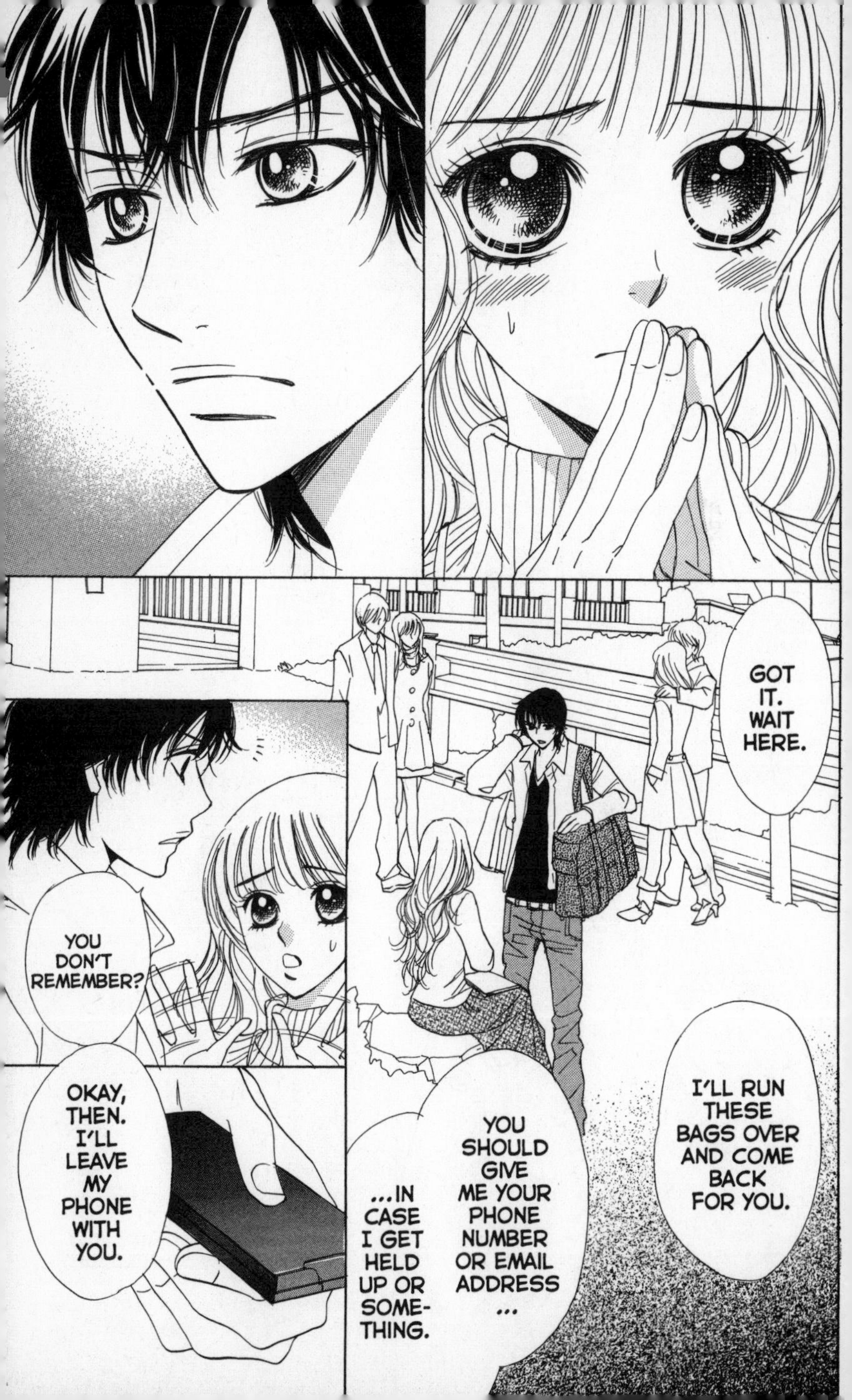
GOT IT. WAIT HERE.
I'LL RUN THESE BAGS OVER AND COME BACK FOR YOU.
YOU SHOULD GIVE ME YOUR PHONE NUMBER OR EMAIL ADDRESS...
...IN CASE I GET HELD UP OR SOME-THING.
YOU DON'T REMEMBER?
OKAY, THEN. I'LL LEAVE MY PHONE WITH YOU.

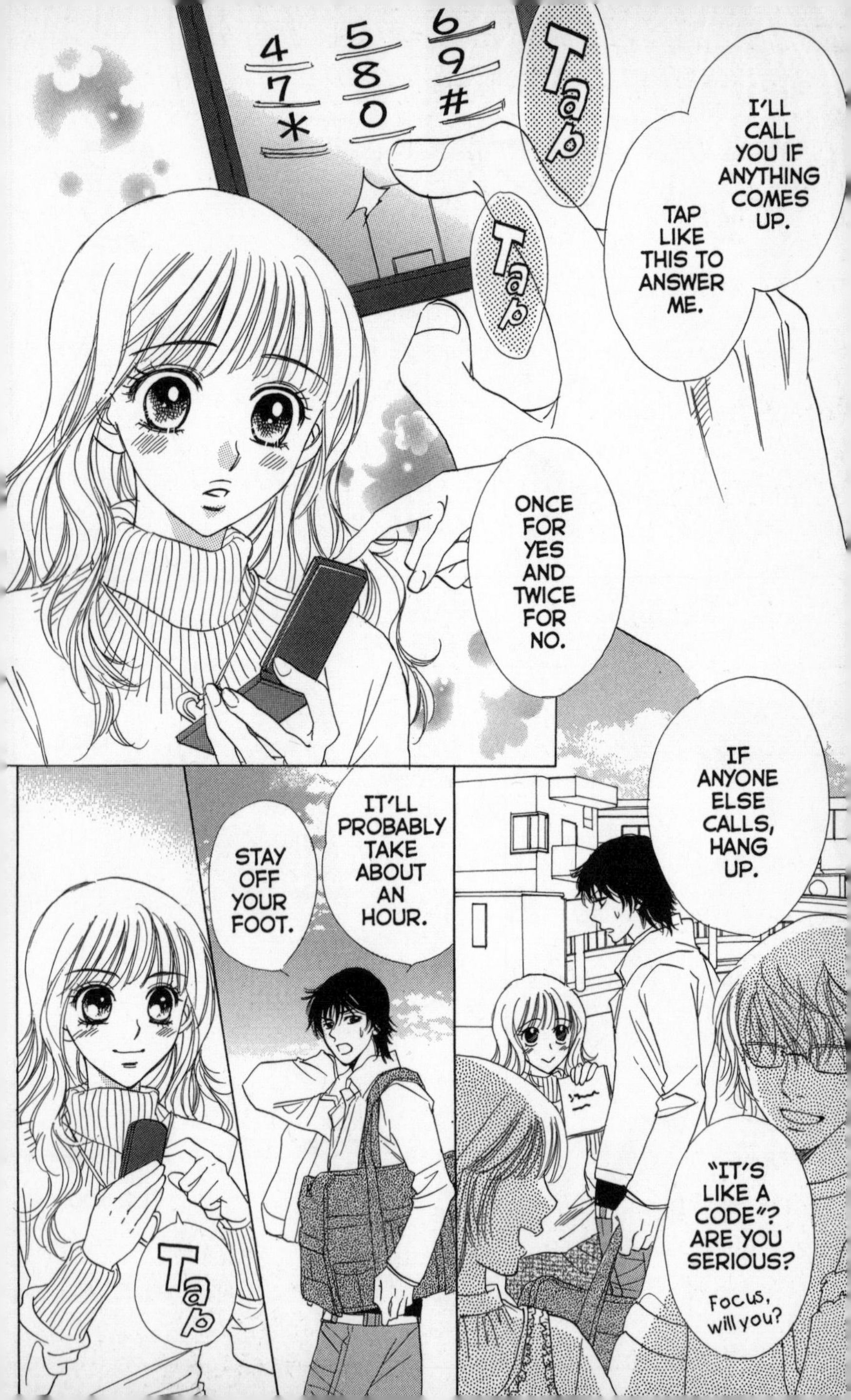
I'LL CALL YOU IF ANYTHING COMES UP.
TAP LIKE THIS TO ANSWER ME.
Tap
Tap
ONCE FOR YES AND TWICE FOR NO.
IF ANYONE ELSE CALLS, HANG UP.
"IT'S LIKE A CODE"? ARE YOU SERIOUS?
Focus, will you?
IT'LL PROBABLY TAKE ABOUT AN HOUR.
STAY OFF YOUR FOOT.
Tap

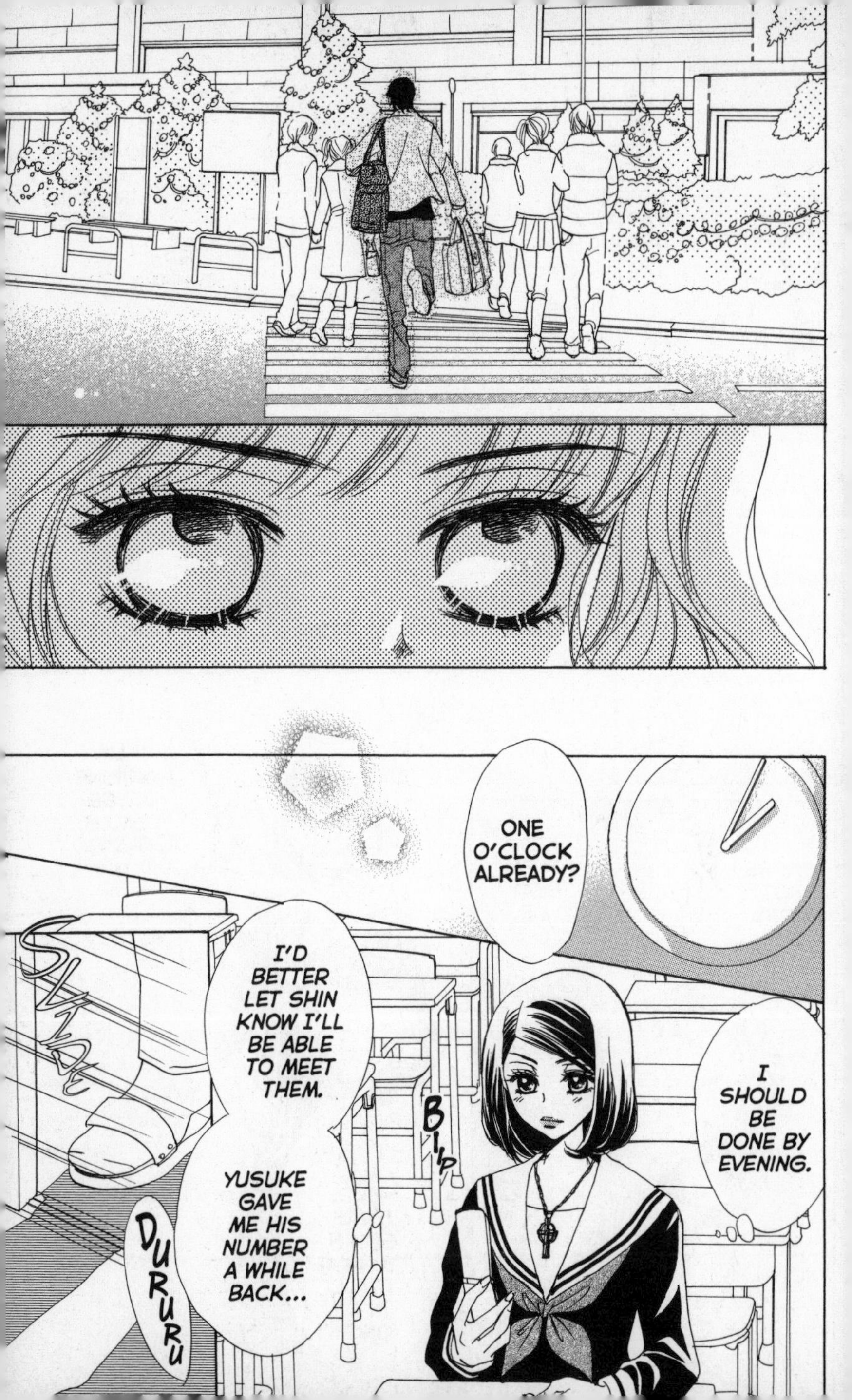
ONE O'CLOCK ALREADY?
I SHOULD BE DONE BY EVENING.
I'D BETTER LET SHIN KNOW I'LL BE ABLE TO MEET THEM.
BIIP
YUSUKE GAVE ME HIS NUMBER A WHILE BACK...
DURURU

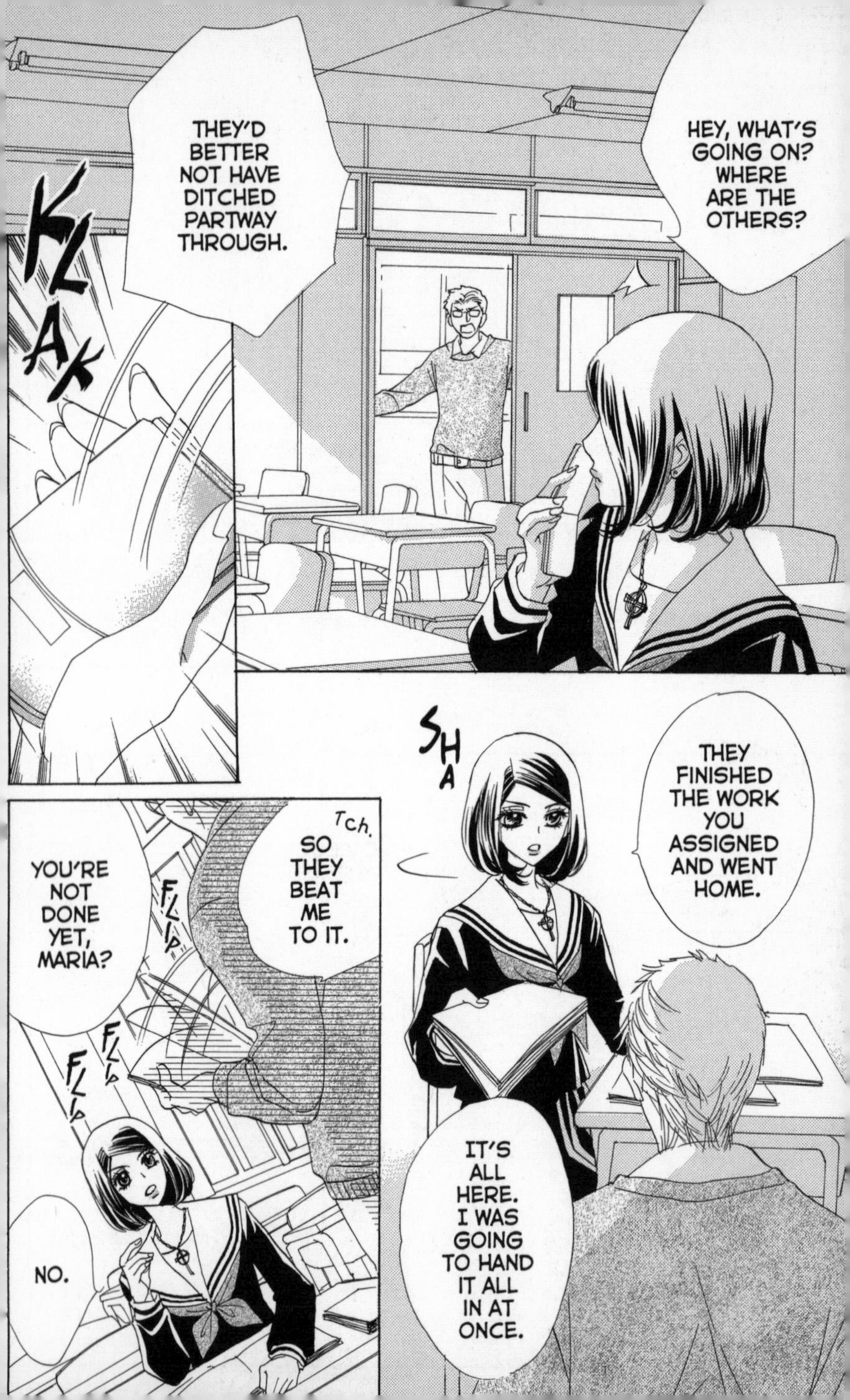

HEY, WHAT'S GOING ON? WHERE ARE THE OTHERS?
THEY'D BETTER NOT HAVE DITCHED PARTWAY THROUGH.
KLAK
SHA
THEY FINISHED THE WORK YOU ASSIGNED AND WENT HOME.
IT'S ALL HERE. I WAS GOING TO HAND IT ALL IN AT ONCE.
Tch.
SO THEY BEAT ME TO IT.
YOU'RE NOT DONE YET, MARIA?
FLIP
FLIP
FLIP
NO.

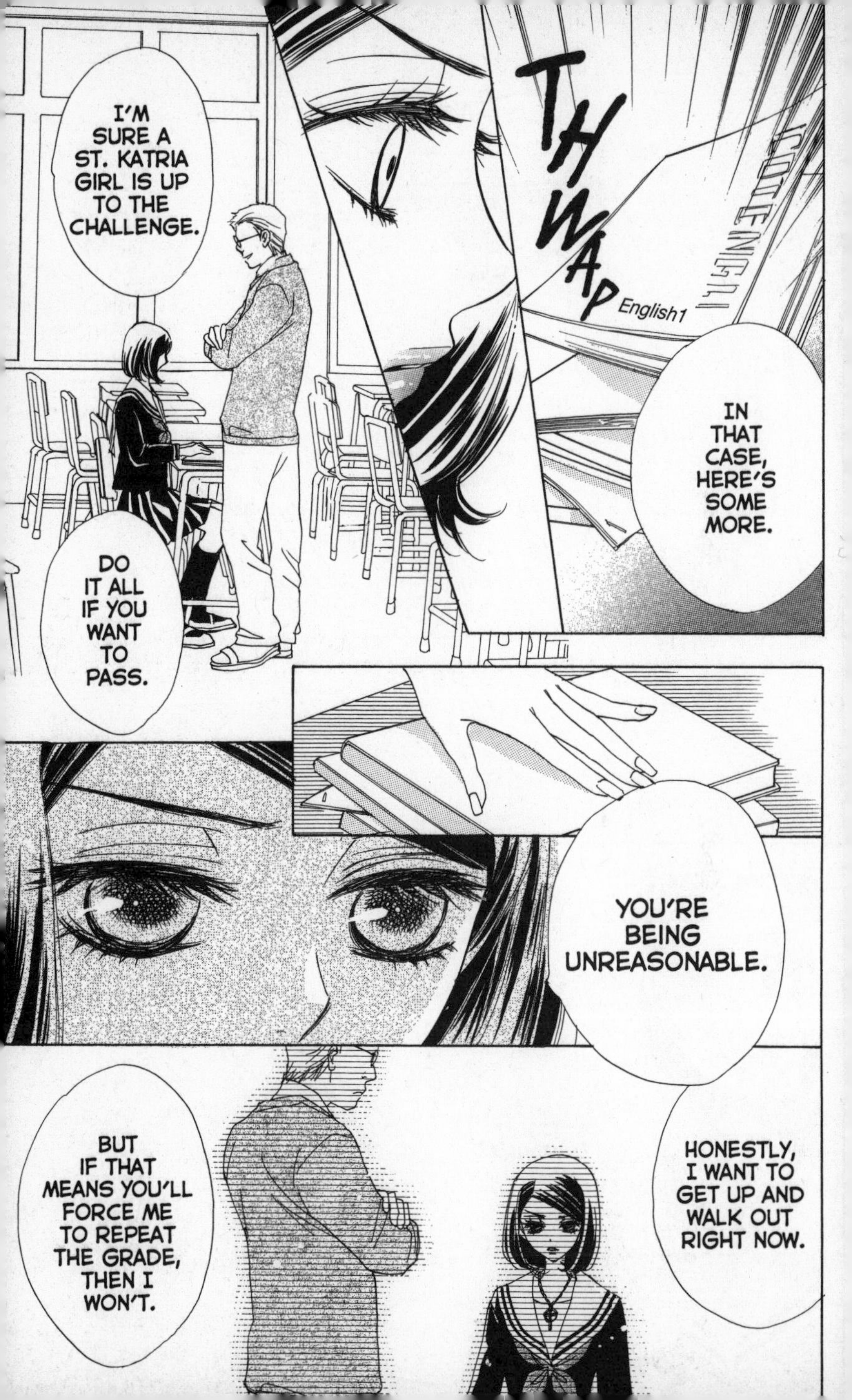
THWAP
English1
IN THAT CASE, HERE'S SOME MORE.
I'M SURE A ST. KATRIA GIRL IS UP TO THE CHALLENGE.
DO IT ALL IF YOU WANT TO PASS.
YOU'RE BEING UNREASONABLE.
HONESTLY, I WANT TO GET UP AND WALK OUT RIGHT NOW.
BUT IF THAT MEANS YOU'LL FORCE ME TO REPEAT THE GRADE, THEN I WON'T.

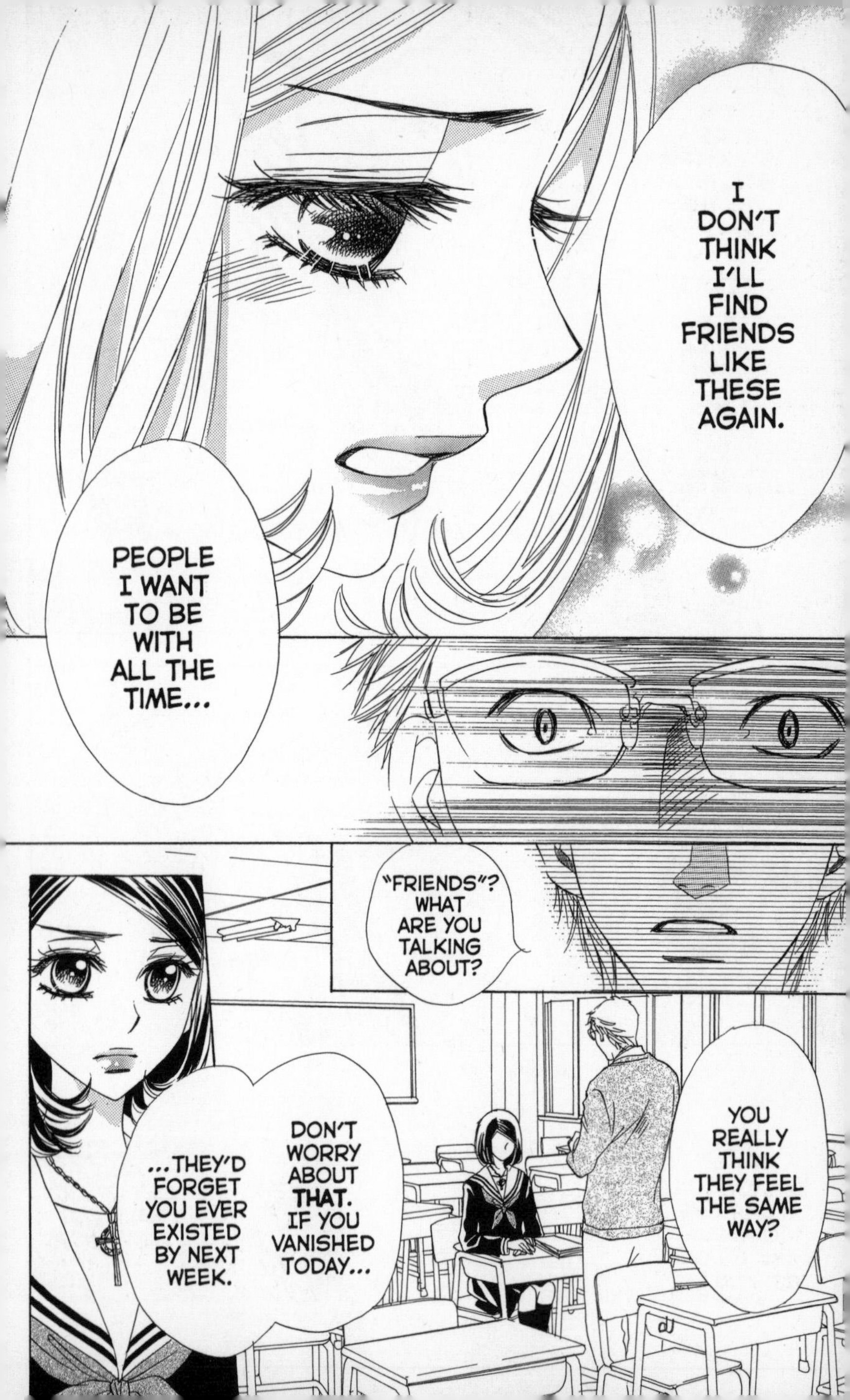
I DON'T THINK I'LL FIND FRIENDS LIKE THESE AGAIN.
PEOPLE I WANT TO BE WITH ALL THE TIME...
"FRIENDS"? WHAT ARE YOU TALKING ABOUT?
YOU REALLY THINK THEY FEEL THE SAME WAY?
DON'T WORRY ABOUT **THAT**. IF YOU VANISHED TODAY...
...THEY'D FORGET YOU EVER EXISTED BY NEXT WEEK.

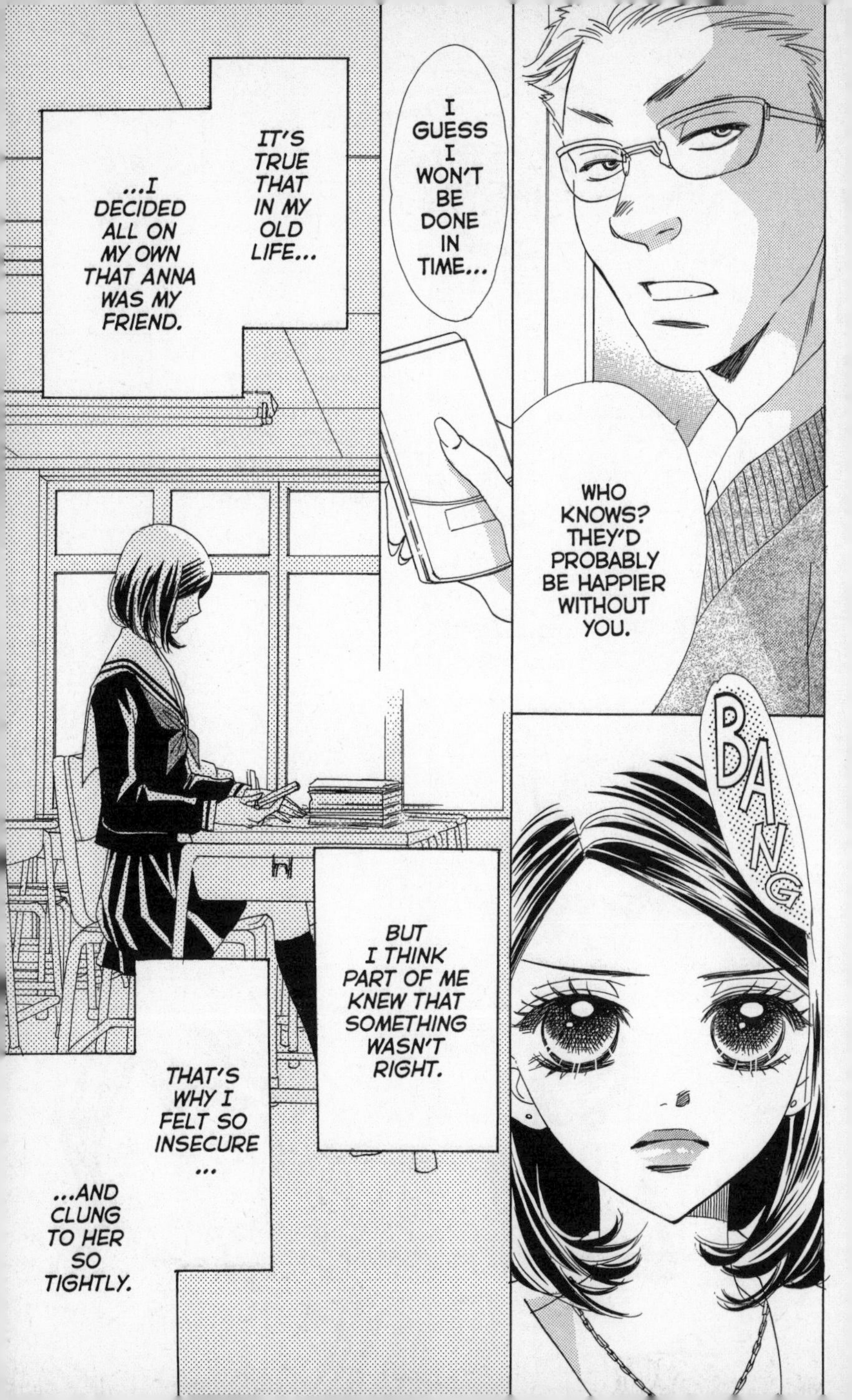
I GUESS I WON'T BE DONE IN TIME...
WHO KNOWS? THEY'D PROBABLY BE HAPPIER WITHOUT YOU.
BANG
IT'S TRUE THAT IN MY OLD LIFE...
...I DECIDED ALL ON MY OWN THAT ANNA WAS MY FRIEND.
BUT I THINK PART OF ME KNEW THAT SOMETHING WASN'T RIGHT.
THAT'S WHY I FELT SO INSECURE...
...AND CLUNG TO HER SO TIGHTLY.

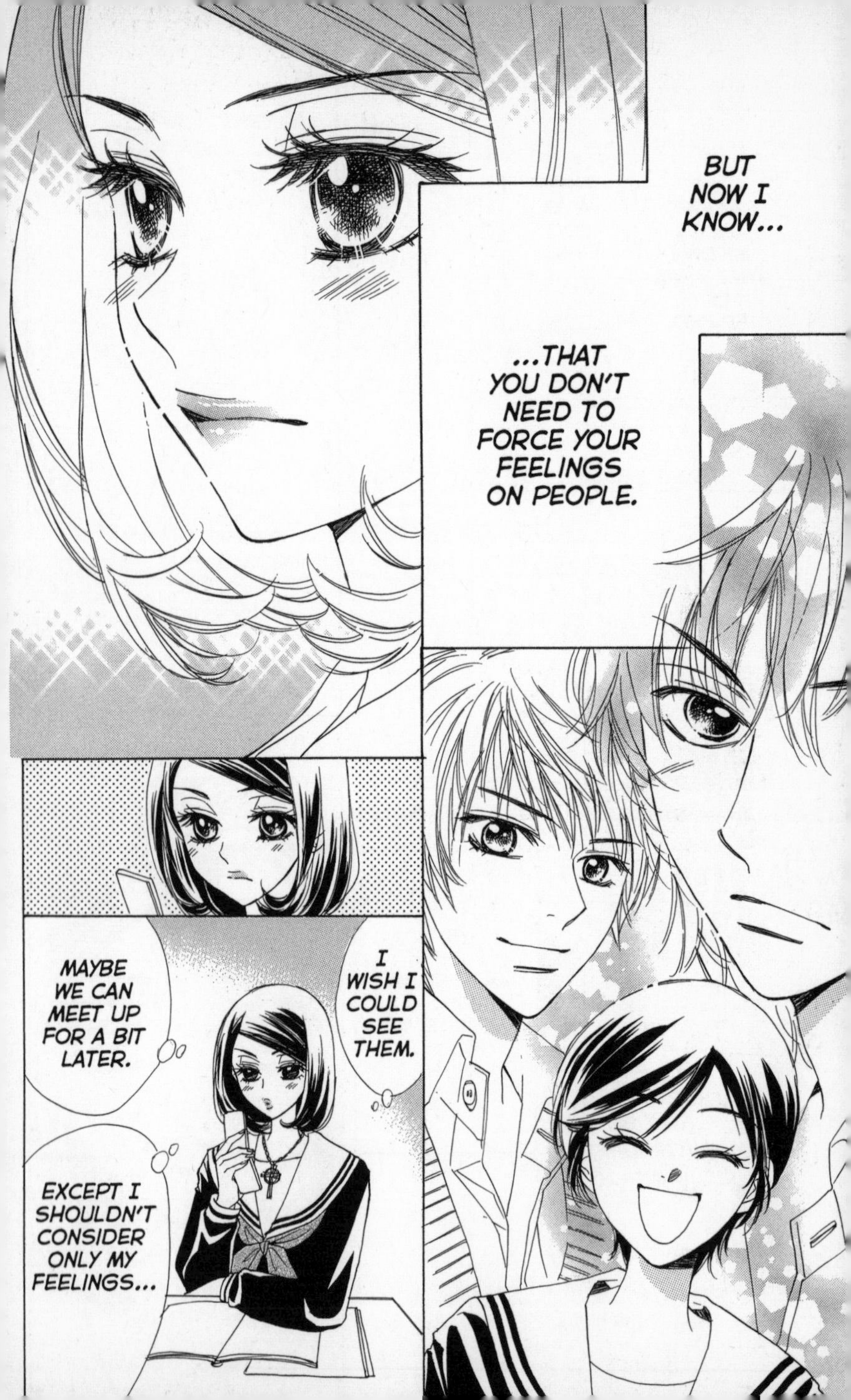
BUT NOW I KNOW...
...THAT YOU DON'T NEED TO FORCE YOUR FEELINGS ON PEOPLE.
I WISH I COULD SEE THEM.
MAYBE WE CAN MEET UP FOR A BIT LATER.
EXCEPT I SHOULDN'T CONSIDER ONLY MY FEELINGS...

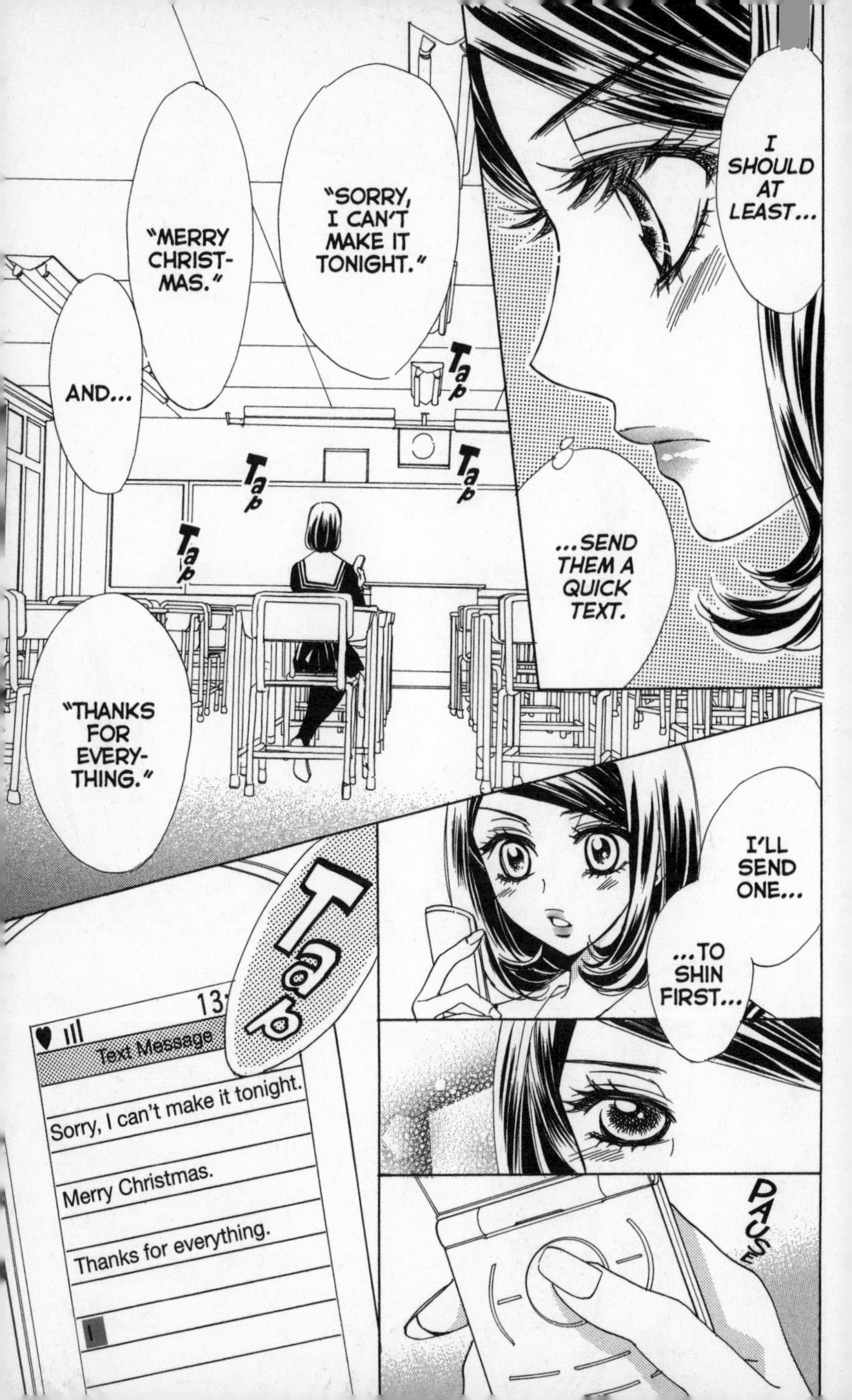
I SHOULD AT LEAST...
...SEND THEM A QUICK TEXT.
"SORRY, I CAN'T MAKE IT TONIGHT."
"MERRY CHRIST-MAS."
AND...
Tap
Tap
Tap
Tap
"THANKS FOR EVERY-THING."
I'LL SEND ONE...
...TO SHIN FIRST...
PAUSE
Tap
13:
Text Message
Sorry, I can't make it tonight.
Merry Christmas.
Thanks for everything.

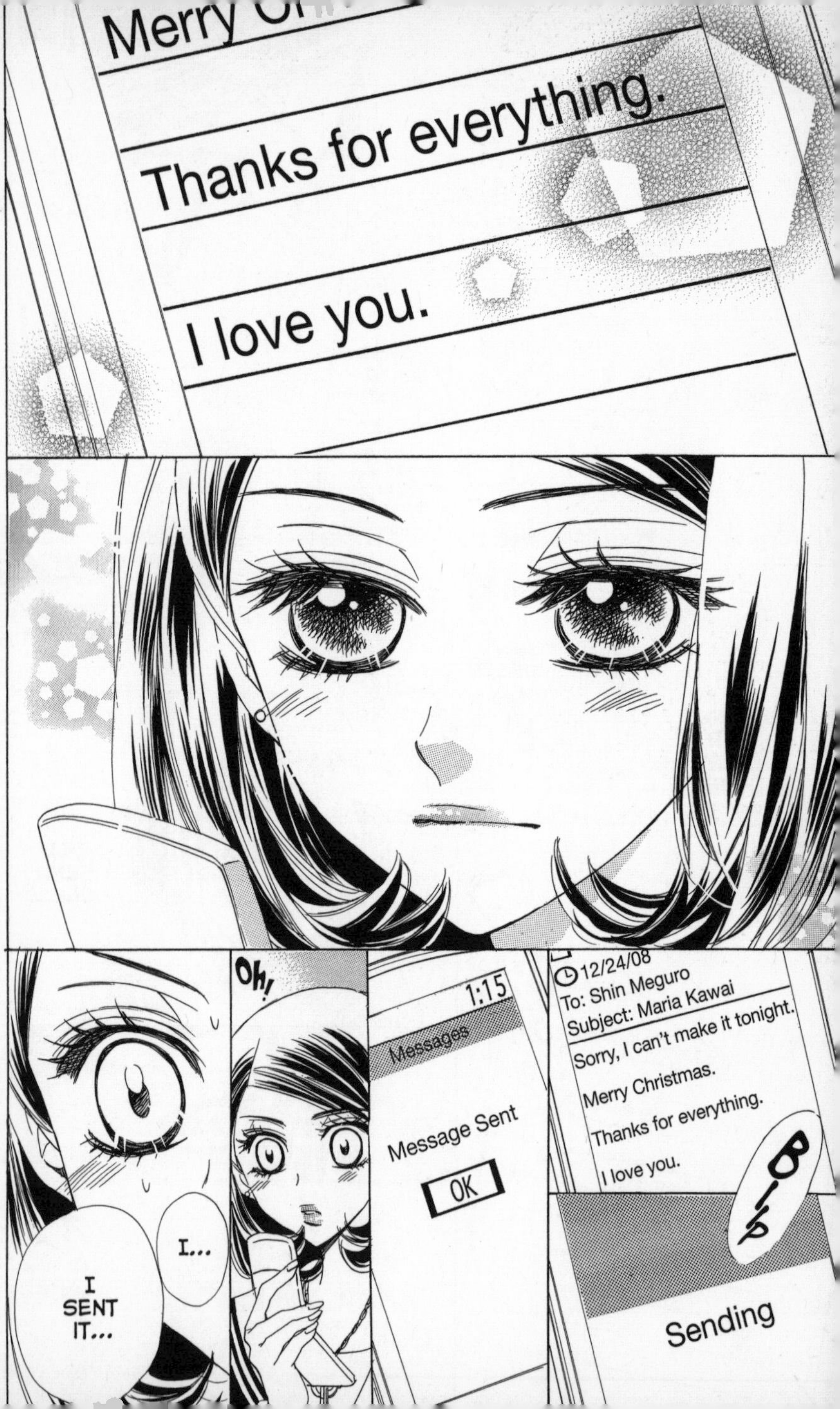

Merry
Thanks for everything.
I love you.
12/24/08
To: Shin Meguro
Subject: Maria Kawai
Sorry, I can't make it tonight.
Merry Christmas.
Thanks for everything.
I love you.
Blip
Sending
1:15
Messages
Message Sent
OK
Oh!
I...
I SENT IT...

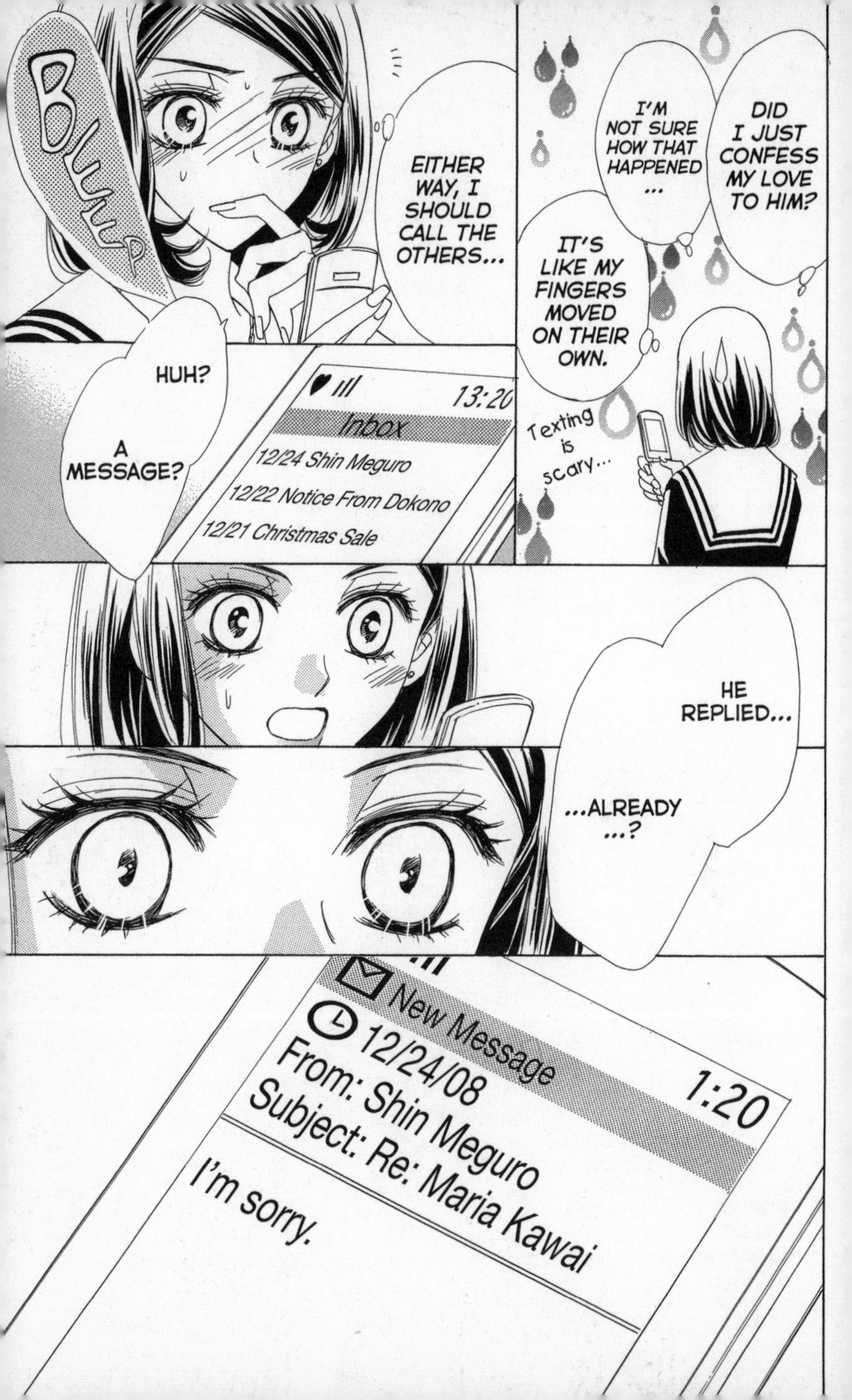
DID I JUST CONFESS MY LOVE TO HIM?
I'M NOT SURE HOW THAT HAPPENED...
IT'S LIKE MY FINGERS MOVED ON THEIR OWN.
Texting is scary...
BLUUP
EITHER WAY, I SHOULD CALL THE OTHERS...
HUH?
A MESSAGE?
13:20
Inbox
12/24 Shin Meguro
12/22 Notice From Dokono
12/21 Christmas Sale
HE REPLIED...
...ALREADY ...?
New Message
1:20
12/24/08
From: Shin Meguro
Subject: Re: Maria Kawai
I'm sorry.

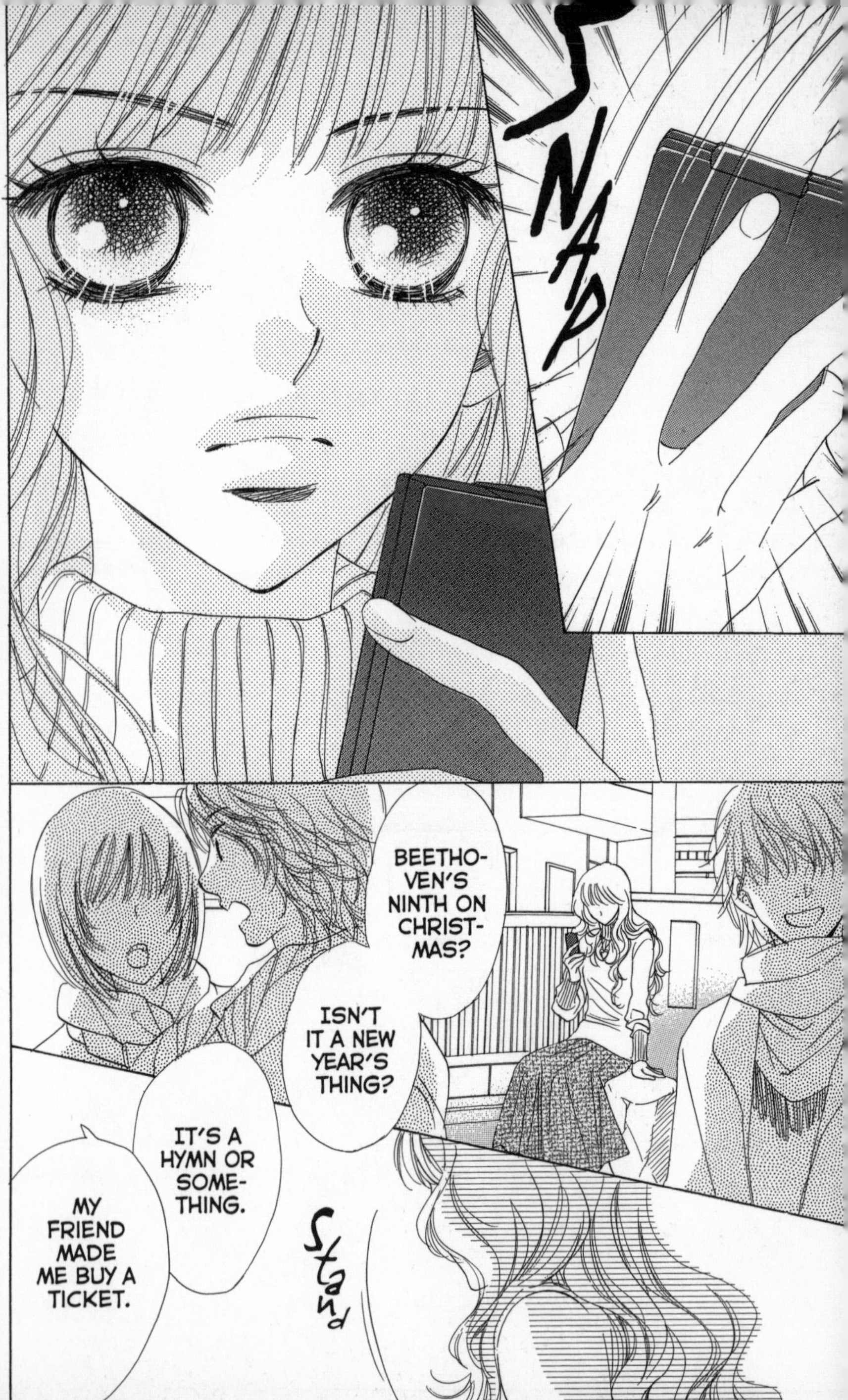
SNAP
BEETHOVEN'S NINTH ON CHRISTMAS?
ISN'T IT A NEW YEAR'S THING?
IT'S A HYMN OR SOMETHING.
MY FRIEND MADE ME BUY A TICKET.
Stand

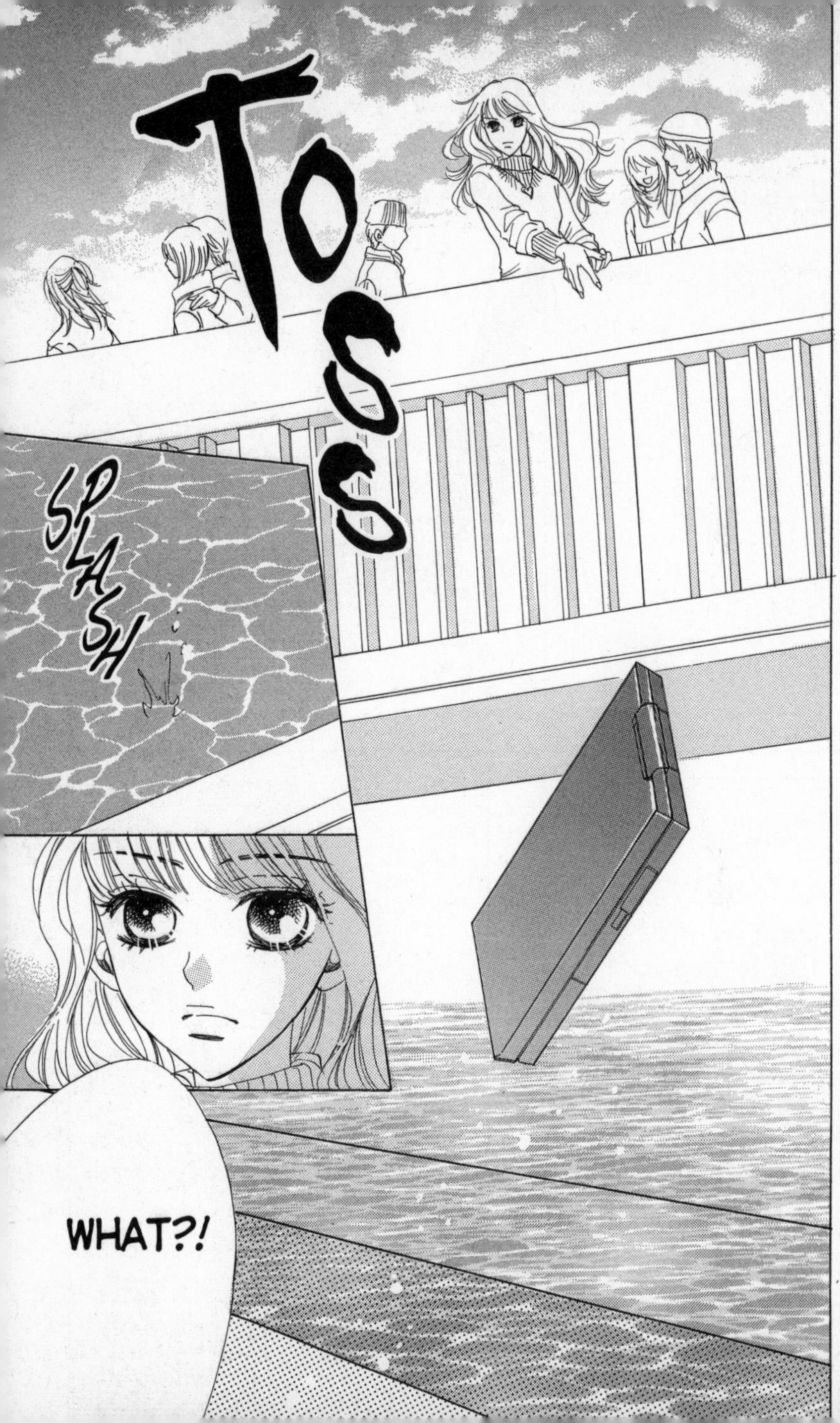
TOSS
SPLASH
WHAT?!

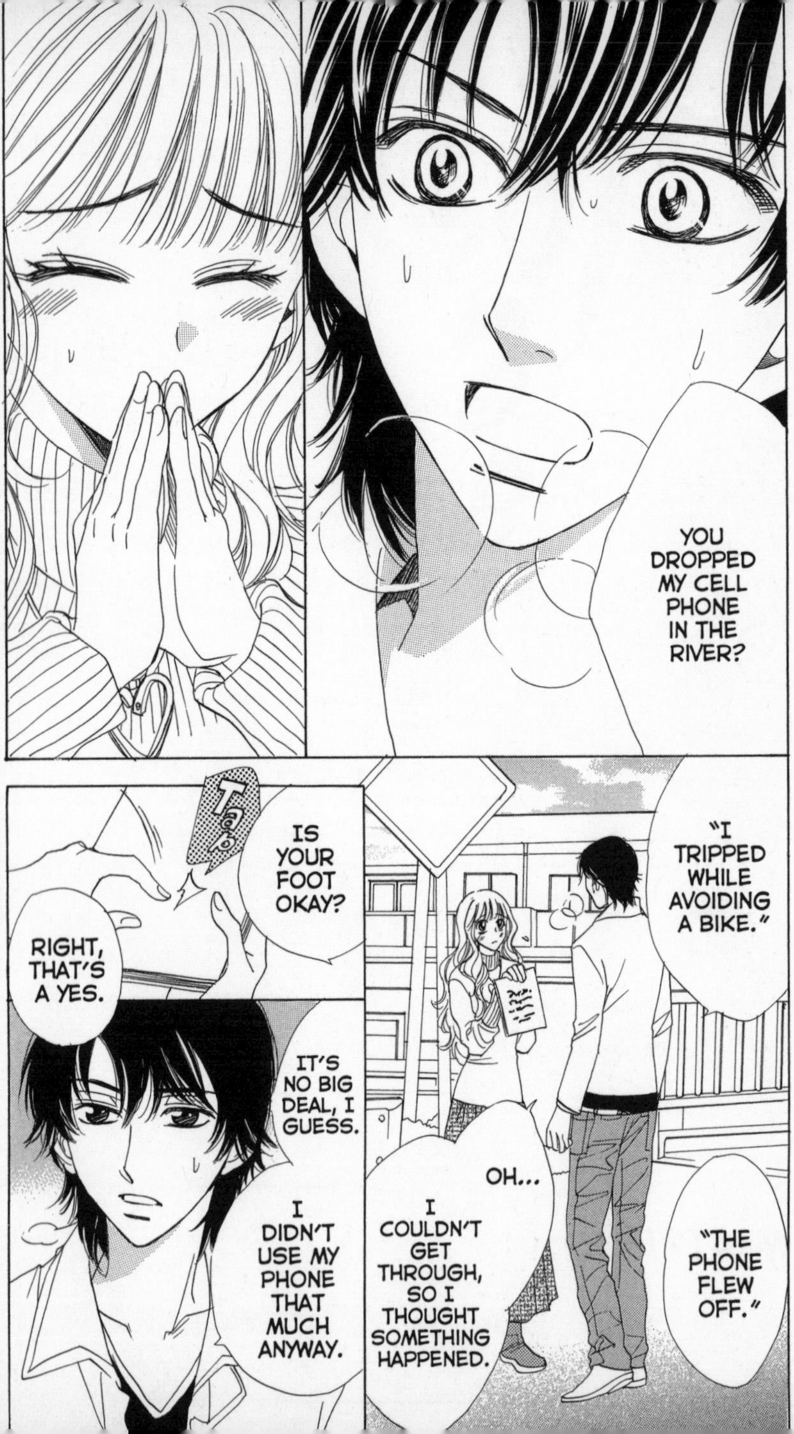
YOU DROPPED MY CELL PHONE IN THE RIVER?
"I TRIPPED WHILE AVOIDING A BIKE."
"THE PHONE FLEW OFF."
OH...
I COULDN'T GET THROUGH, SO I THOUGHT SOMETHING HAPPENED.
IS YOUR FOOT OKAY?
Tap
RIGHT, THAT'S A YES.
IT'S NO BIG DEAL, I GUESS.
I DIDN'T USE MY PHONE THAT MUCH ANYWAY.

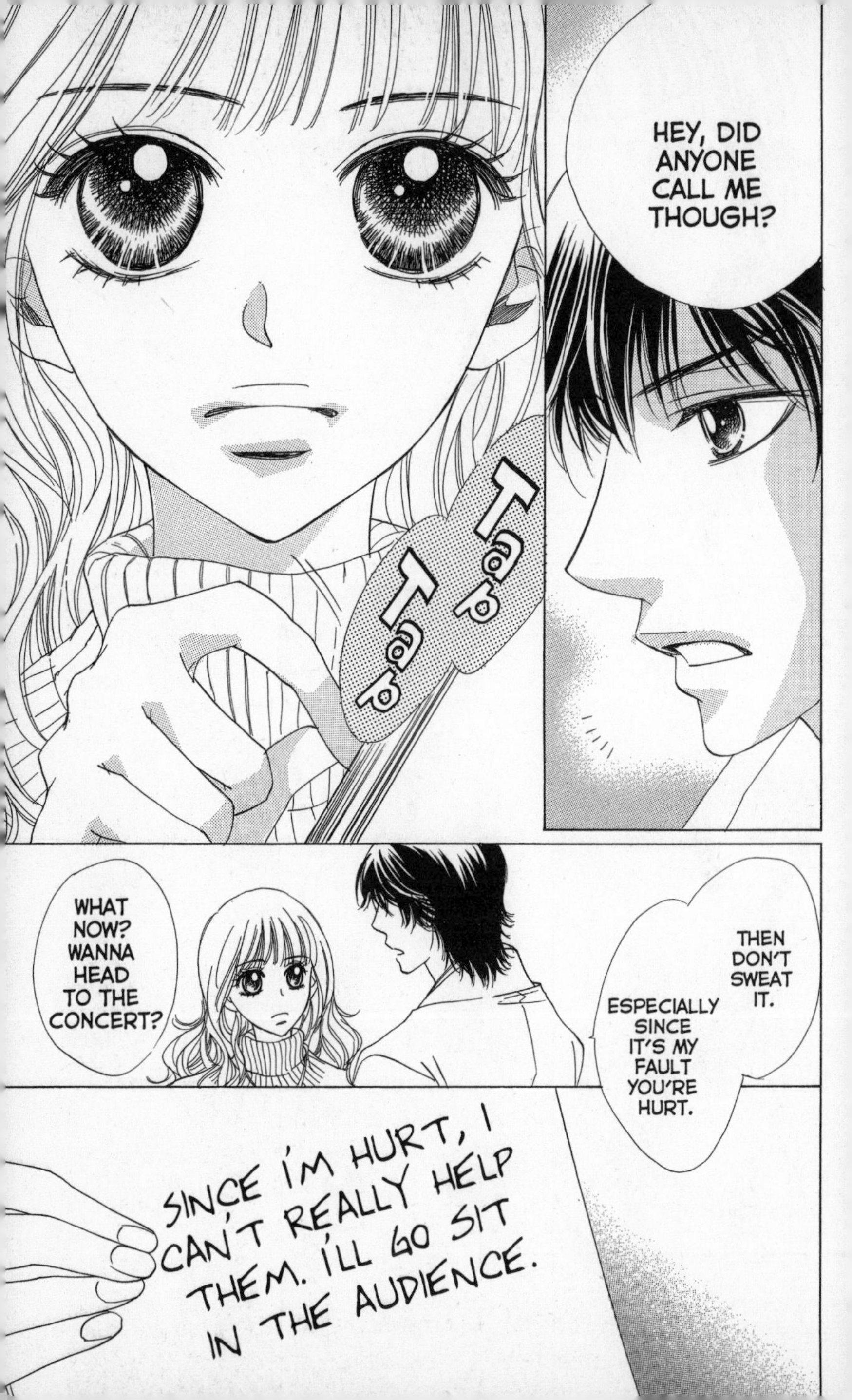
HEY, DID ANYONE CALL ME THOUGH?
Tap Tap
THEN DON'T SWEAT IT.
ESPECIALLY SINCE IT'S MY FAULT YOU'RE HURT.
WHAT NOW? WANNA HEAD TO THE CONCERT?
SINCE I'M HURT, I CAN'T REALLY HELP THEM. I'LL GO SIT IN THE AUDIENCE.

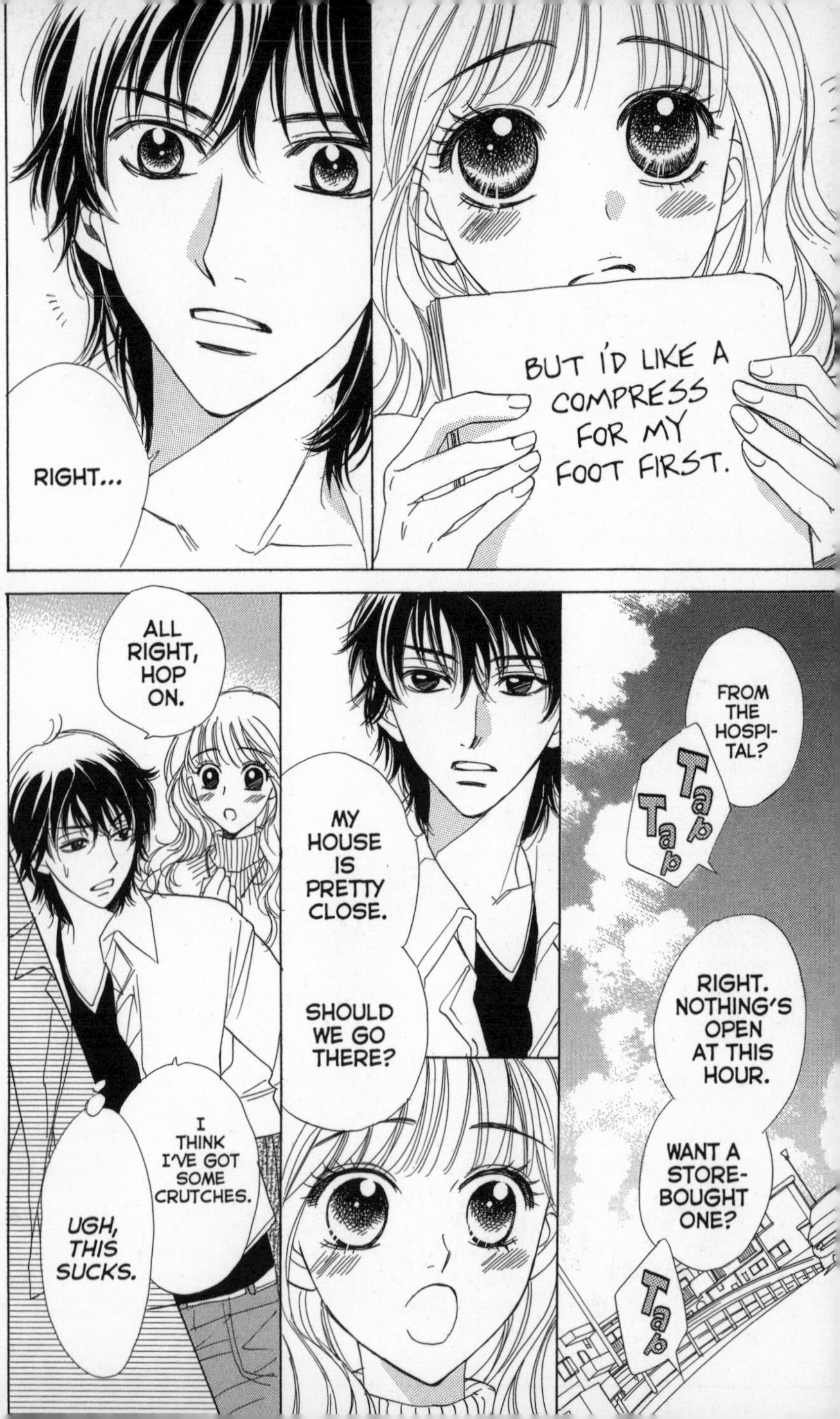
BUT I'D LIKE A COMPRESS FOR MY FOOT FIRST.
RIGHT...
FROM THE HOSPITAL?
Tap Tap
RIGHT. NOTHING'S OPEN AT THIS HOUR.
WANT A STORE-BOUGHT ONE?
Tap
MY HOUSE IS PRETTY CLOSE.
SHOULD WE GO THERE?
ALL RIGHT, HOP ON.
I THINK I'VE GOT SOME CRUTCHES.
UGH, THIS SUCKS.

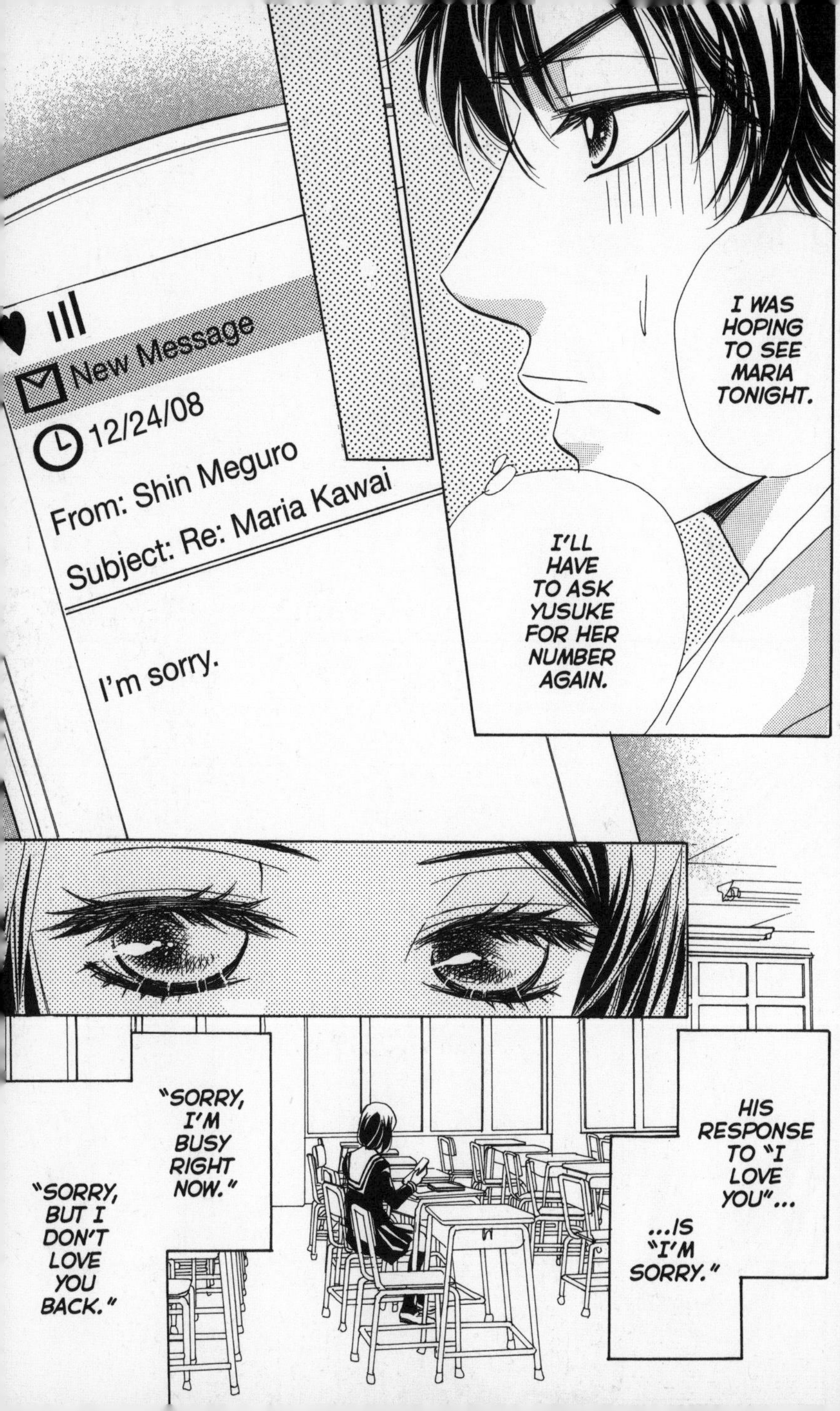
I WAS HOPING TO SEE MARIA TONIGHT.
I'LL HAVE TO ASK YUSUKE FOR HER NUMBER AGAIN.
New Message
12/24/08
From: Shin Meguro
Subject: Re: Maria Kawai
I'm sorry.
HIS RESPONSE TO "I LOVE YOU"...
...IS "I'M SORRY."
"SORRY, I'M BUSY RIGHT NOW."
"SORRY, BUT I DON'T LOVE YOU BACK."

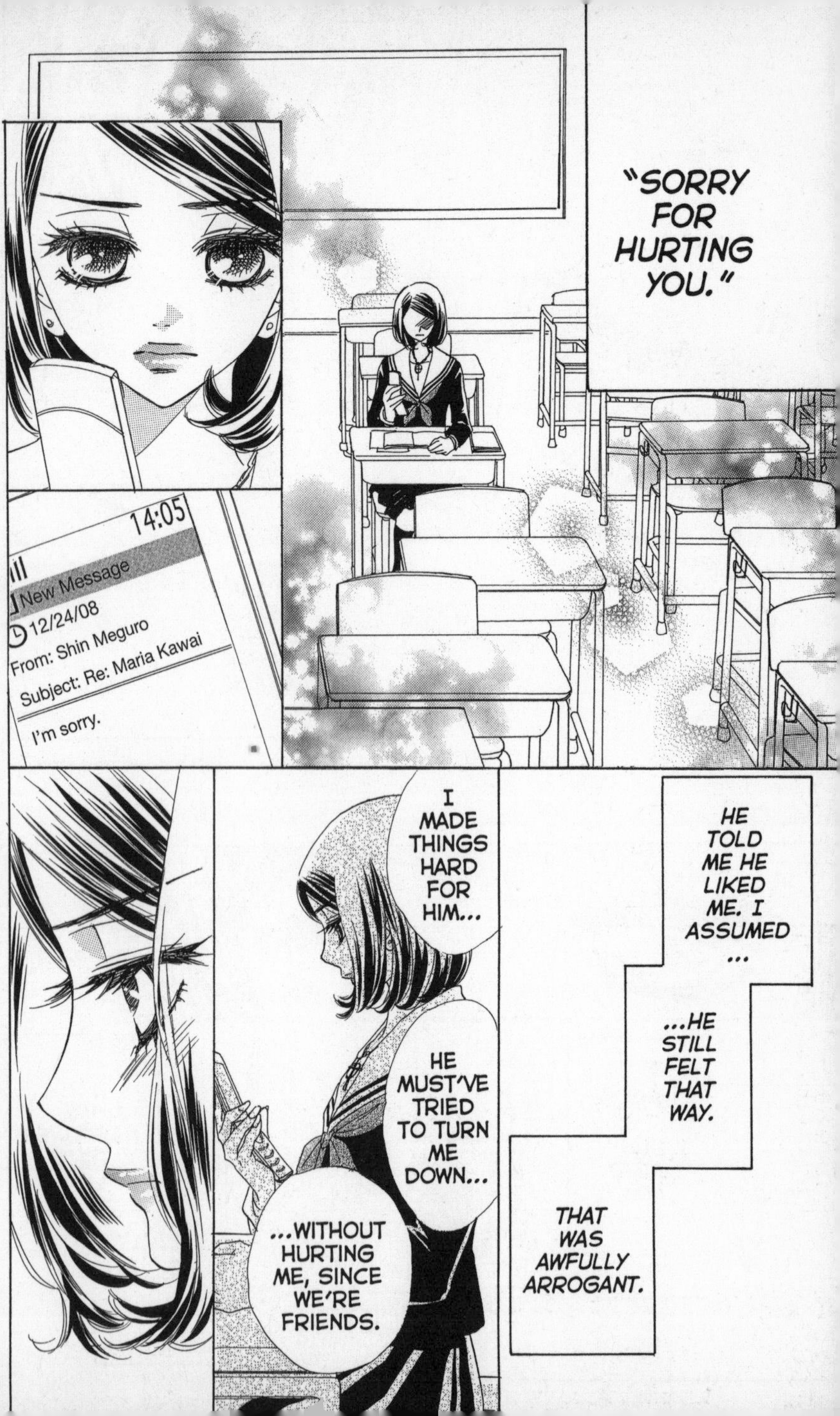
"SORRY FOR HURTING YOU."
14:05
New Message
12/24/08
From: Shin Meguro
Subject: Re: Maria Kawai
I'm sorry.
HE TOLD ME HE LIKED ME. I ASSUMED ...
...HE STILL FELT THAT WAY.
THAT WAS AWFULLY ARROGANT.
I MADE THINGS HARD FOR HIM...
HE MUST'VE TRIED TO TURN ME DOWN...
...WITHOUT HURTING ME, SINCE WE'RE FRIENDS.

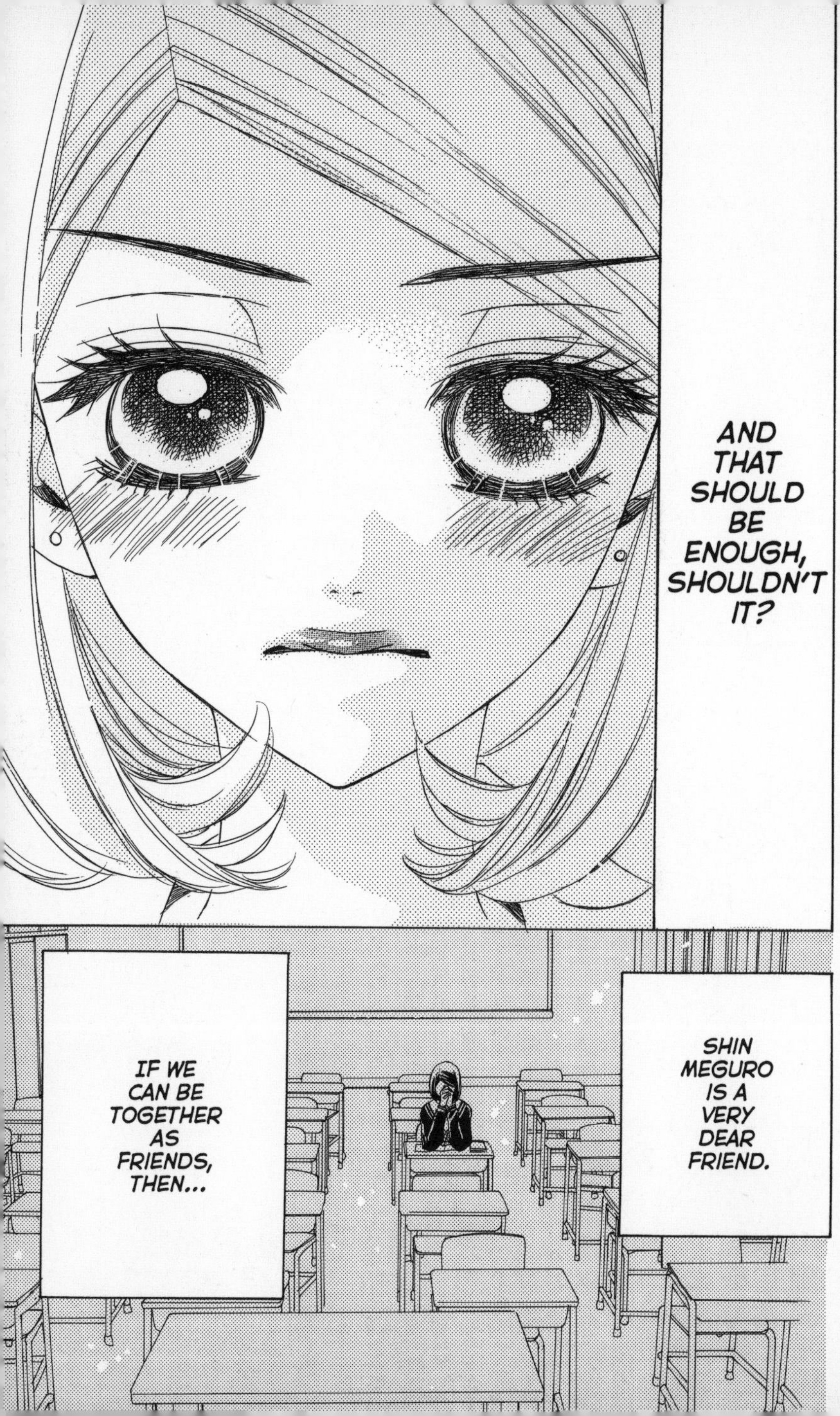
AND THAT SHOULD BE ENOUGH, SHOULDN'T IT?
SHIN MEGURO IS A VERY DEAR FRIEND.
IF WE CAN BE TOGETHER AS FRIENDS, THEN...

A Devil and
Her Love Song

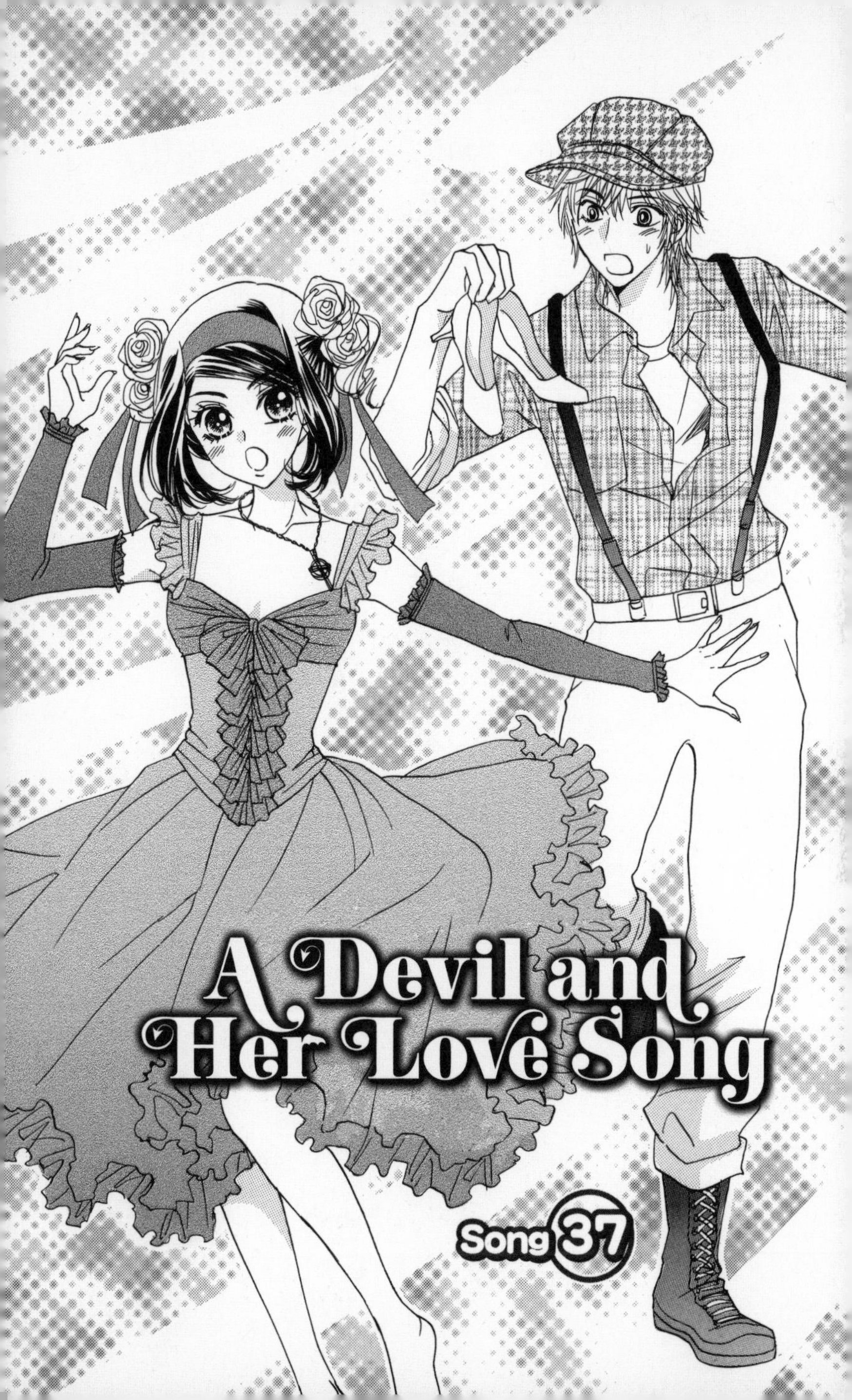
A Devil and Her Love Song
Song 37

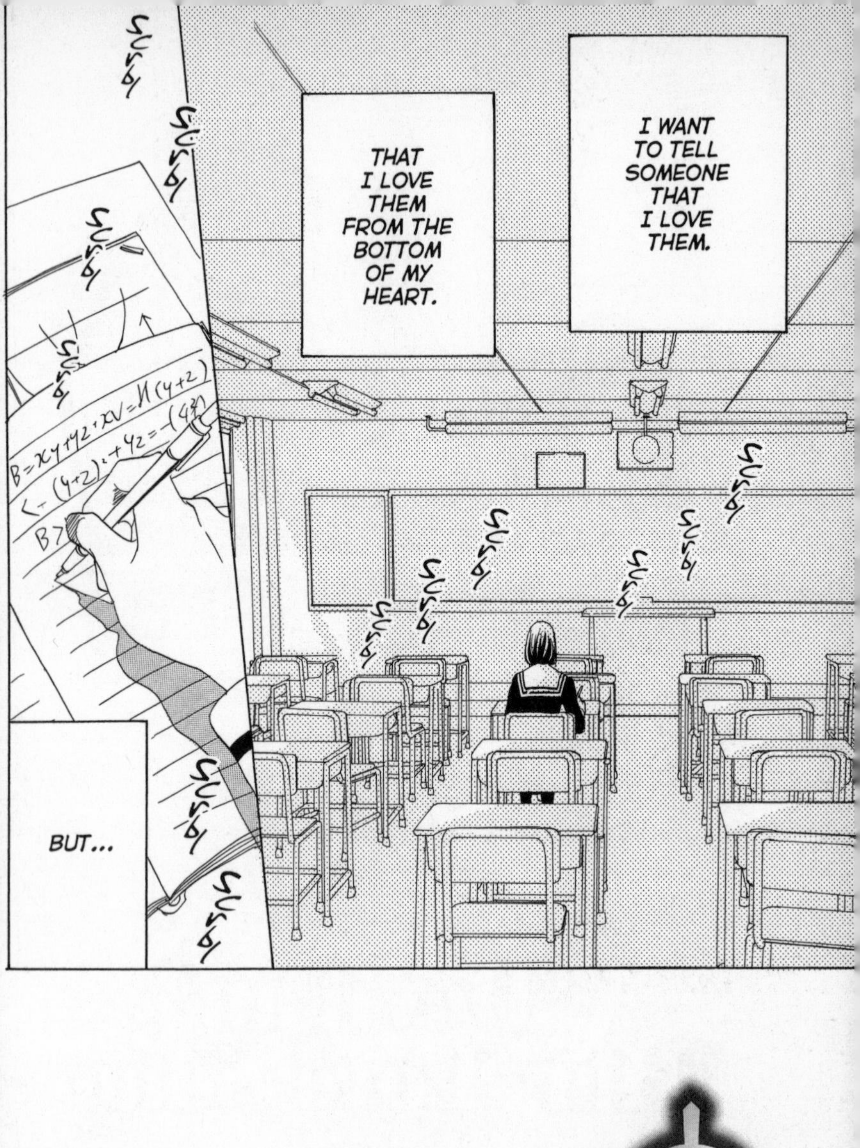
I WANT TO TELL SOMEONE THAT I LOVE THEM.
THAT I LOVE THEM FROM THE BOTTOM OF MY HEART.
BUT...

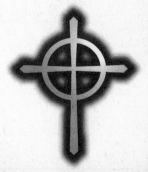

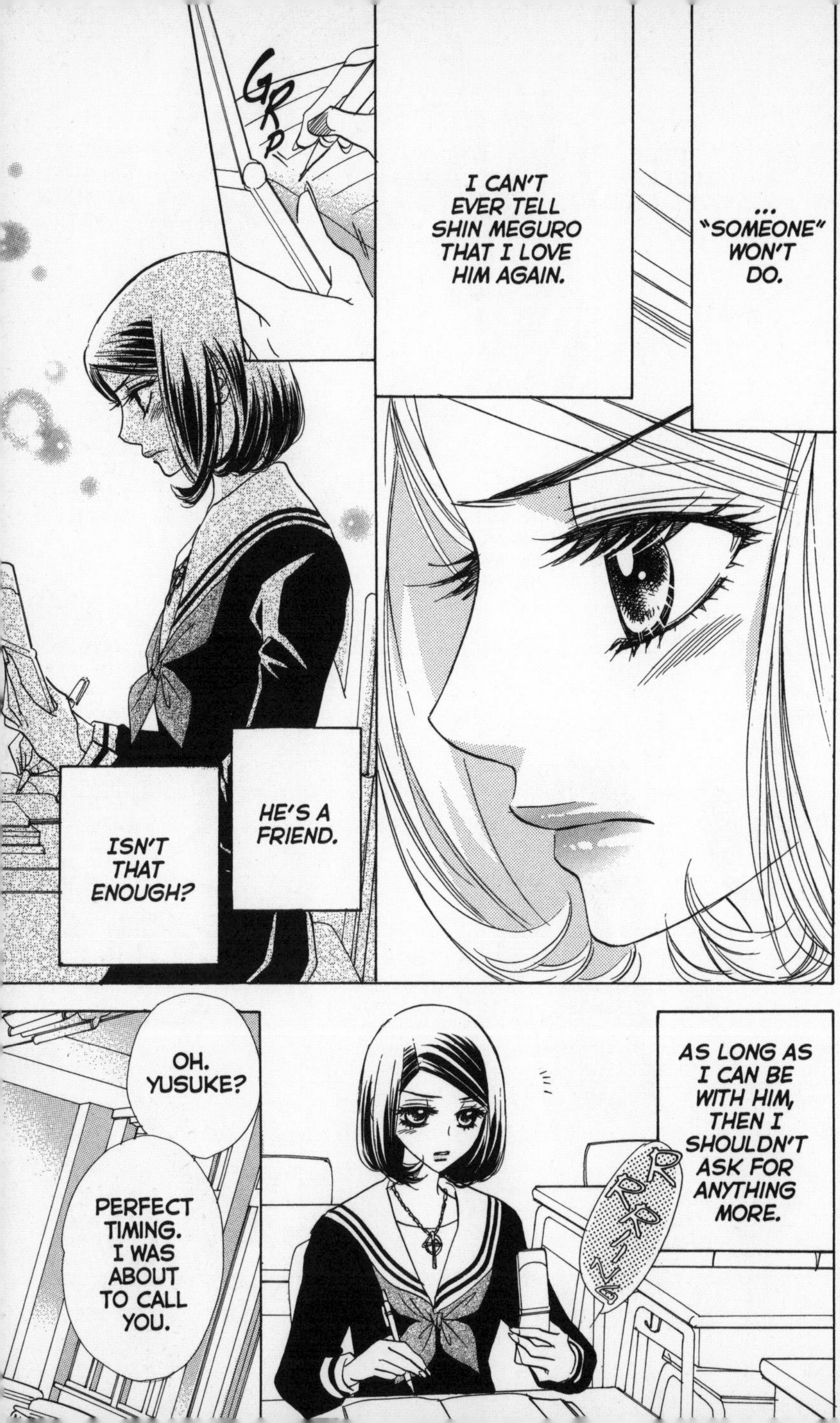

... "SOMEONE" WON'T DO.
I CAN'T EVER TELL SHIN MEGURO THAT I LOVE HIM AGAIN.
GRP
HE'S A FRIEND.
ISN'T THAT ENOUGH?
AS LONG AS I CAN BE WITH HIM, THEN I SHOULDN'T ASK FOR ANYTHING MORE.
RRRING
OH. YUSUKE?
PERFECT TIMING. I WAS ABOUT TO CALL YOU.

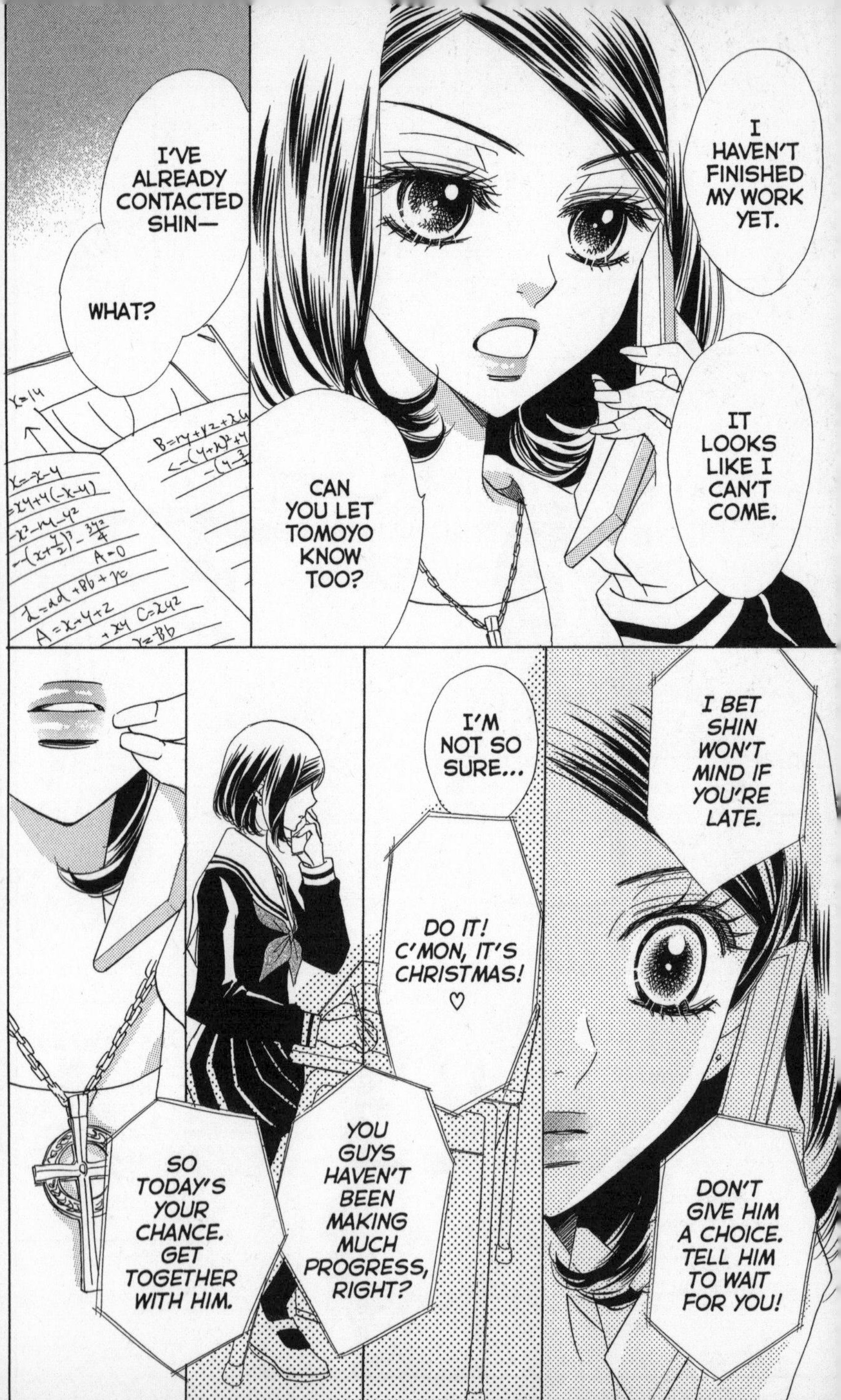
I HAVEN'T FINISHED MY WORK YET.
IT LOOKS LIKE I CAN'T COME.
CAN YOU LET TOMOYO KNOW TOO?
I'VE ALREADY CONTACTED SHIN—
WHAT?
I BET SHIN WON'T MIND IF YOU'RE LATE.
DON'T GIVE HIM A CHOICE. TELL HIM TO WAIT FOR YOU!
I'M NOT SO SURE...
DO IT! C'MON, IT'S CHRISTMAS! ♡
YOU GUYS HAVEN'T BEEN MAKING MUCH PROGRESS, RIGHT?
SO TODAY'S YOUR CHANCE. GET TOGETHER WITH HIM.

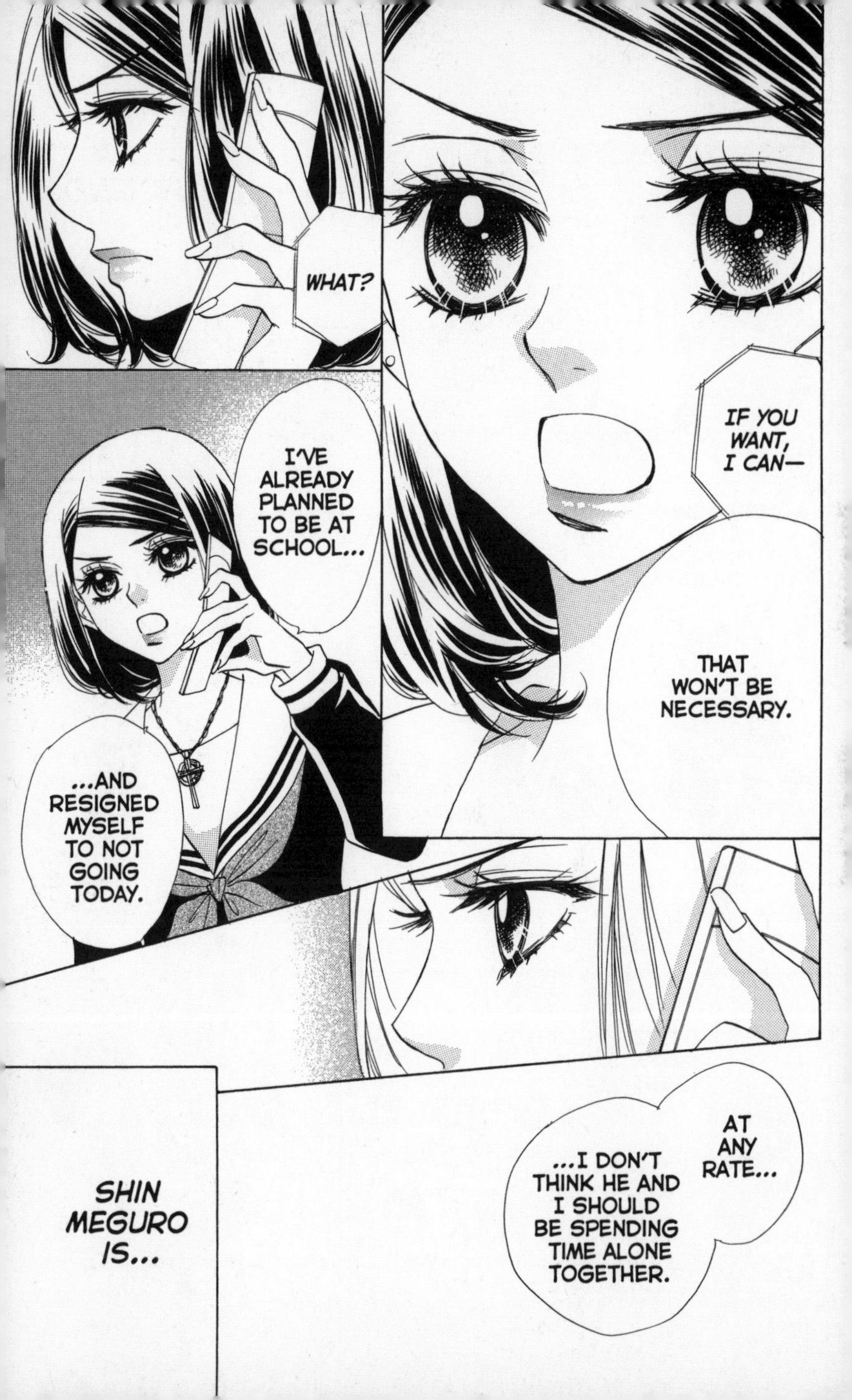
IF YOU WANT, I CAN—
THAT WON'T BE NECESSARY.
WHAT?
I'VE ALREADY PLANNED TO BE AT SCHOOL...
...AND RESIGNED MYSELF TO NOT GOING TODAY.
AT ANY RATE...
...I DON'T THINK HE AND I SHOULD BE SPENDING TIME ALONE TOGETHER.
SHIN MEGURO IS...

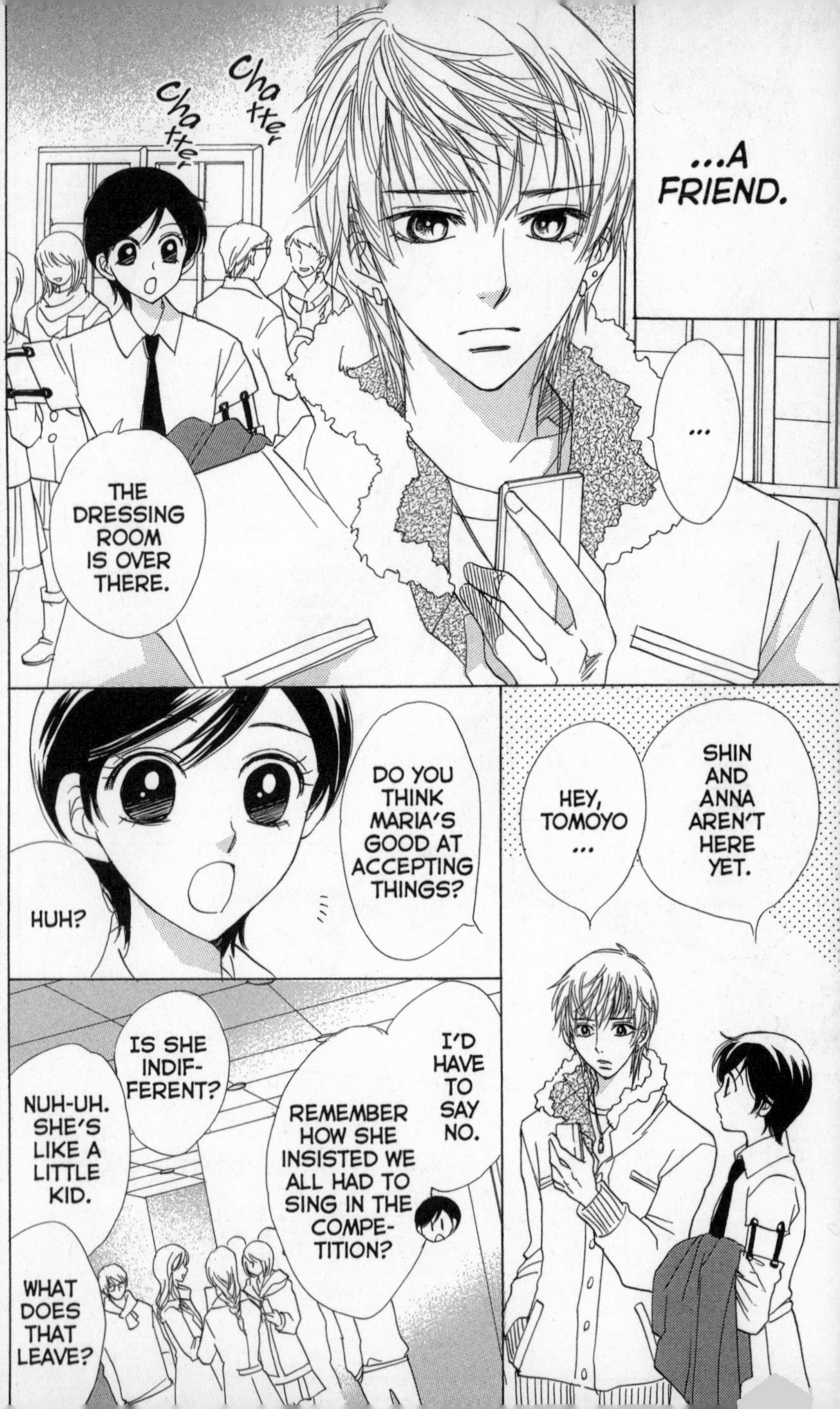
...A FRIEND.
...
Chatter Chatter
THE DRESSING ROOM IS OVER THERE.
SHIN AND ANNA AREN'T HERE YET.
HEY, TOMOYO...
DO YOU THINK MARIA'S GOOD AT ACCEPTING THINGS?
HUH?
I'D HAVE TO SAY NO.
REMEMBER HOW SHE INSISTED WE ALL HAD TO SING IN THE COMPETITION?
IS SHE INDIFFERENT?
NUH-UH. SHE'S LIKE A LITTLE KID.
WHAT DOES THAT LEAVE?

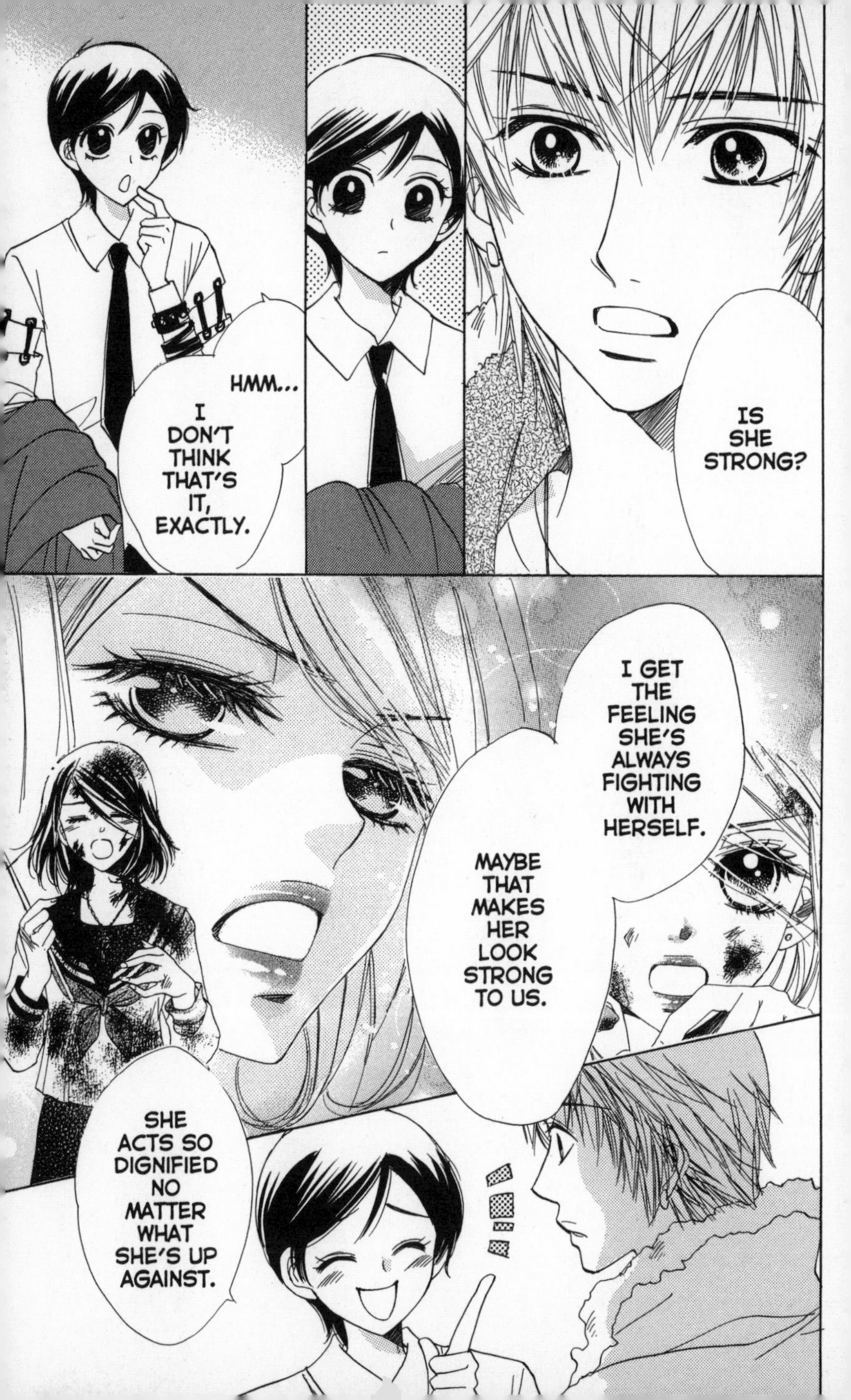
IS SHE STRONG?
HMM...
I DON'T THINK THAT'S IT, EXACTLY.
I GET THE FEELING SHE'S ALWAYS FIGHTING WITH HERSELF.
MAYBE THAT MAKES HER LOOK STRONG TO US.
SHE ACTS SO DIGNIFIED NO MATTER WHAT SHE'S UP AGAINST.

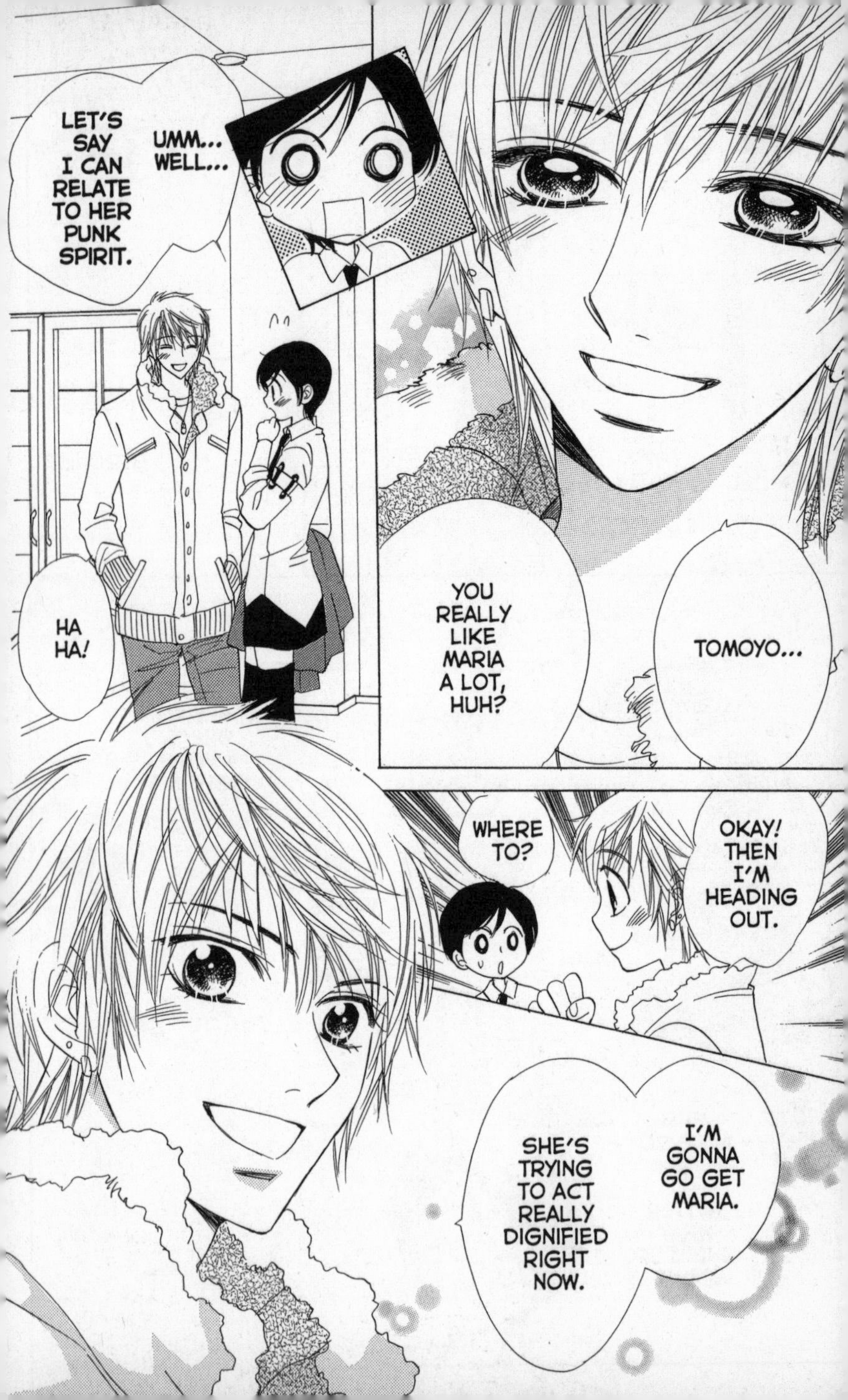
TOMOYO...
YOU REALLY LIKE MARIA A LOT, HUH?
UMM... WELL...
LET'S SAY I CAN RELATE TO HER PUNK SPIRIT.
HA HA!
OKAY! THEN I'M HEADING OUT.
WHERE TO?
I'M GONNA GO GET MARIA.
SHE'S TRYING TO ACT REALLY DIGNIFIED RIGHT NOW.

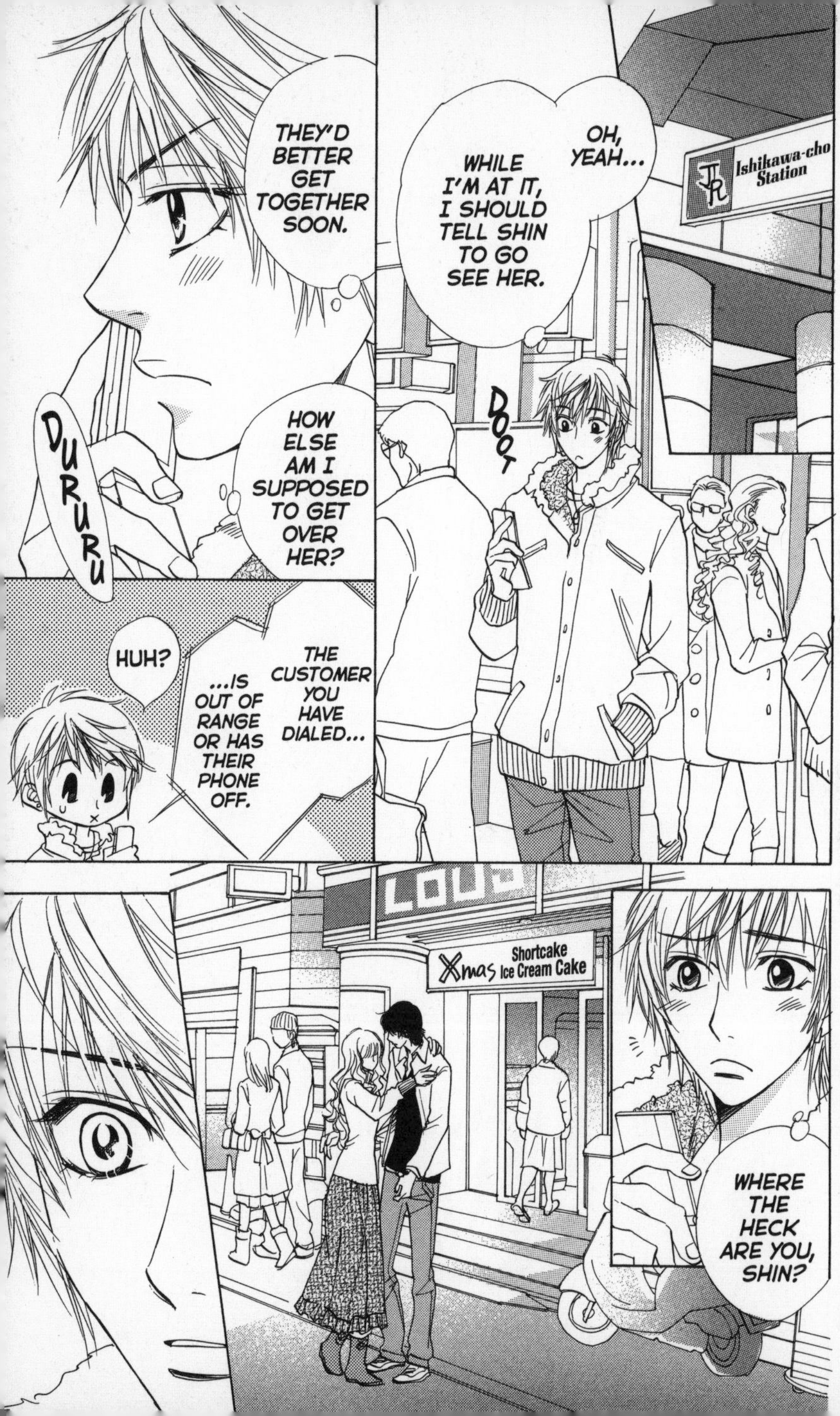
Ishikawa-cho Station
OH, YEAH...
WHILE I'M AT IT, I SHOULD TELL SHIN TO GO SEE HER.
DOOT
THEY'D BETTER GET TOGETHER SOON.
HOW ELSE AM I SUPPOSED TO GET OVER HER?
DURURU
HUH?
THE CUSTOMER YOU HAVE DIALED...
...IS OUT OF RANGE OR HAS THEIR PHONE OFF.
WHERE THE HECK ARE YOU, SHIN?
Xmas Shortcake Ice Cream Cake

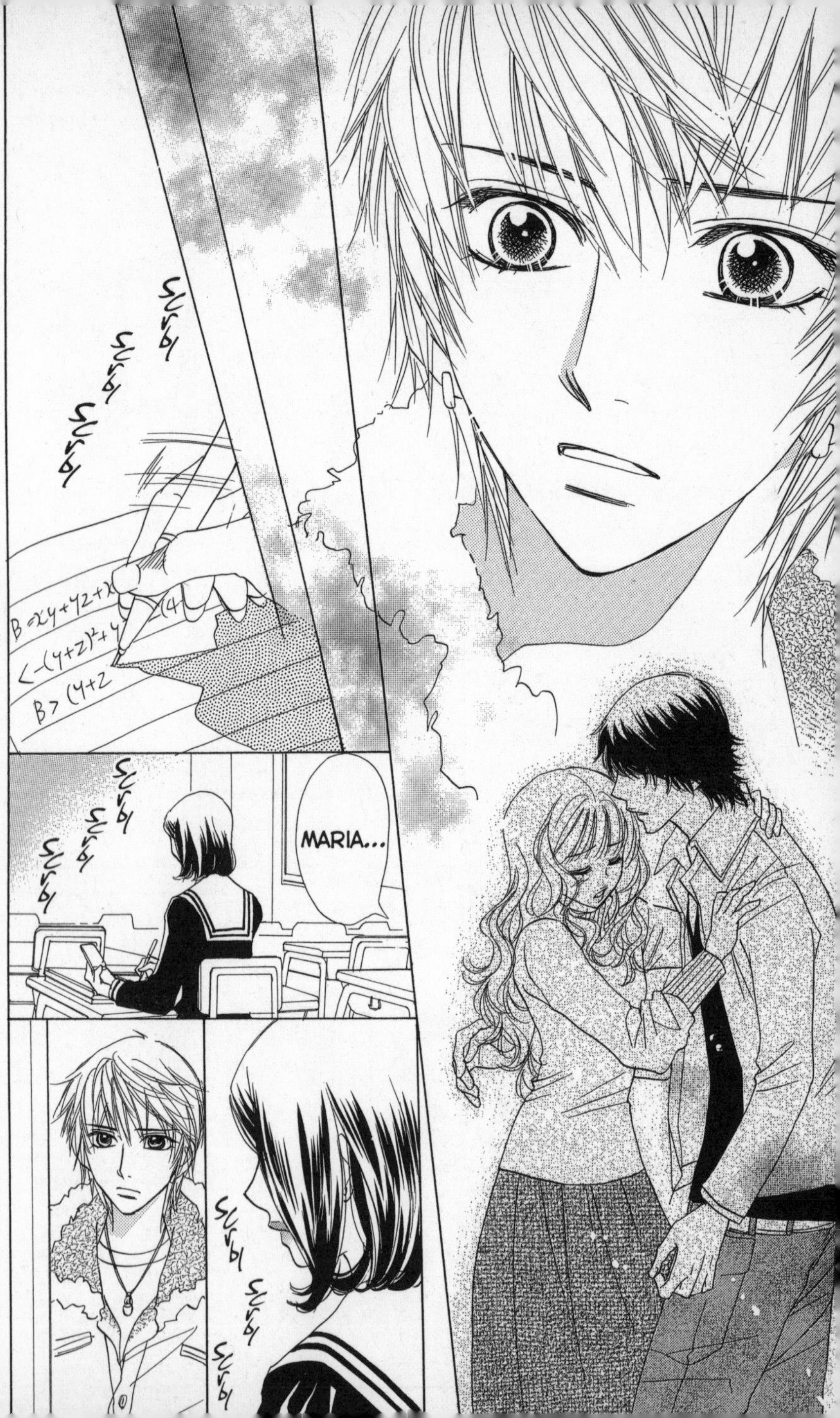
MARIA...

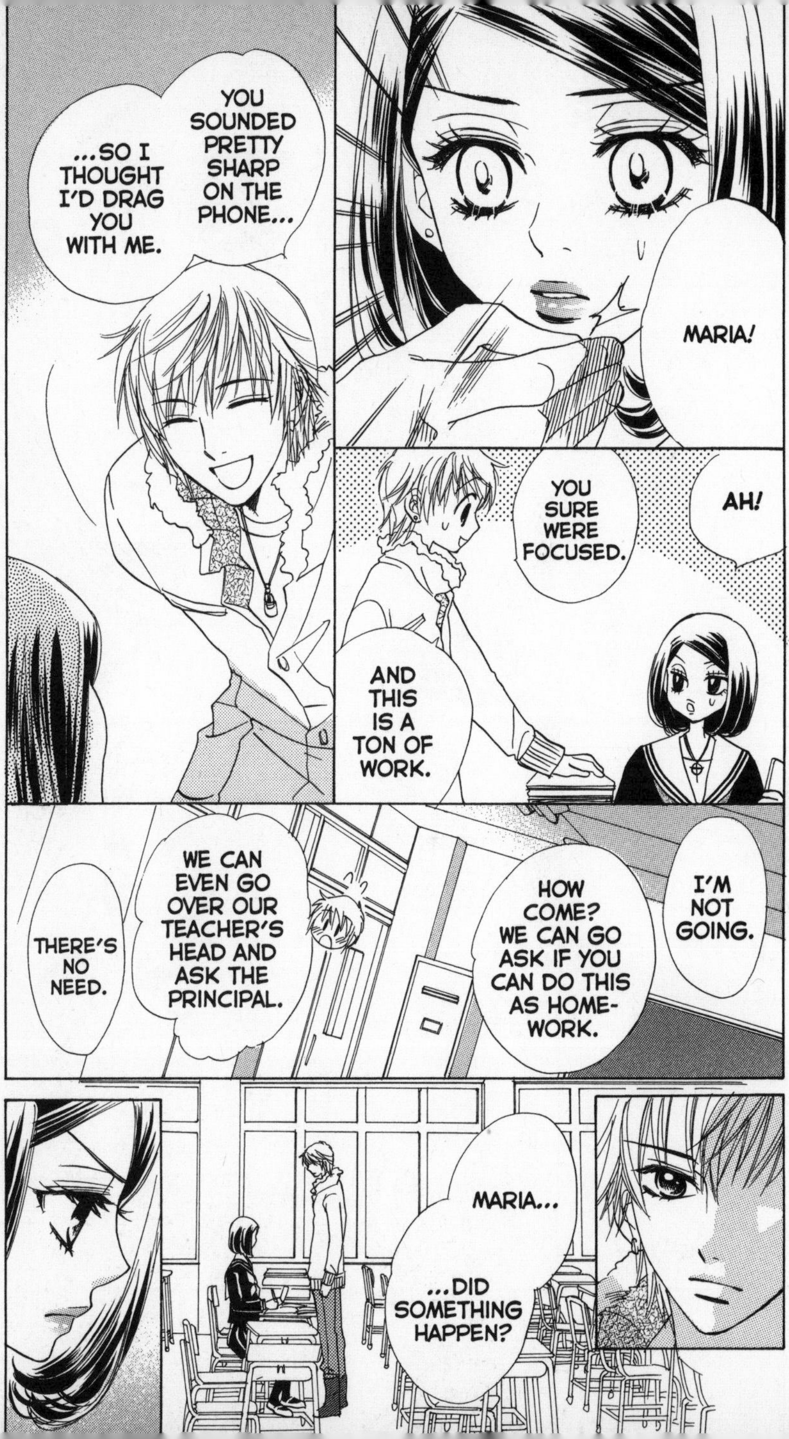
MARIA!
AH!
YOU SURE WERE FOCUSED.
AND THIS IS A TON OF WORK.
YOU SOUNDED PRETTY SHARP ON THE PHONE...
...SO I THOUGHT I'D DRAG YOU WITH ME.
I'M NOT GOING.
HOW COME? WE CAN GO ASK IF YOU CAN DO THIS AS HOME-WORK.
WE CAN EVEN GO OVER OUR TEACHER'S HEAD AND ASK THE PRINCIPAL.
THERE'S NO NEED.
MARIA...
...DID SOMETHING HAPPEN?

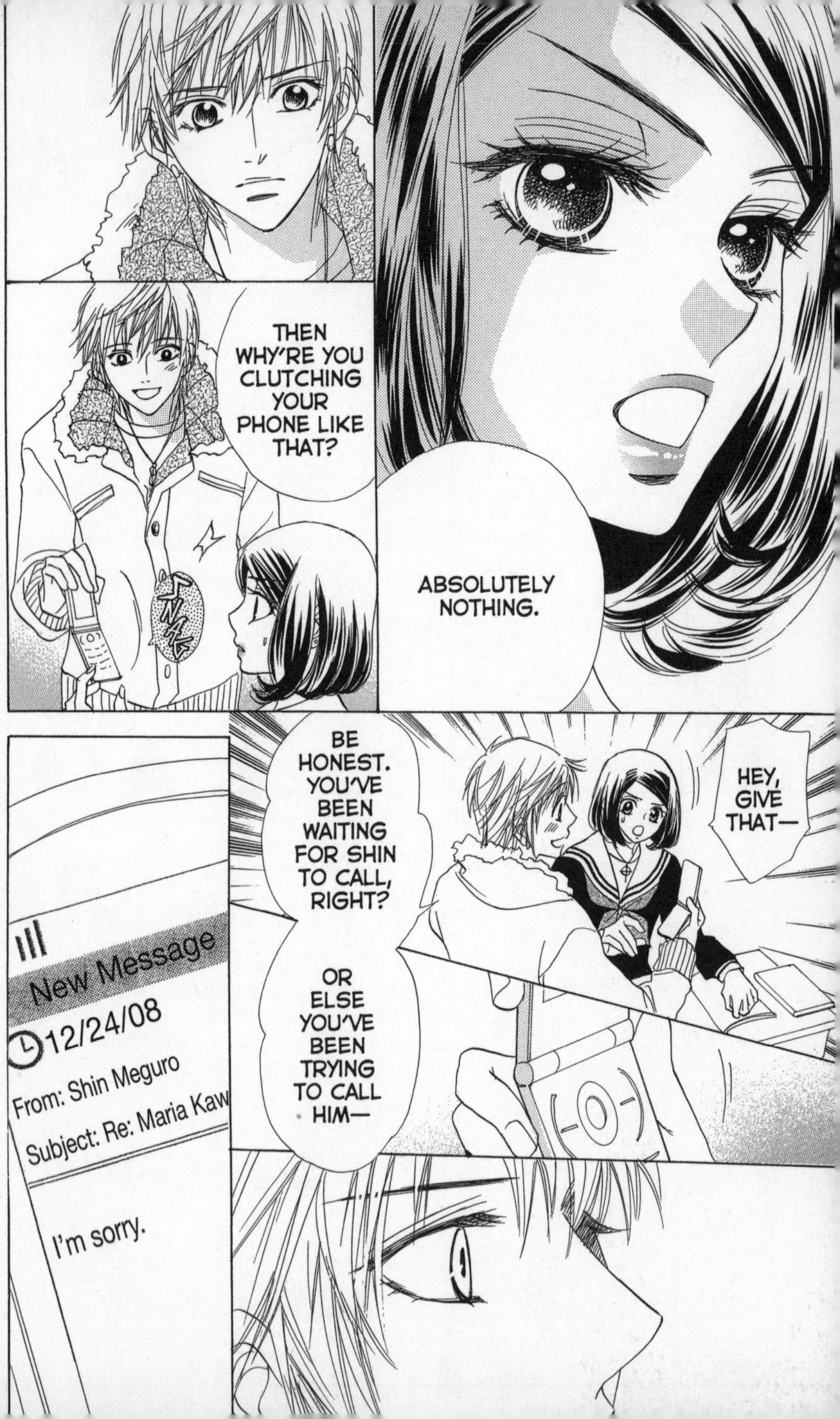
ABSOLUTELY NOTHING.
THEN WHY'RE YOU CLUTCHING YOUR PHONE LIKE THAT?
HEY, GIVE THAT—
BE HONEST. YOU'VE BEEN WAITING FOR SHIN TO CALL, RIGHT?
OR ELSE YOU'VE BEEN TRYING TO CALL HIM—
New Message
12/24/08
From: Shin Meguro
Subject: Re: Maria Kaw
I'm sorry.

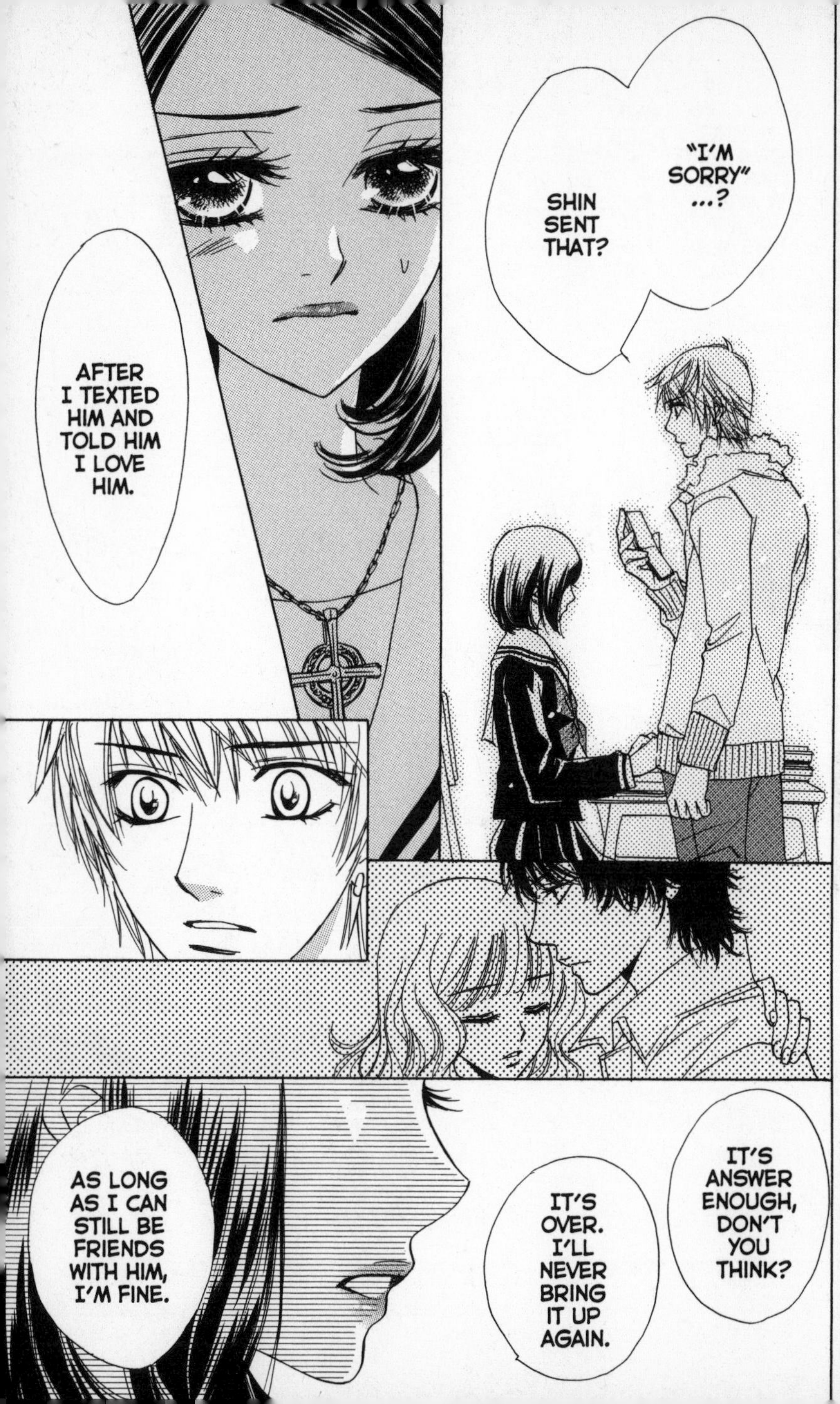
"I'M SORRY" ...?
SHIN SENT THAT?
AFTER I TEXTED HIM AND TOLD HIM I LOVE HIM.
IT'S ANSWER ENOUGH, DON'T YOU THINK?
IT'S OVER. I'LL NEVER BRING IT UP AGAIN.
AS LONG AS I CAN STILL BE FRIENDS WITH HIM, I'M FINE.

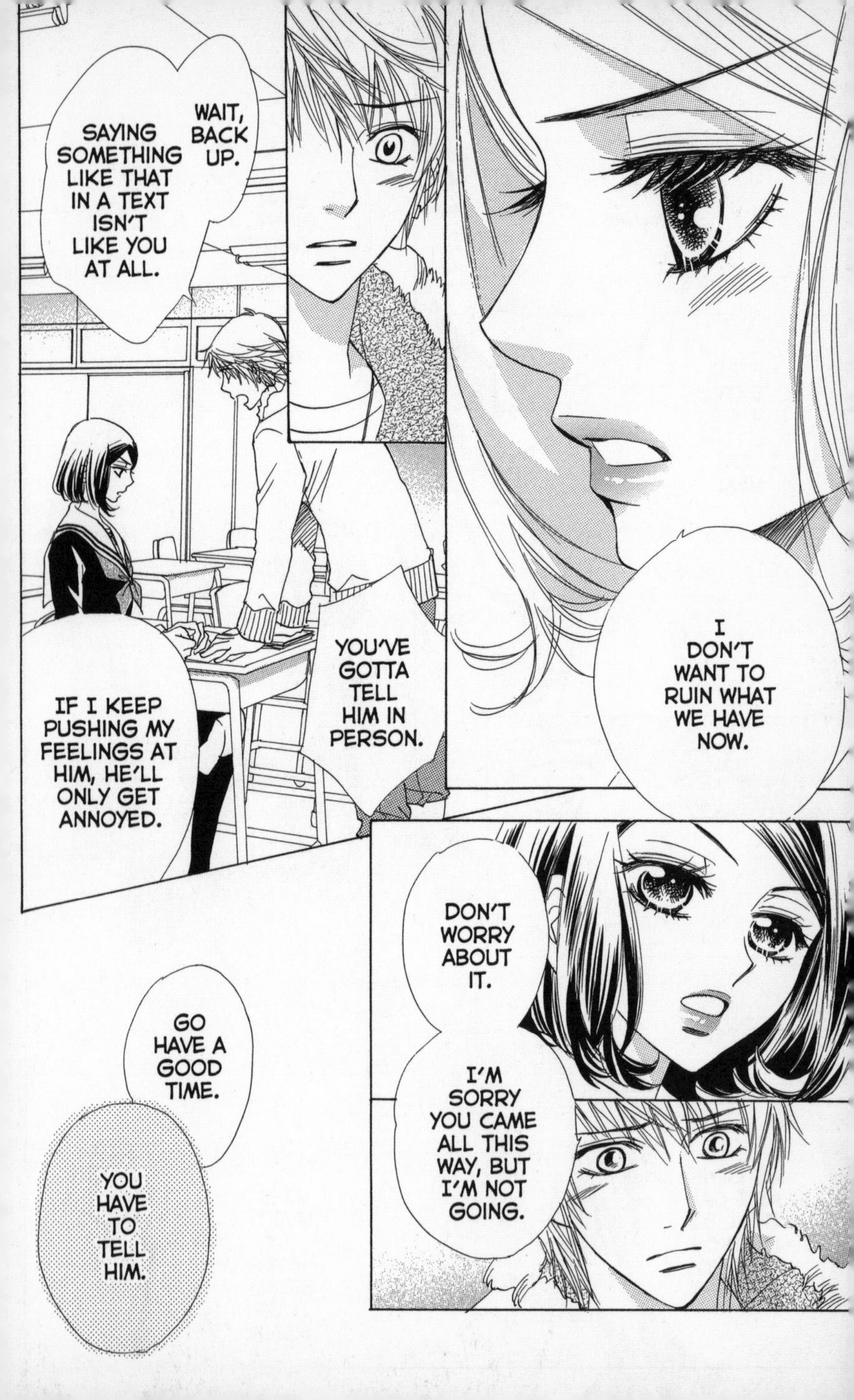
WAIT, BACK UP.
SAYING SOMETHING LIKE THAT IN A TEXT ISN'T LIKE YOU AT ALL.
YOU'VE GOTTA TELL HIM IN PERSON.
IF I KEEP PUSHING MY FEELINGS AT HIM, HE'LL ONLY GET ANNOYED.
I DON'T WANT TO RUIN WHAT WE HAVE NOW.
DON'T WORRY ABOUT IT.
I'M SORRY YOU CAME ALL THIS WAY, BUT I'M NOT GOING.
GO HAVE A GOOD TIME.
YOU HAVE TO TELL HIM.

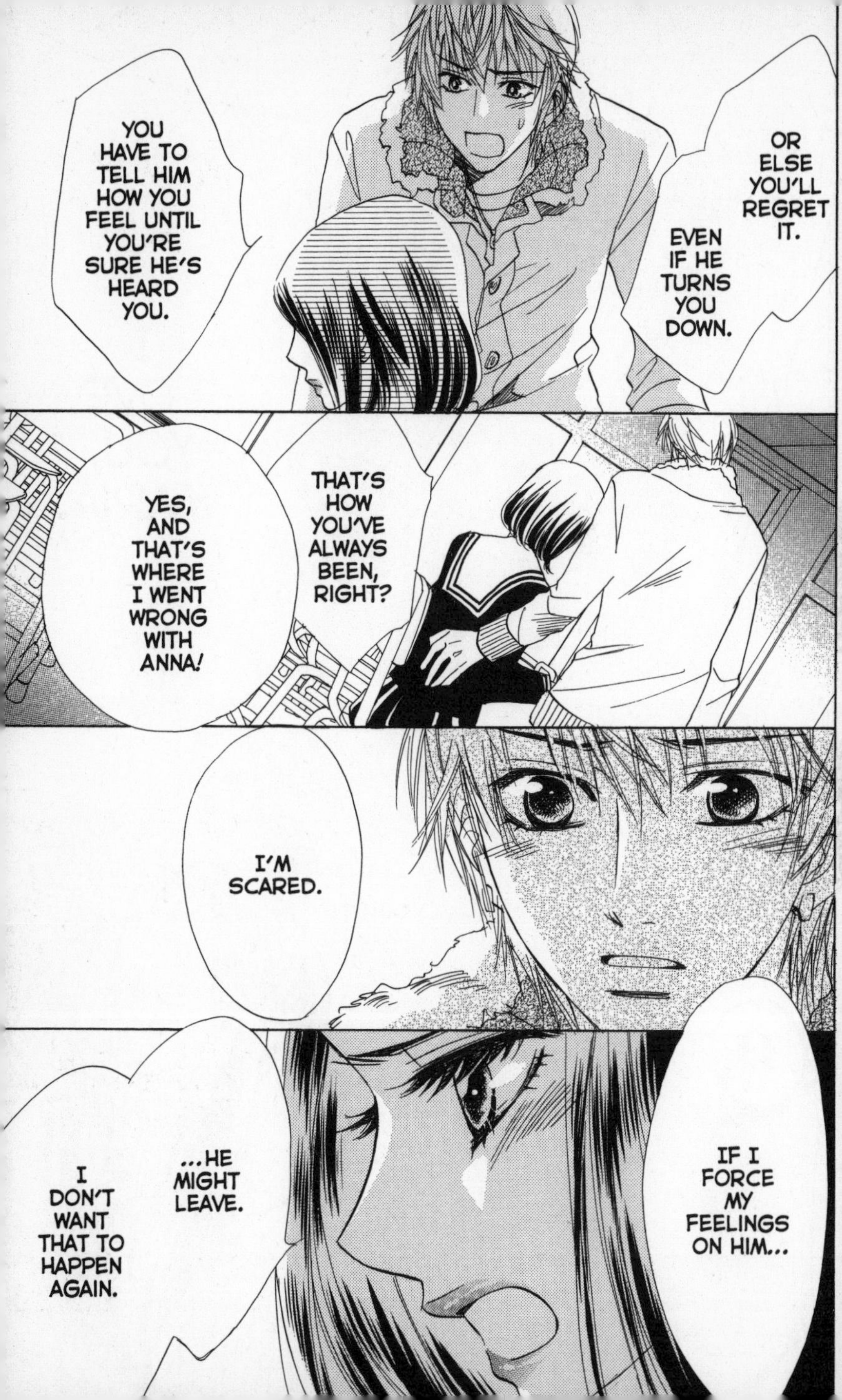
OR ELSE YOU'LL REGRET IT.
EVEN IF HE TURNS YOU DOWN.
YOU HAVE TO TELL HIM HOW YOU FEEL UNTIL YOU'RE SURE HE'S HEARD YOU.
THAT'S HOW YOU'VE ALWAYS BEEN, RIGHT?
YES, AND THAT'S WHERE I WENT WRONG WITH ANNA!
I'M SCARED.
IF I FORCE MY FEELINGS ON HIM...
...HE MIGHT LEAVE.
I DON'T WANT THAT TO HAPPEN AGAIN.

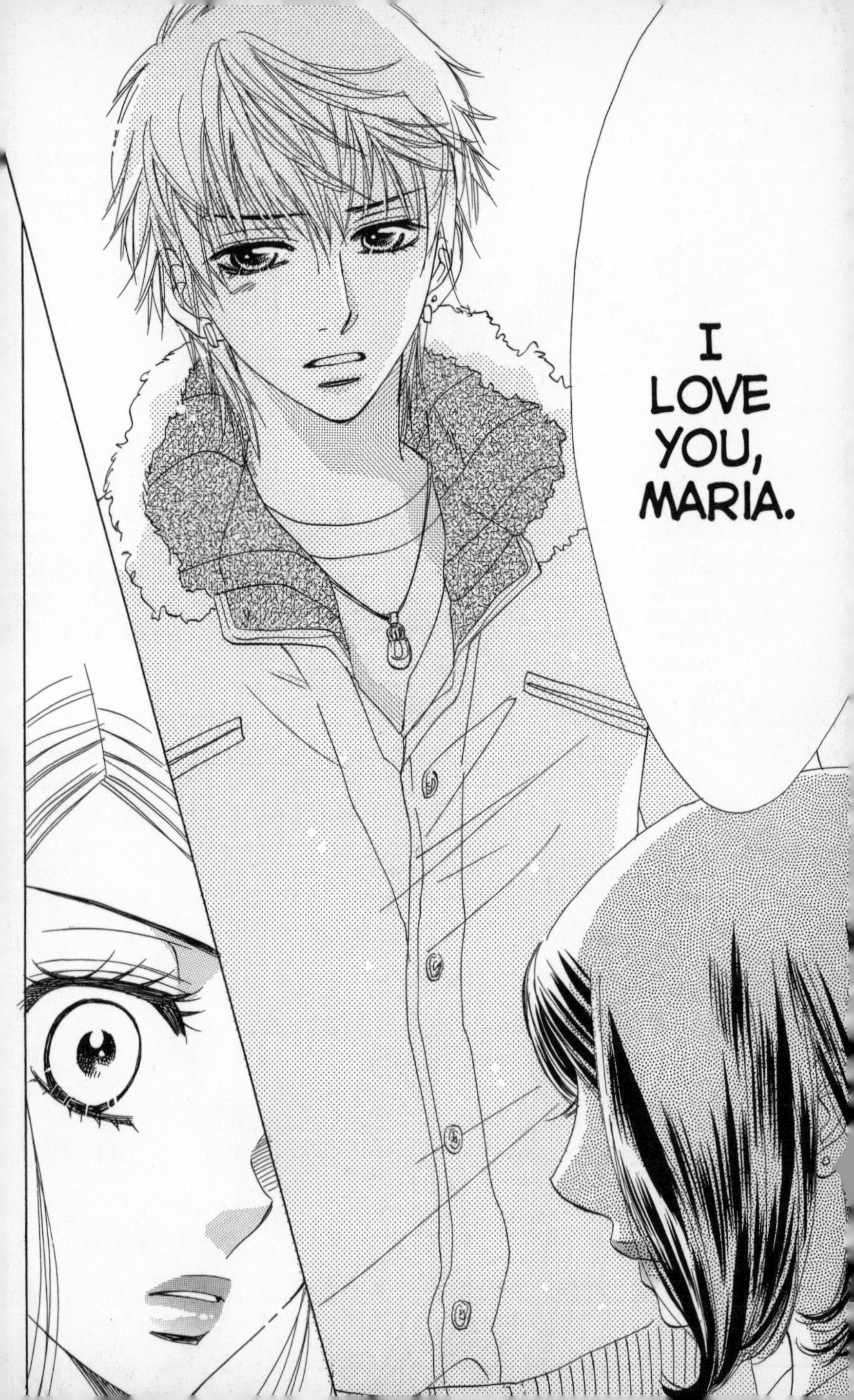
I LOVE YOU, MARIA.

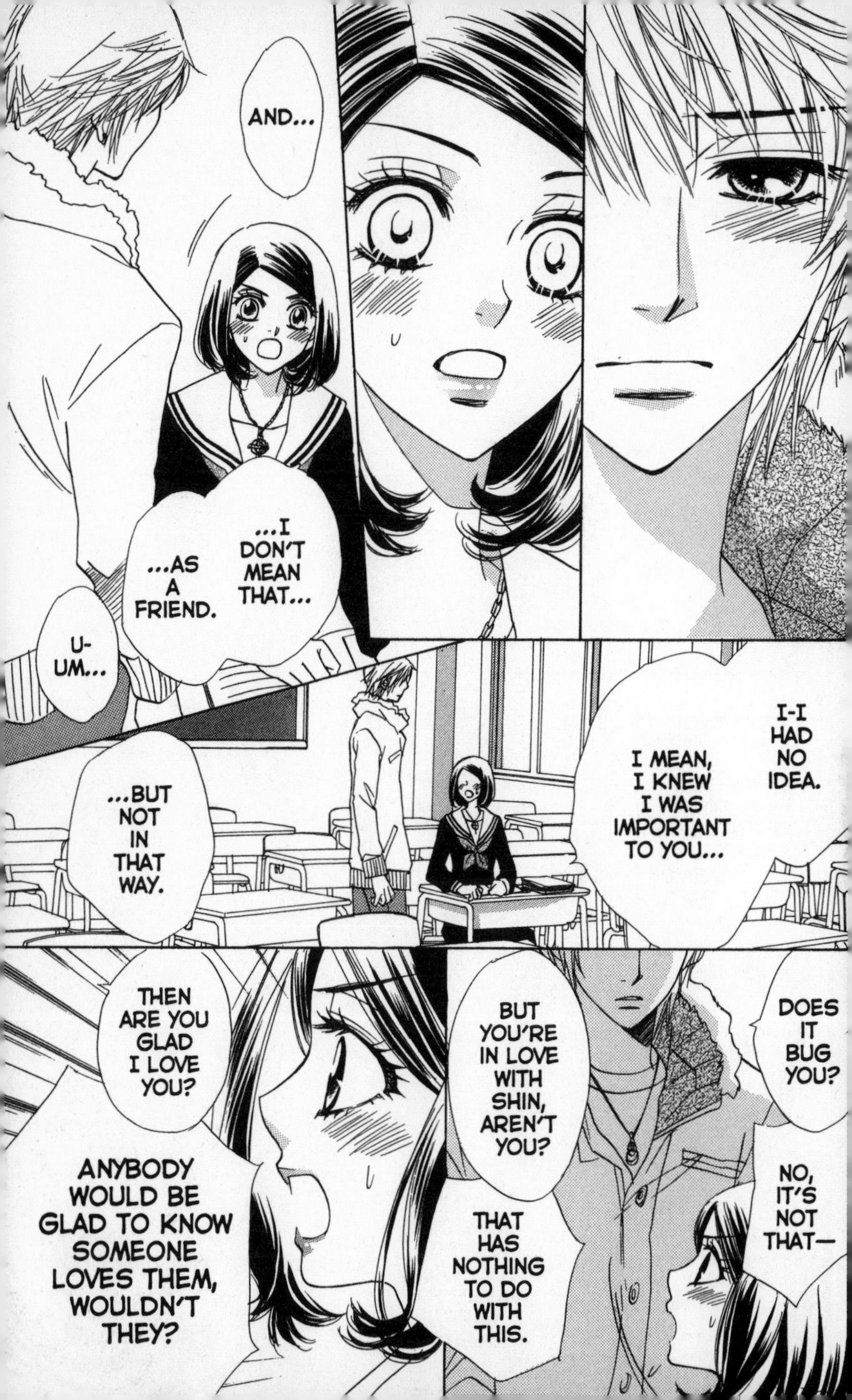
AND...
...I DON'T MEAN THAT...
...AS A FRIEND.
U-UM...
I-I HAD NO IDEA.
I MEAN, I KNEW I WAS IMPORTANT TO YOU...
...BUT NOT IN THAT WAY.
DOES IT BUG YOU?
NO, IT'S NOT THAT—
BUT YOU'RE IN LOVE WITH SHIN, AREN'T YOU?
THAT HAS NOTHING TO DO WITH THIS.
THEN ARE YOU GLAD I LOVE YOU?
ANYBODY WOULD BE GLAD TO KNOW SOMEONE LOVES THEM, WOULDN'T THEY?

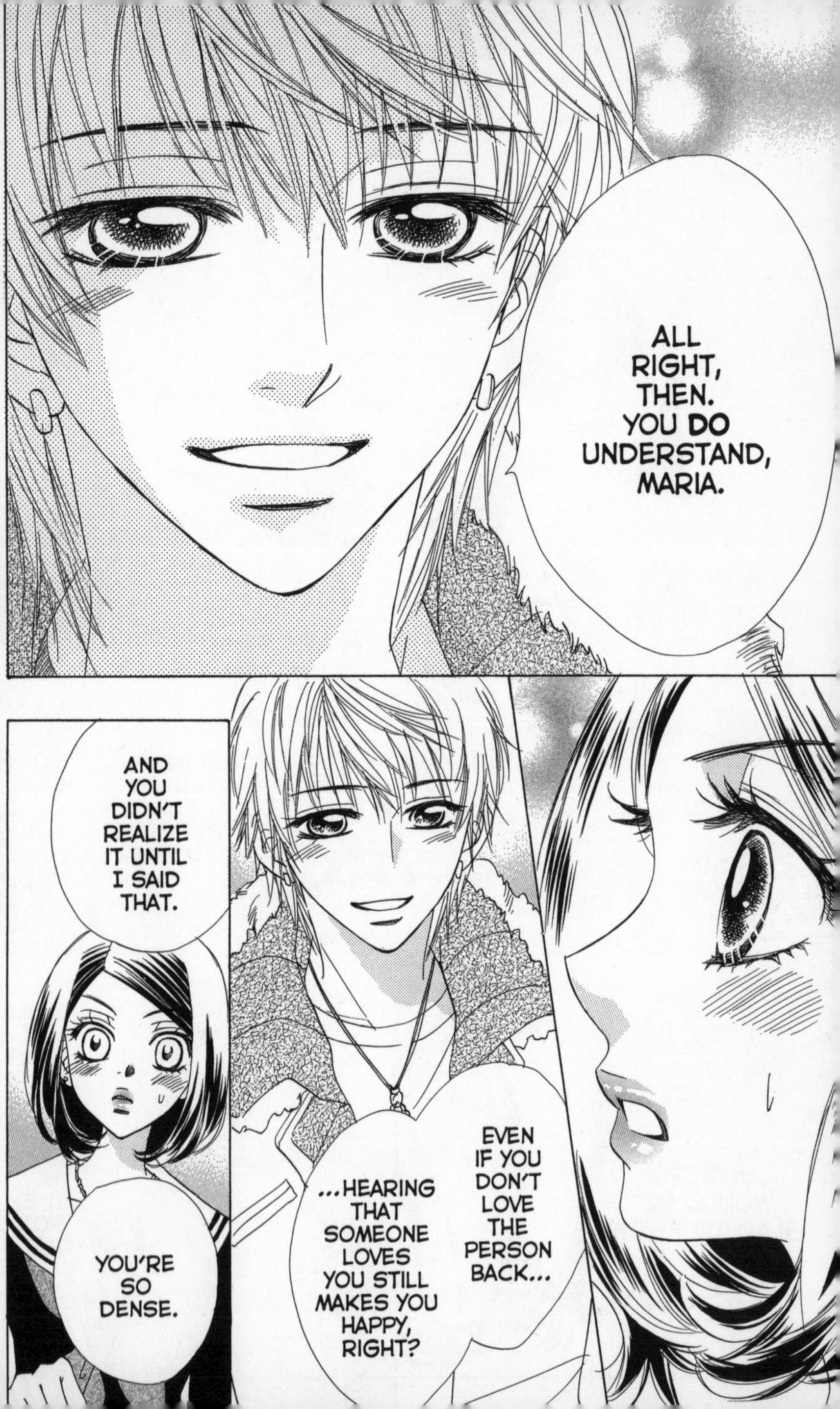
ALL RIGHT, THEN. YOU DO UNDERSTAND, MARIA.
EVEN IF YOU DON'T LOVE THE PERSON BACK...
...HEARING THAT SOMEONE LOVES YOU STILL MAKES YOU HAPPY, RIGHT?
AND YOU DIDN'T REALIZE IT UNTIL I SAID THAT.
YOU'RE SO DENSE.

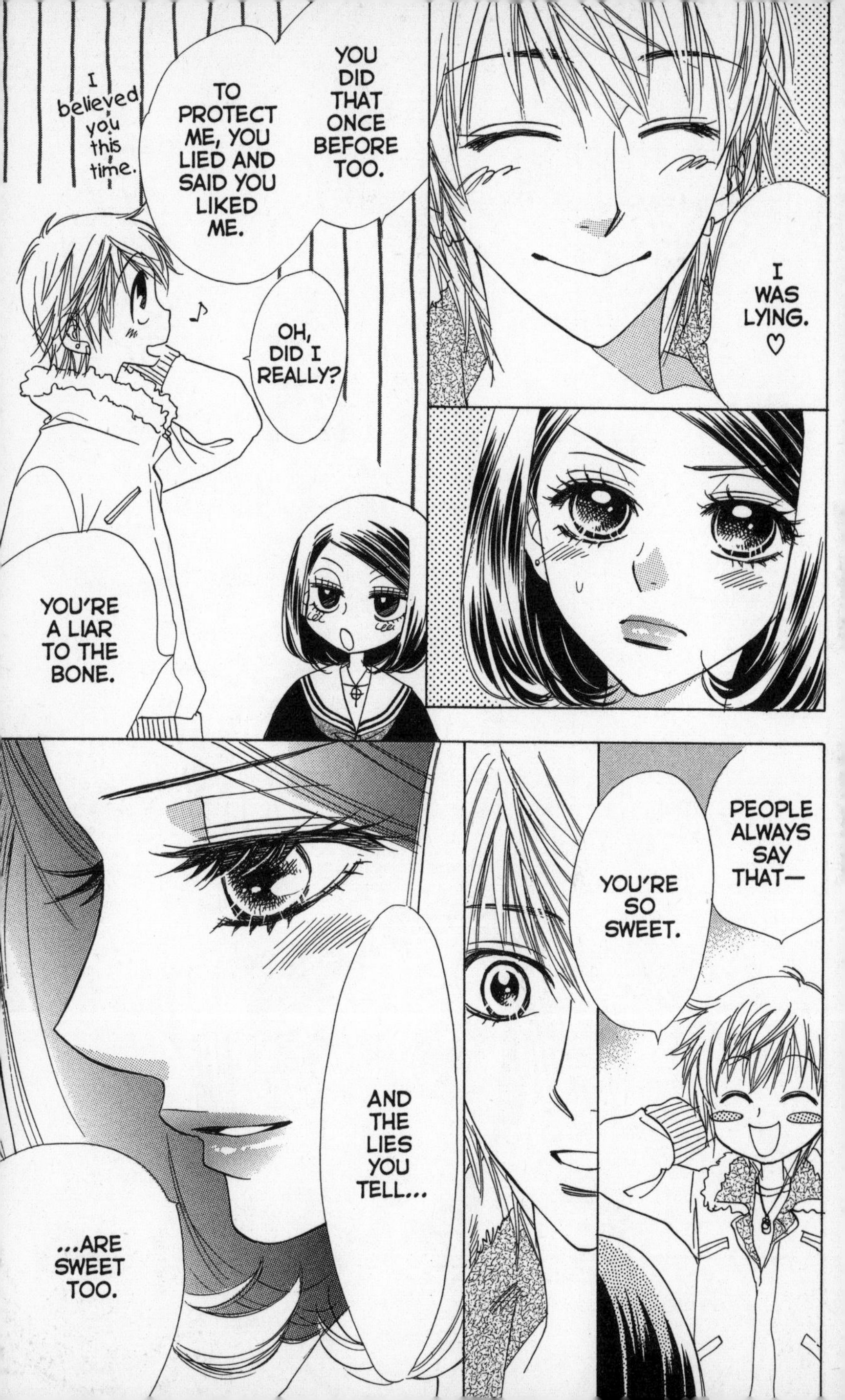
I WAS LYING. ♡
YOU DID THAT ONCE BEFORE TOO.
TO PROTECT ME, YOU LIED AND SAID YOU LIKED ME.
I believed you this time.
OH, DID I REALLY?
YOU'RE A LIAR TO THE BONE.
PEOPLE ALWAYS SAY THAT—
YOU'RE SO SWEET.
AND THE LIES YOU TELL...
...ARE SWEET TOO.

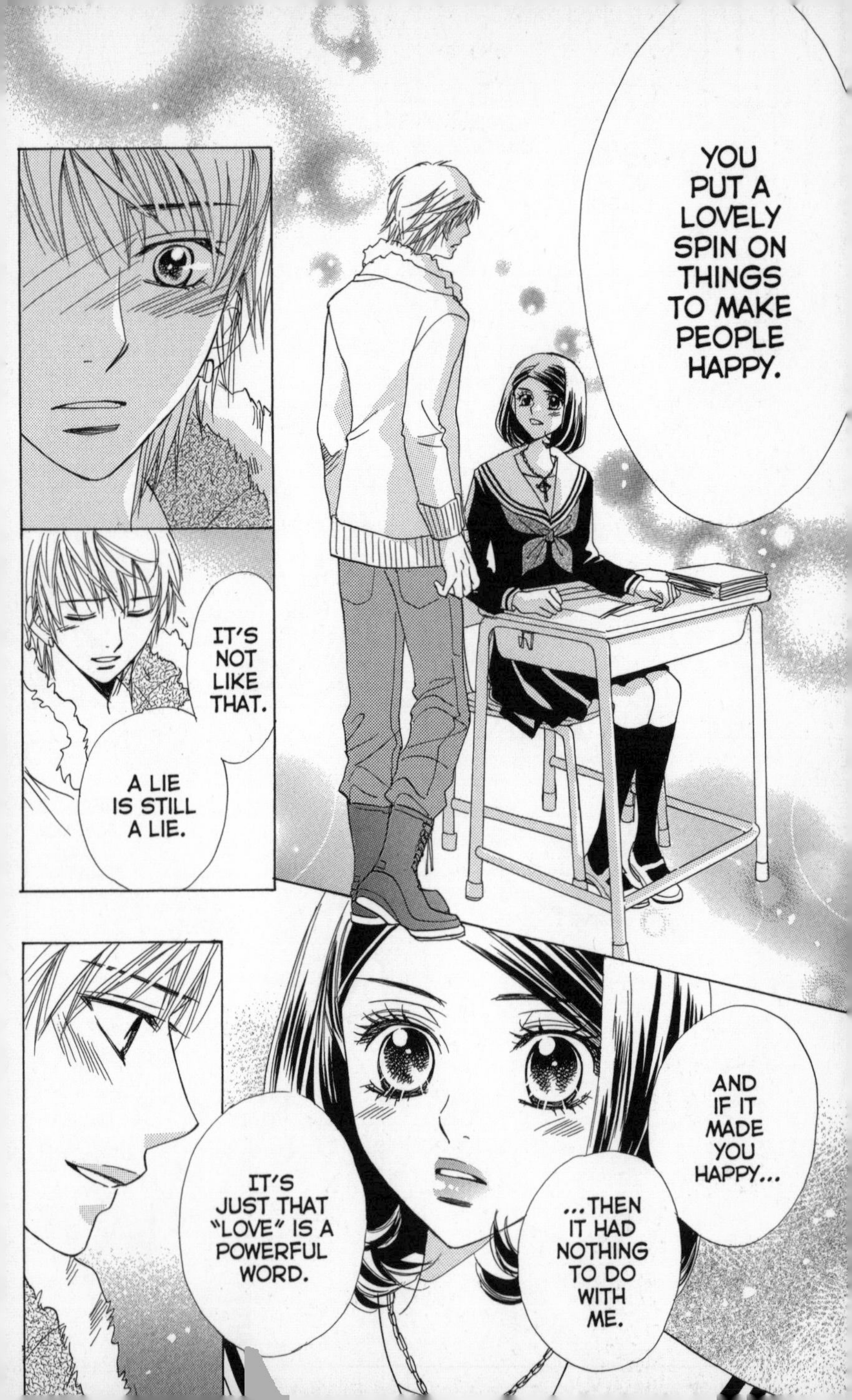
YOU PUT A LOVELY SPIN ON THINGS TO MAKE PEOPLE HAPPY.
IT'S NOT LIKE THAT.
A LIE IS STILL A LIE.
AND IF IT MADE YOU HAPPY...
...THEN IT HAD NOTHING TO DO WITH ME.
IT'S JUST THAT "LOVE" IS A POWERFUL WORD.

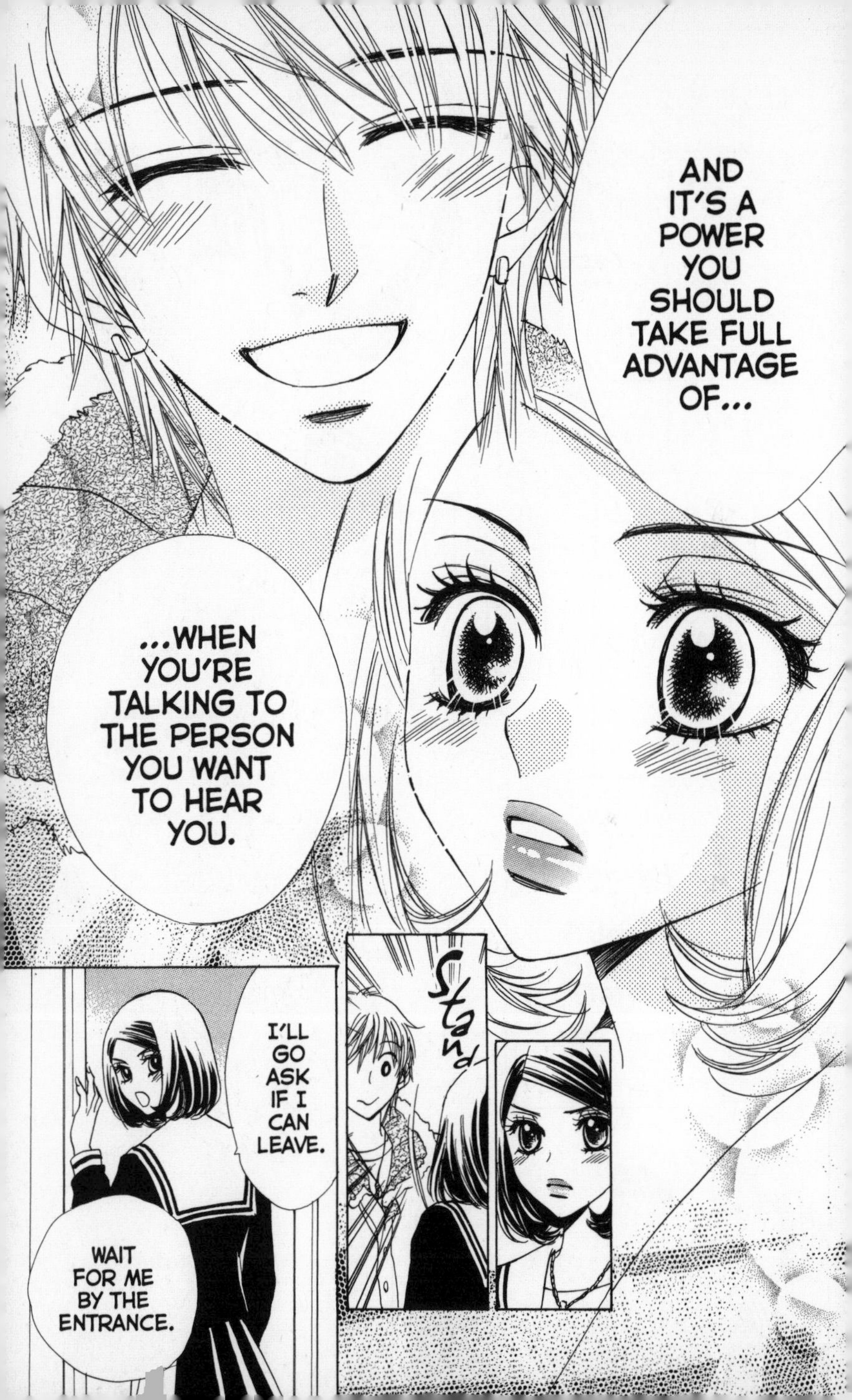
AND IT'S A POWER YOU SHOULD TAKE FULL ADVANTAGE OF...
...WHEN YOU'RE TALKING TO THE PERSON YOU WANT TO HEAR YOU.
Stand
I'LL GO ASK IF I CAN LEAVE.
WAIT FOR ME BY THE ENTRANCE.

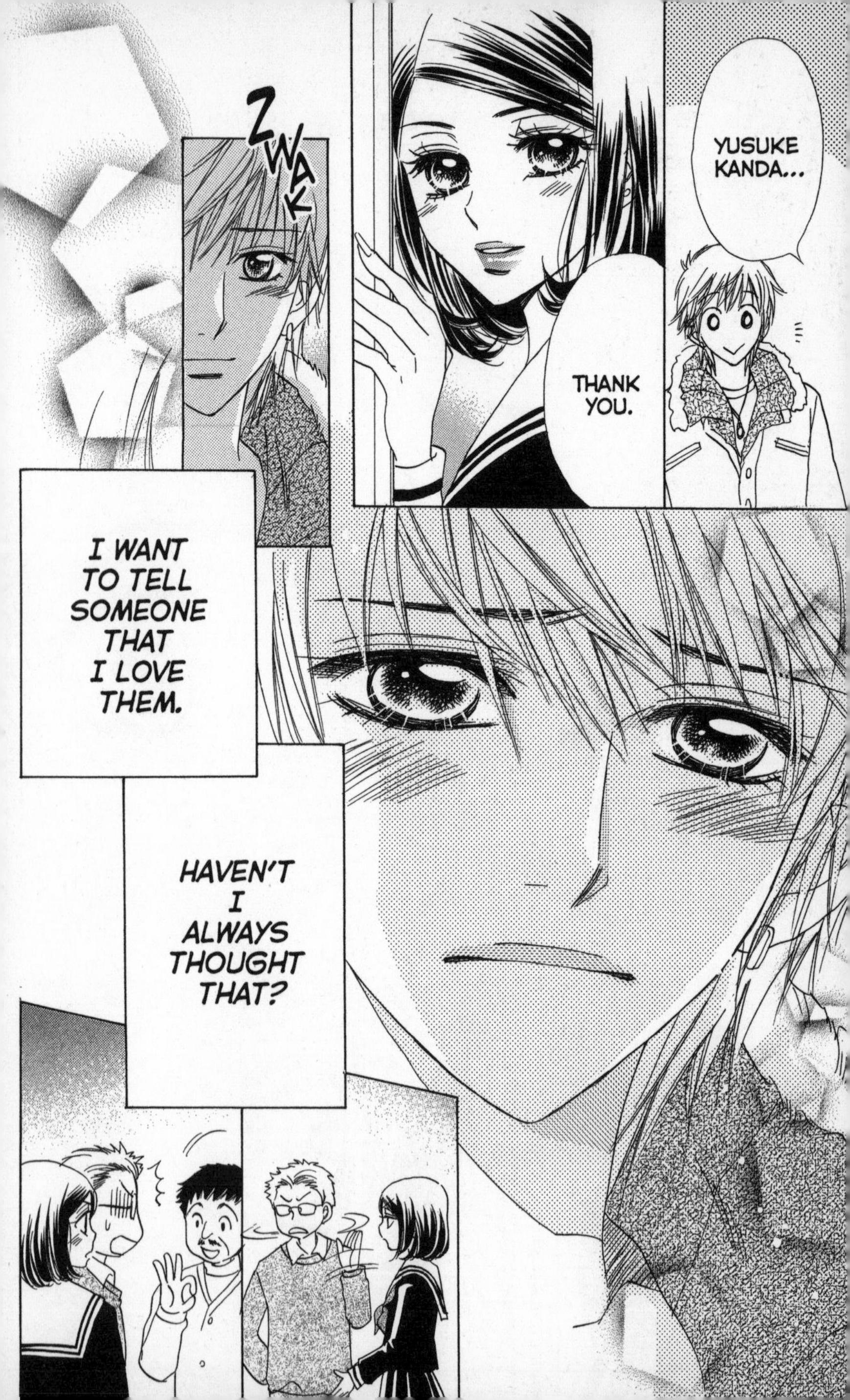
YUSUKE KANDA...
THANK YOU.
ZWAK
I WANT TO TELL SOMEONE THAT I LOVE THEM.
HAVEN'T I ALWAYS THOUGHT THAT?

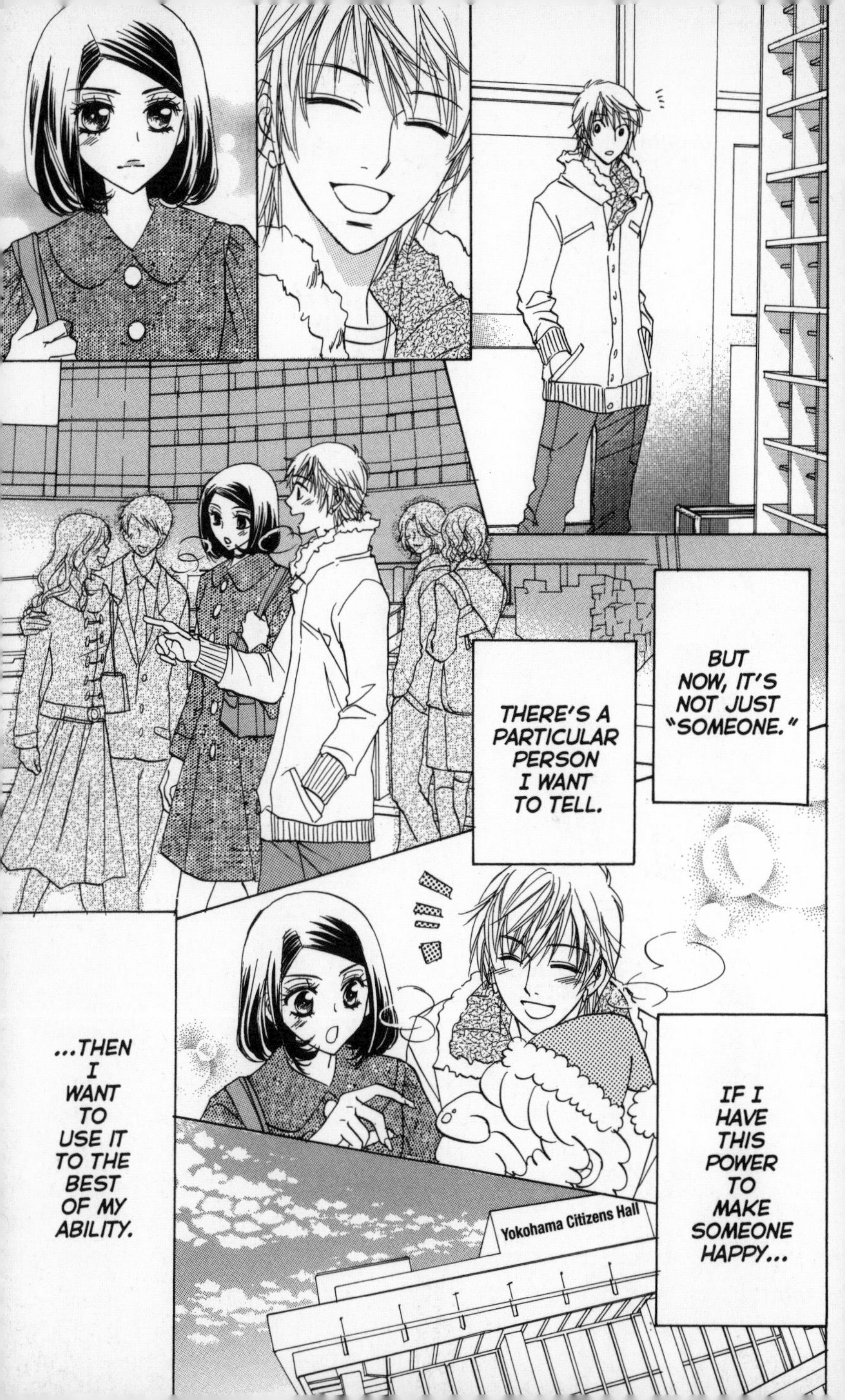
BUT NOW, IT'S NOT JUST "SOMEONE."
THERE'S A PARTICULAR PERSON I WANT TO TELL.
IF I HAVE THIS POWER TO MAKE SOMEONE HAPPY...
Yokohama Citizens Hall
...THEN I WANT TO USE IT TO THE BEST OF MY ABILITY.

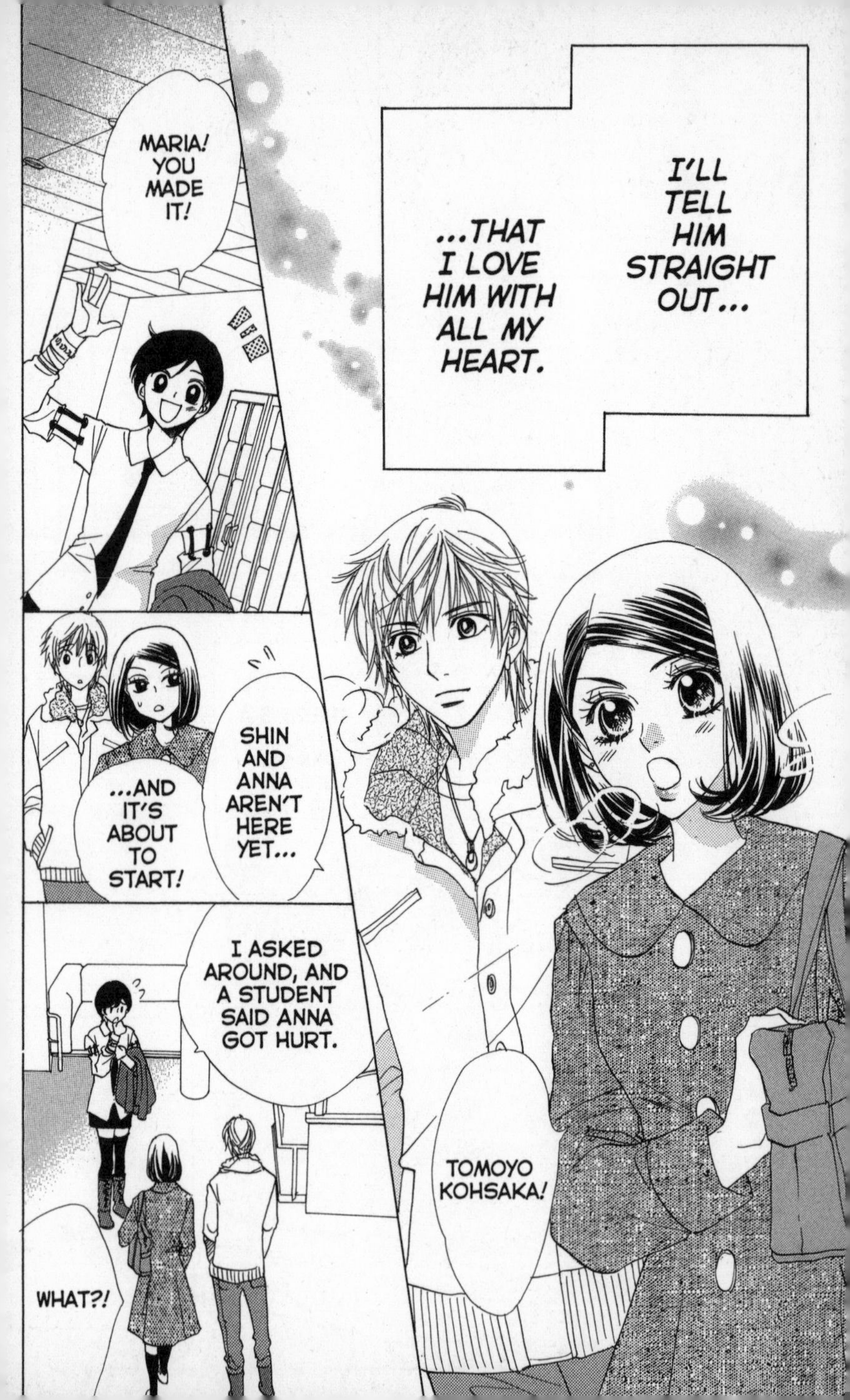
I'LL TELL HIM STRAIGHT OUT...
...THAT I LOVE HIM WITH ALL MY HEART.
TOMOYO KOHSAKA!
MARIA! YOU MADE IT!
SHIN AND ANNA AREN'T HERE YET...
...AND IT'S ABOUT TO START!
I ASKED AROUND, AND A STUDENT SAID ANNA GOT HURT.
WHAT?!

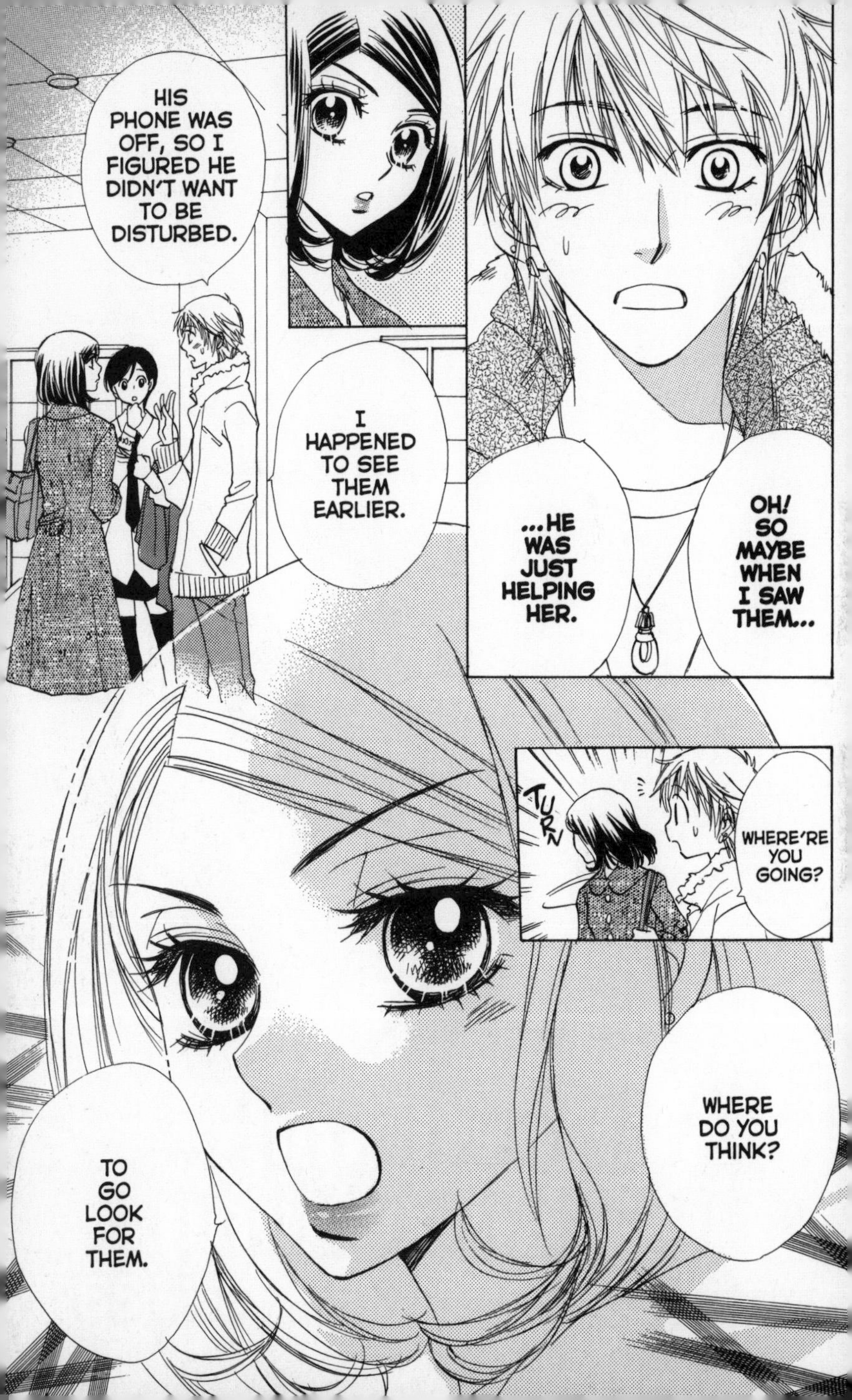
OH! SO MAYBE WHEN I SAW THEM...
...HE WAS JUST HELPING HER.
HIS PHONE WAS OFF, SO I FIGURED HE DIDN'T WANT TO BE DISTURBED.
I HAPPENED TO SEE THEM EARLIER.
TURN
WHERE'RE YOU GOING?
WHERE DO YOU THINK?
TO GO LOOK FOR THEM.

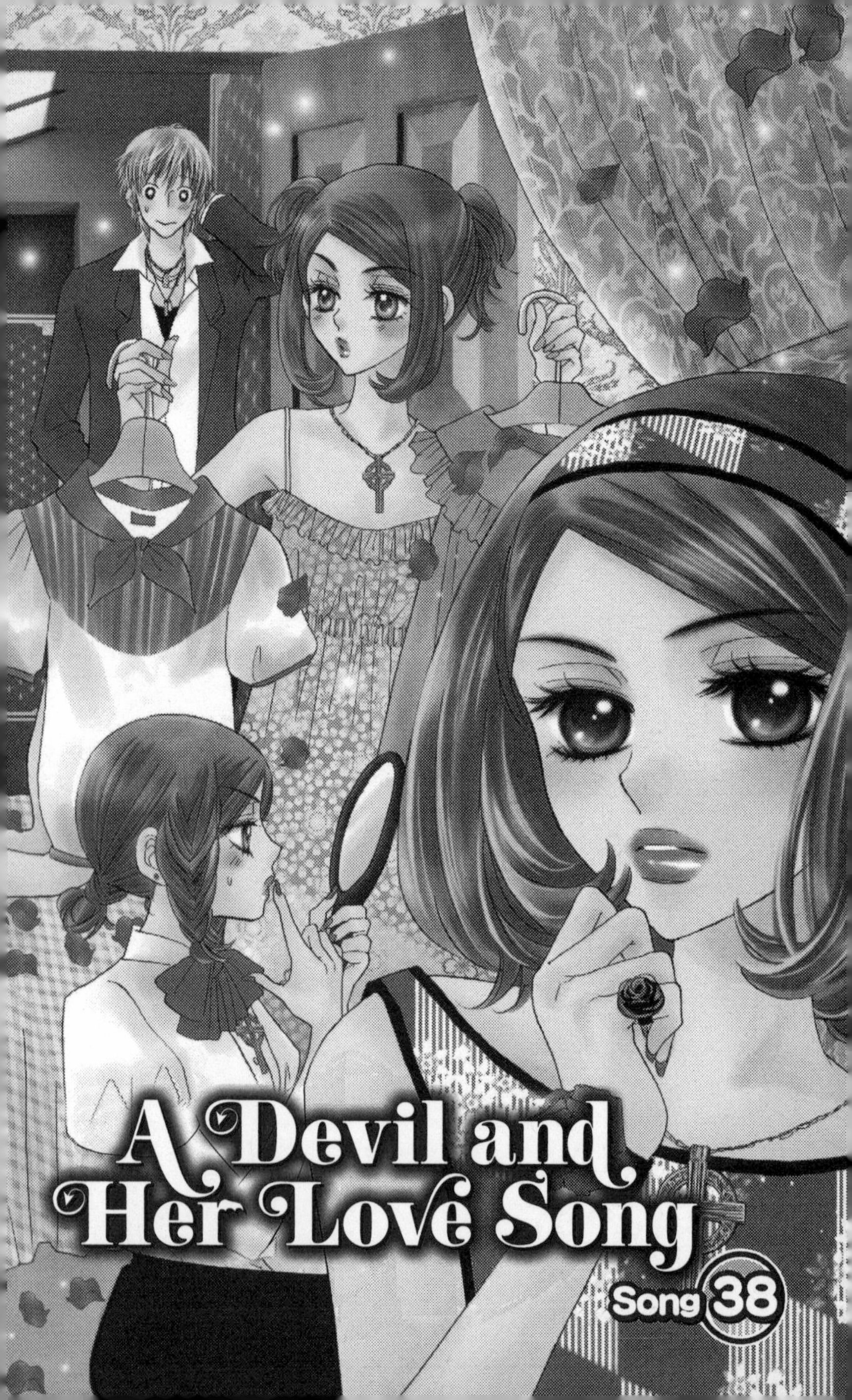
A Devil and Her Love Song
Song 38

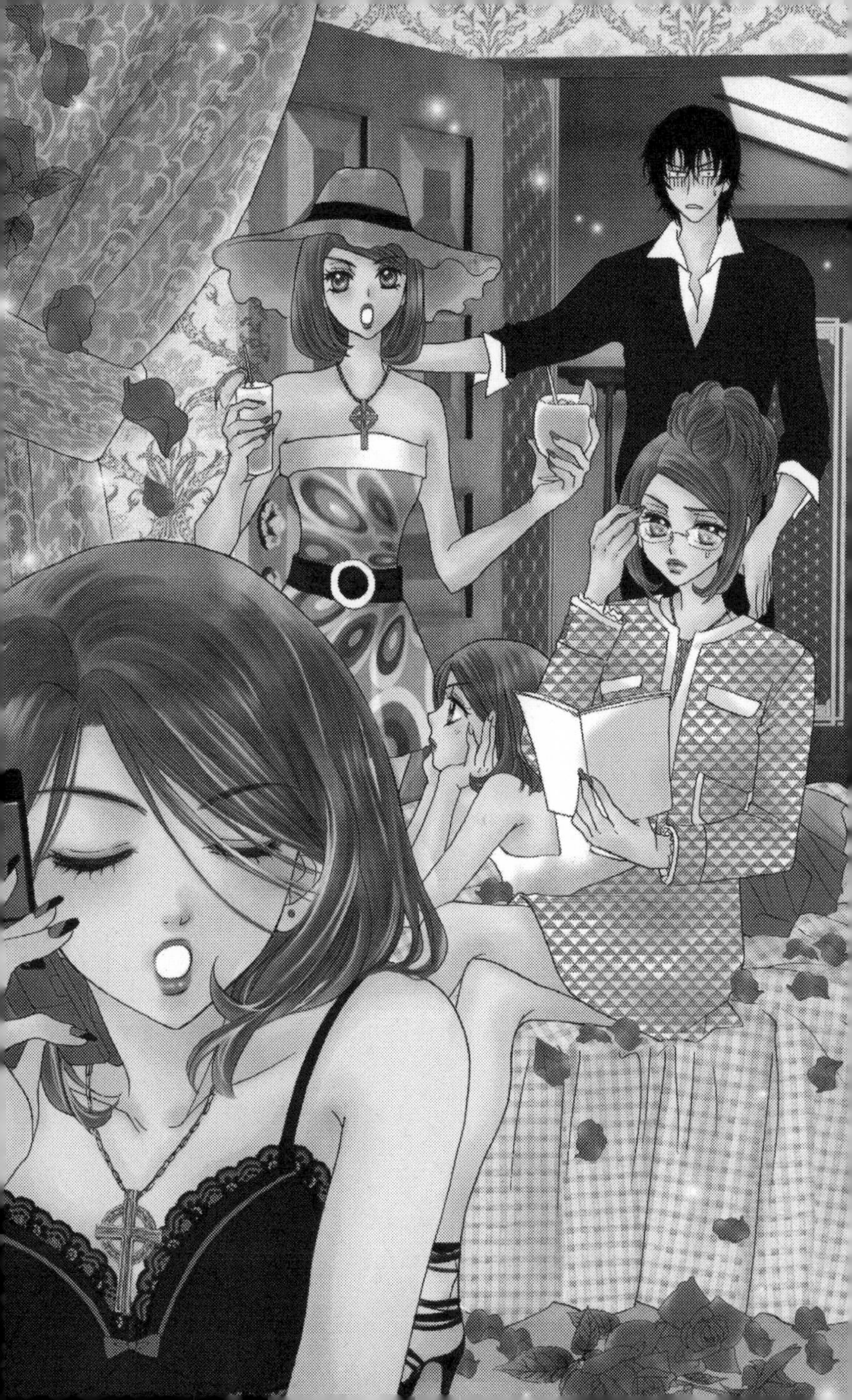

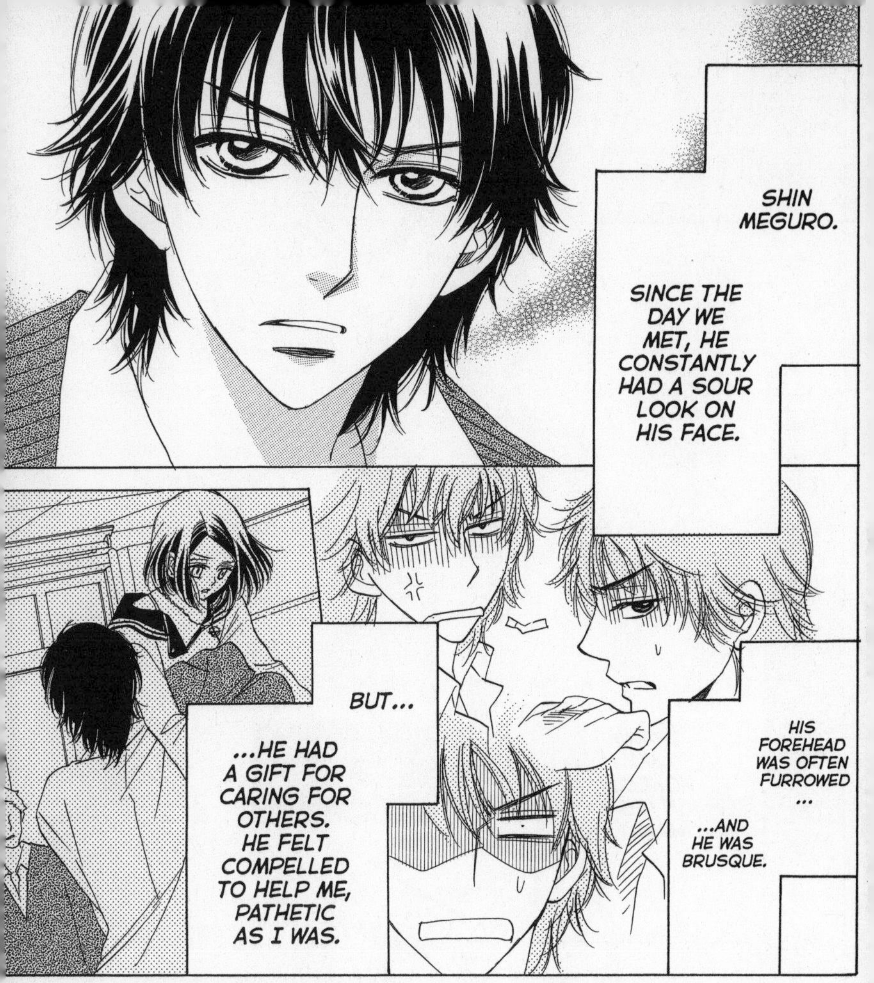
SHIN MEGURO.
SINCE THE DAY WE MET, HE CONSTANTLY HAD A SOUR LOOK ON HIS FACE.
HIS FOREHEAD WAS OFTEN FURROWED ...
...AND HE WAS BRUSQUE.
BUT...
...HE HAD A GIFT FOR CARING FOR OTHERS. HE FELT COMPELLED TO HELP ME, PATHETIC AS I WAS.

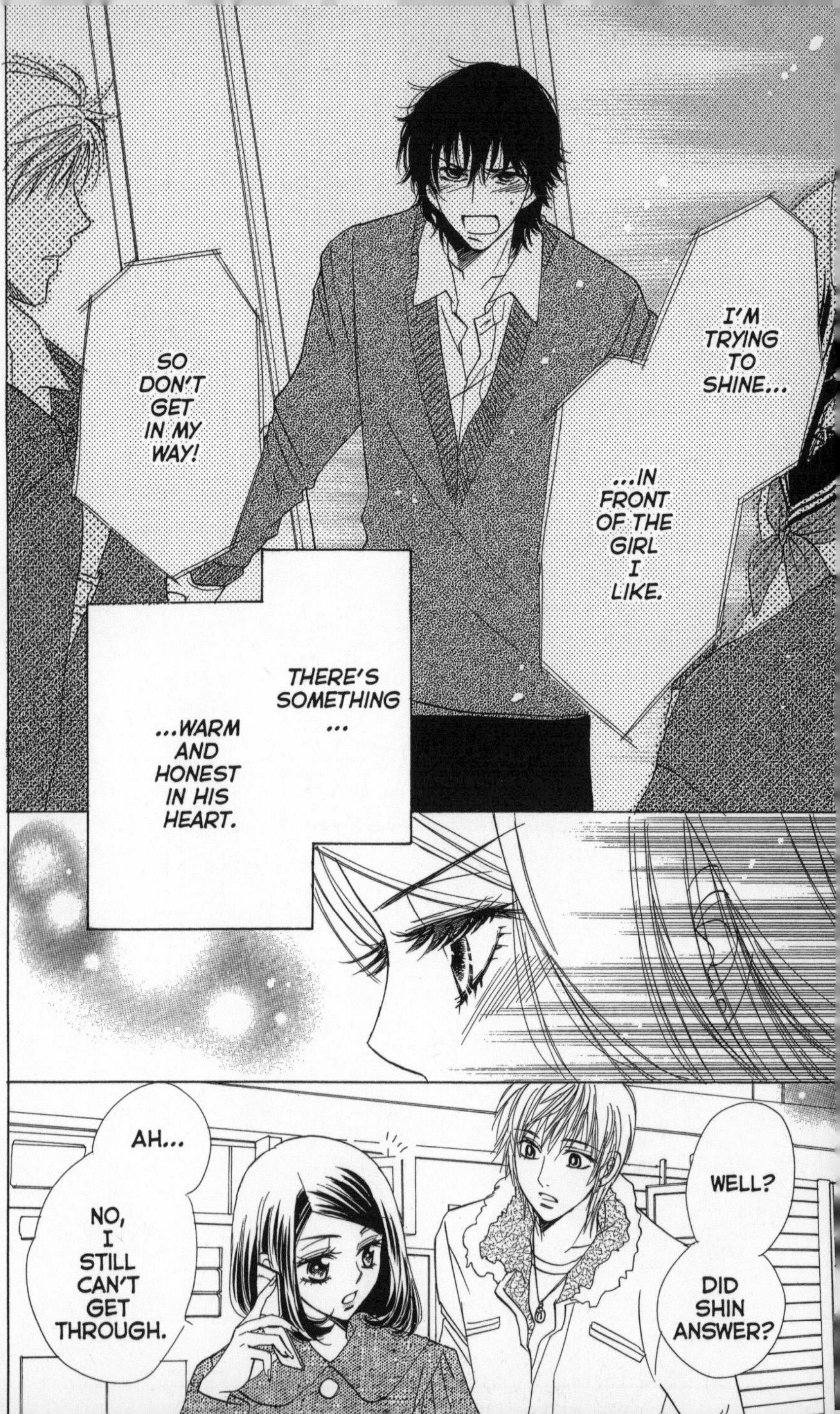
I'M TRYING TO SHINE...
...IN FRONT OF THE GIRL I LIKE.
SO DON'T GET IN MY WAY!
THERE'S SOMETHING...
...WARM AND HONEST IN HIS HEART.
WELL?
DID SHIN ANSWER?
AH...
NO, I STILL CAN'T GET THROUGH.

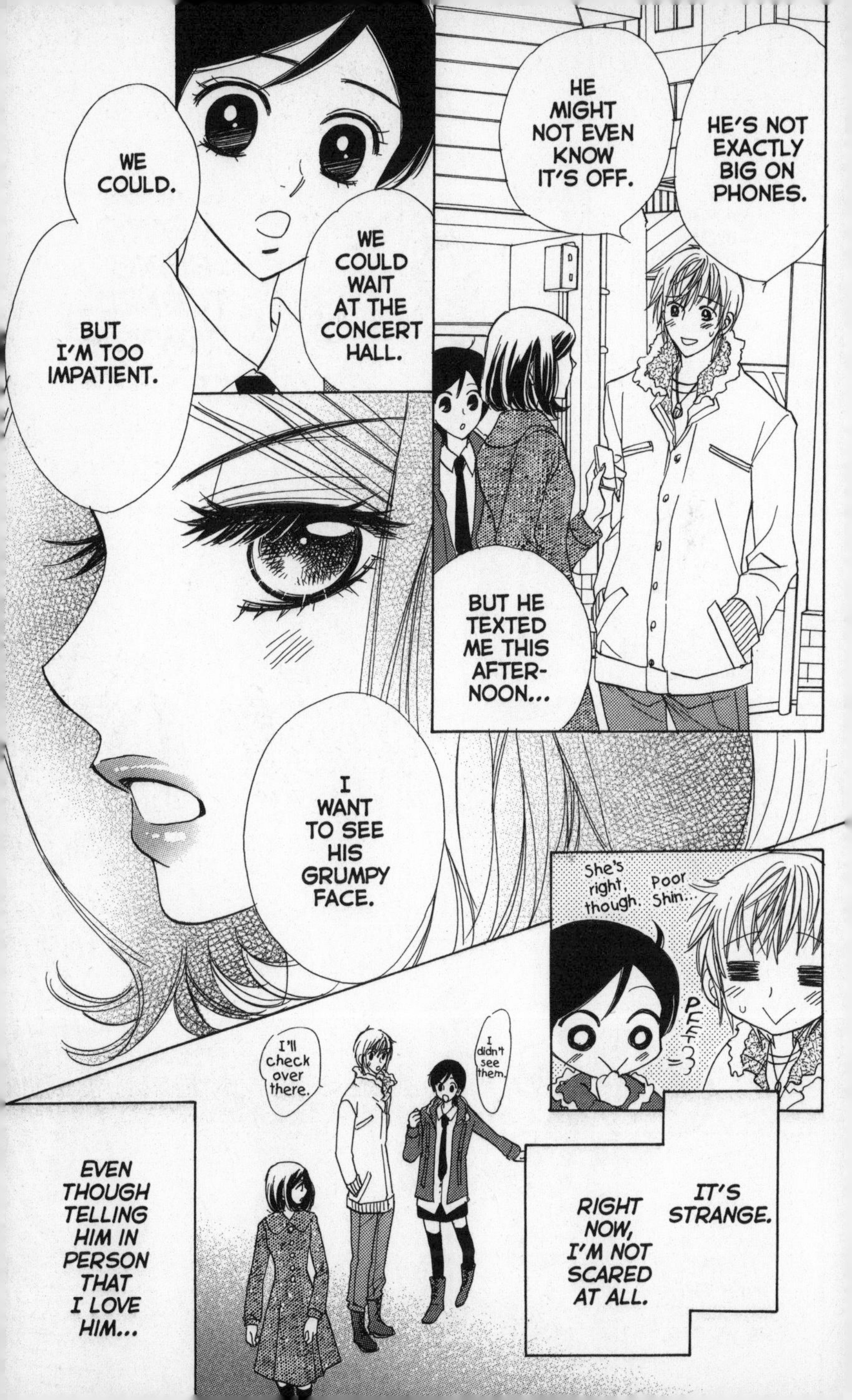
HE'S NOT EXACTLY BIG ON PHONES.
HE MIGHT NOT EVEN KNOW IT'S OFF.
BUT HE TEXTED ME THIS AFTERNOON...
WE COULD WAIT AT THE CONCERT HALL.
WE COULD.
BUT I'M TOO IMPATIENT.
I WANT TO SEE HIS GRUMPY FACE.
Poor Shin...
She's right, though.
PFFT
IT'S STRANGE.
RIGHT NOW, I'M NOT SCARED AT ALL.
I didn't see them.
I'll check over there.
EVEN THOUGH TELLING HIM IN PERSON THAT I LOVE HIM...

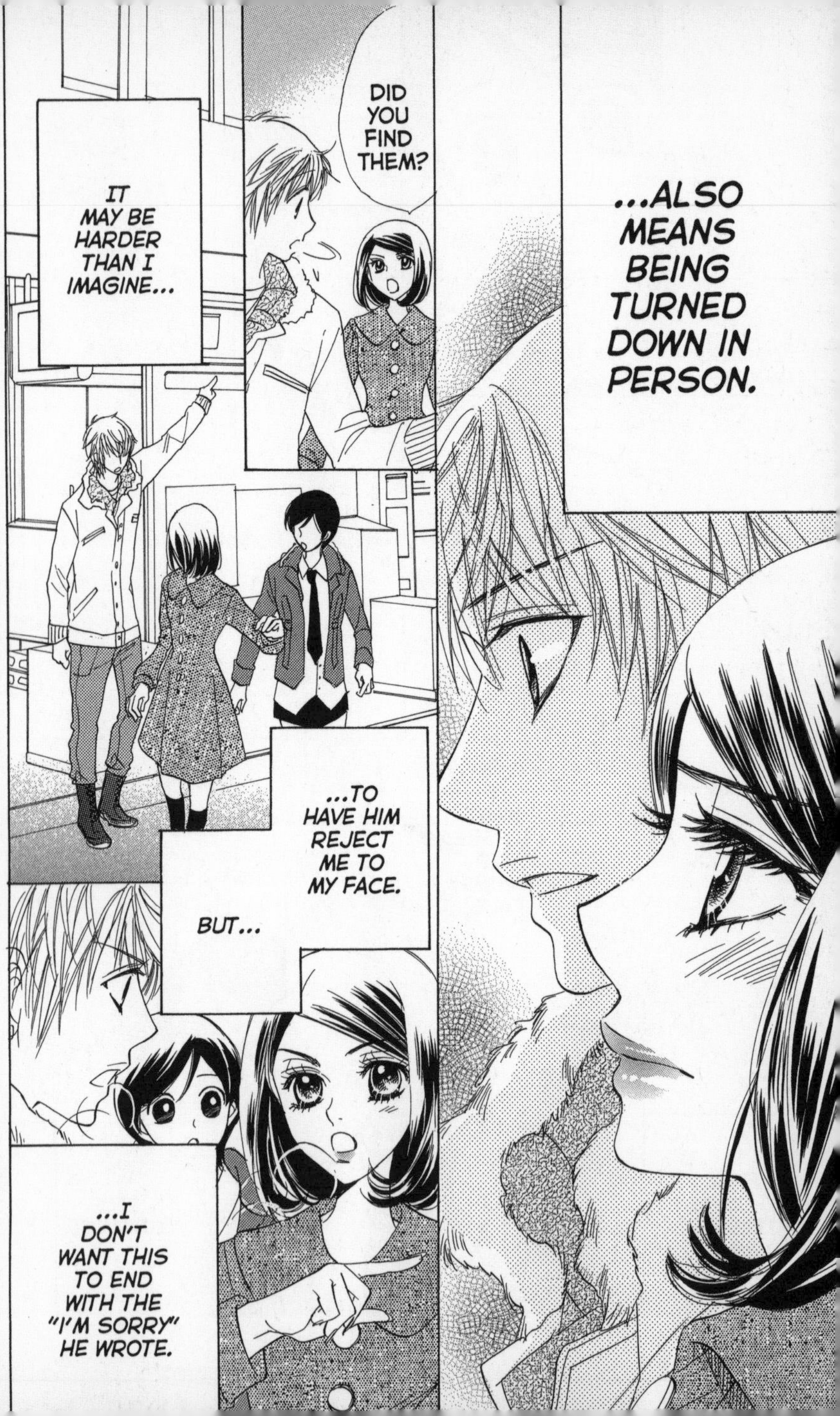
...ALSO MEANS BEING TURNED DOWN IN PERSON.
DID YOU FIND THEM?
IT MAY BE HARDER THAN I IMAGINE...
...TO HAVE HIM REJECT ME TO MY FACE.
BUT...
...I DON'T WANT THIS TO END WITH THE "I'M SORRY" HE WROTE.

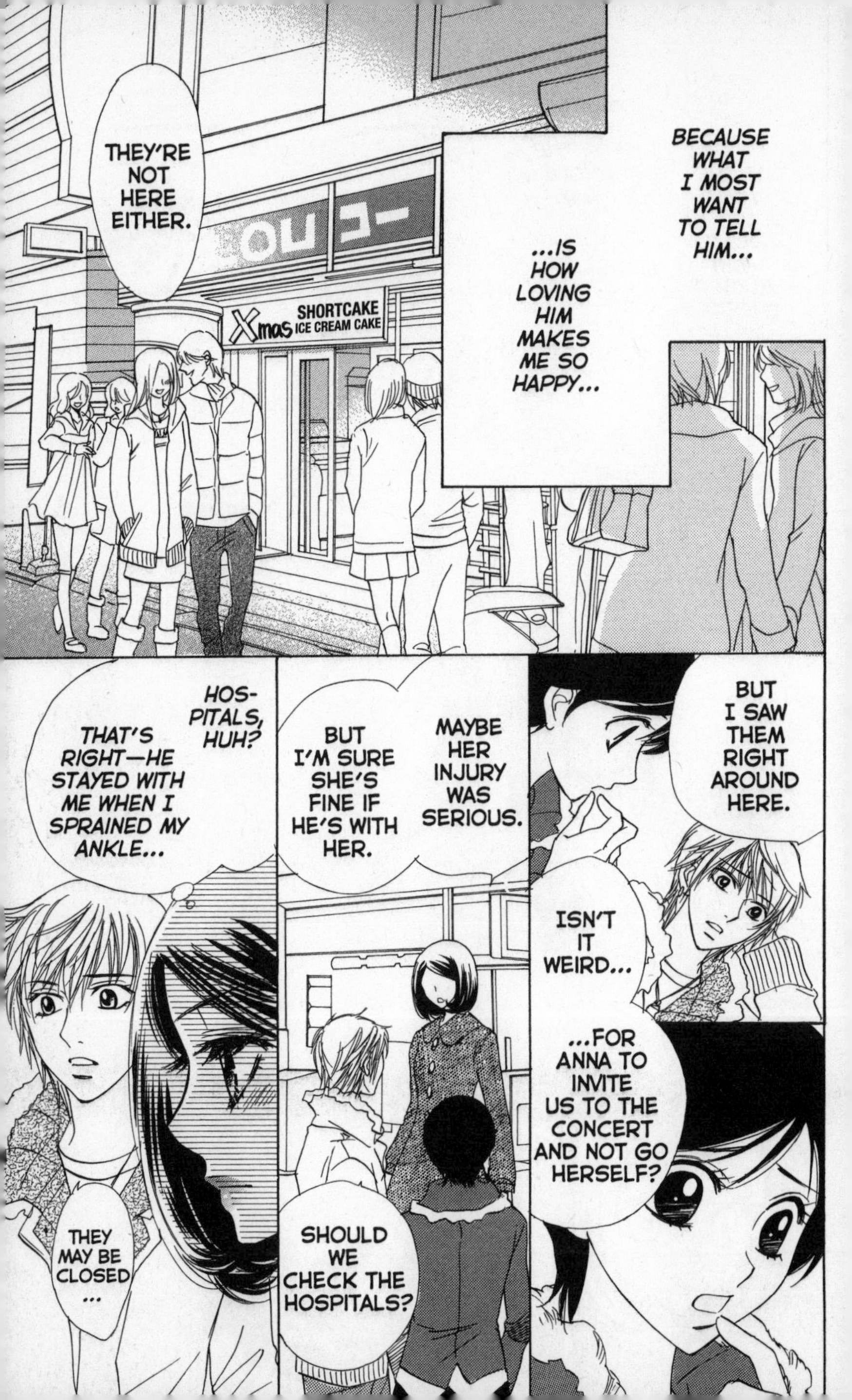
BECAUSE WHAT I MOST WANT TO TELL HIM...
...IS HOW LOVING HIM MAKES ME SO HAPPY...
THEY'RE NOT HERE EITHER.
Xmas SHORTCAKE ICE CREAM CAKE
BUT I SAW THEM RIGHT AROUND HERE.
ISN'T IT WEIRD...
...FOR ANNA TO INVITE US TO THE CONCERT AND NOT GO HERSELF?
MAYBE HER INJURY WAS SERIOUS.
BUT I'M SURE SHE'S FINE IF HE'S WITH HER.
SHOULD WE CHECK THE HOSPITALS?
HOS-PITALS, HUH?
THAT'S RIGHT—HE STAYED WITH ME WHEN I SPRAINED MY ANKLE...
THEY MAY BE CLOSED...

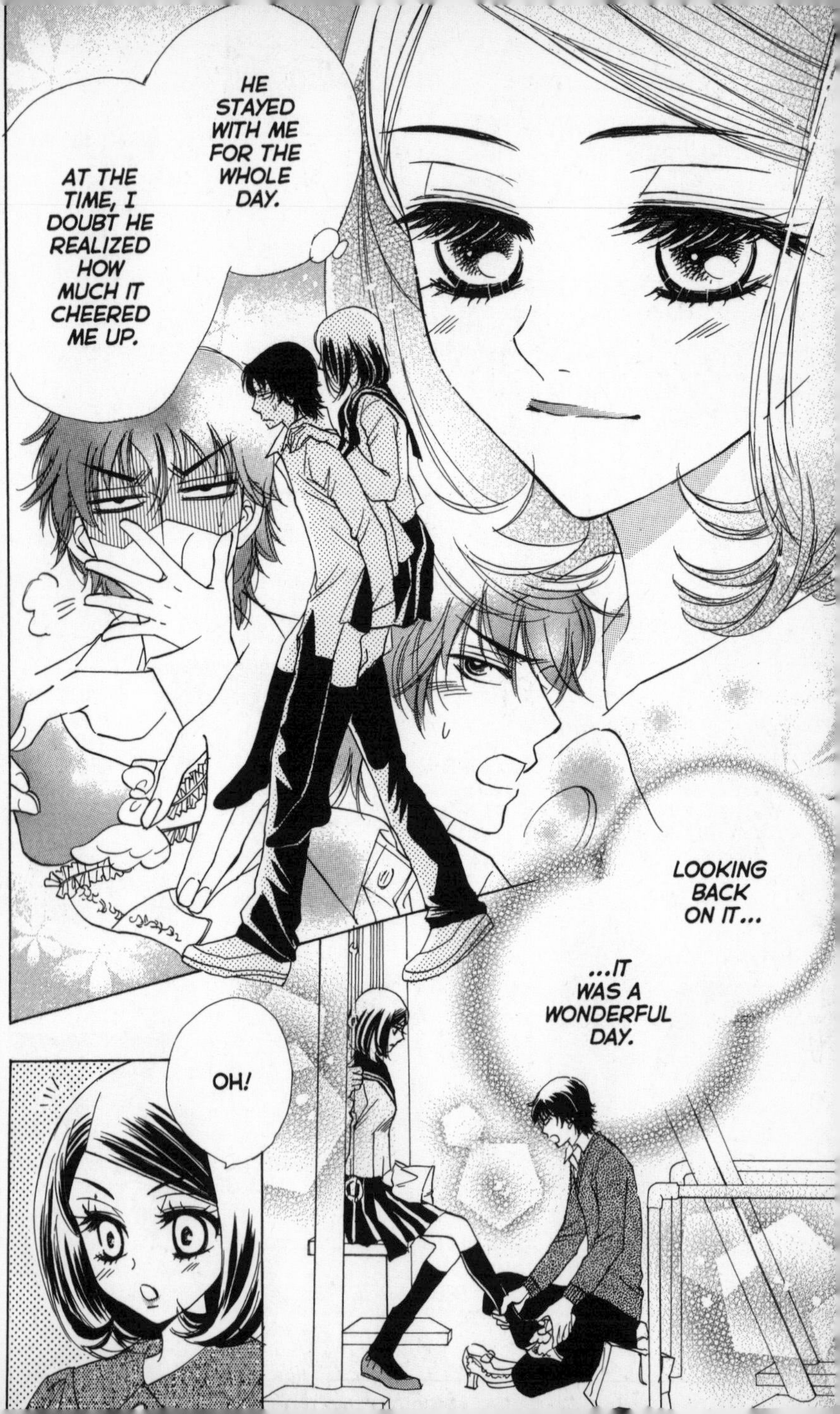
HE STAYED WITH ME FOR THE WHOLE DAY.
AT THE TIME, I DOUBT HE REALIZED HOW MUCH IT CHEERED ME UP.
LOOKING BACK ON IT...
...IT WAS A WONDERFUL DAY.
OH!

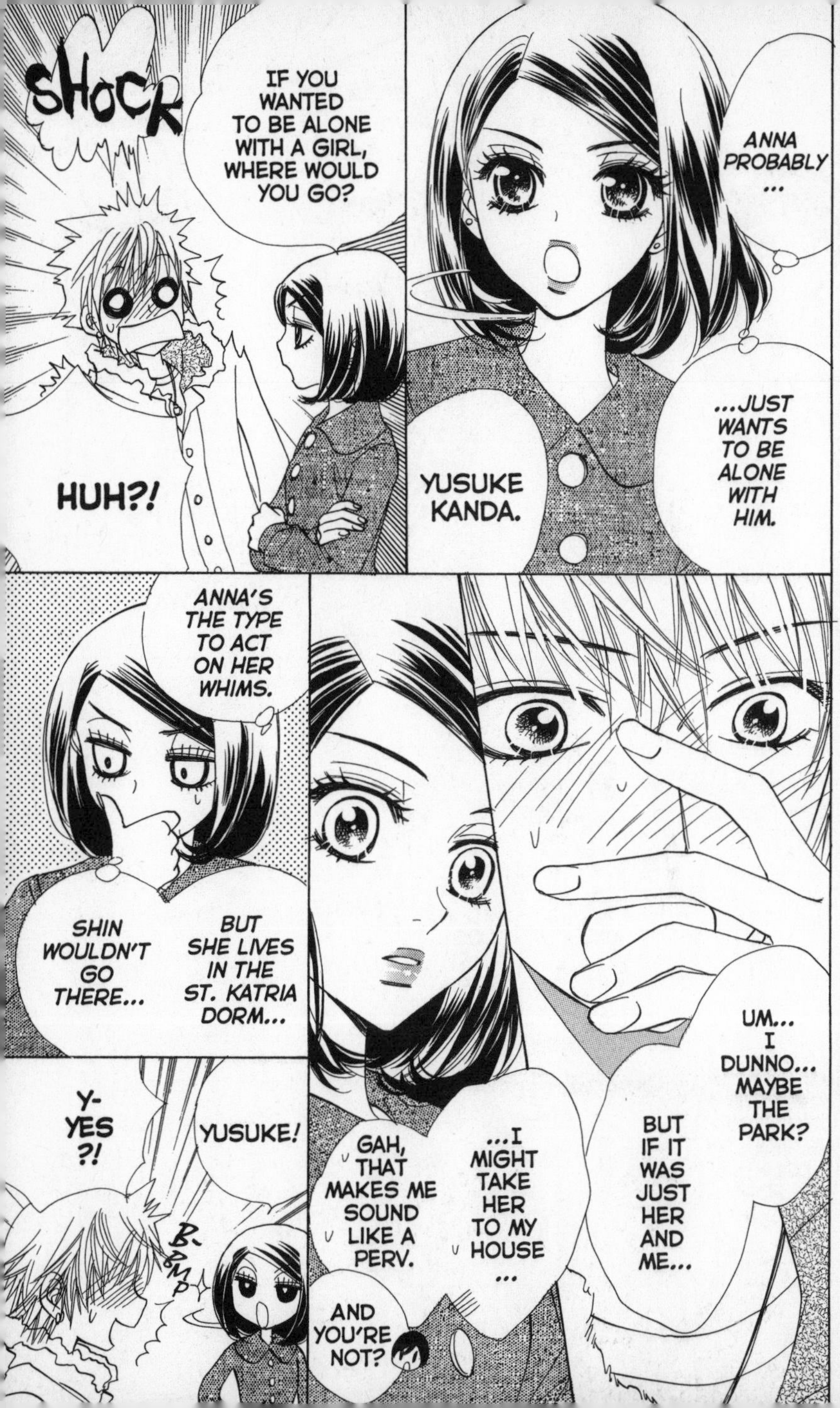
ANNA PROBABLY ...
...JUST WANTS TO BE ALONE WITH HIM.
YUSUKE KANDA.
IF YOU WANTED TO BE ALONE WITH A GIRL, WHERE WOULD YOU GO?
SHOCK
HUH?!
UM... I DUNNO... MAYBE THE PARK?
BUT IF IT WAS JUST HER AND ME...
...I MIGHT TAKE HER TO MY HOUSE ...
GAH, THAT MAKES ME SOUND LIKE A PERV.
AND YOU'RE NOT?
ANNA'S THE TYPE TO ACT ON HER WHIMS.
BUT SHE LIVES IN THE ST. KATRIA DORM...
SHIN WOULDN'T GO THERE...
YUSUKE!
Y-YES?!
B-BMP

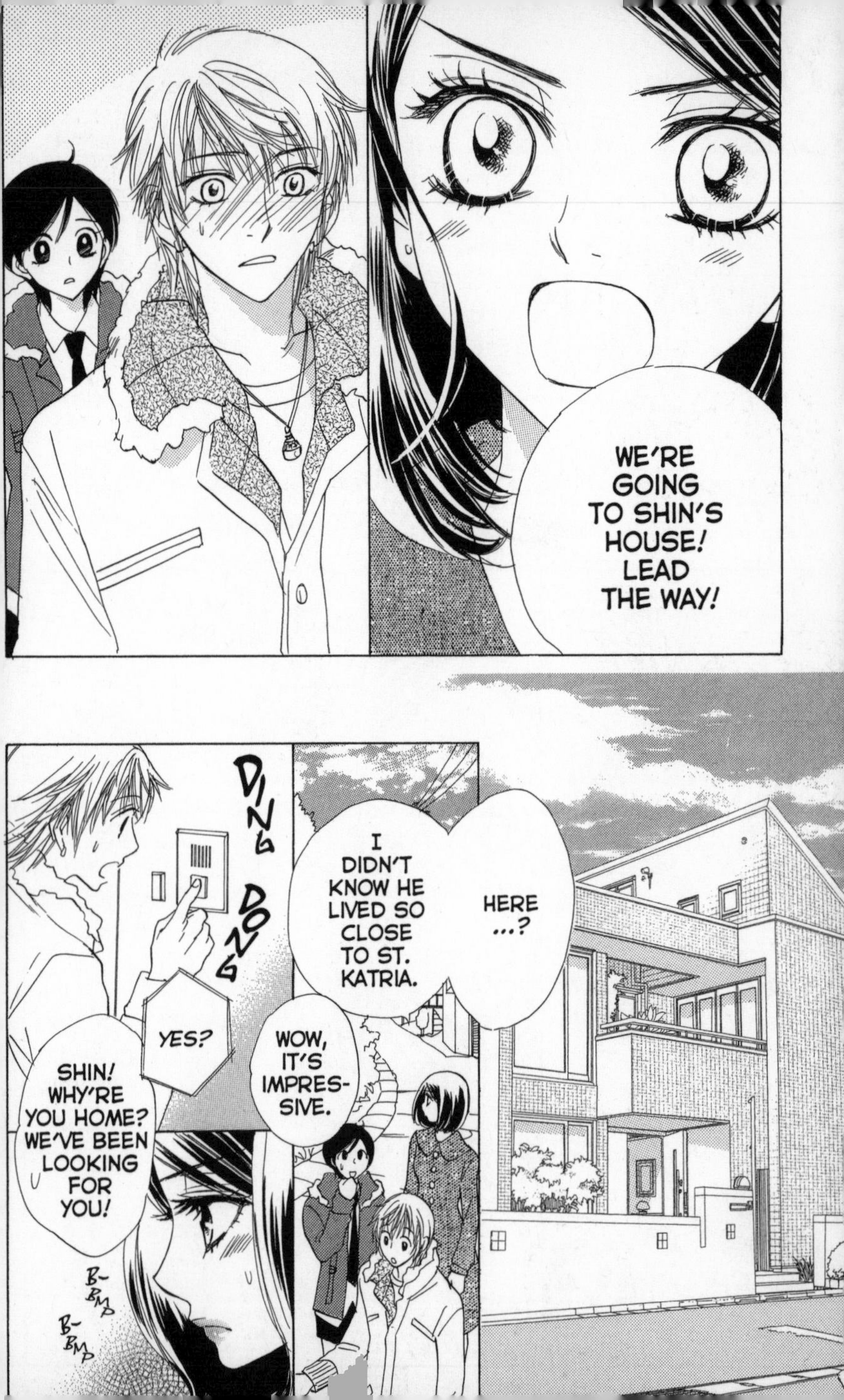
WE'RE GOING TO SHIN'S HOUSE! LEAD THE WAY!
HERE ...?
I DIDN'T KNOW HE LIVED SO CLOSE TO ST. KATRIA.
WOW, IT'S IMPRES-SIVE.
DING DONG
YES?
SHIN! WHY'RE YOU HOME? WE'VE BEEN LOOKING FOR YOU!
B-BMP
B-BMP

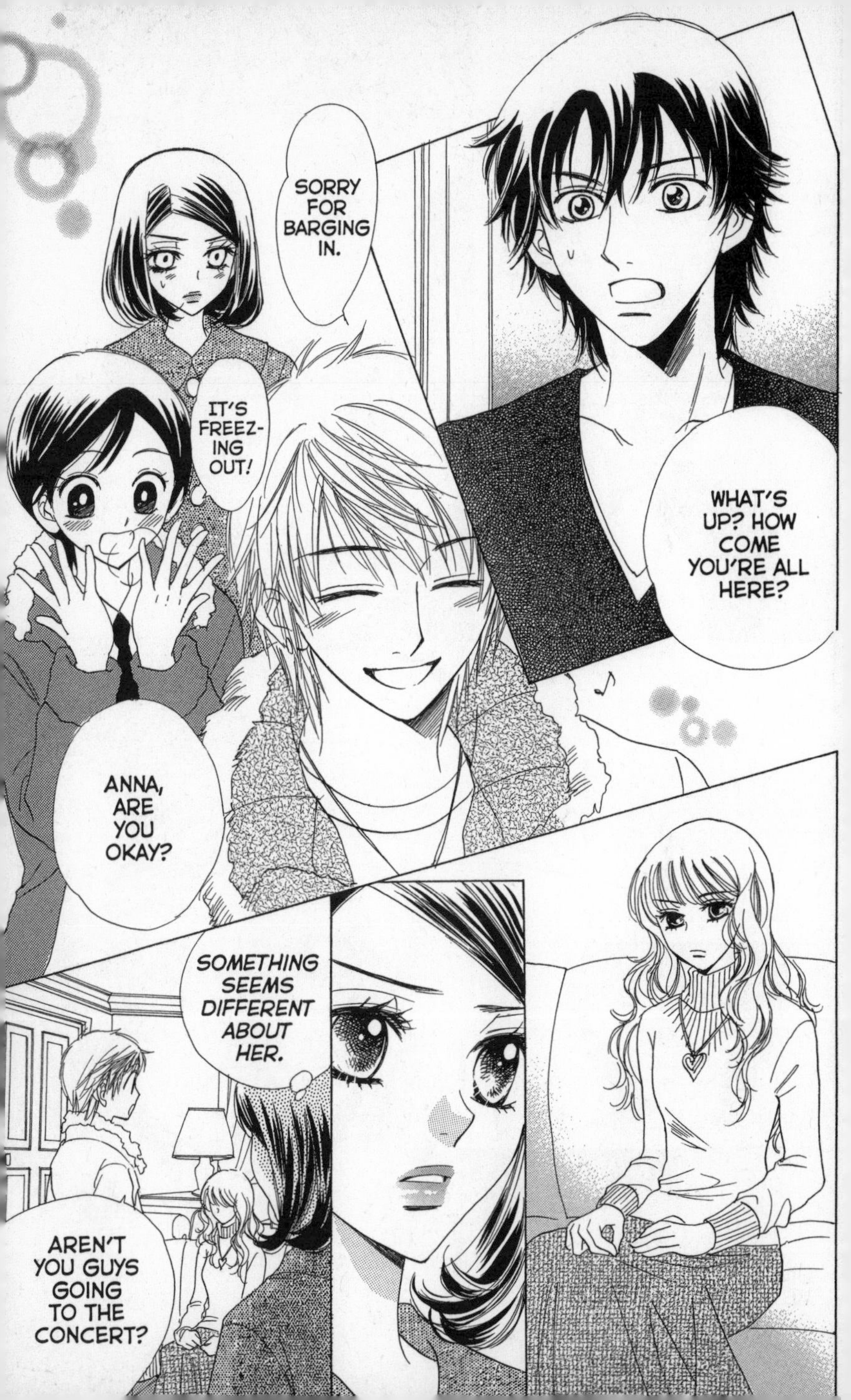
WHAT'S UP? HOW COME YOU'RE ALL HERE?
SORRY FOR BARGING IN.
IT'S FREEZ-ING OUT!
ANNA, ARE YOU OKAY?
SOMETHING SEEMS DIFFERENT ABOUT HER.
AREN'T YOU GUYS GOING TO THE CONCERT?

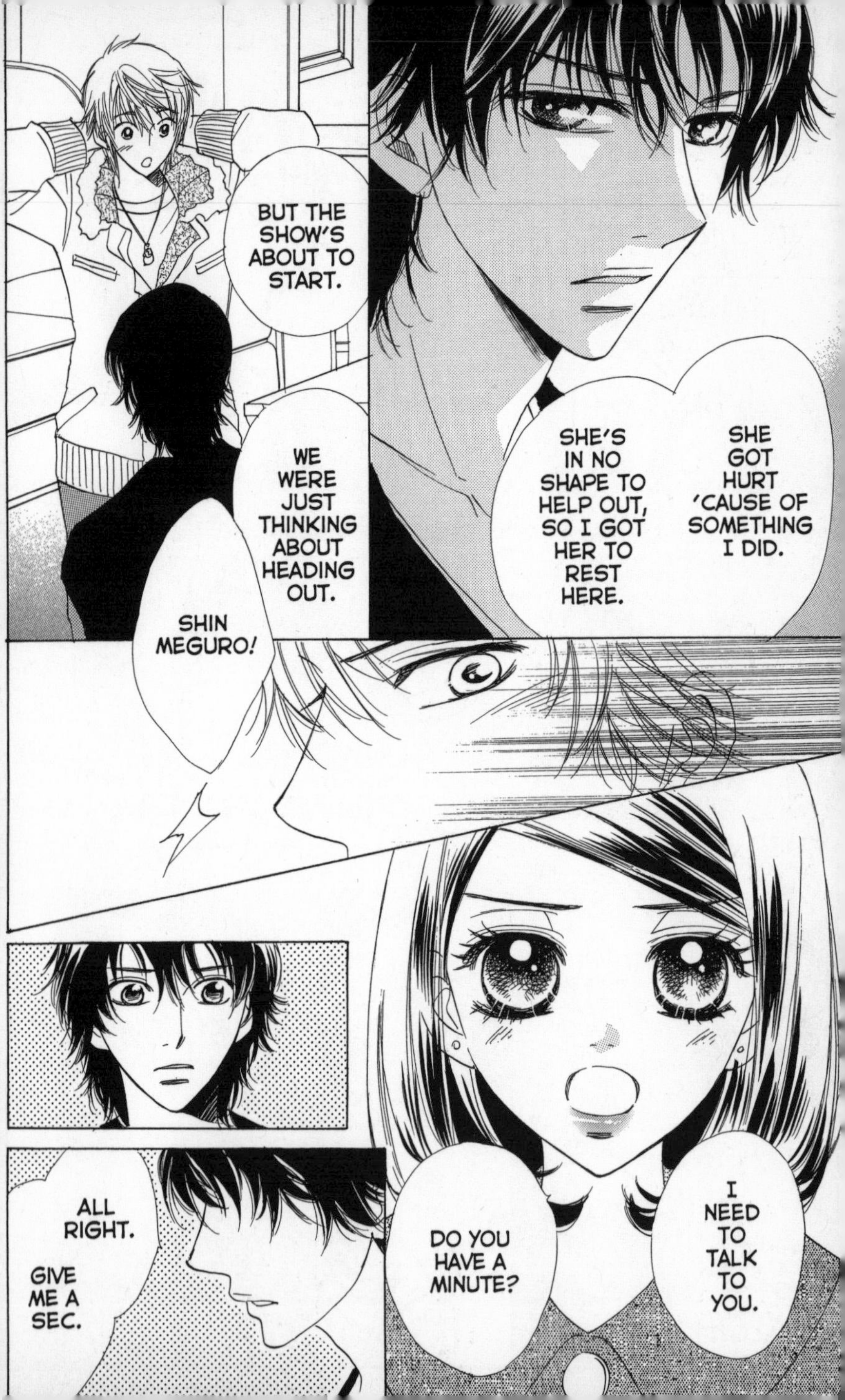
SHE GOT HURT 'CAUSE OF SOMETHING I DID.
SHE'S IN NO SHAPE TO HELP OUT, SO I GOT HER TO REST HERE.
BUT THE SHOW'S ABOUT TO START.
WE WERE JUST THINKING ABOUT HEADING OUT.
SHIN MEGURO!
I NEED TO TALK TO YOU.
DO YOU HAVE A MINUTE?
ALL RIGHT.
GIVE ME A SEC.

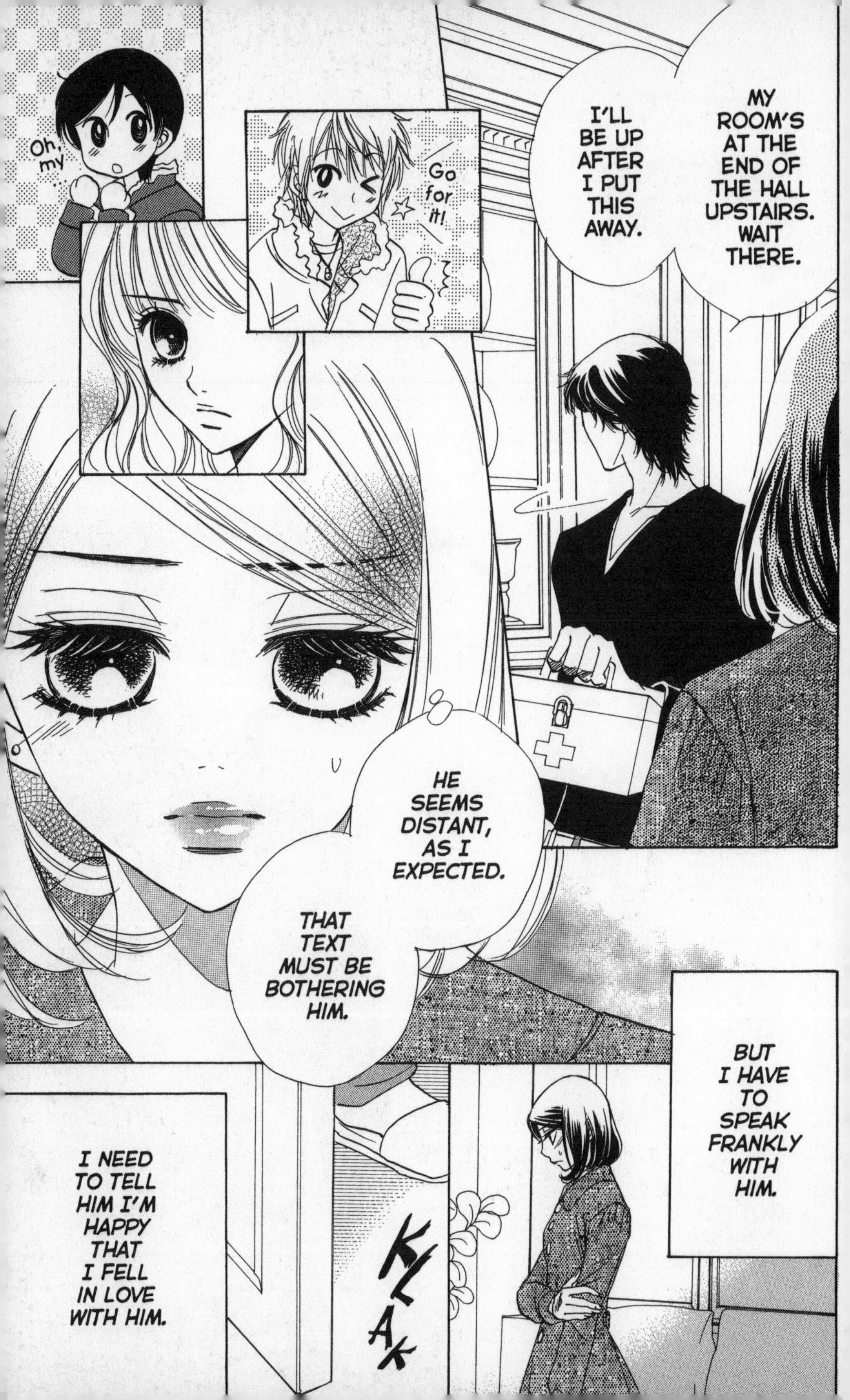
MY ROOM'S AT THE END OF THE HALL UPSTAIRS. WAIT THERE.
I'LL BE UP AFTER I PUT THIS AWAY.
Go for it!
Oh, my
HE SEEMS DISTANT, AS I EXPECTED.
THAT TEXT MUST BE BOTHERING HIM.
BUT I HAVE TO SPEAK FRANKLY WITH HIM.
KLAK
I NEED TO TELL HIM I'M HAPPY THAT I FELL IN LOVE WITH HIM.

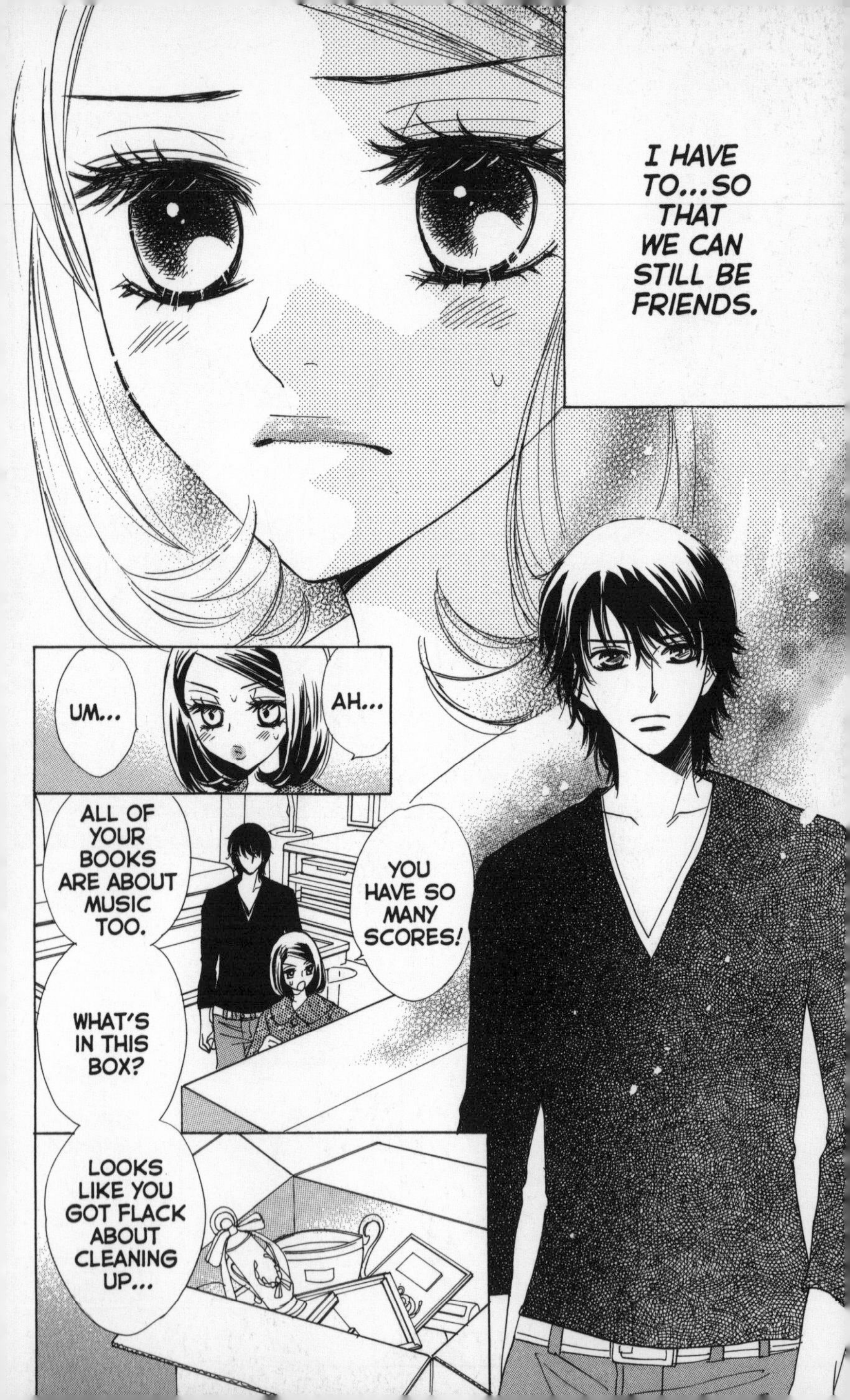
I HAVE TO...SO THAT WE CAN STILL BE FRIENDS.
AH...
UM...
YOU HAVE SO MANY SCORES!
ALL OF YOUR BOOKS ARE ABOUT MUSIC TOO.
WHAT'S IN THIS BOX?
LOOKS LIKE YOU GOT FLACK ABOUT CLEANING UP...

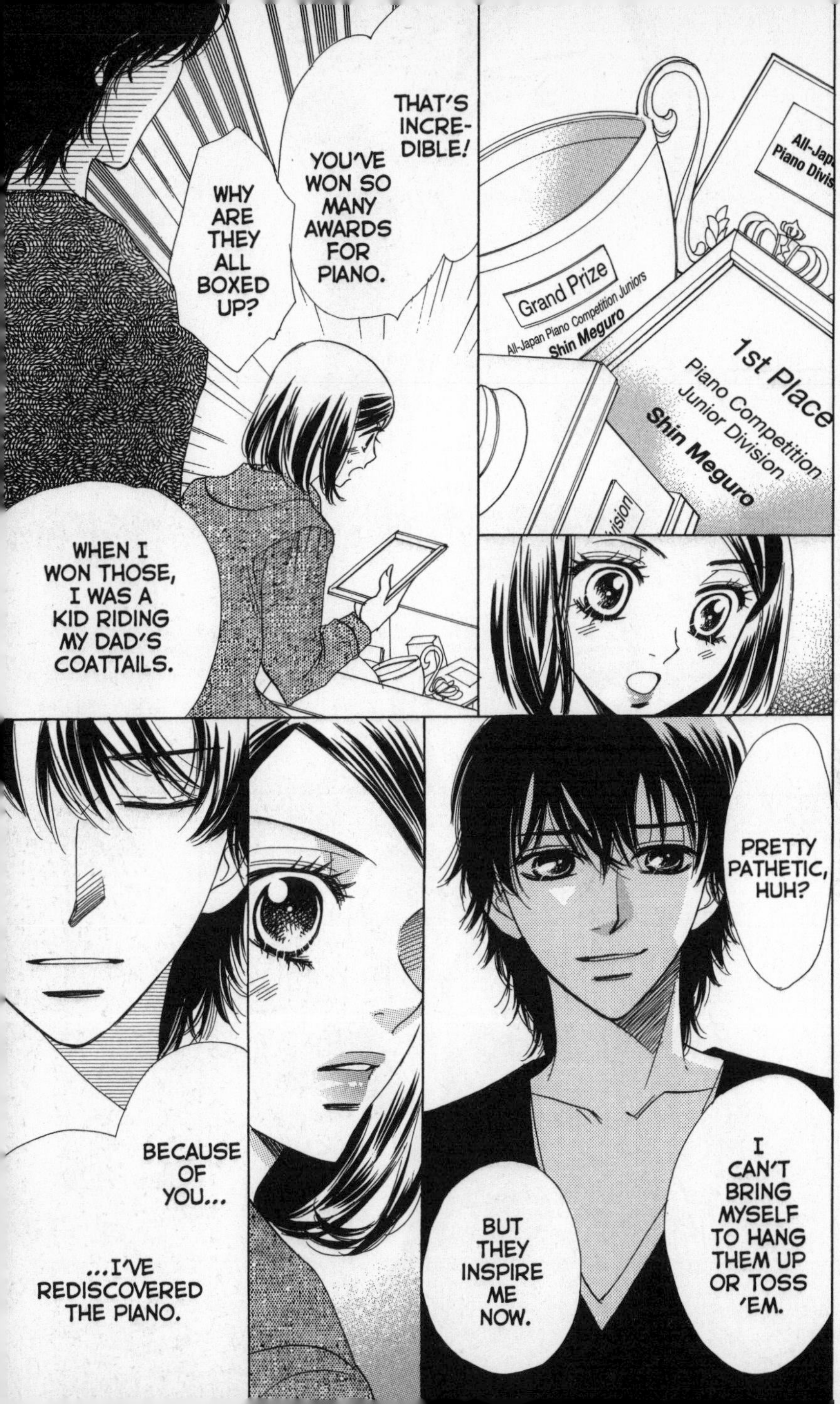

Grand Prize
All-Japan Piano Competition Juniors
Shin Meguro
1st Place
Piano Competition
Junior Division
Shin Meguro
THAT'S INCREDIBLE!
YOU'VE WON SO MANY AWARDS FOR PIANO.
WHY ARE THEY ALL BOXED UP?
WHEN I WON THOSE, I WAS A KID RIDING MY DAD'S COATTAILS.
PRETTY PATHETIC, HUH?
I CAN'T BRING MYSELF TO HANG THEM UP OR TOSS 'EM.
BUT THEY INSPIRE ME NOW.
BECAUSE OF YOU...
...I'VE REDISCOVERED THE PIANO.

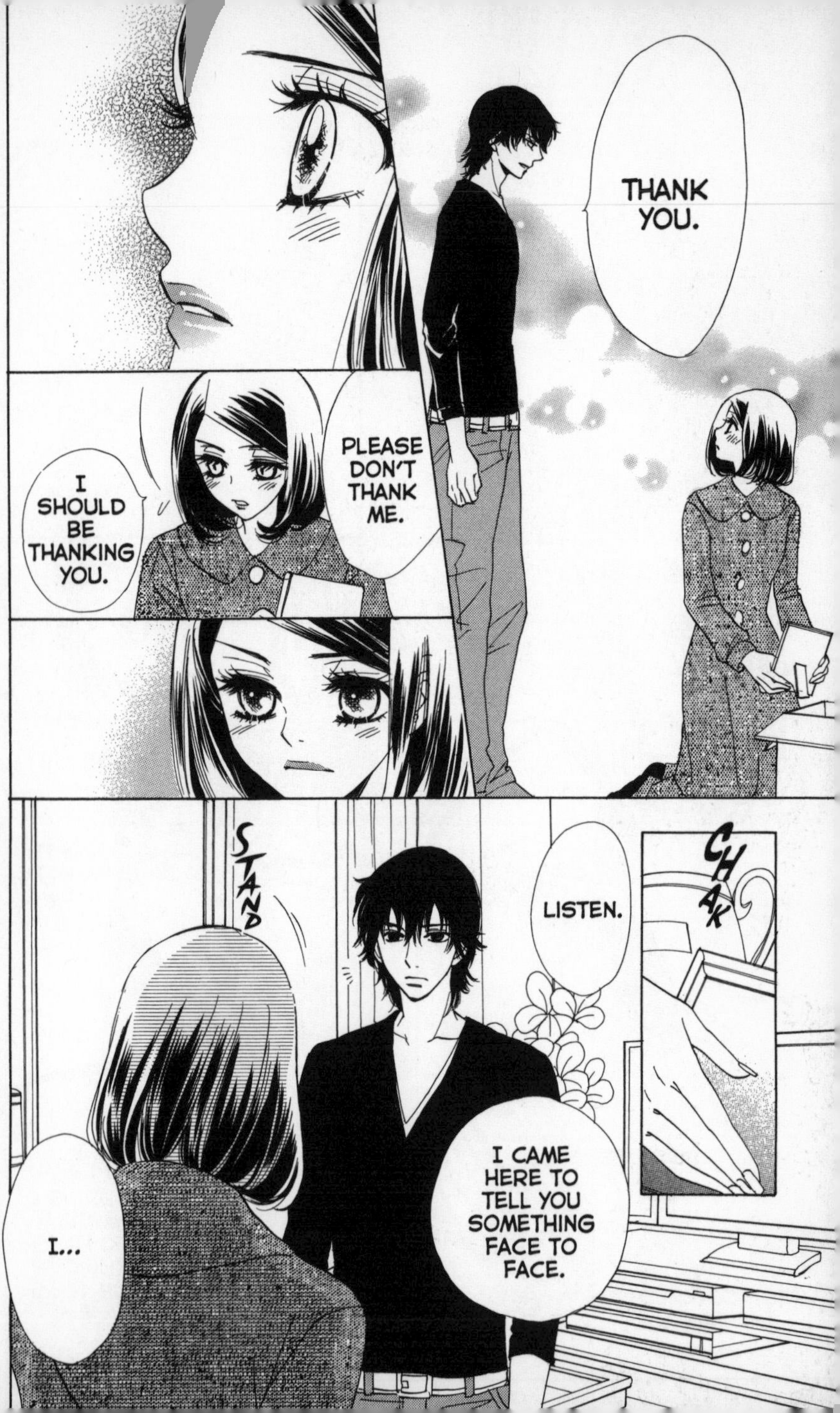
THANK YOU.
PLEASE DON'T THANK ME.
I SHOULD BE THANKING YOU.
CHAK
LISTEN.
STAND
I CAME HERE TO TELL YOU SOMETHING FACE TO FACE.
I...

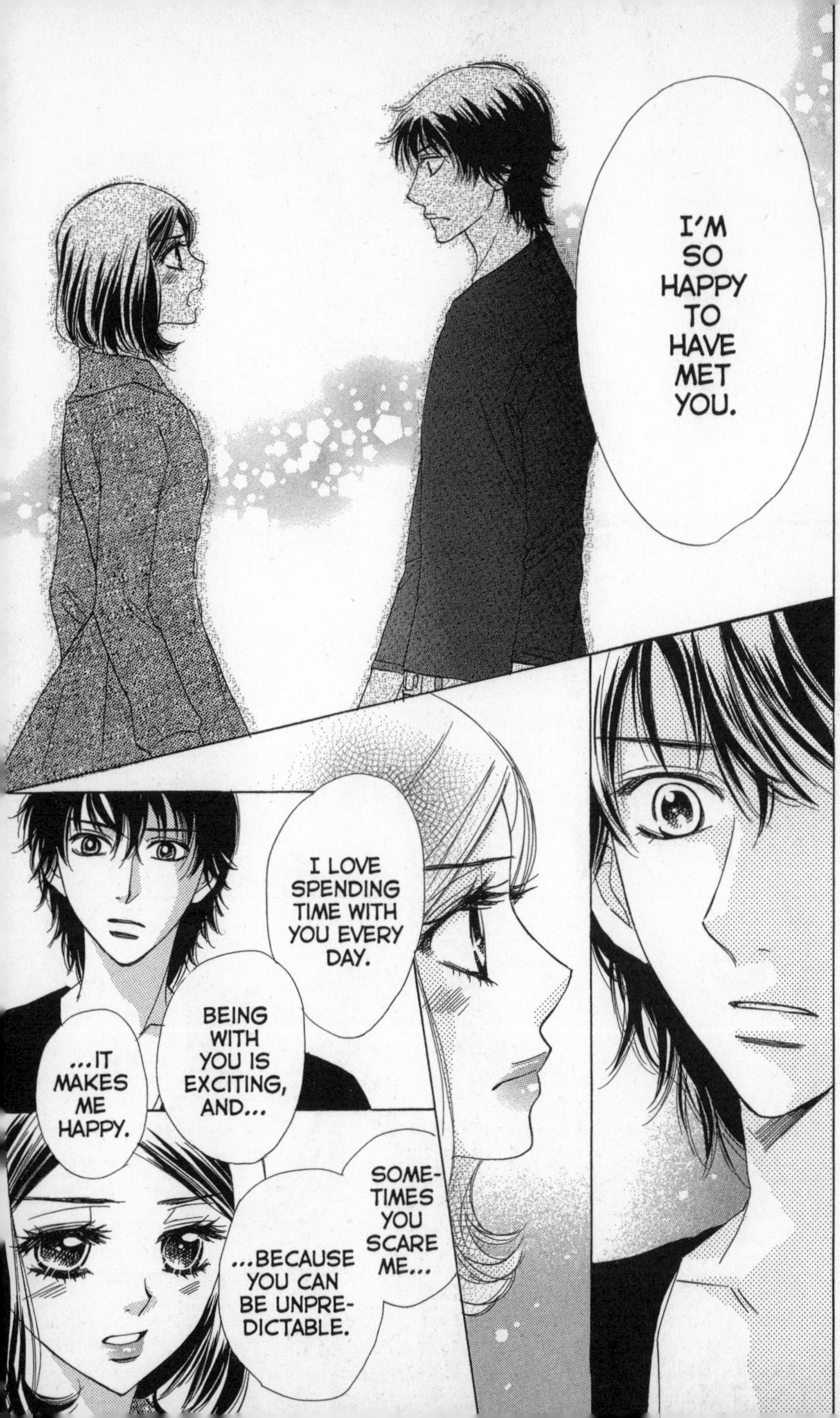
I'M SO HAPPY TO HAVE MET YOU.
I LOVE SPENDING TIME WITH YOU EVERY DAY.
BEING WITH YOU IS EXCITING, AND...
...IT MAKES ME HAPPY.
SOME-TIMES YOU SCARE ME...
...BECAUSE YOU CAN BE UNPRE-DICTABLE.

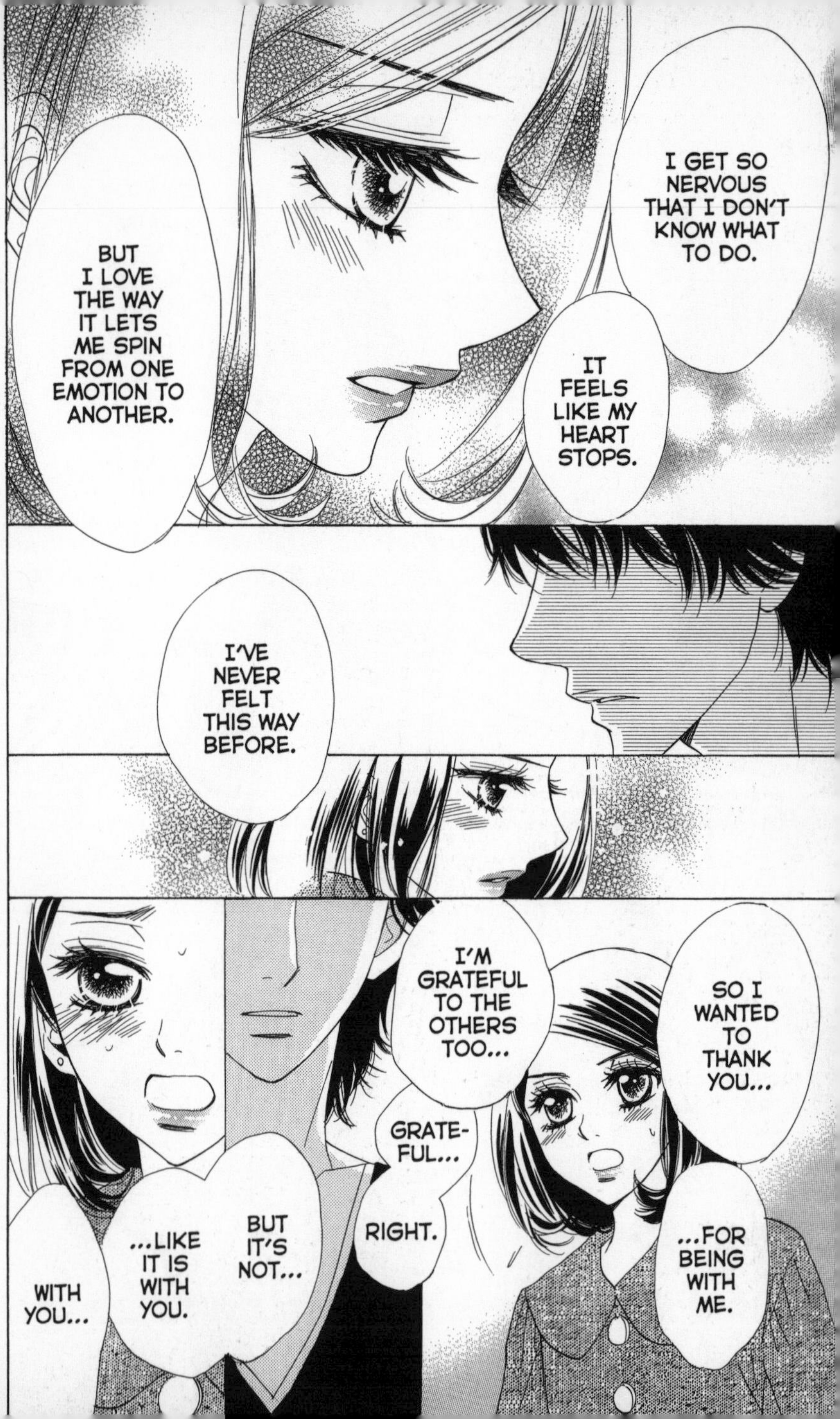
I GET SO NERVOUS THAT I DON'T KNOW WHAT TO DO.
IT FEELS LIKE MY HEART STOPS.
BUT I LOVE THE WAY IT LETS ME SPIN FROM ONE EMOTION TO ANOTHER.
I'VE NEVER FELT THIS WAY BEFORE.
SO I WANTED TO THANK YOU...
...FOR BEING WITH ME.
I'M GRATEFUL TO THE OTHERS TOO...
GRATE-FUL...
RIGHT.
BUT IT'S NOT...
...LIKE IT IS WITH YOU.
WITH YOU...

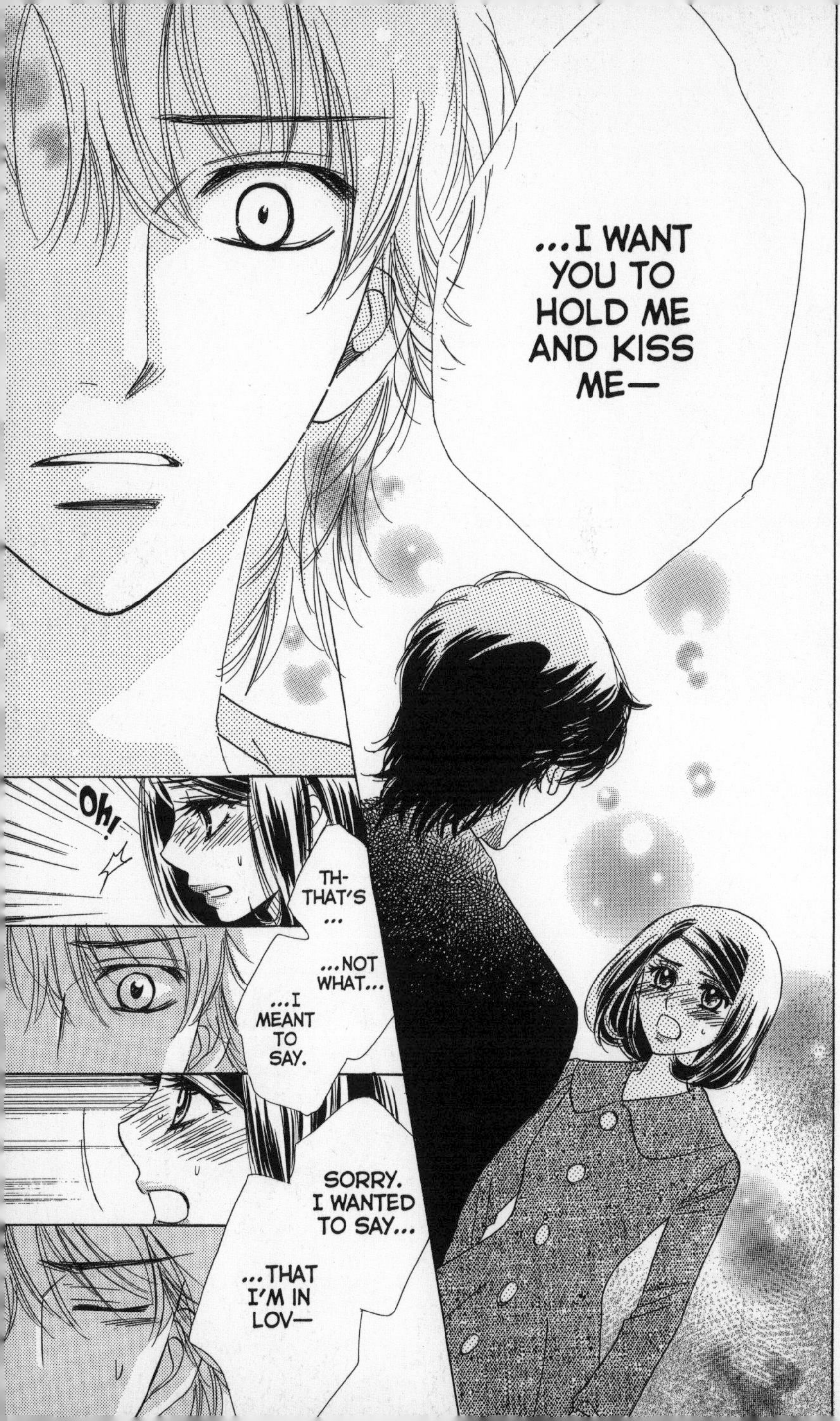
...I WANT YOU TO HOLD ME AND KISS ME—
Oh!
TH-THAT'S...
...NOT WHAT...
...I MEANT TO SAY.
SORRY. I WANTED TO SAY...
...THAT I'M IN LOV—

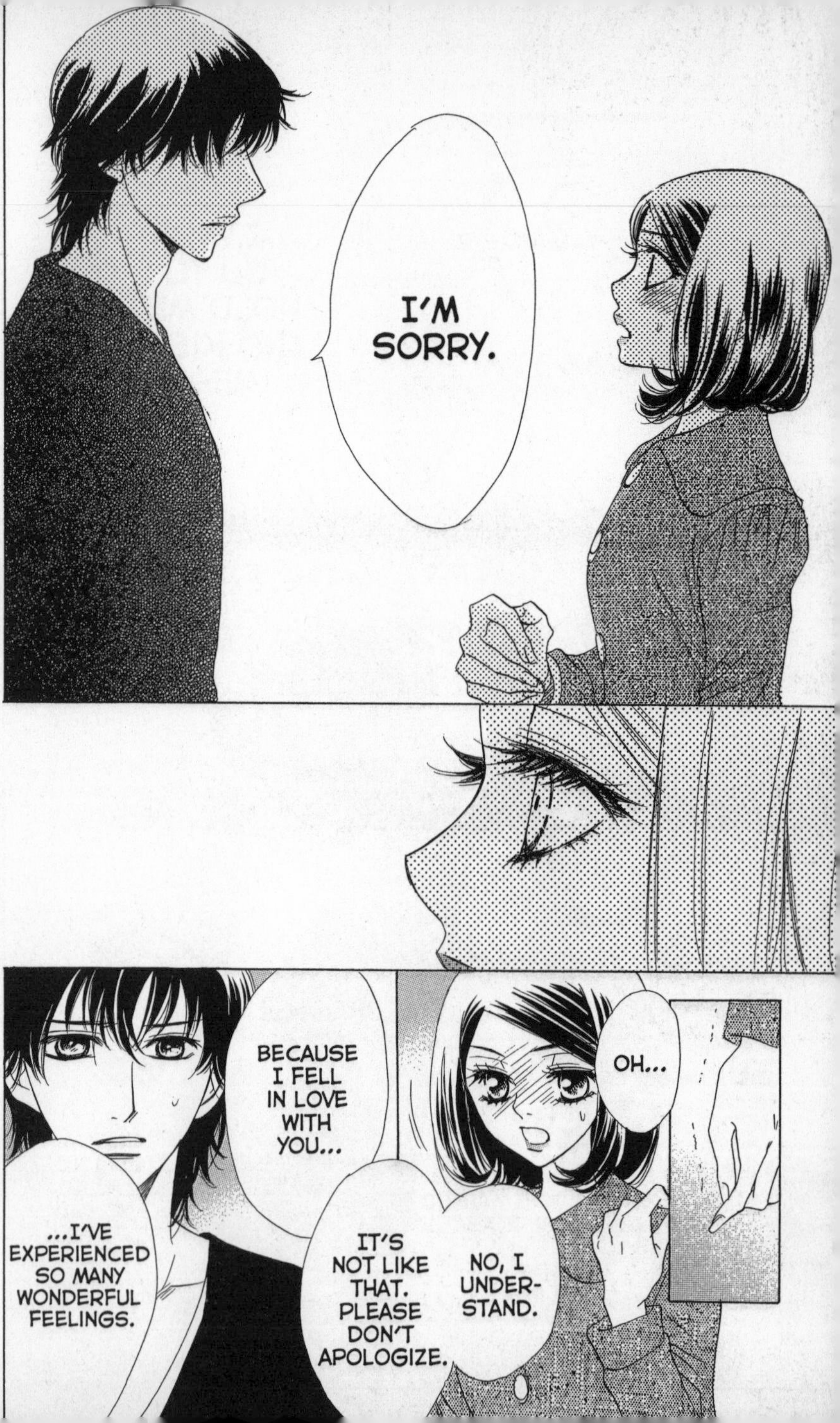
I'M SORRY.
OH...
NO, I UNDER-STAND.
IT'S NOT LIKE THAT. PLEASE DON'T APOLOGIZE.
BECAUSE I FELL IN LOVE WITH YOU...
...I'VE EXPERIENCED SO MANY WONDERFUL FEELINGS.

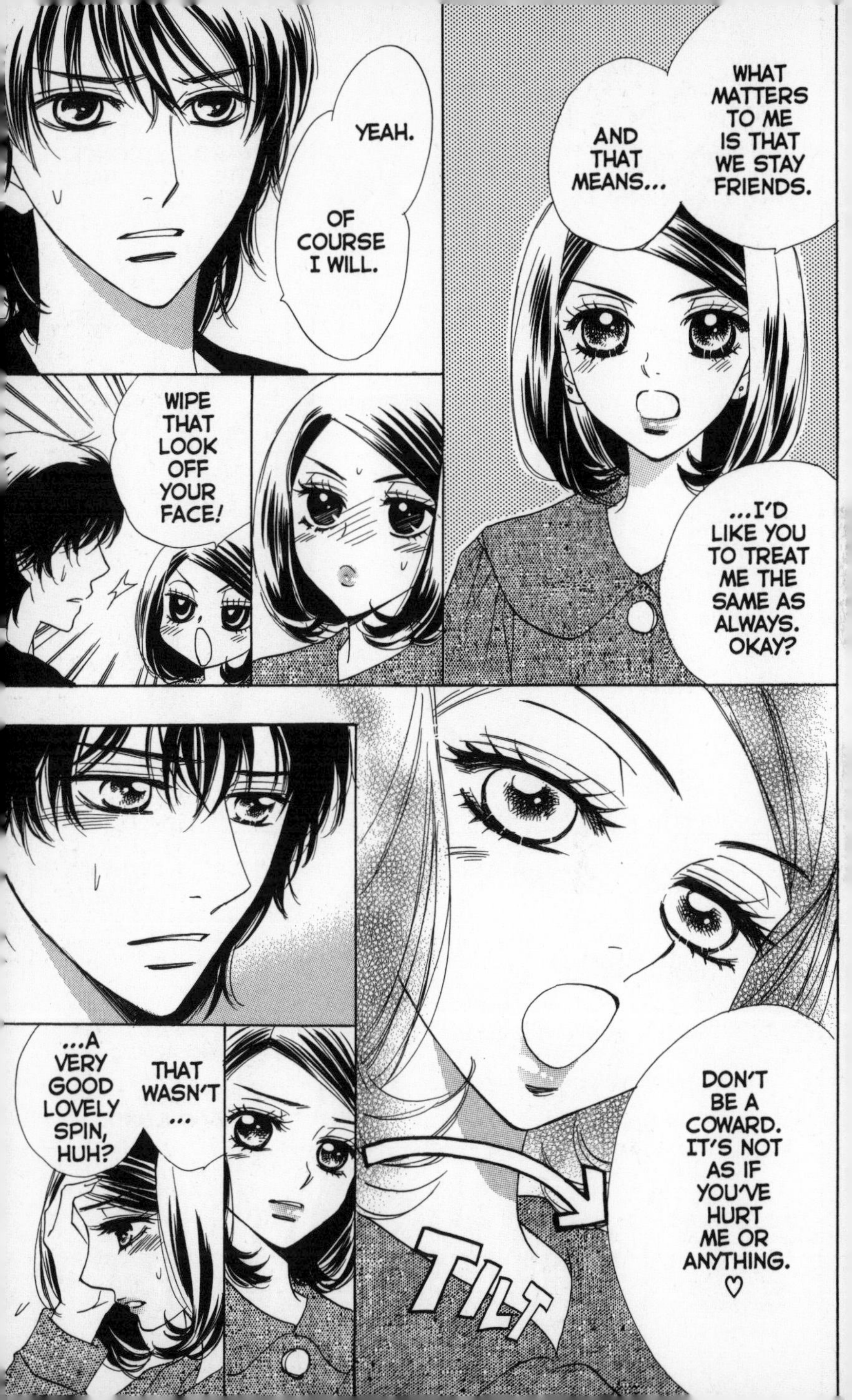
WHAT MATTERS TO ME IS THAT WE STAY FRIENDS.
AND THAT MEANS...
...I'D LIKE YOU TO TREAT ME THE SAME AS ALWAYS. OKAY?
YEAH.
OF COURSE I WILL.
WIPE THAT LOOK OFF YOUR FACE!
DON'T BE A COWARD. IT'S NOT AS IF YOU'VE HURT ME OR ANYTHING. ♡
TILT
THAT WASN'T ...
...A VERY GOOD LOVELY SPIN, HUH?

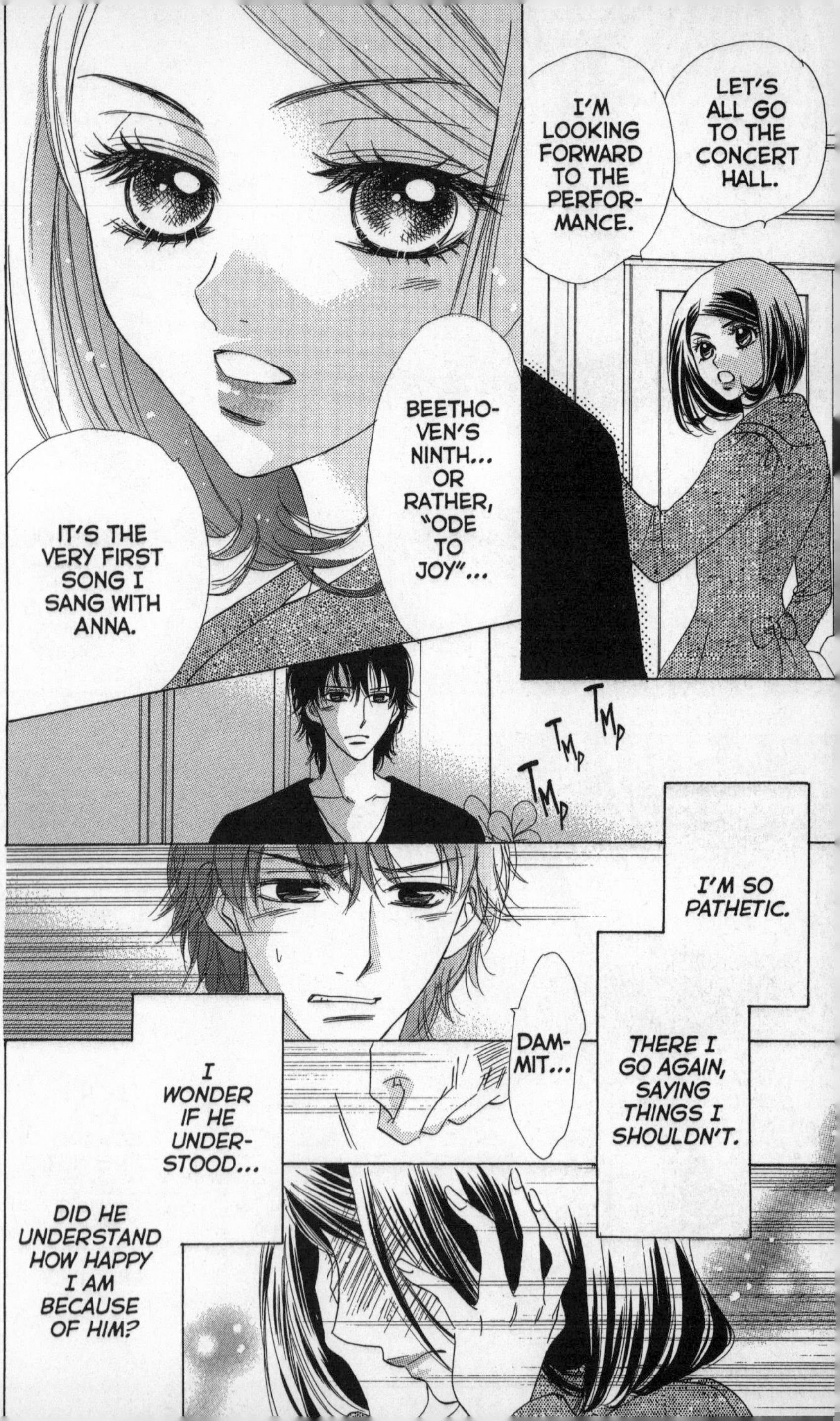
LET'S ALL GO TO THE CONCERT HALL.
I'M LOOKING FORWARD TO THE PERFORMANCE.
BEETHOVEN'S NINTH... OR RATHER, "ODE TO JOY"...
IT'S THE VERY FIRST SONG I SANG WITH ANNA.
TMP TMP TMP
I'M SO PATHETIC.
DAMMIT...
THERE I GO AGAIN, SAYING THINGS I SHOULDN'T.
I WONDER IF HE UNDERSTOOD...
DID HE UNDERSTAND HOW HAPPY I AM BECAUSE OF HIM?

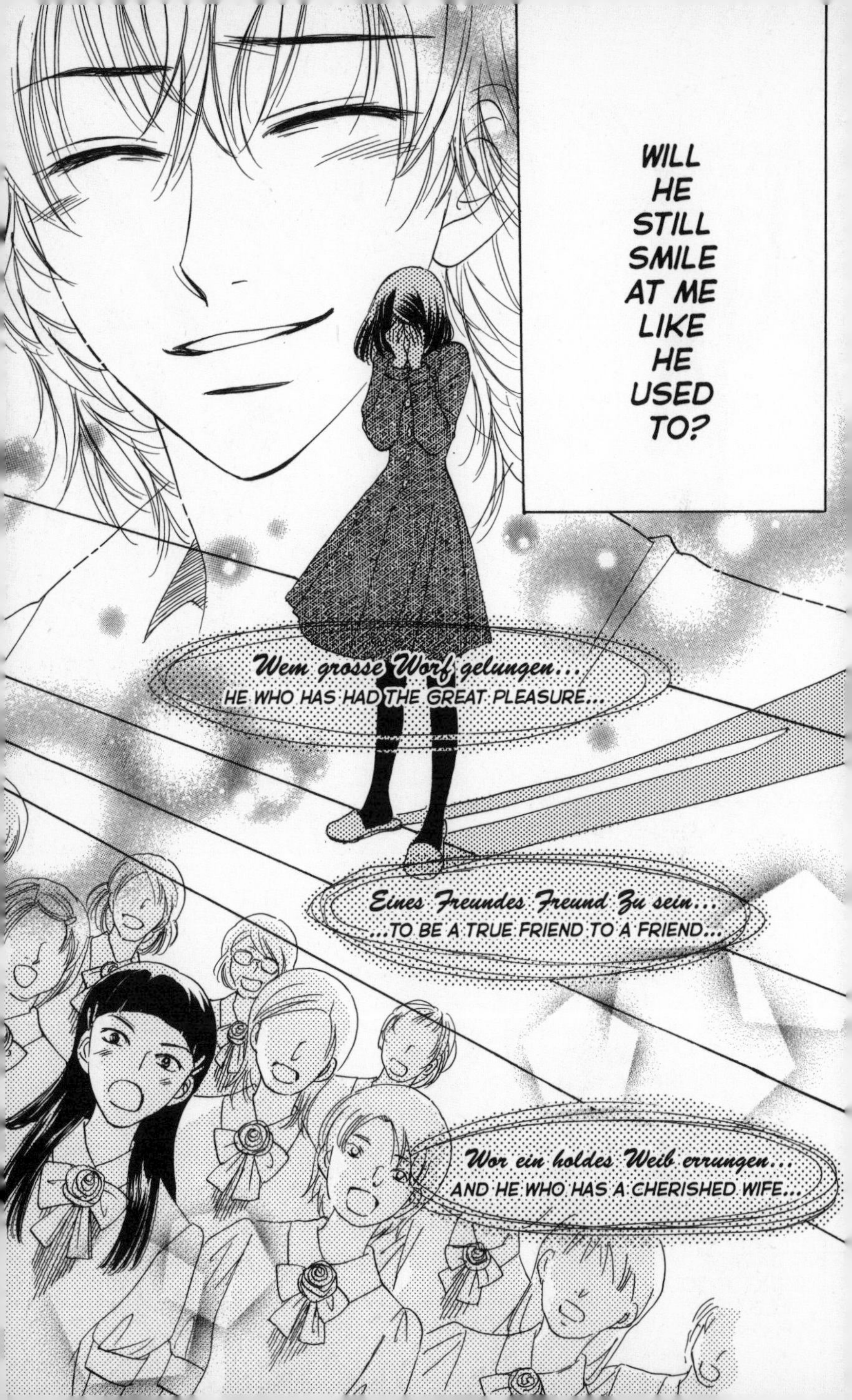
WILL HE STILL SMILE AT ME LIKE HE USED TO?
Wem grosse Worf gelungen...
HE WHO HAS HAD THE GREAT PLEASURE...
Eines Freundes Freund Zu sein...
...TO BE A TRUE FRIEND TO A FRIEND...
Wor ein holdes Weib errungen...
AND HE WHO HAS A CHERISHED WIFE...

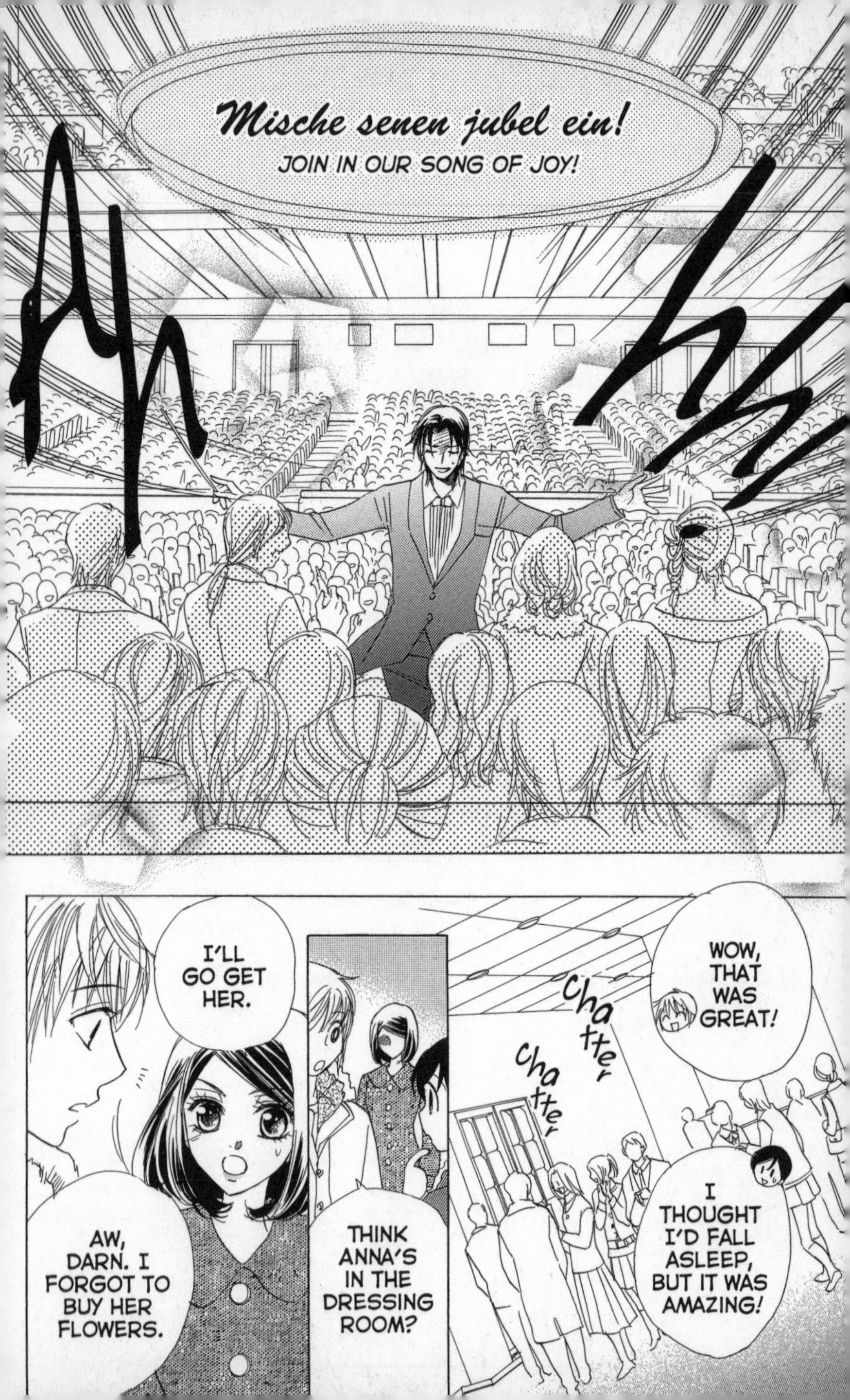
Mische senen jubel ein!
JOIN IN OUR SONG OF JOY!
WOW, THAT WAS GREAT!
Chatter
Chatter
I THOUGHT I'D FALL ASLEEP, BUT IT WAS AMAZING!
THINK ANNA'S IN THE DRESSING ROOM?
I'LL GO GET HER.
AW, DARN. I FORGOT TO BUY HER FLOWERS.

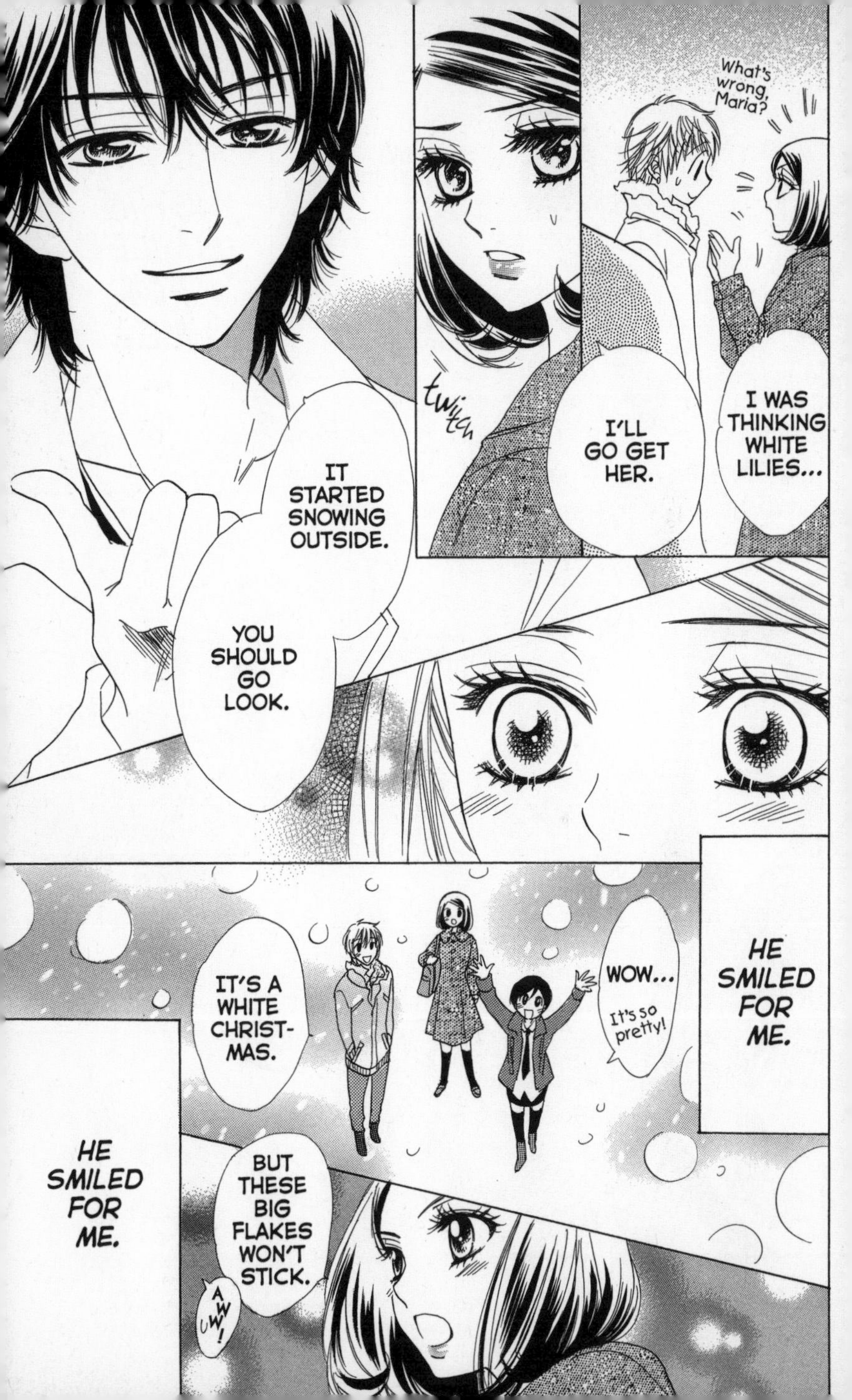
What's wrong, Maria?
I WAS THINKING WHITE LILIES...
I'LL GO GET HER.
twitch
IT STARTED SNOWING OUTSIDE.
YOU SHOULD GO LOOK.
HE SMILED FOR ME.
WOW...
It's so pretty!
IT'S A WHITE CHRISTMAS.
BUT THESE BIG FLAKES WON'T STICK.
AWW!
HE SMILED FOR ME.

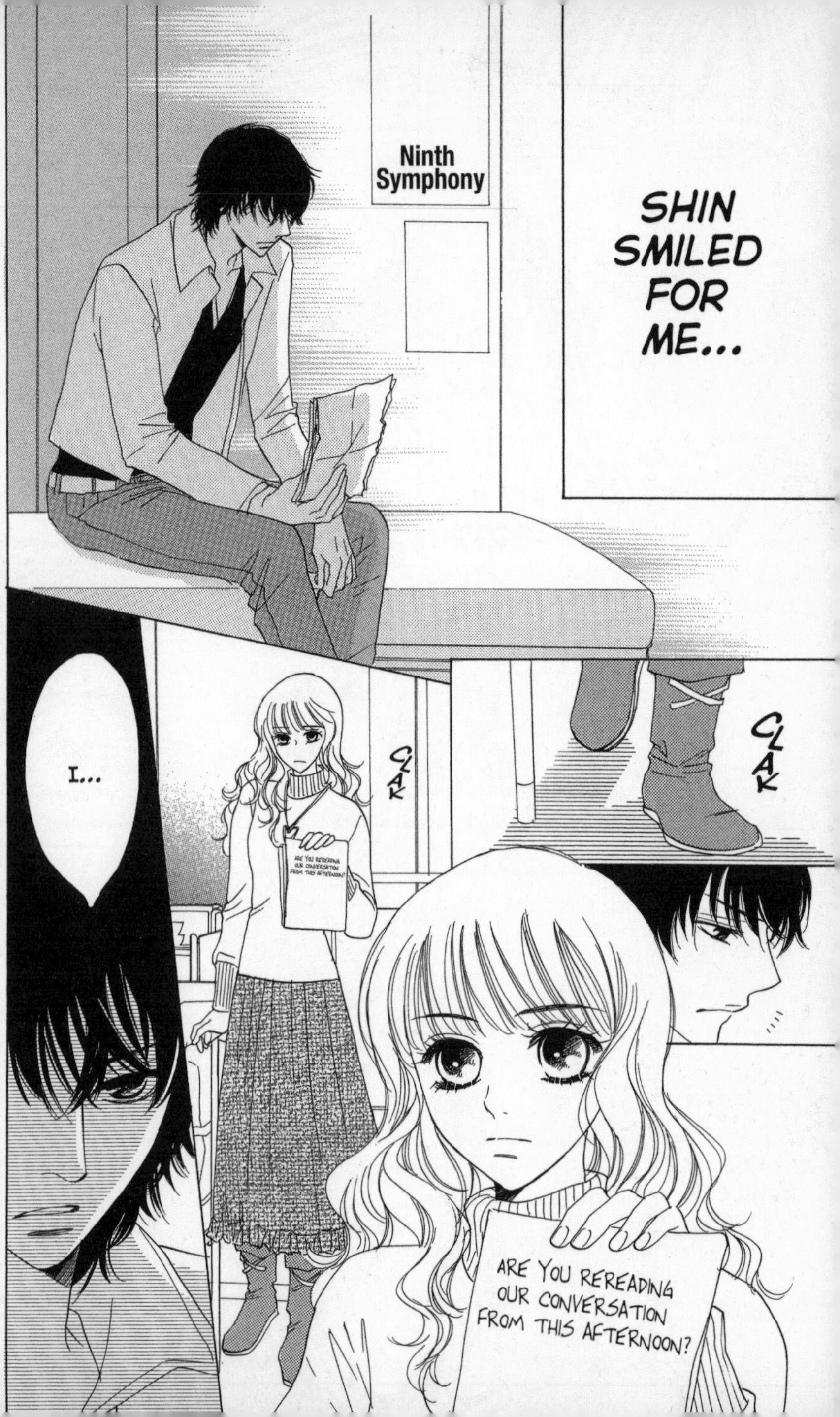
SHIN SMILED FOR ME...
Ninth Symphony
CLAK
ARE YOU REREADING OUR CONVERSATION FROM THIS AFTERNOON?
CLAK
ARE YOU REREADING OUR CONVERSATION FROM THIS AFTERNOON?
I...

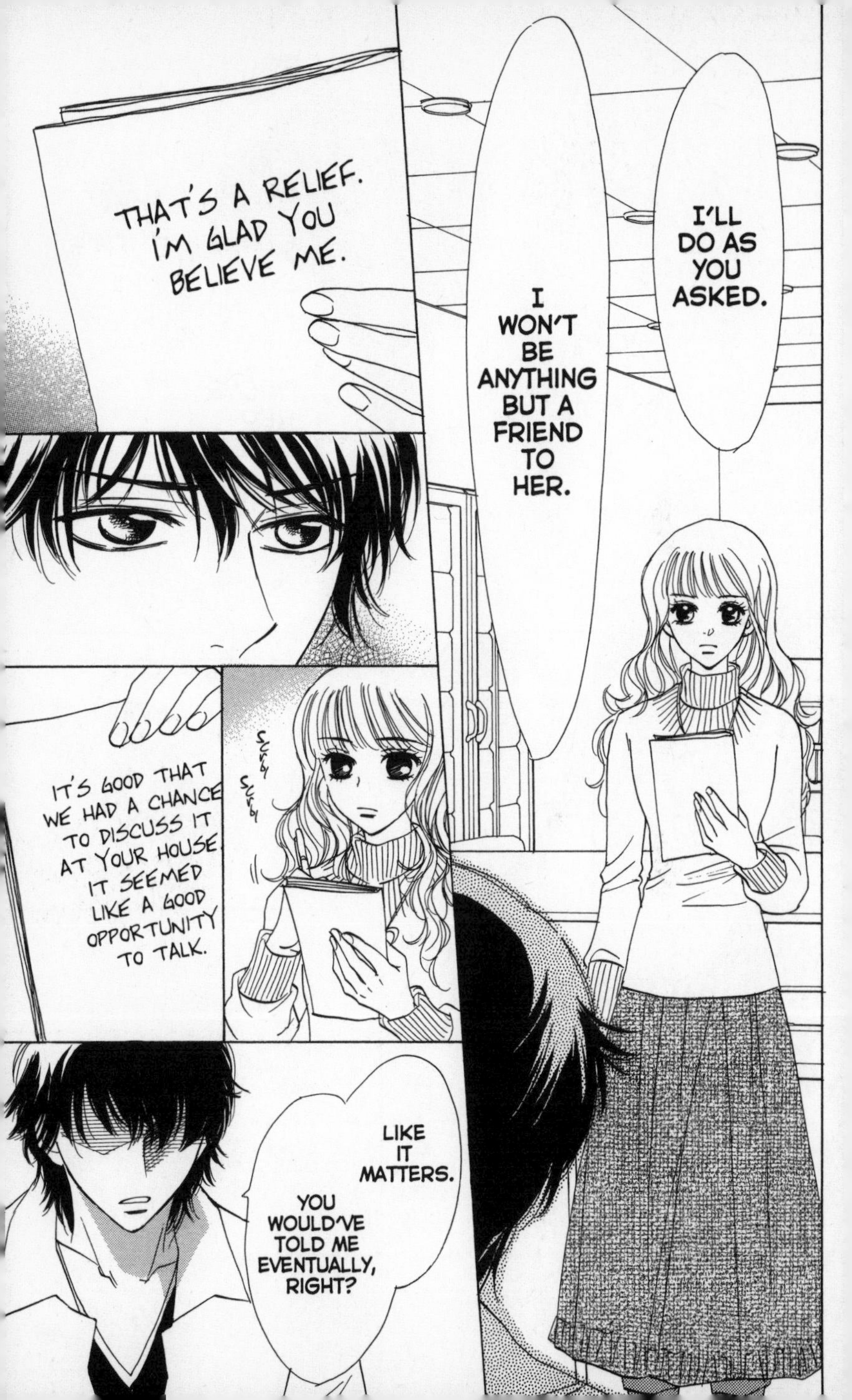
I'LL DO AS YOU ASKED.
I WON'T BE ANYTHING BUT A FRIEND TO HER.
THAT'S A RELIEF. I'M GLAD YOU BELIEVE ME.
IT'S GOOD THAT WE HAD A CHANCE TO DISCUSS IT AT YOUR HOUSE. IT SEEMED LIKE A GOOD OPPORTUNITY TO TALK.
LIKE IT MATTERS.
YOU WOULD'VE TOLD ME EVENTUALLY, RIGHT?

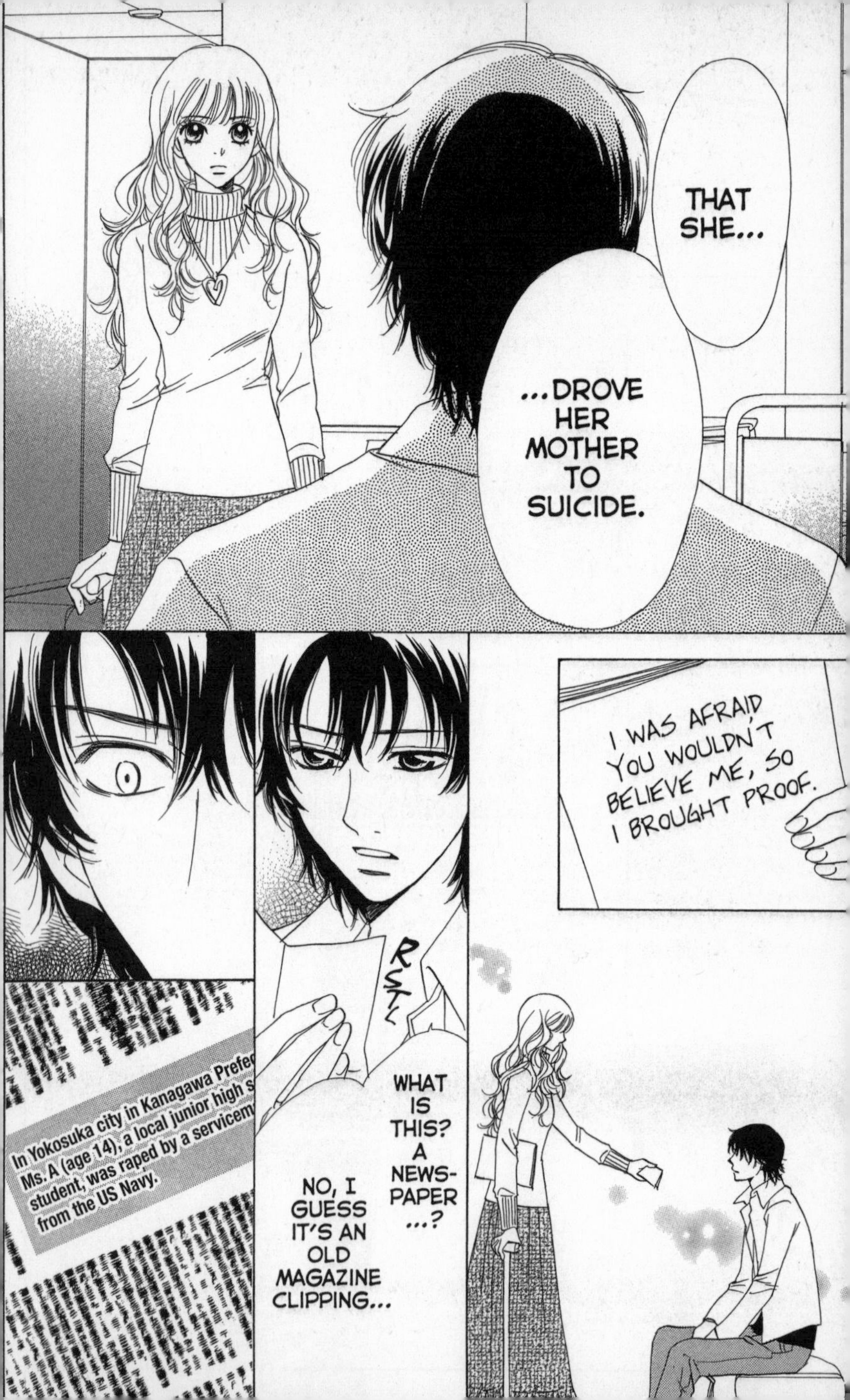
THAT SHE...
...DROVE HER MOTHER TO SUICIDE.
I WAS AFRAID YOU WOULDN'T BELIEVE ME, SO I BROUGHT PROOF.
RSTL
WHAT IS THIS? A NEWS-PAPER ...?
NO, I GUESS IT'S AN OLD MAGAZINE CLIPPING...
In Yokosuka city in Kanagawa Prefec
Ms. A (age 14), a local junior high s
student, was raped by a servicem
from the US Navy.

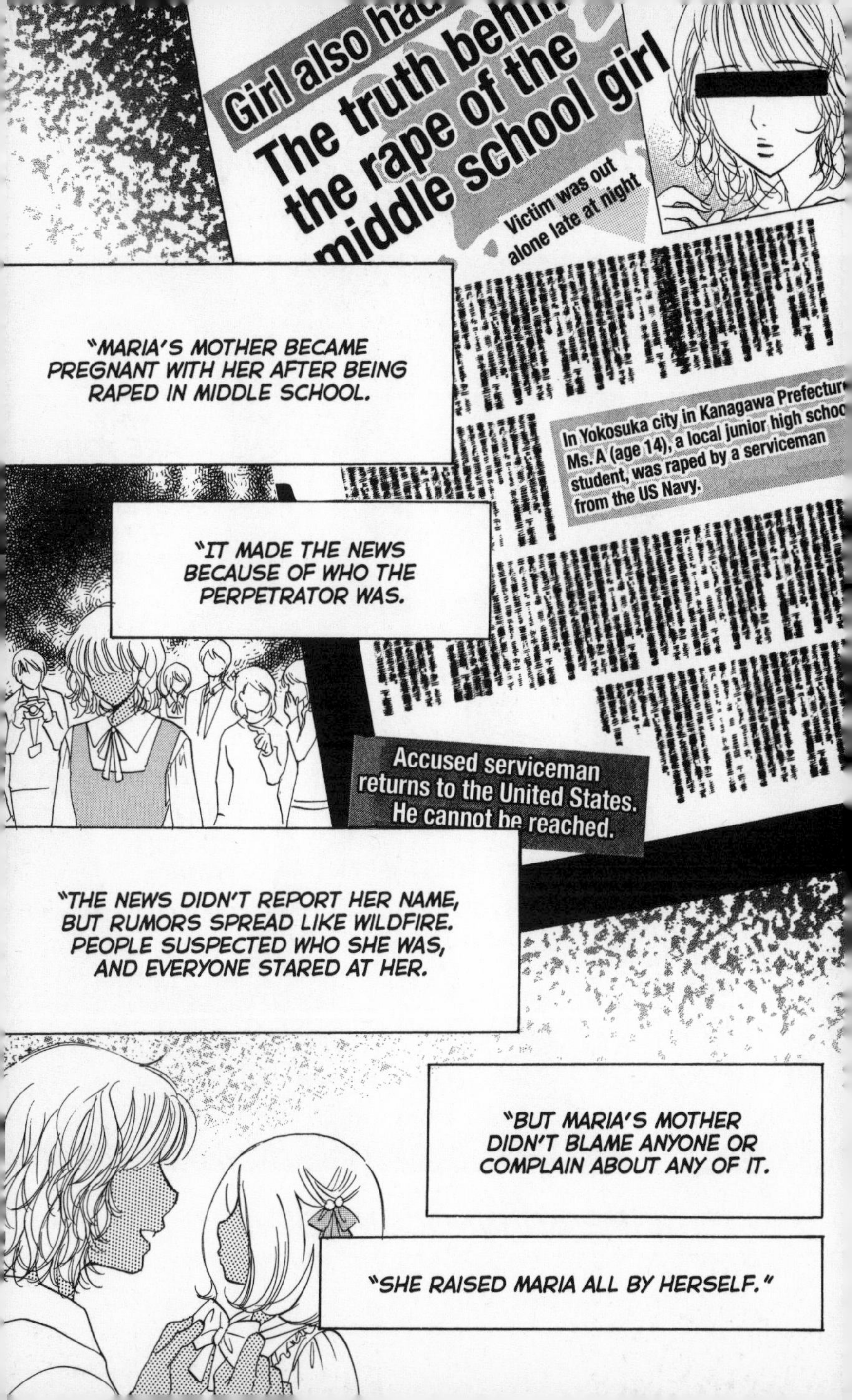

Girl also
The truth
the rape of the
middle school girl
Victim was out alone late at night
In Yokosuka city in Kanagawa Prefecture, Ms. A (age 14), a local junior high school student, was raped by a serviceman from the US Navy.
"MARIA'S MOTHER BECAME PREGNANT WITH HER AFTER BEING RAPED IN MIDDLE SCHOOL.
Accused serviceman returns to the United States. He cannot be reached.
"IT MADE THE NEWS BECAUSE OF WHO THE PERPETRATOR WAS.
"THE NEWS DIDN'T REPORT HER NAME, BUT RUMORS SPREAD LIKE WILDFIRE. PEOPLE SUSPECTED WHO SHE WAS, AND EVERYONE STARED AT HER.
"BUT MARIA'S MOTHER DIDN'T BLAME ANYONE OR COMPLAIN ABOUT ANY OF IT.
"SHE RAISED MARIA ALL BY HERSELF."

"AND MARIA, BEING MARIA, SPOKE THE TRUTH...

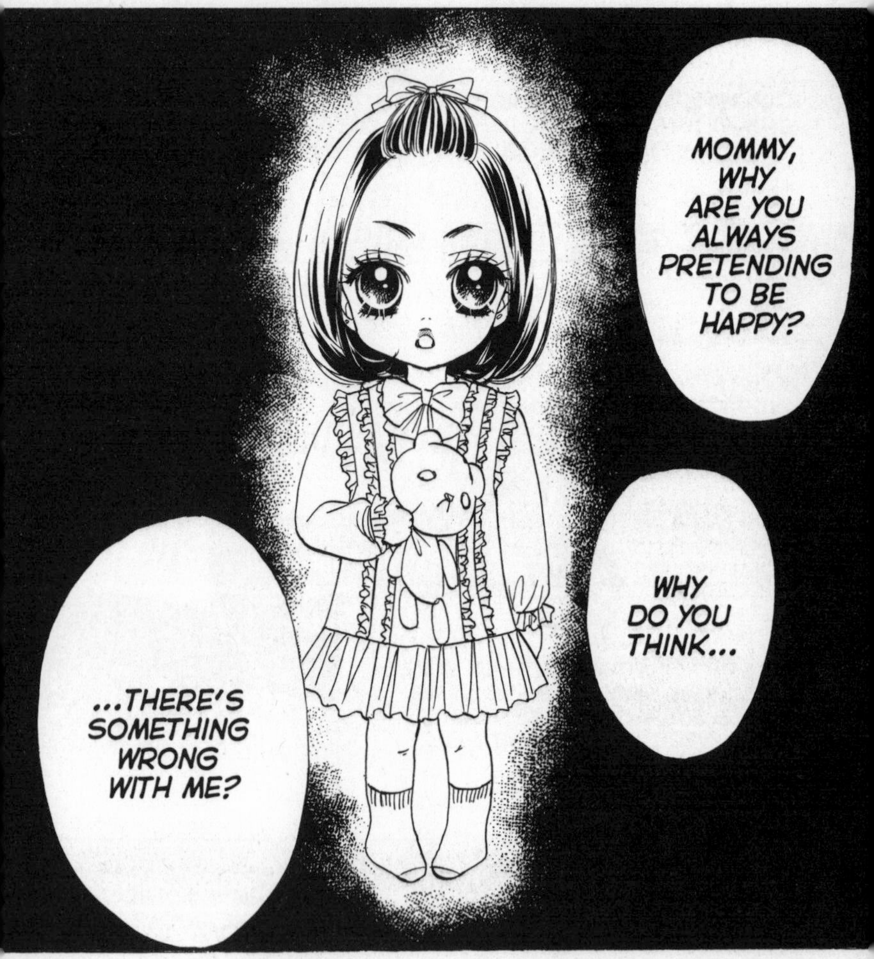
MOMMY, WHY ARE YOU ALWAYS PRETENDING TO BE HAPPY?
WHY DO YOU THINK...
...THERE'S SOMETHING WRONG WITH ME?

"...LIKE AN INNOCENT DEVIL."

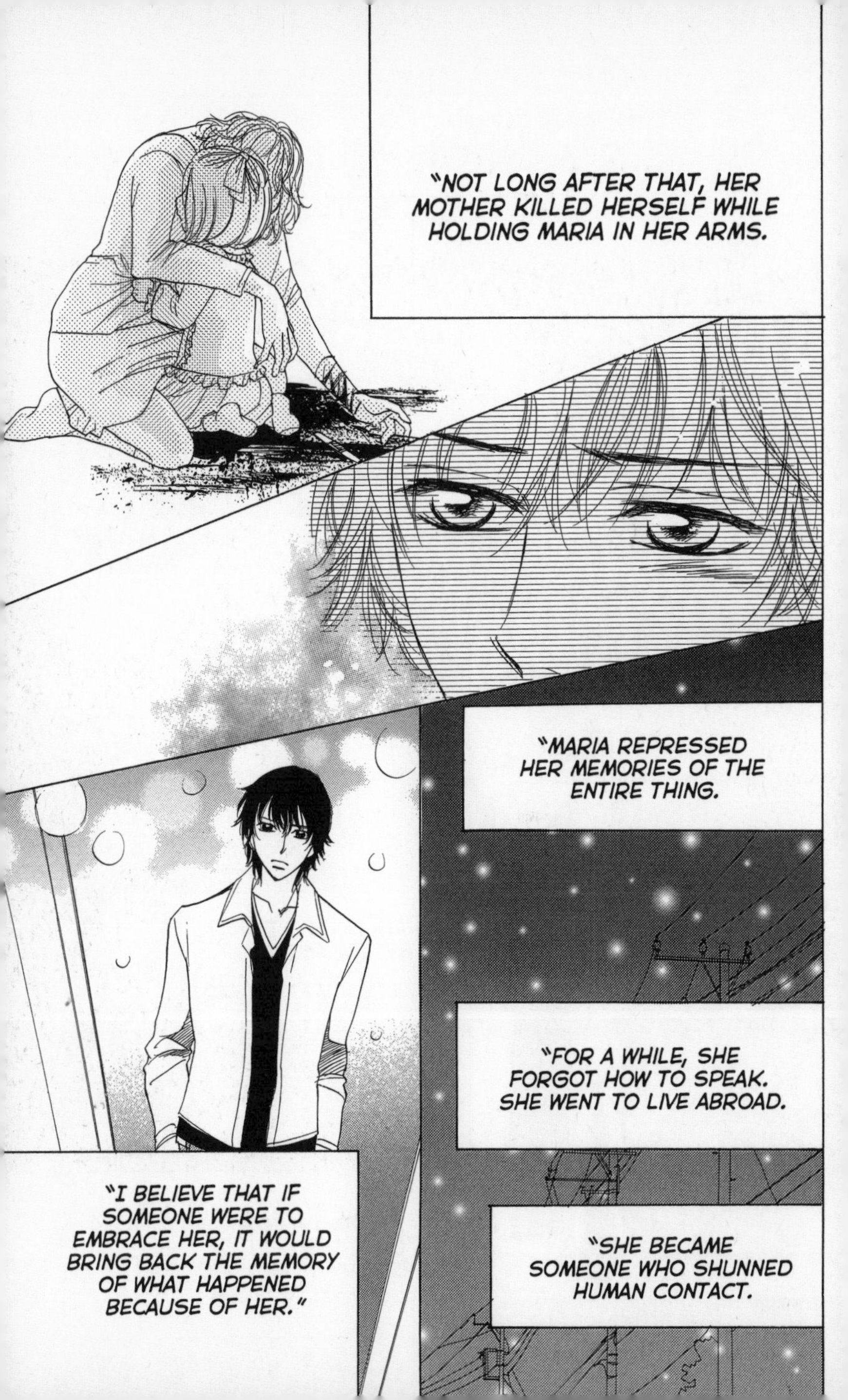
"NOT LONG AFTER THAT, HER MOTHER KILLED HERSELF WHILE HOLDING MARIA IN HER ARMS.
"MARIA REPRESSED HER MEMORIES OF THE ENTIRE THING.
"FOR A WHILE, SHE FORGOT HOW TO SPEAK. SHE WENT TO LIVE ABROAD.
"SHE BECAME SOMEONE WHO SHUNNED HUMAN CONTACT.
"I BELIEVE THAT IF SOMEONE WERE TO EMBRACE HER, IT WOULD BRING BACK THE MEMORY OF WHAT HAPPENED BECAUSE OF HER."

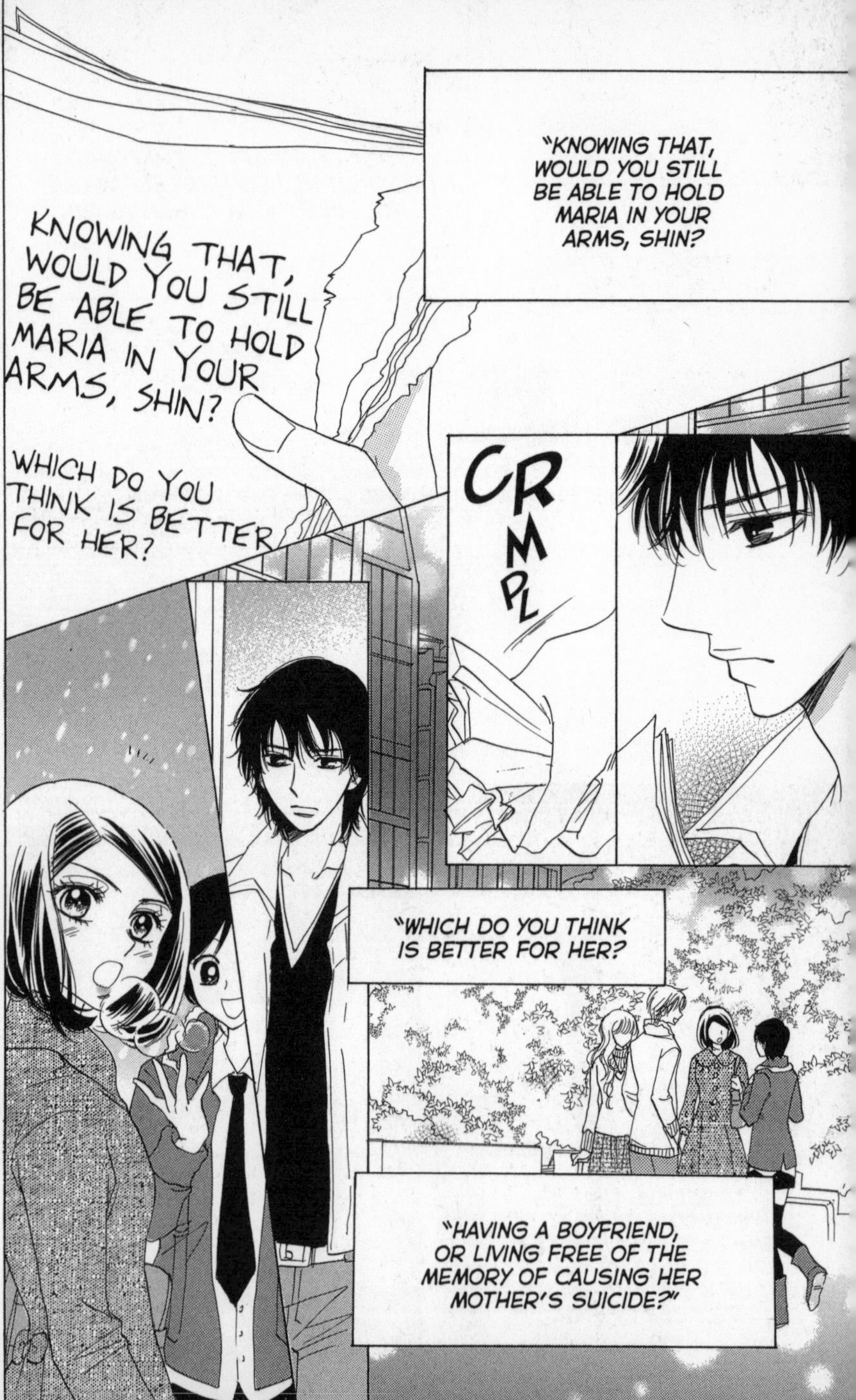
"KNOWING THAT, WOULD YOU STILL BE ABLE TO HOLD MARIA IN YOUR ARMS, SHIN?
KNOWING THAT, WOULD YOU STILL BE ABLE TO HOLD MARIA IN YOUR ARMS, SHIN?
WHICH DO YOU THINK IS BETTER FOR HER?
CRMPL
"WHICH DO YOU THINK IS BETTER FOR HER?
"HAVING A BOYFRIEND, OR LIVING FREE OF THE MEMORY OF CAUSING HER MOTHER'S SUICIDE?"

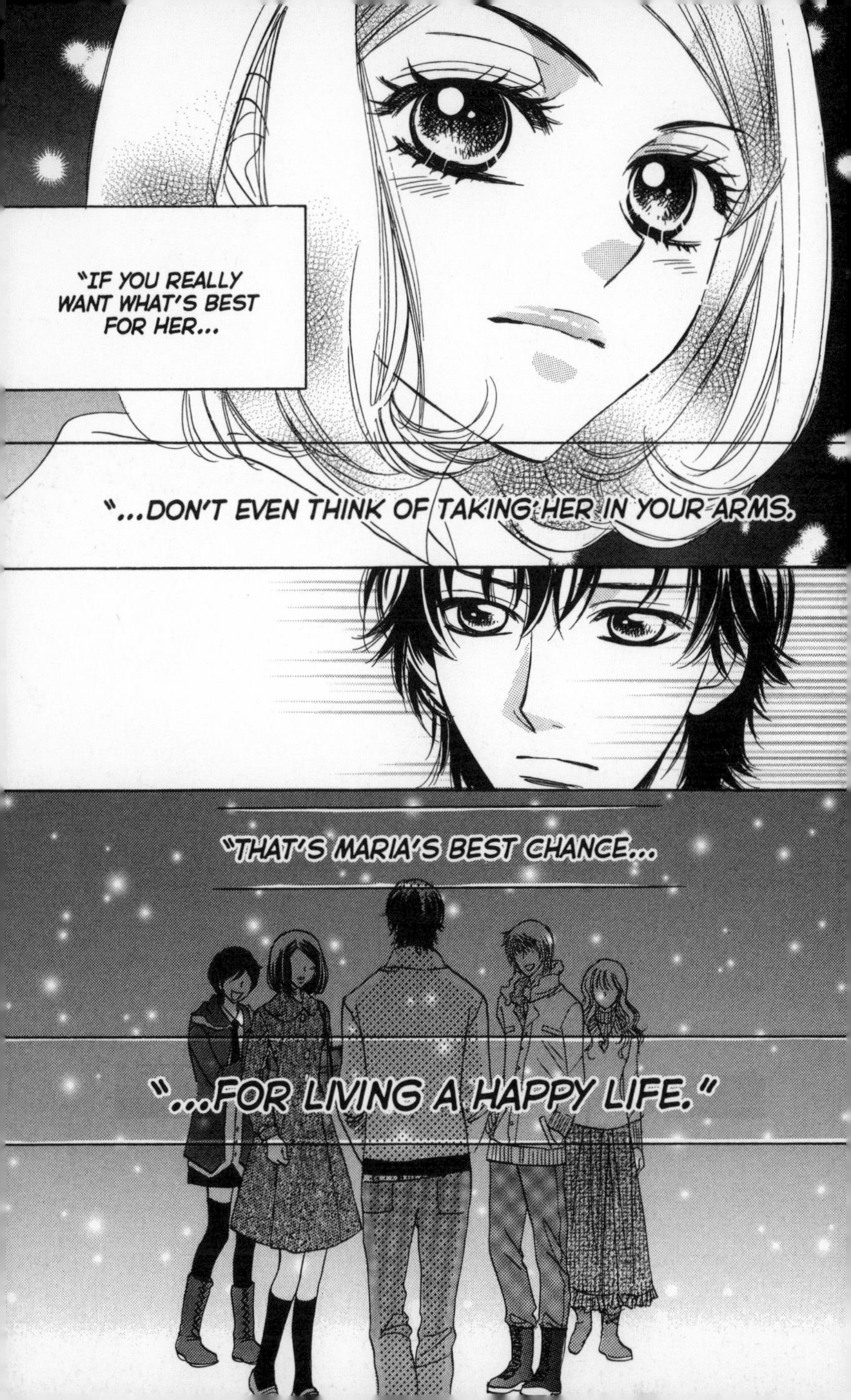
"IF YOU REALLY WANT WHAT'S BEST FOR HER...
"...DON'T EVEN THINK OF TAKING HER IN YOUR ARMS.
"THAT'S MARIA'S BEST CHANCE...
"...FOR LIVING A HAPPY LIFE."

A Devil and
Her Love Song

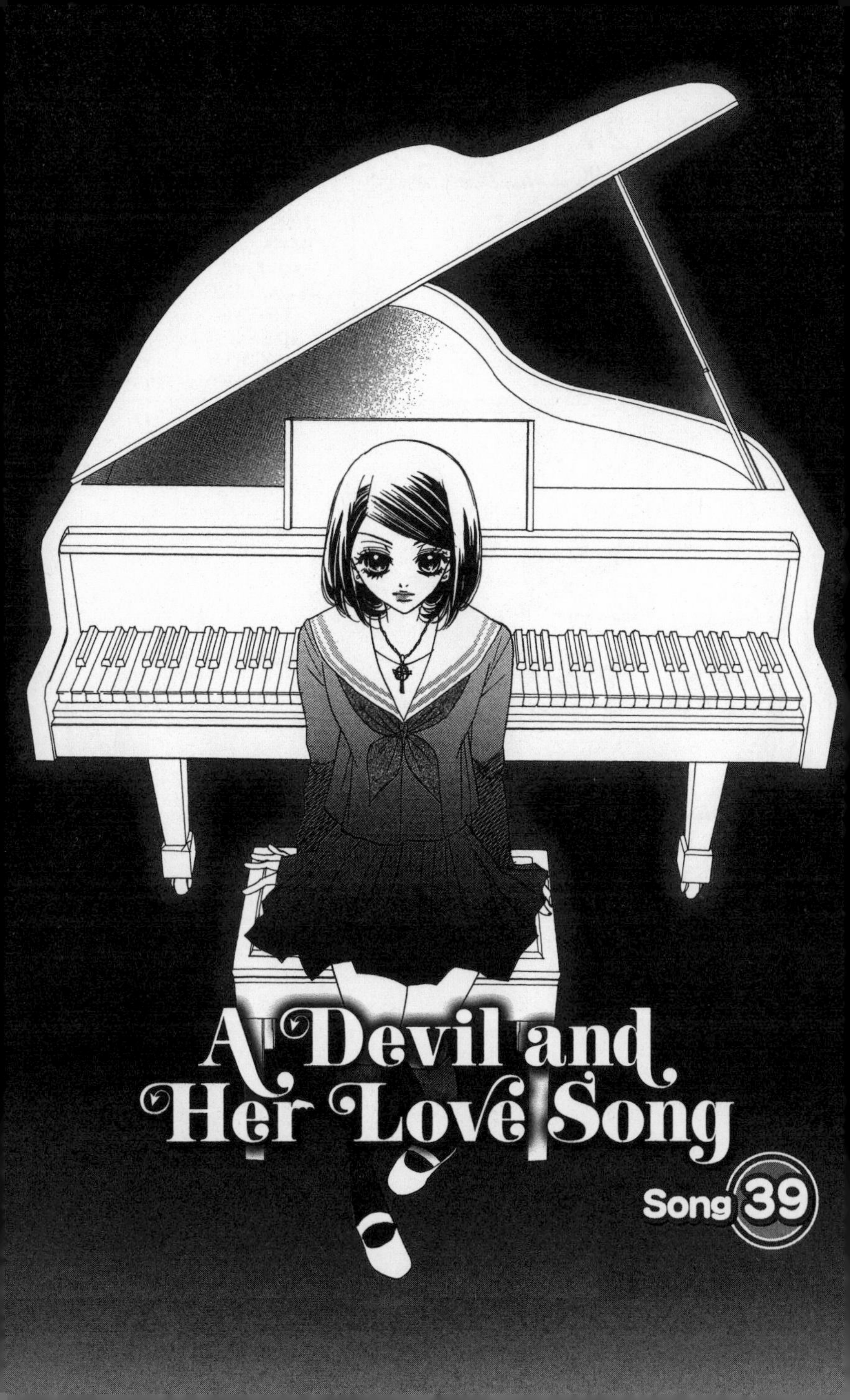
A Devil and Her Love Song
Song 39

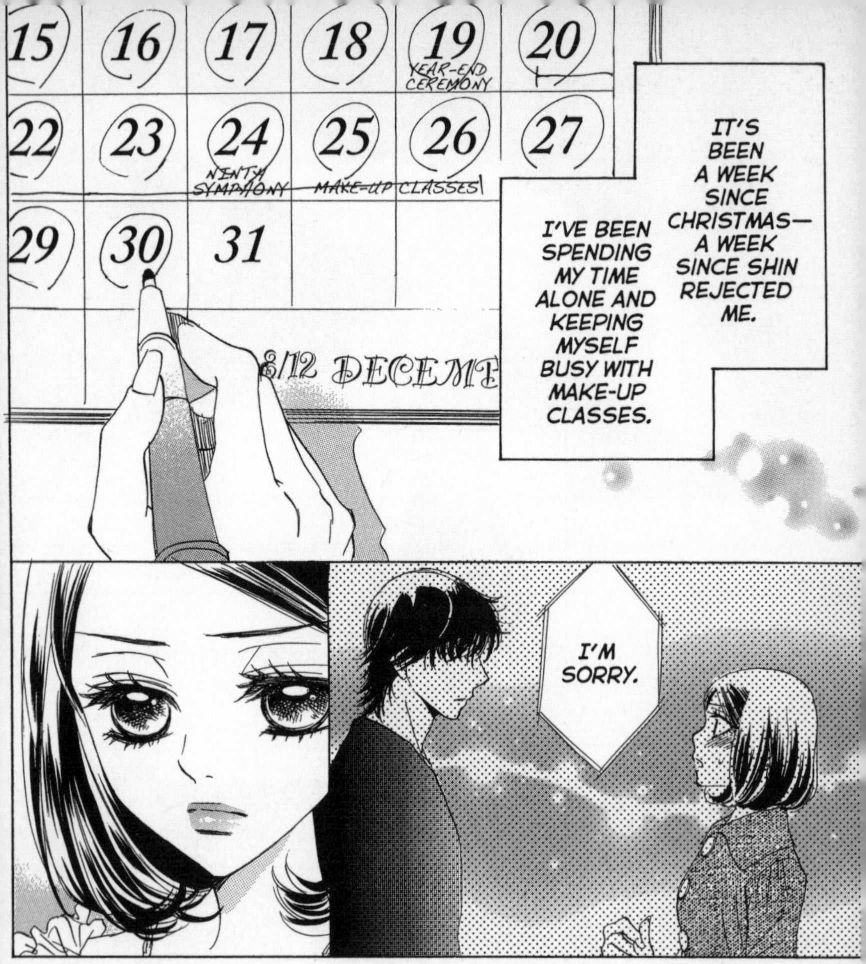
15 16 17 18 19 20
YEAR-END CEREMONY
22 23 24 25 26 27
NINTH SYMPHONY
MAKE-UP CLASSES
29 30 31
8/12 DECEMB
IT'S BEEN A WEEK SINCE CHRISTMAS— A WEEK SINCE SHIN REJECTED ME.
I'VE BEEN SPENDING MY TIME ALONE AND KEEPING MYSELF BUSY WITH MAKE-UP CLASSES.
I'M SORRY.

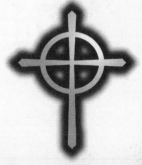

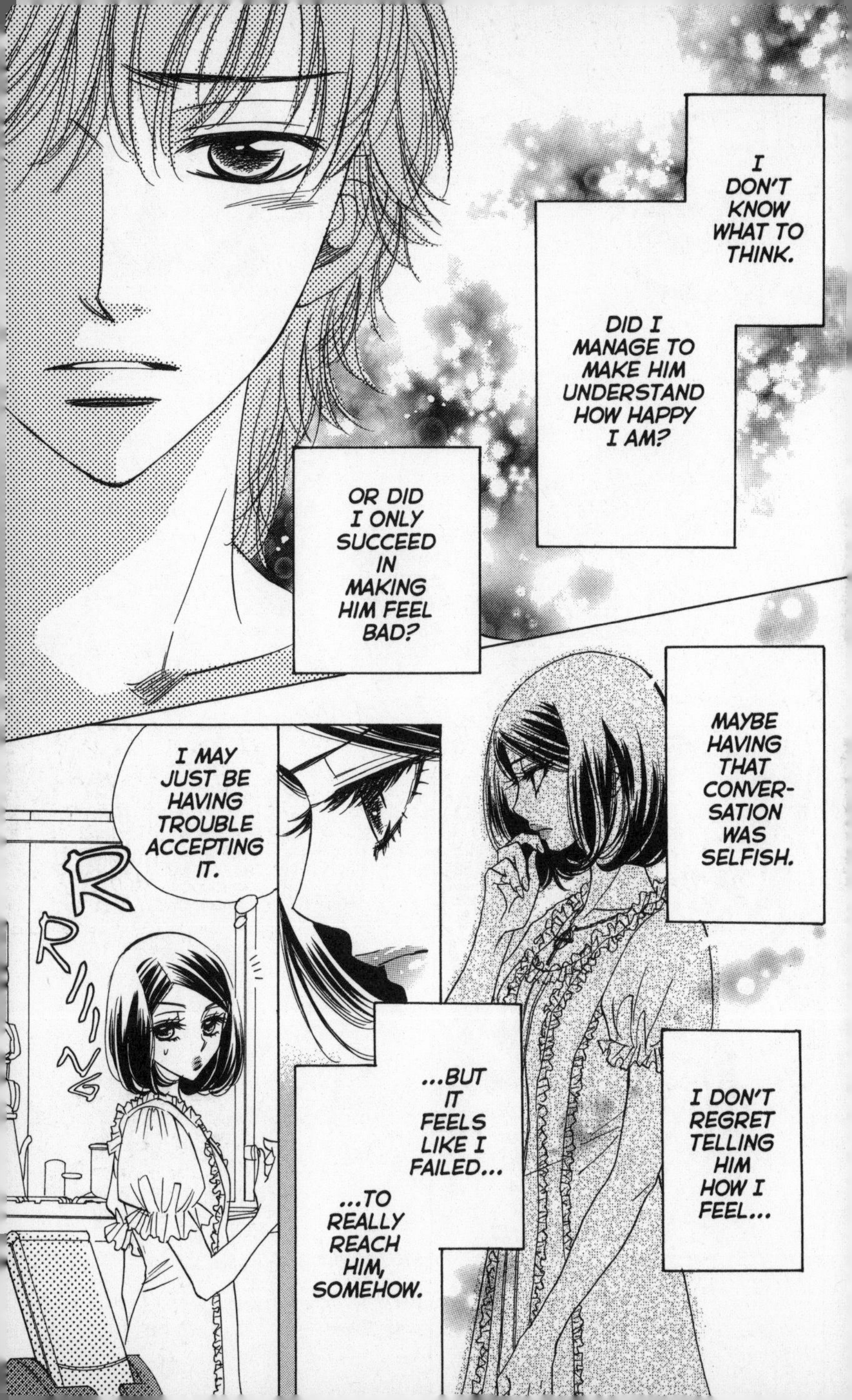
I DON'T KNOW WHAT TO THINK.
DID I MANAGE TO MAKE HIM UNDERSTAND HOW HAPPY I AM?
OR DID I ONLY SUCCEED IN MAKING HIM FEEL BAD?
MAYBE HAVING THAT CONVER-SATION WAS SELFISH.
I DON'T REGRET TELLING HIM HOW I FEEL...
...BUT IT FEELS LIKE I FAILED...
...TO REALLY REACH HIM, SOMEHOW.
I MAY JUST BE HAVING TROUBLE ACCEPTING IT.
RRIIIING

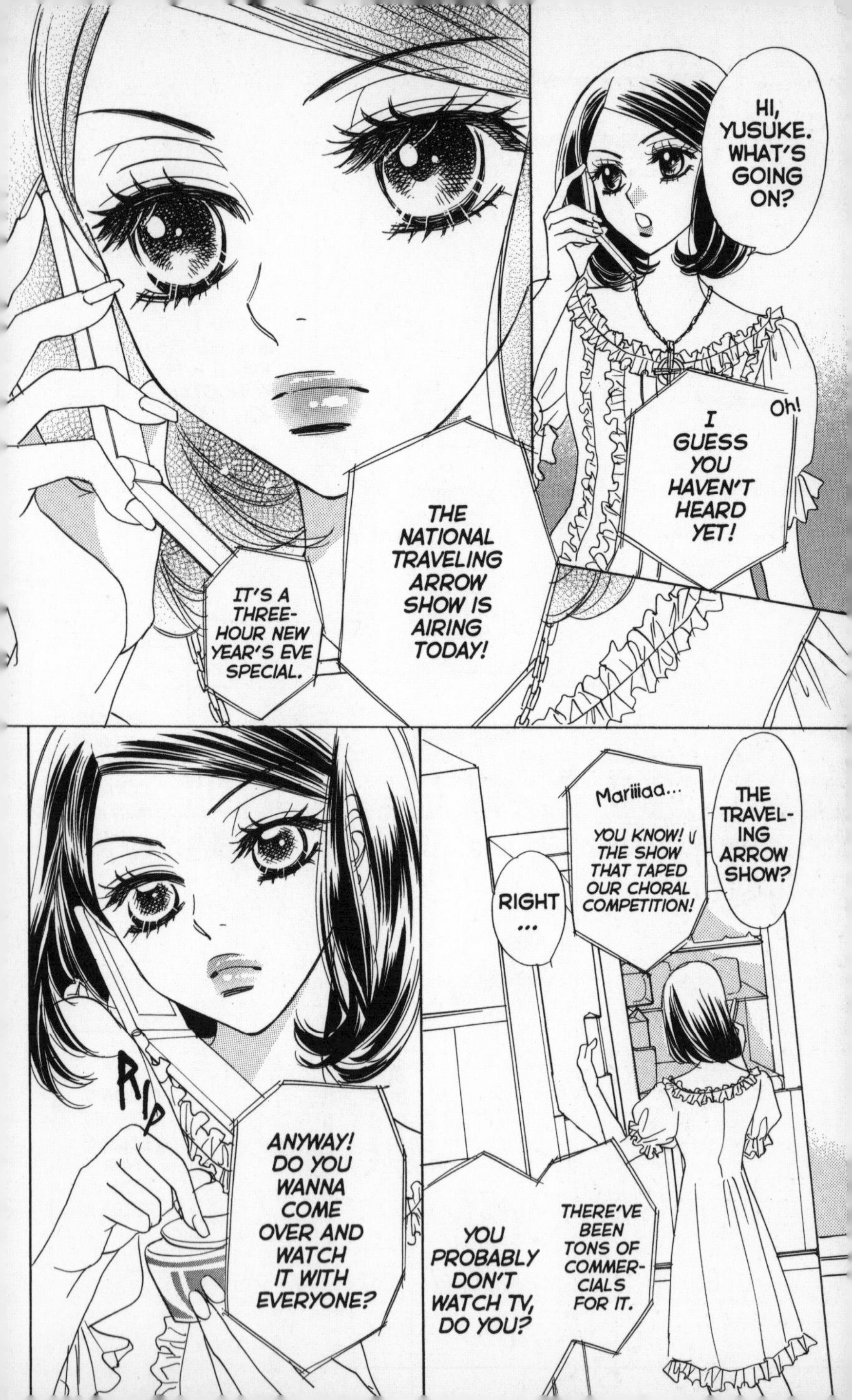
HI, YUSUKE. WHAT'S GOING ON?
Oh!
I GUESS YOU HAVEN'T HEARD YET!
THE NATIONAL TRAVELING ARROW SHOW IS AIRING TODAY!
IT'S A THREE-HOUR NEW YEAR'S EVE SPECIAL.
THE TRAVEL-ING ARROW SHOW?
Mariiiaa...
YOU KNOW! THE SHOW THAT TAPED OUR CHORAL COMPETITION!
RIGHT...
THERE'VE BEEN TONS OF COMMER-CIALS FOR IT.
YOU PROBABLY DON'T WATCH TV, DO YOU?
RIP
ANYWAY! DO YOU WANNA COME OVER AND WATCH IT WITH EVERYONE?

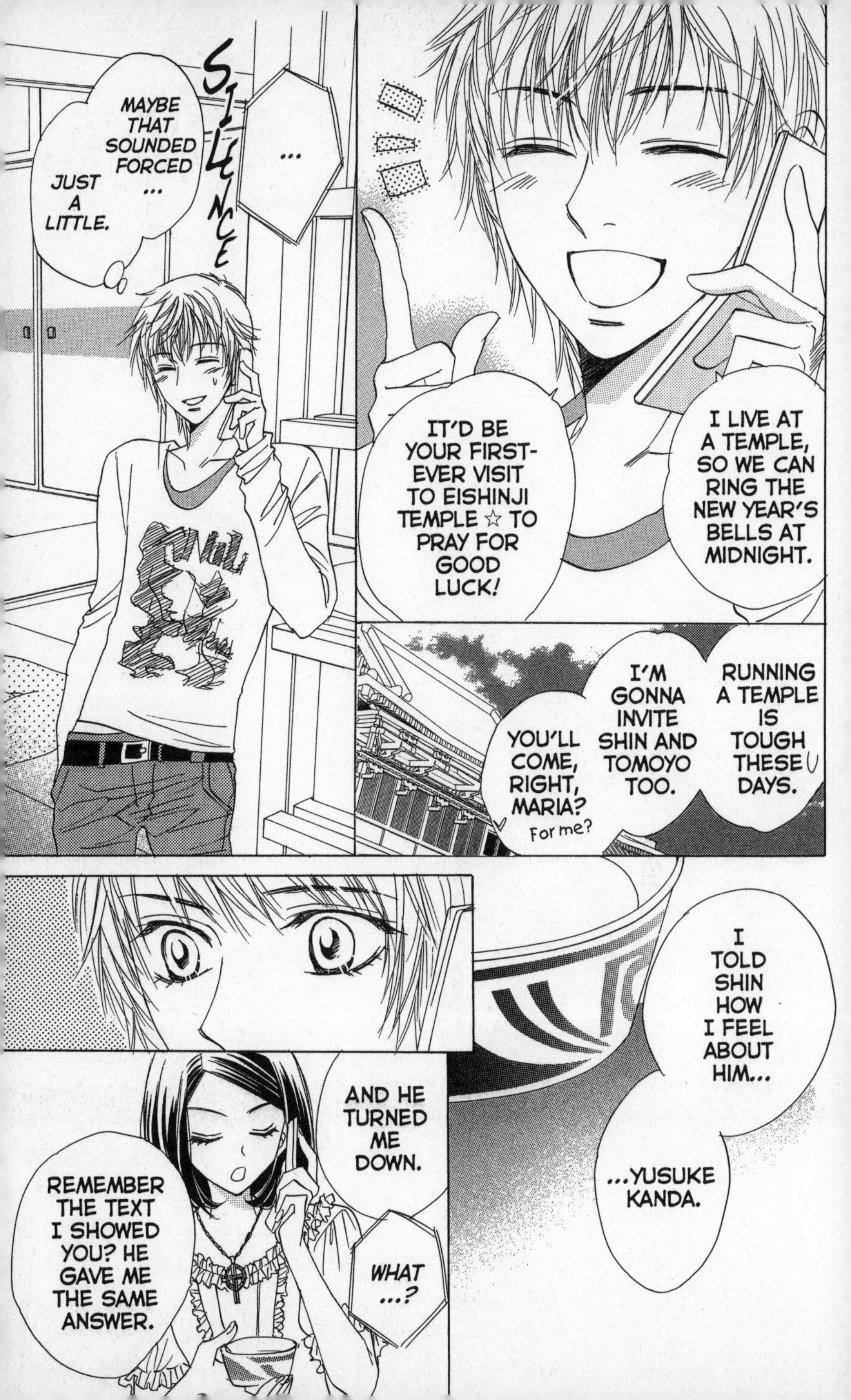
I LIVE AT A TEMPLE, SO WE CAN RING THE NEW YEAR'S BELLS AT MIDNIGHT.
IT'D BE YOUR FIRST-EVER VISIT TO EISHINJI TEMPLE ☆ TO PRAY FOR GOOD LUCK!
RUNNING A TEMPLE IS TOUGH THESE DAYS.
I'M GONNA INVITE SHIN AND TOMOYO TOO.
YOU'LL COME, RIGHT, MARIA?
For me?
...
SILENCE
MAYBE THAT SOUNDED FORCED ... JUST A LITTLE.
I TOLD SHIN HOW I FEEL ABOUT HIM...
...YUSUKE KANDA.
AND HE TURNED ME DOWN.
WHAT ...?
REMEMBER THE TEXT I SHOWED YOU? HE GAVE ME THE SAME ANSWER.

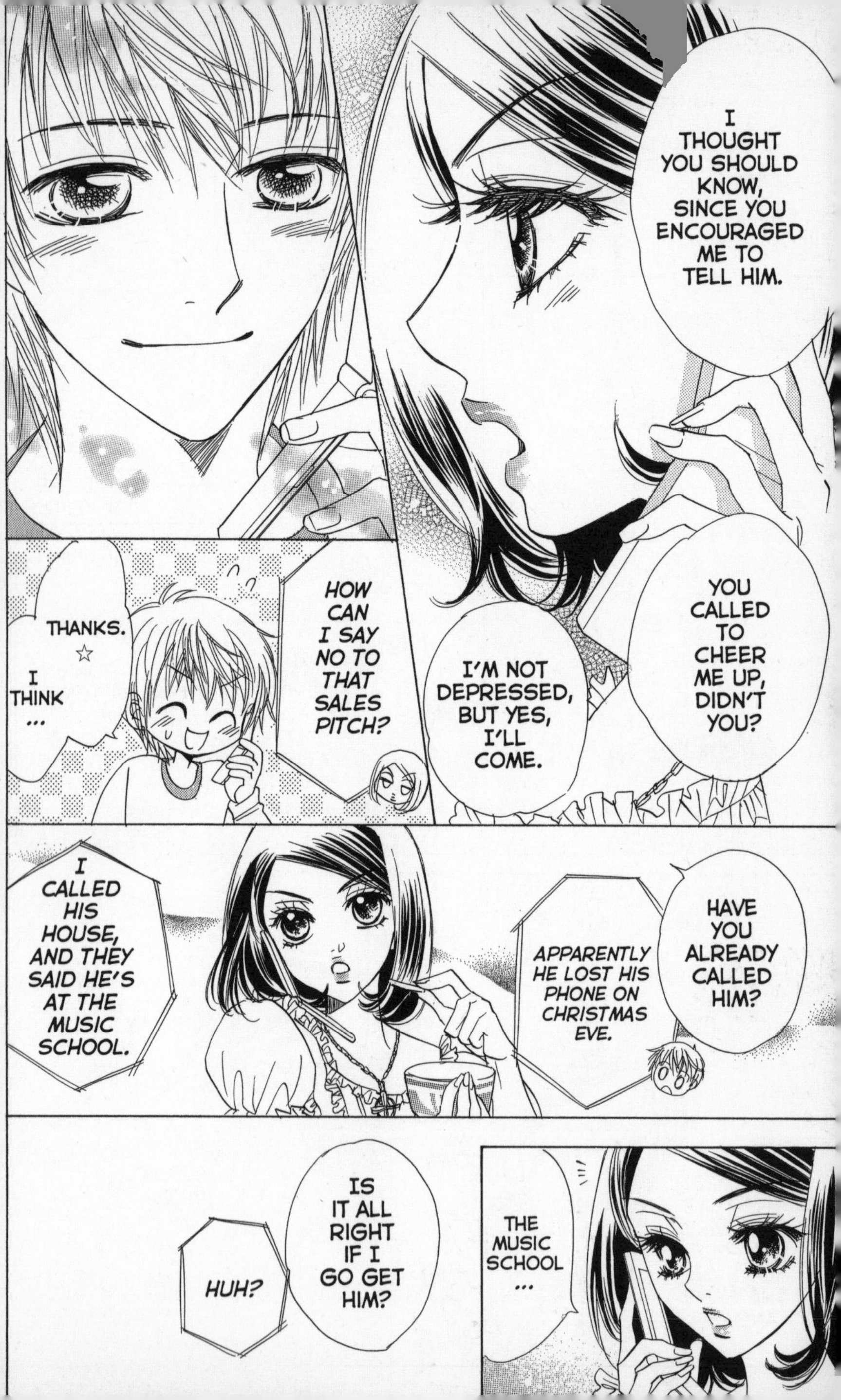
I THOUGHT YOU SHOULD KNOW, SINCE YOU ENCOURAGED ME TO TELL HIM.
YOU CALLED TO CHEER ME UP, DIDN'T YOU?
I'M NOT DEPRESSED, BUT YES, I'LL COME.
HOW CAN I SAY NO TO THAT SALES PITCH?
THANKS. ☆
I THINK ...
HAVE YOU ALREADY CALLED HIM?
APPARENTLY HE LOST HIS PHONE ON CHRISTMAS EVE.
I CALLED HIS HOUSE, AND THEY SAID HE'S AT THE MUSIC SCHOOL.
THE MUSIC SCHOOL ...
IS IT ALL RIGHT IF I GO GET HIM?
HUH?

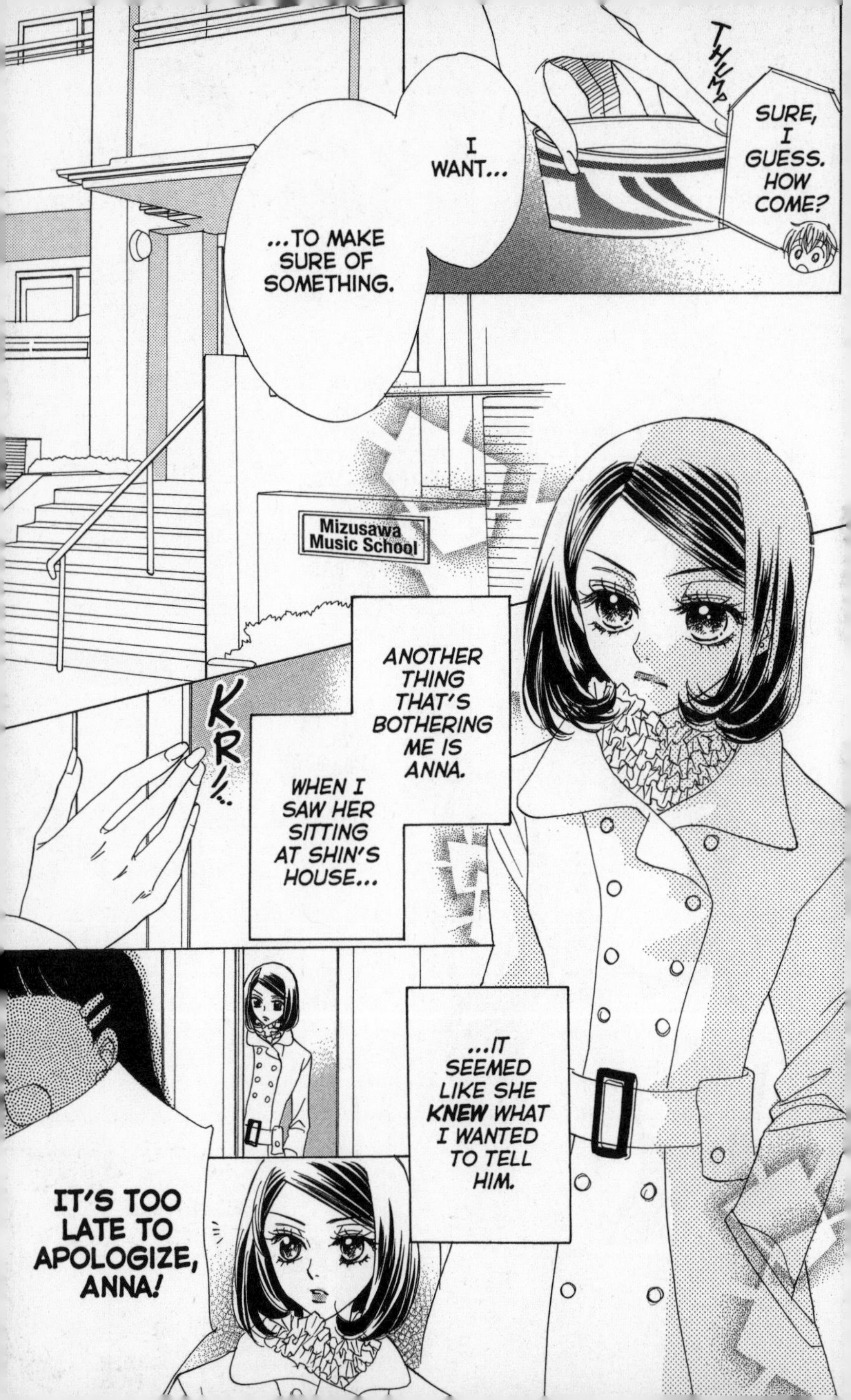
THUMP
SURE, I GUESS. HOW COME?
I WANT...
...TO MAKE SURE OF SOMETHING.
Mizusawa Music School
ANOTHER THING THAT'S BOTHERING ME IS ANNA.
WHEN I SAW HER SITTING AT SHIN'S HOUSE...
KRI...
...IT SEEMED LIKE SHE KNEW WHAT I WANTED TO TELL HIM.
IT'S TOO LATE TO APOLOGIZE, ANNA!

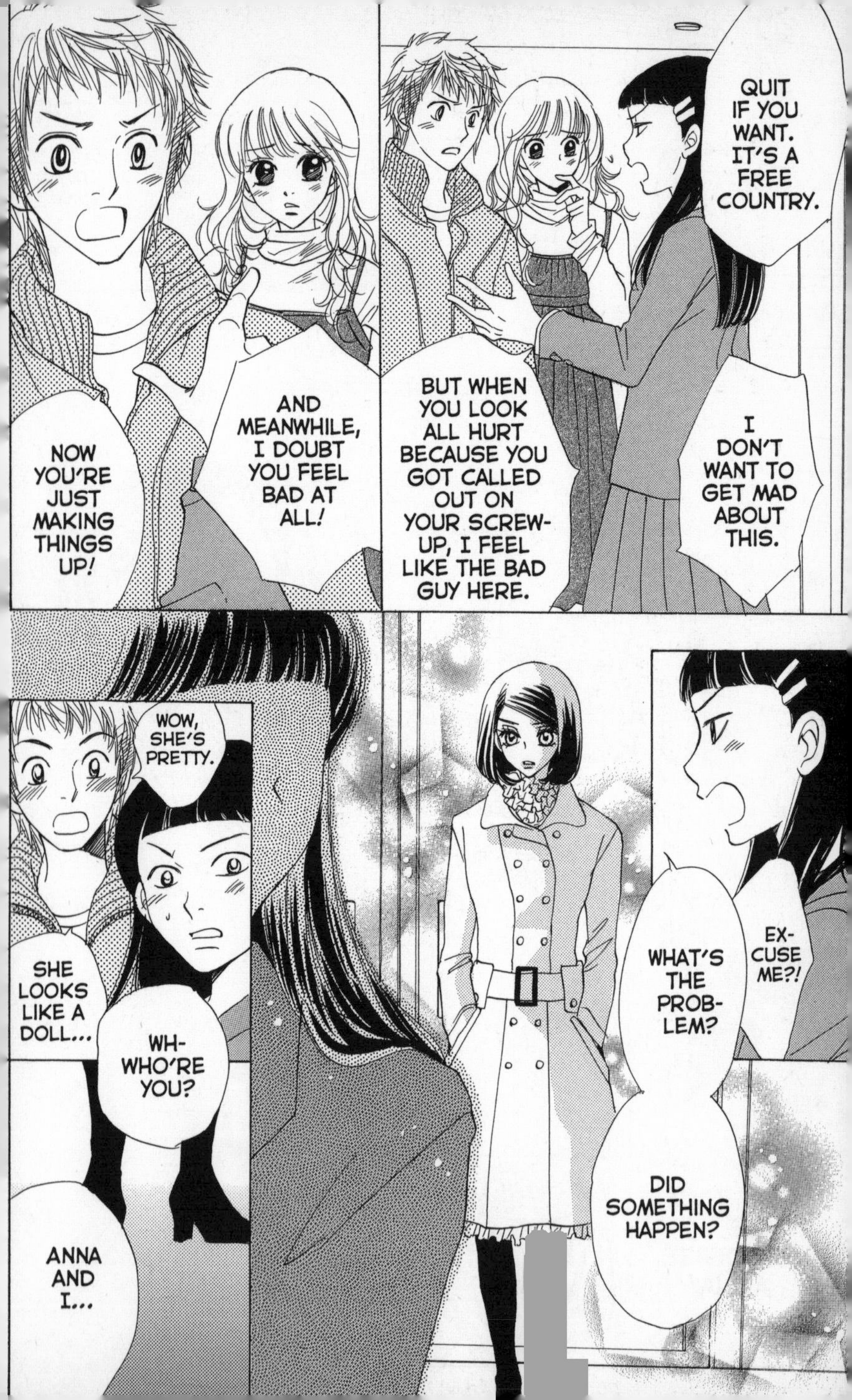
QUIT IF YOU WANT. IT'S A FREE COUNTRY.
I DON'T WANT TO GET MAD ABOUT THIS.
BUT WHEN YOU LOOK ALL HURT BECAUSE YOU GOT CALLED OUT ON YOUR SCREW-UP, I FEEL LIKE THE BAD GUY HERE.
AND MEANWHILE, I DOUBT YOU FEEL BAD AT ALL!
NOW YOU'RE JUST MAKING THINGS UP!
EX-CUSE ME?!
WHAT'S THE PROB-LEM?
DID SOMETHING HAPPEN?
WOW, SHE'S PRETTY.
SHE LOOKS LIKE A DOLL...
WH-WHO'RE YOU?
ANNA AND I...

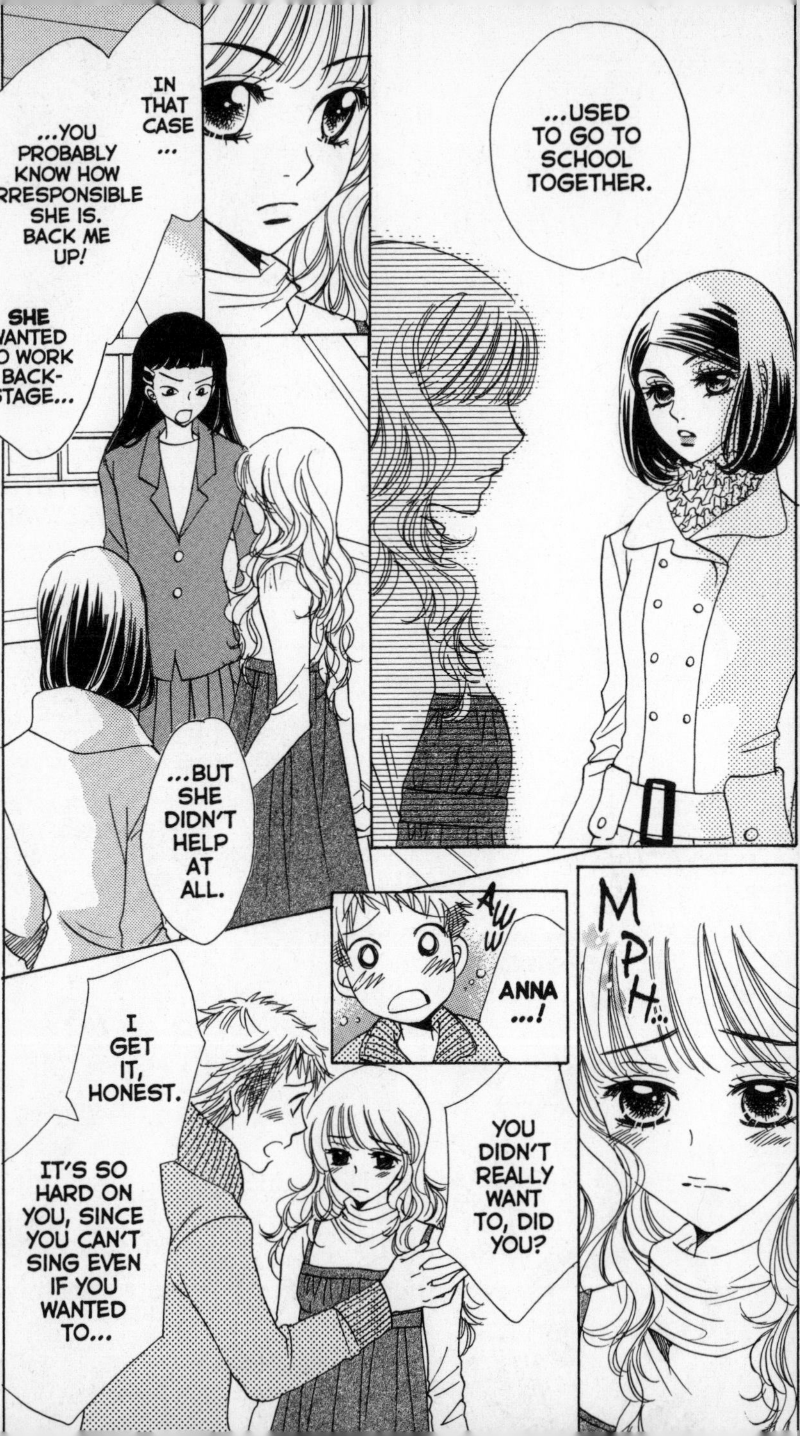
...USED TO GO TO SCHOOL TOGETHER.
IN THAT CASE...
...YOU PROBABLY KNOW HOW IRRESPONSIBLE SHE IS. BACK ME UP!
SHE WANTED TO WORK BACK-STAGE...
...BUT SHE DIDN'T HELP AT ALL.
MPH...
AWW
ANNA...!
YOU DIDN'T REALLY WANT TO, DID YOU?
I GET IT, HONEST.
IT'S SO HARD ON YOU, SINCE YOU CAN'T SING EVEN IF YOU WANTED TO...

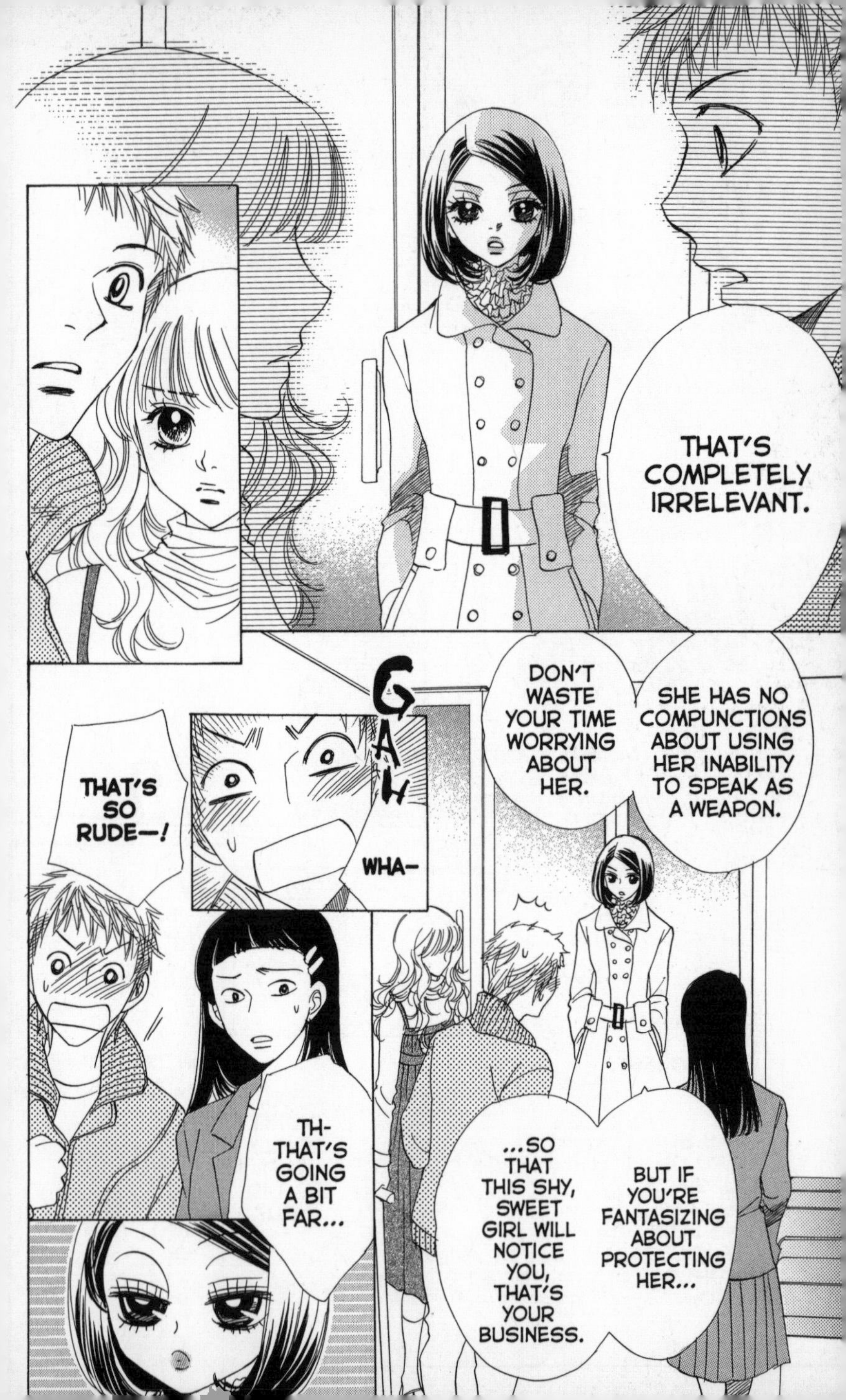
THAT'S COMPLETELY IRRELEVANT.
SHE HAS NO COMPUNCTIONS ABOUT USING HER INABILITY TO SPEAK AS A WEAPON.
DON'T WASTE YOUR TIME WORRYING ABOUT HER.
GAH
WHA-
THAT'S SO RUDE—!
BUT IF YOU'RE FANTASIZING ABOUT PROTECTING HER...
...SO THAT THIS SHY, SWEET GIRL WILL NOTICE YOU, THAT'S YOUR BUSINESS.
TH- THAT'S GOING A BIT FAR...

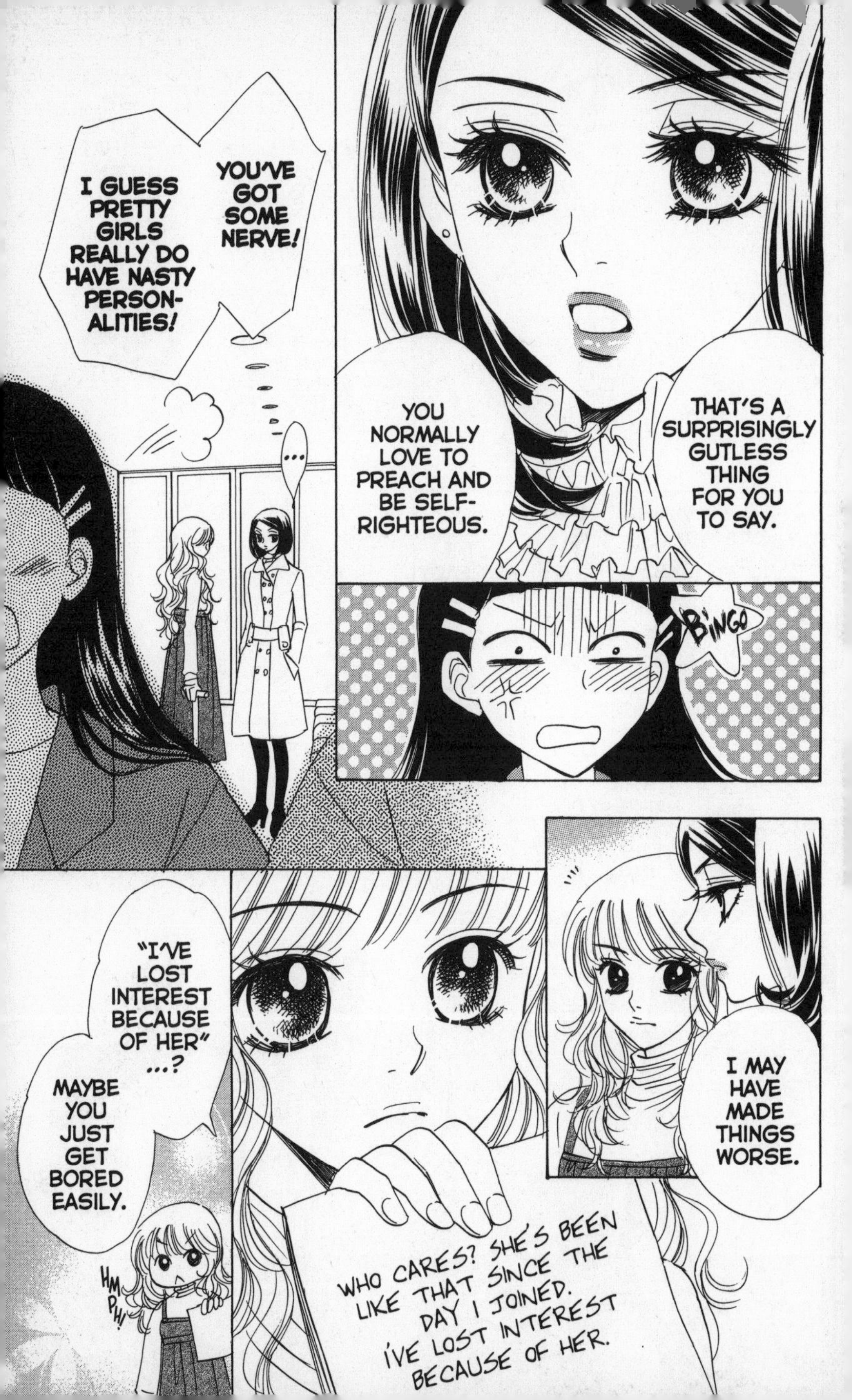
THAT'S A SURPRISINGLY GUTLESS THING FOR YOU TO SAY.
YOU NORMALLY LOVE TO PREACH AND BE SELF-RIGHTEOUS.
BINGO
YOU'VE GOT SOME NERVE!
I GUESS PRETTY GIRLS REALLY DO HAVE NASTY PERSONALITIES!
...
I MAY HAVE MADE THINGS WORSE.
WHO CARES? SHE'S BEEN LIKE THAT SINCE THE DAY I JOINED. I'VE LOST INTEREST BECAUSE OF HER.
"I'VE LOST INTEREST BECAUSE OF HER" ...?
MAYBE YOU JUST GET BORED EASILY.
HMPH!

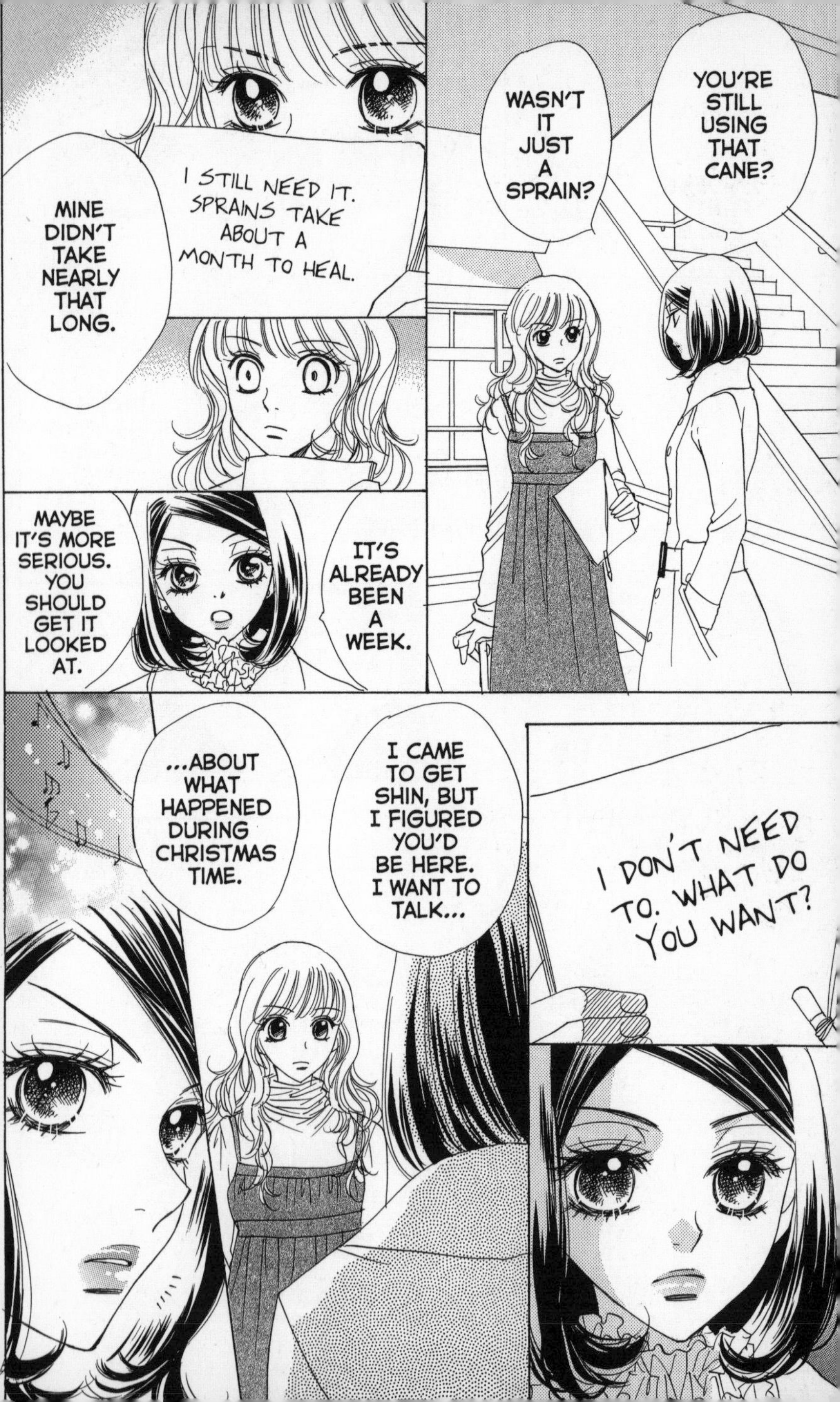
YOU'RE STILL USING THAT CANE?
WASN'T IT JUST A SPRAIN?
I STILL NEED IT. SPRAINS TAKE ABOUT A MONTH TO HEAL.
MINE DIDN'T TAKE NEARLY THAT LONG.
IT'S ALREADY BEEN A WEEK.
MAYBE IT'S MORE SERIOUS. YOU SHOULD GET IT LOOKED AT.
I DON'T NEED TO. WHAT DO YOU WANT?
I CAME TO GET SHIN, BUT I FIGURED YOU'D BE HERE. I WANT TO TALK...
...ABOUT WHAT HAPPENED DURING CHRISTMAS TIME.

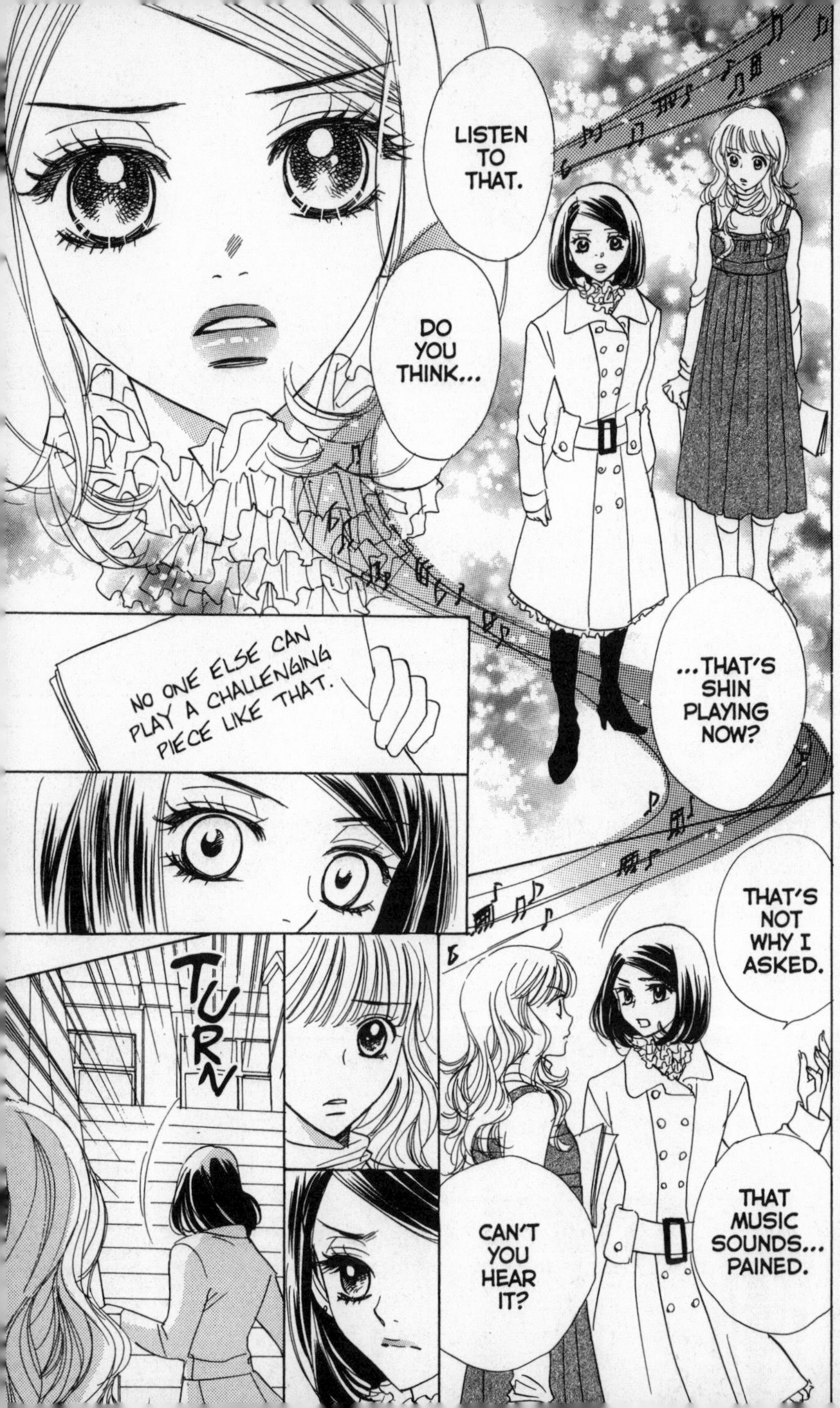
LISTEN TO THAT.
DO YOU THINK...
...THAT'S SHIN PLAYING NOW?
NO ONE ELSE CAN PLAY A CHALLENGING PIECE LIKE THAT.
THAT'S NOT WHY I ASKED.
THAT MUSIC SOUNDS... PAINED.
CAN'T YOU HEAR IT?
TURN

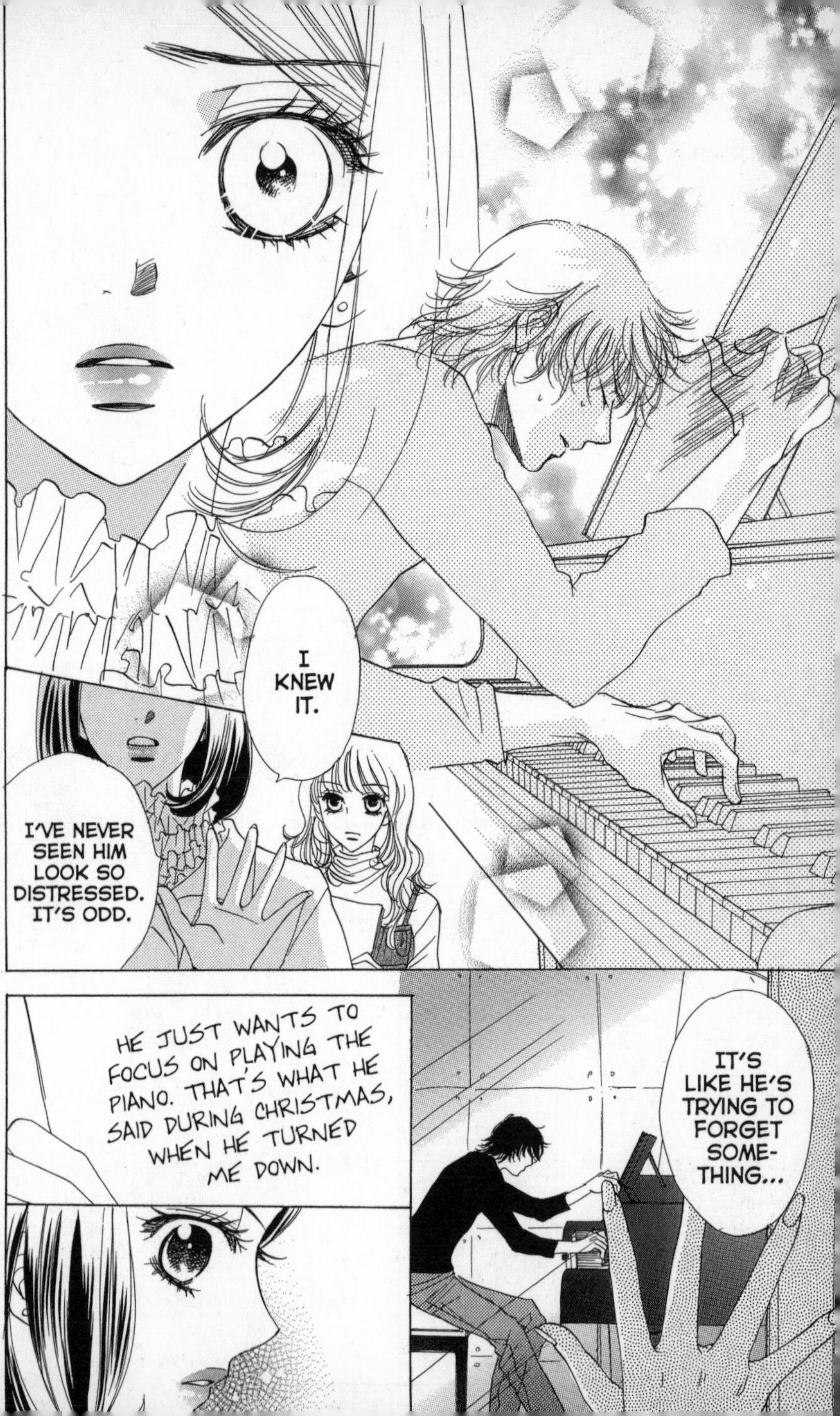
I KNEW IT.
I'VE NEVER SEEN HIM LOOK SO DISTRESSED. IT'S ODD.
IT'S LIKE HE'S TRYING TO FORGET SOME-THING...
HE JUST WANTS TO FOCUS ON PLAYING THE PIANO. THAT'S WHAT HE SAID DURING CHRISTMAS, WHEN HE TURNED ME DOWN.

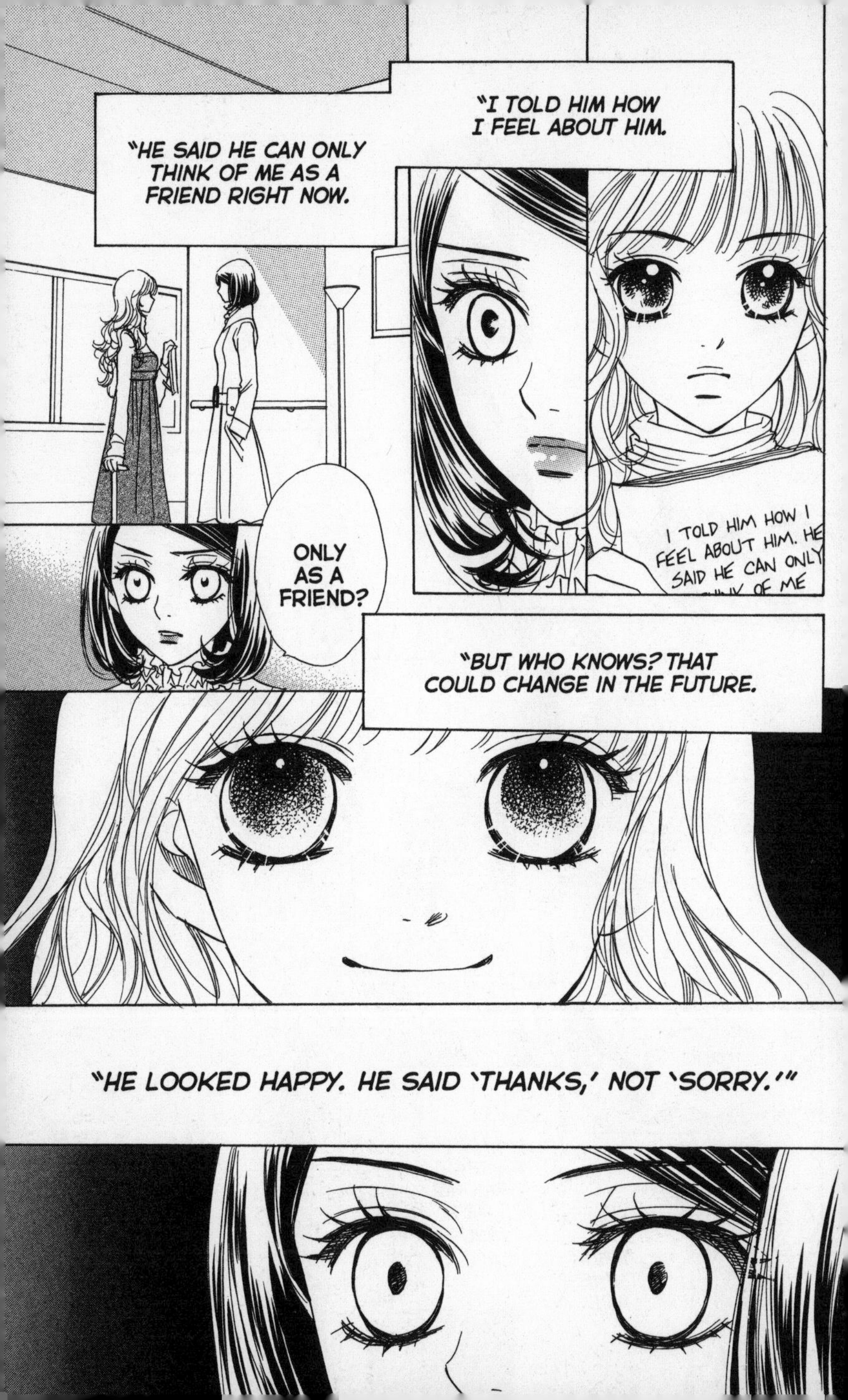
"I TOLD HIM HOW I FEEL ABOUT HIM.
I TOLD HIM HOW I FEEL ABOUT HIM. HE SAID HE CAN ONLY
"HE SAID HE CAN ONLY THINK OF ME AS A FRIEND RIGHT NOW.
ONLY AS A FRIEND?
"BUT WHO KNOWS? THAT COULD CHANGE IN THE FUTURE.
"HE LOOKED HAPPY. HE SAID 'THANKS,' NOT 'SORRY.'"

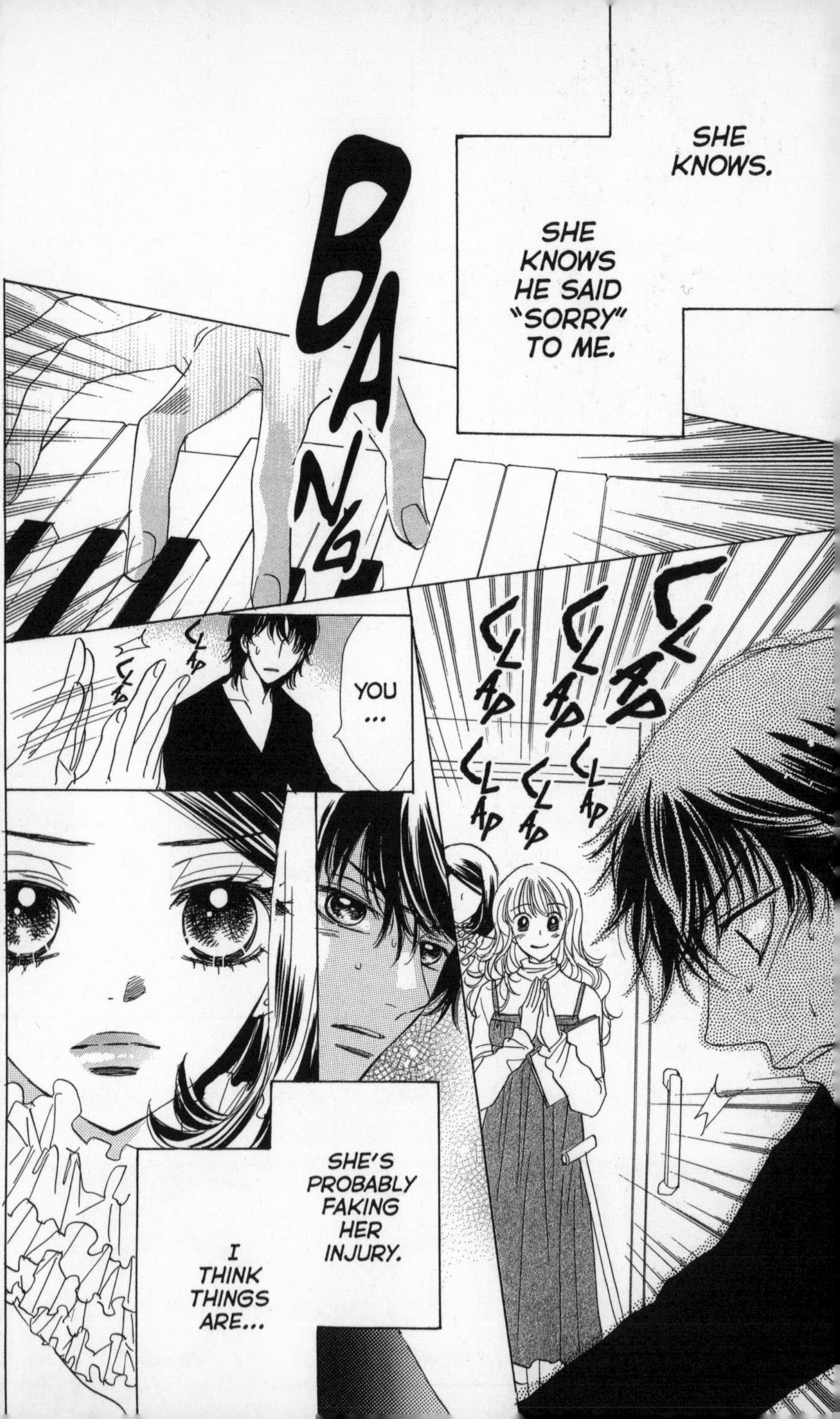

SHE KNOWS.
SHE KNOWS HE SAID "SORRY" TO ME.
BANG
CLAP
CLAP
CLAP
CLAP
CLAP
CLAP
CLAP
CLAP
YOU ...
SHE'S PROBABLY FAKING HER INJURY.
I THINK THINGS ARE...

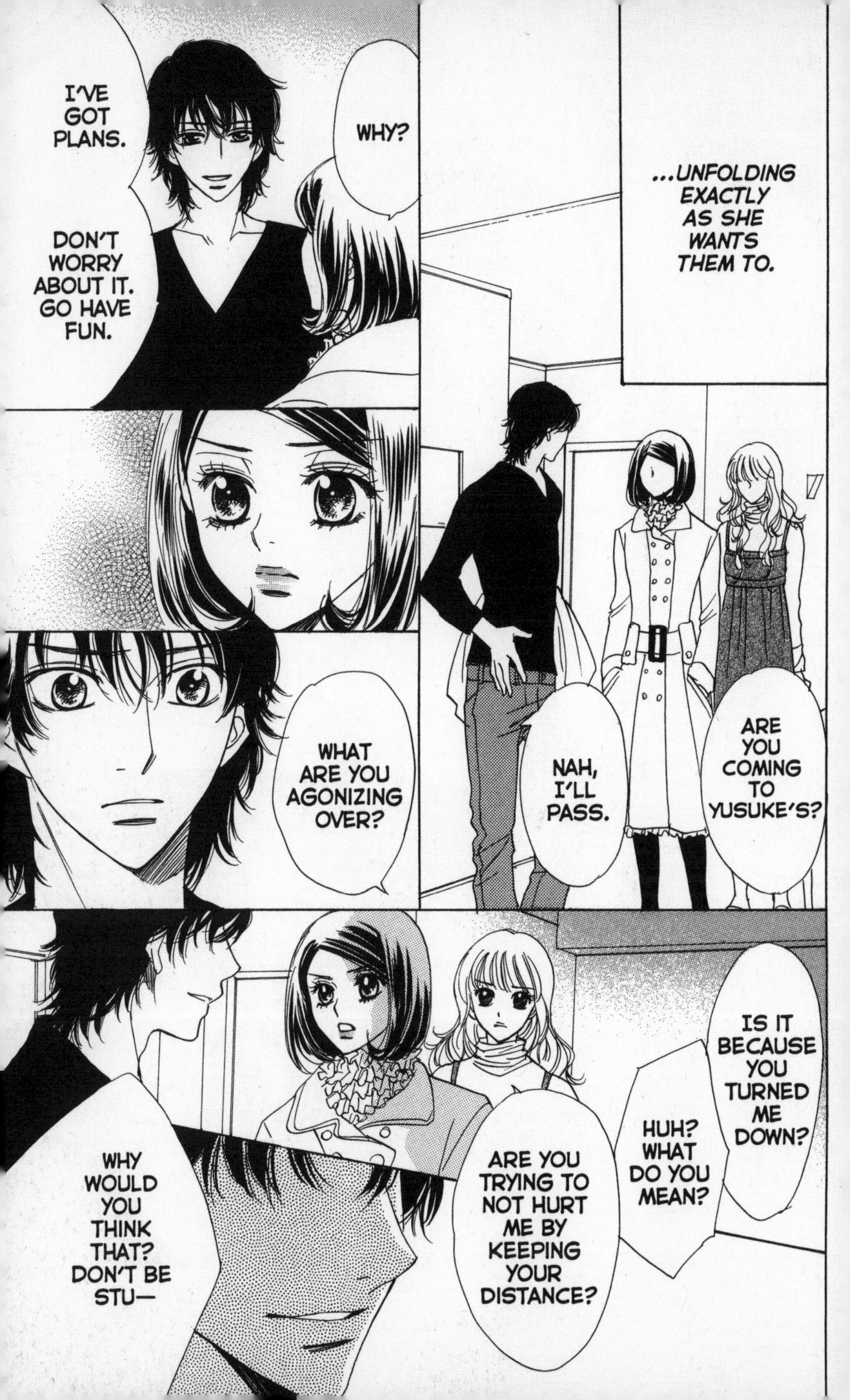
...UNFOLDING EXACTLY AS SHE WANTS THEM TO.
ARE YOU COMING TO YUSUKE'S?
NAH, I'LL PASS.
WHY?
I'VE GOT PLANS.
DON'T WORRY ABOUT IT. GO HAVE FUN.
WHAT ARE YOU AGONIZING OVER?
IS IT BECAUSE YOU TURNED ME DOWN?
HUH? WHAT DO YOU MEAN?
ARE YOU TRYING TO NOT HURT ME BY KEEPING YOUR DISTANCE?
WHY WOULD YOU THINK THAT? DON'T BE STU—

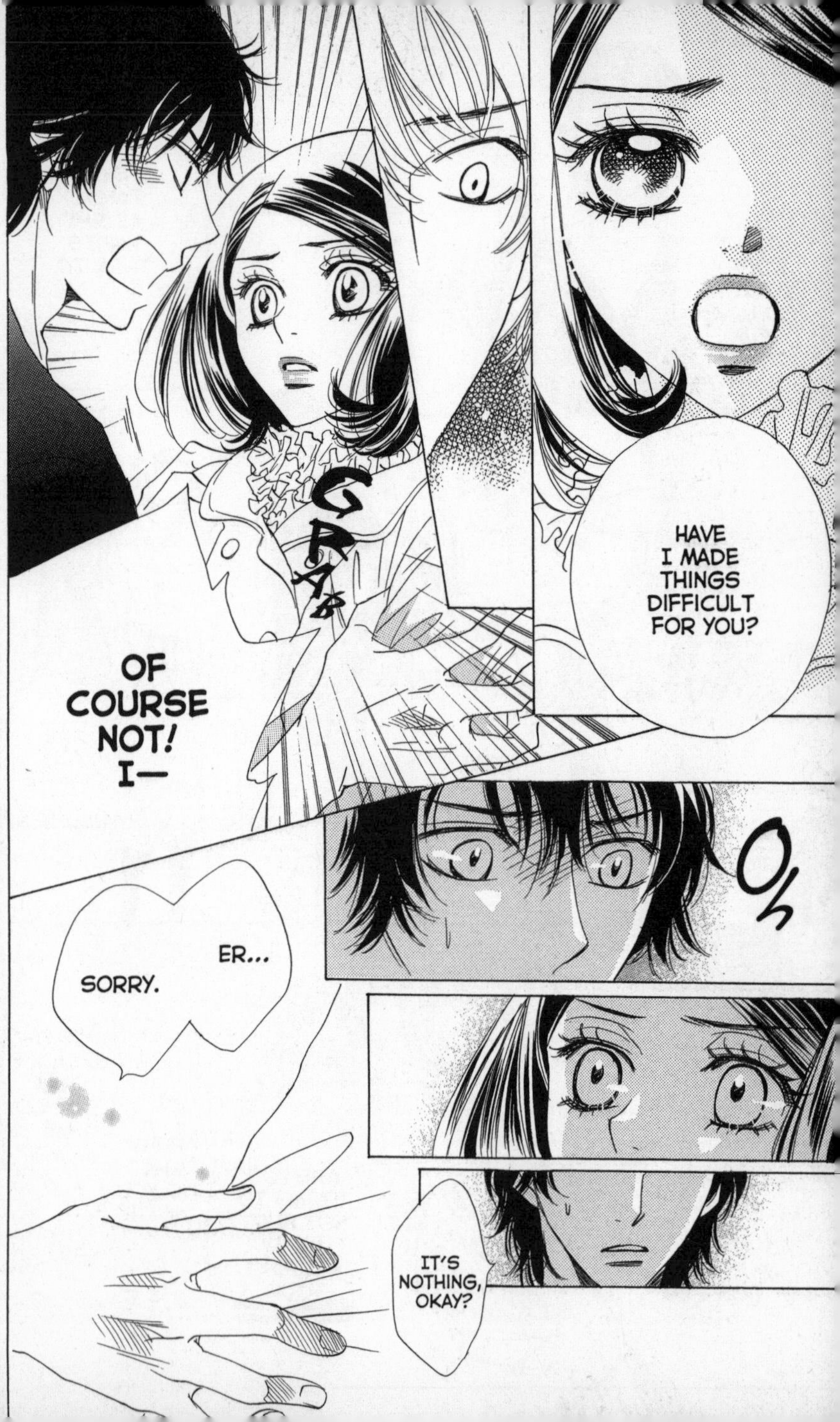
HAVE I MADE THINGS DIFFICULT FOR YOU?
GRAB
OF COURSE NOT! I—
Oh
IT'S NOTHING, OKAY?
ER...
SORRY.

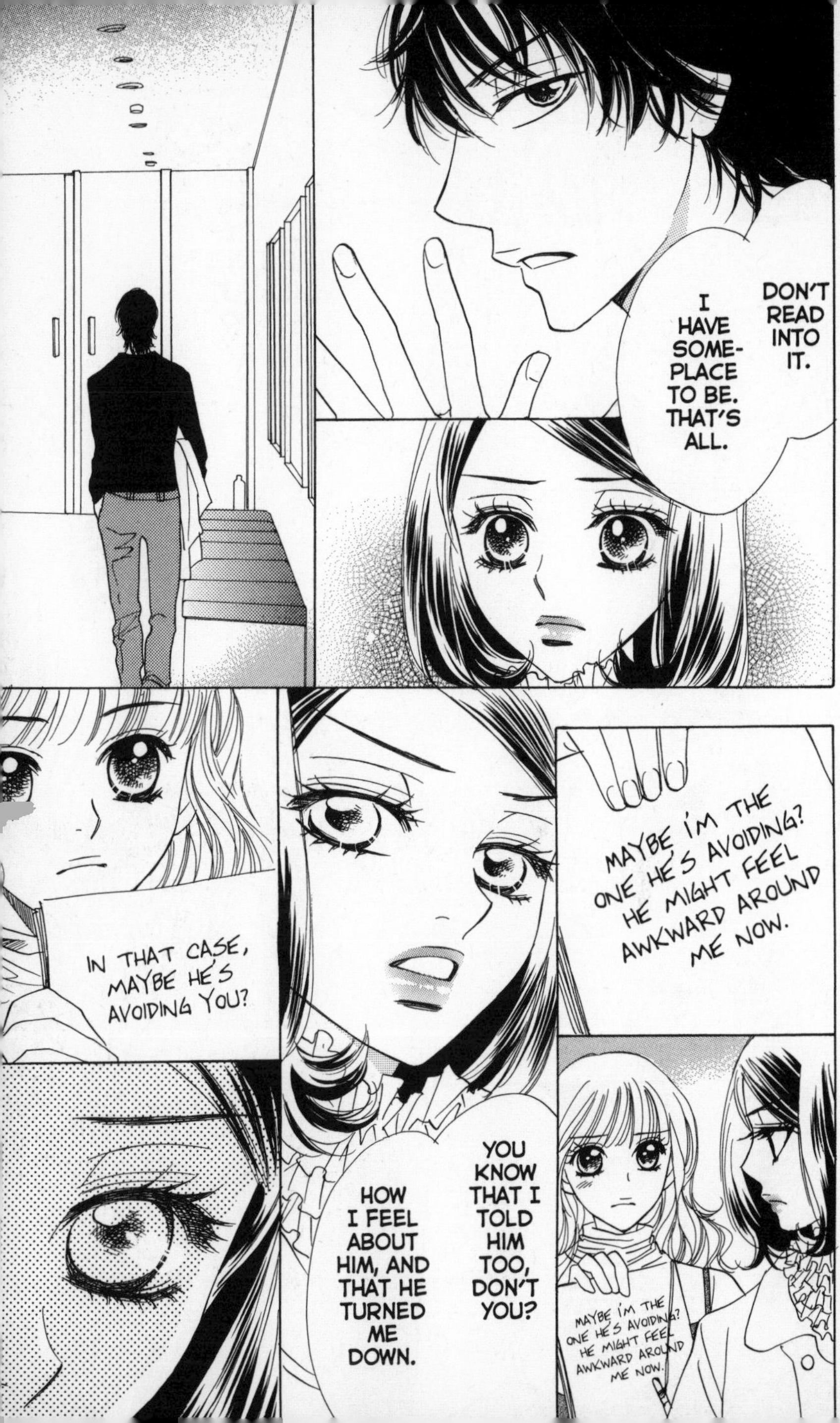
DON'T READ INTO IT.
I HAVE SOME-PLACE TO BE. THAT'S ALL.
MAYBE I'M THE ONE HE'S AVOIDING? HE MIGHT FEEL AWKWARD AROUND ME NOW.
MAYBE I'M THE ONE HE'S AVOIDING? HE MIGHT FEEL AWKWARD AROUND ME NOW.
YOU KNOW THAT I TOLD HIM TOO, DON'T YOU?
HOW I FEEL ABOUT HIM, AND THAT HE TURNED ME DOWN.
IN THAT CASE, MAYBE HE'S AVOIDING YOU?

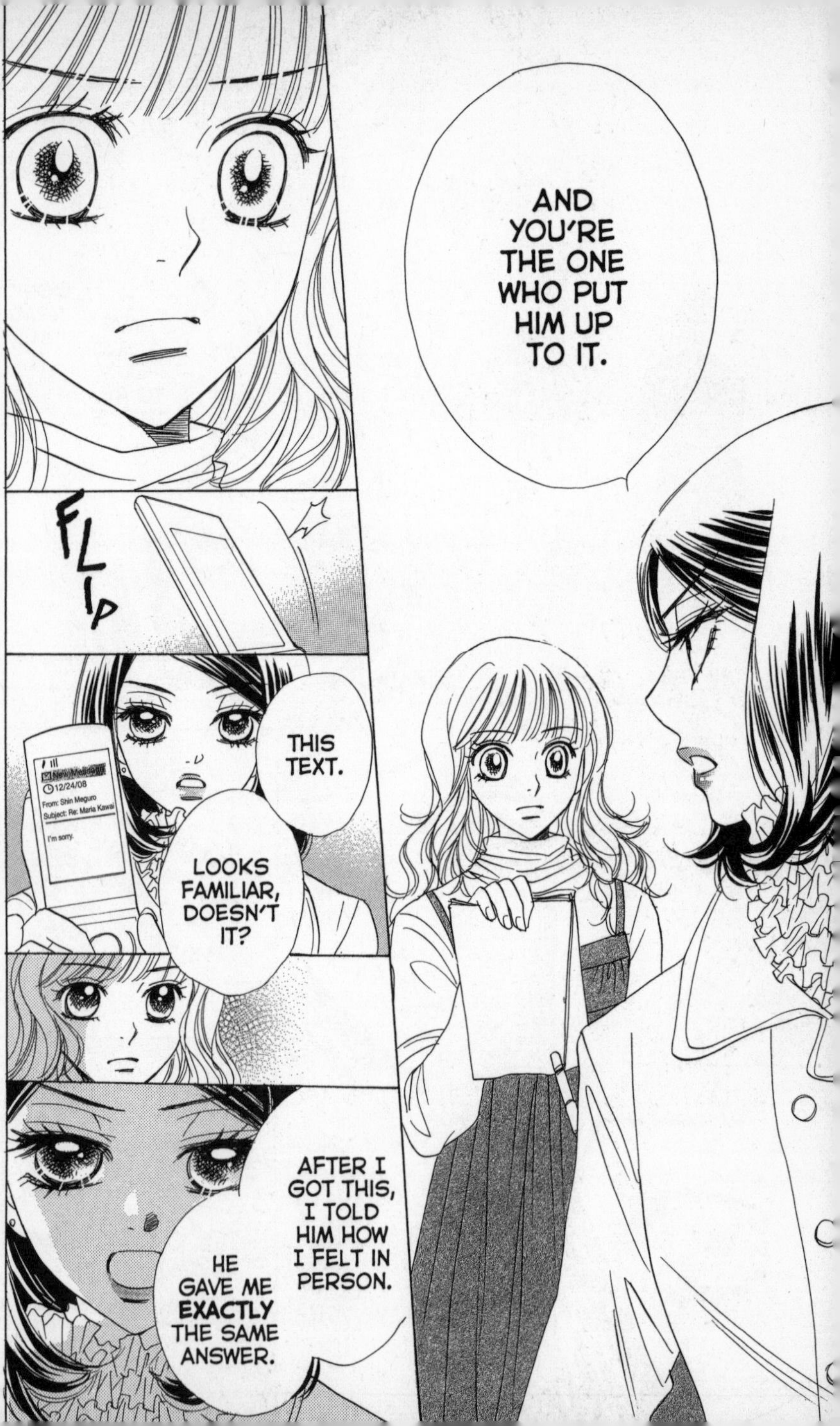
AND YOU'RE THE ONE WHO PUT HIM UP TO IT.
FLIP
12/24/08
From: Shin Meguro
Subject: Re: Maria Kawai
I'm sorry.
THIS TEXT.
LOOKS FAMILIAR, DOESN'T IT?
AFTER I GOT THIS, I TOLD HIM HOW I FELT IN PERSON.
HE GAVE ME **EXACTLY** THE SAME ANSWER.

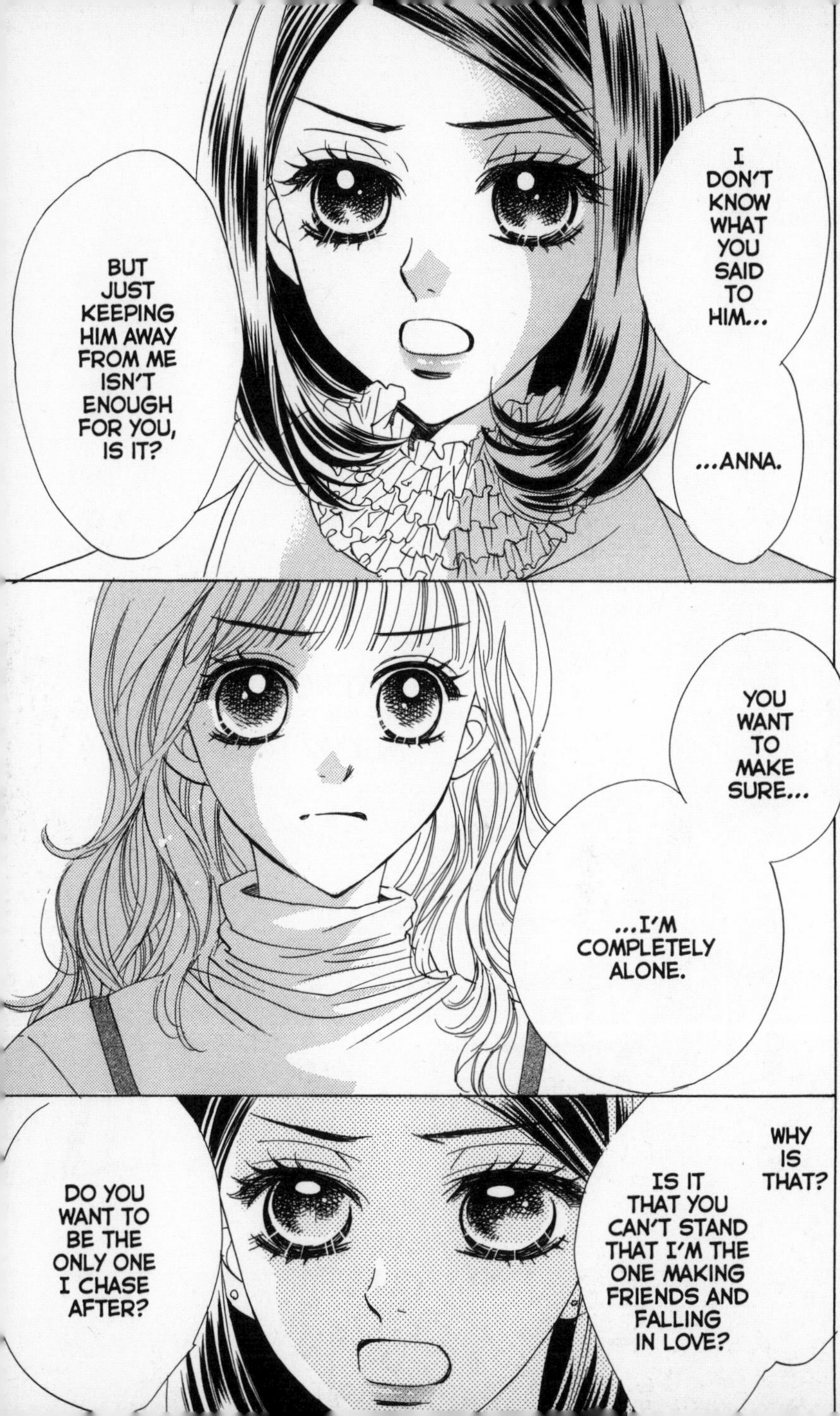
I DON'T KNOW WHAT YOU SAID TO HIM...
...ANNA.
BUT JUST KEEPING HIM AWAY FROM ME ISN'T ENOUGH FOR YOU, IS IT?
YOU WANT TO MAKE SURE...
...I'M COMPLETELY ALONE.
WHY IS THAT?
IS IT THAT YOU CAN'T STAND THAT I'M THE ONE MAKING FRIENDS AND FALLING IN LOVE?
DO YOU WANT TO BE THE ONLY ONE I CHASE AFTER?

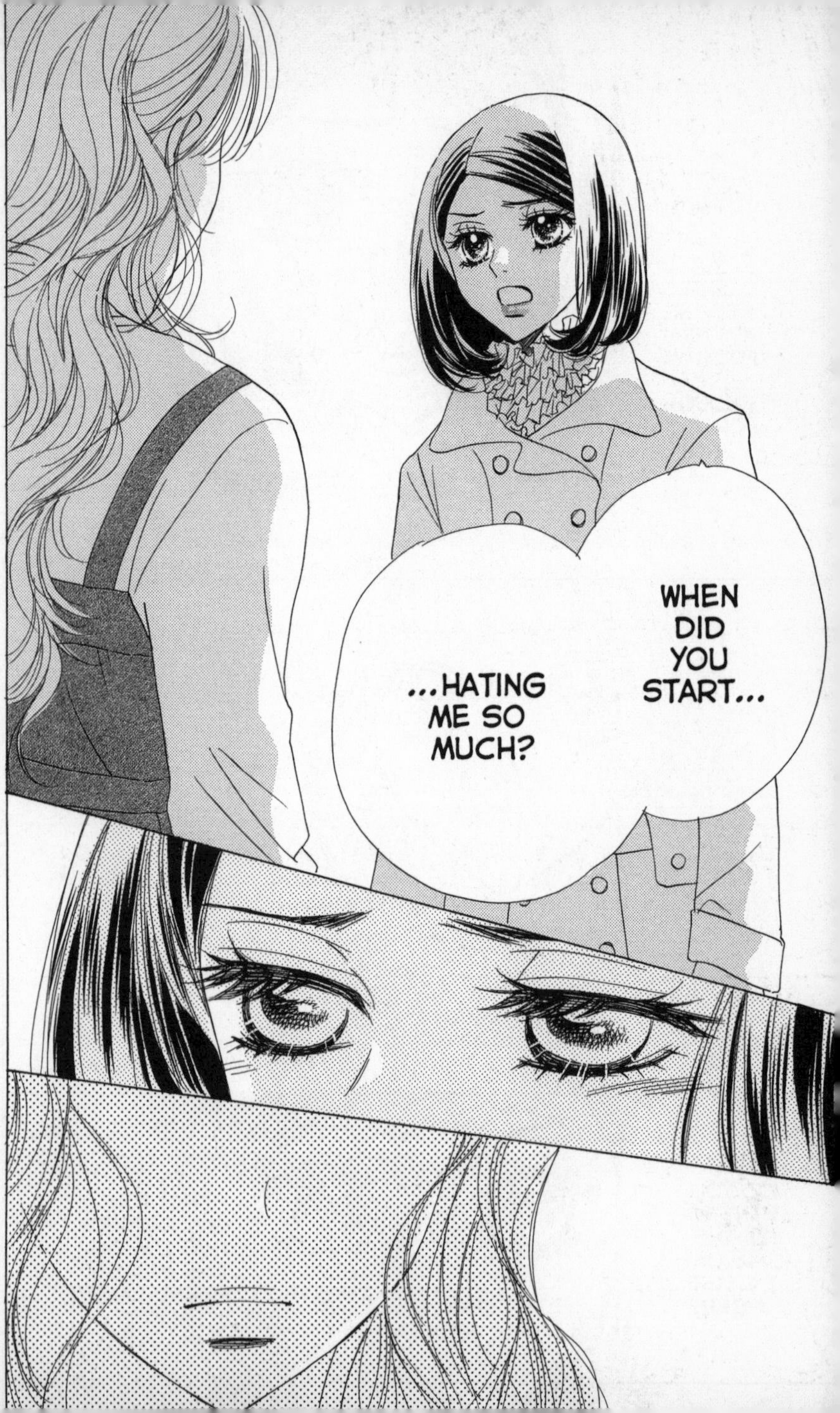
WHEN DID YOU START...
...HATING ME SO MUCH?

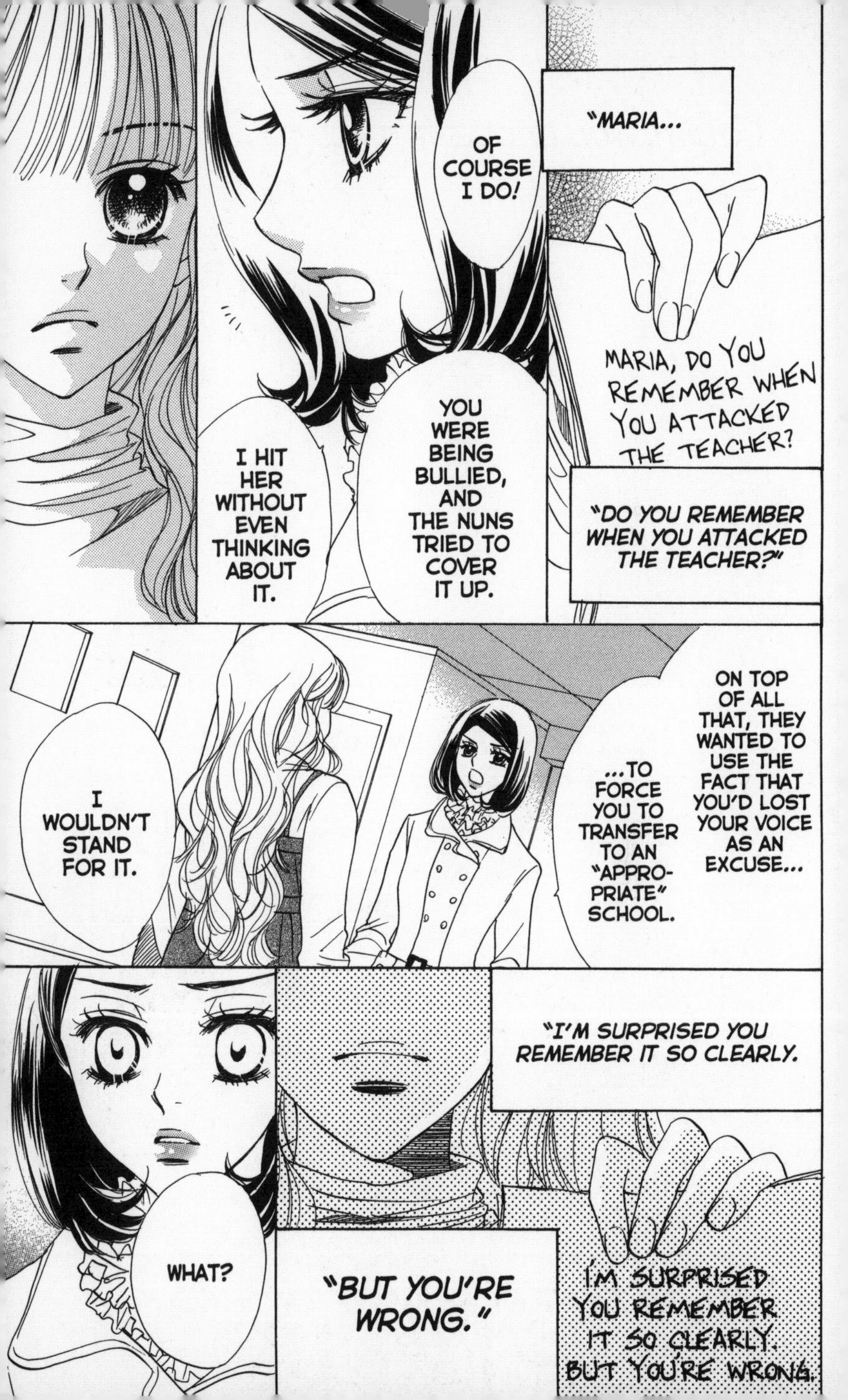
"MARIA...
MARIA, DO YOU REMEMBER WHEN YOU ATTACKED THE TEACHER?
"DO YOU REMEMBER WHEN YOU ATTACKED THE TEACHER?"
OF COURSE I DO!
YOU WERE BEING BULLIED, AND THE NUNS TRIED TO COVER IT UP.
I HIT HER WITHOUT EVEN THINKING ABOUT IT.
ON TOP OF ALL THAT, THEY WANTED TO USE THE FACT THAT YOU'D LOST YOUR VOICE AS AN EXCUSE...
...TO FORCE YOU TO TRANSFER TO AN "APPROPRIATE" SCHOOL.
I WOULDN'T STAND FOR IT.
"I'M SURPRISED YOU REMEMBER IT SO CLEARLY.
I'M SURPRISED YOU REMEMBER IT SO CLEARLY. BUT YOU'RE WRONG.
"BUT YOU'RE WRONG."
WHAT?

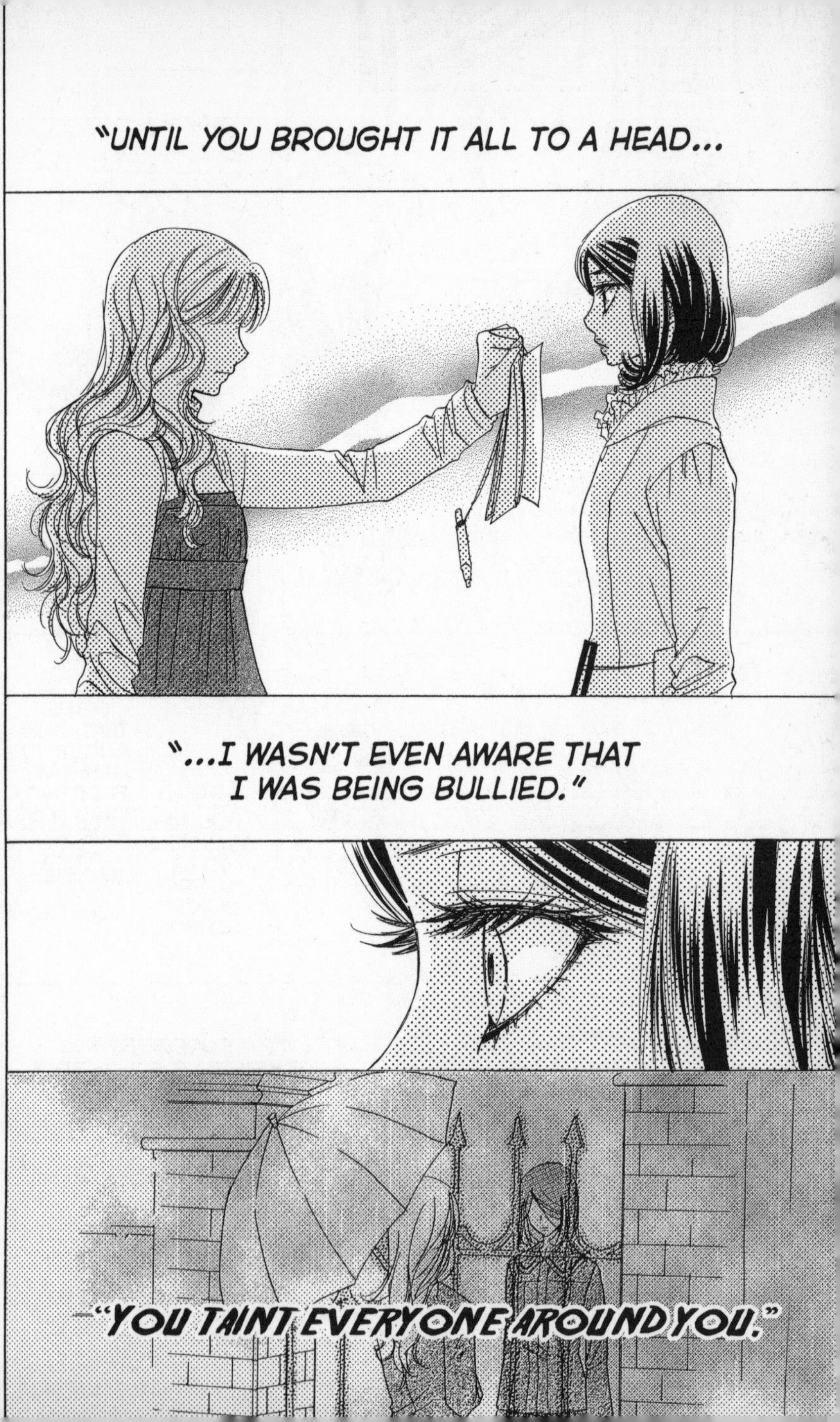
"UNTIL YOU BROUGHT IT ALL TO A HEAD...
"...I WASN'T EVEN AWARE THAT I WAS BEING BULLIED."
"YOU TAINT EVERYONE AROUND YOU."

A Devil and
Her Love Song

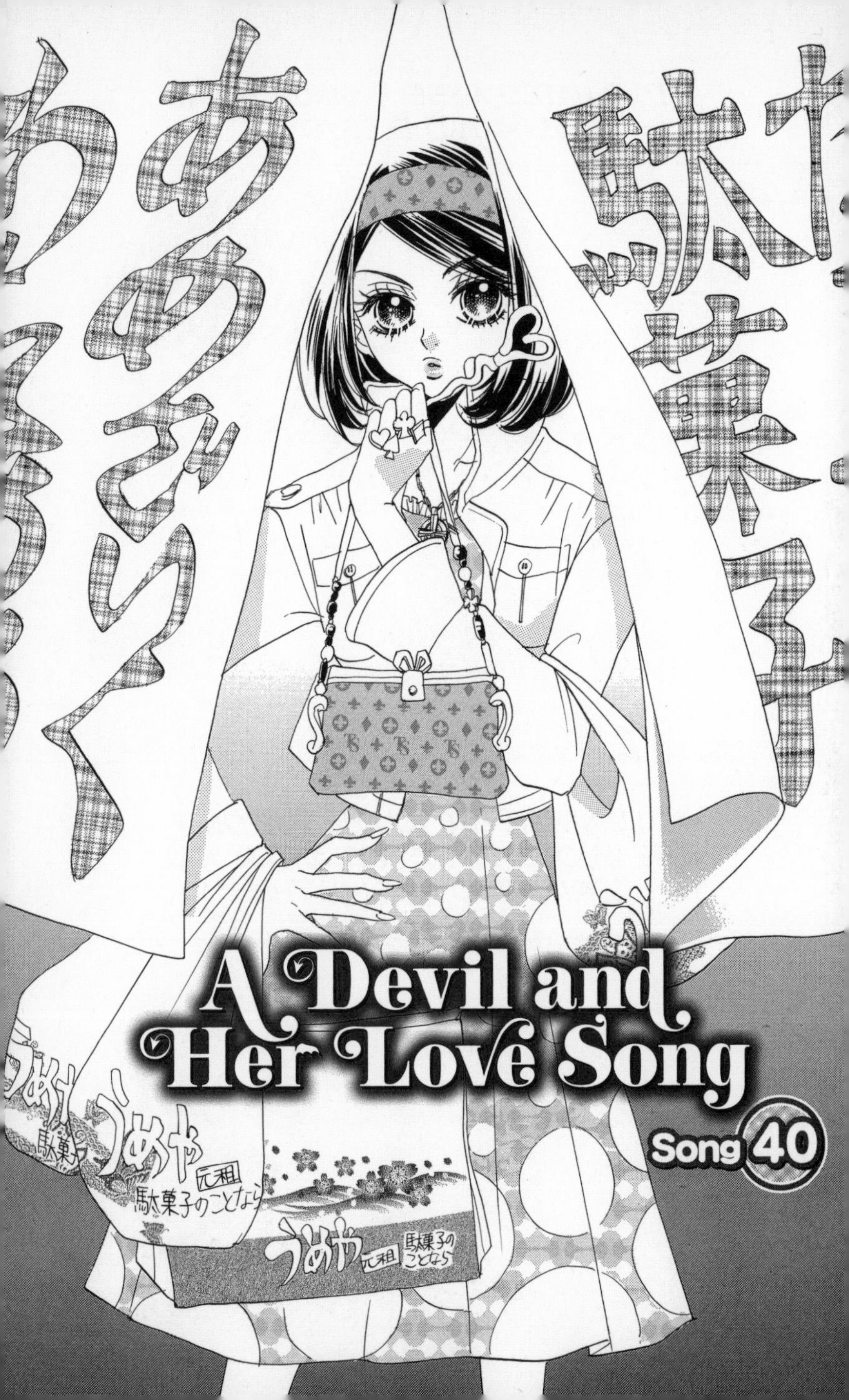
A Devil and Her Love Song
Song 40
駄菓子
うめや
元祖
駄菓子のことなら
うめや
元祖
駄菓子のことなら

"I'VE HATED MYSELF SINCE THEN.
I'VE HATED EVERYONE.

I'VE HATED MYSELF SINCE THEN. I'VE HATED EVERYONE.
I'LL NEVER LET YOU BE THE ONLY ONE WHO'S HAPPY. NOT AFTER YOU CORRUPTED ME LIKE THIS.

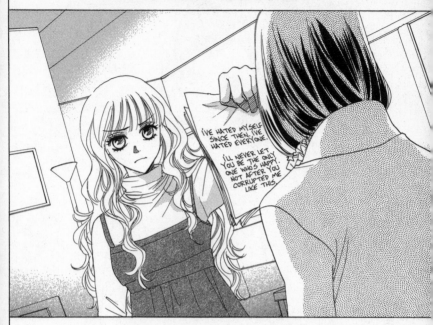

"I'LL NEVER LET YOU BE THE ONLY ONE WHO'S HAPPY. NOT AFTER YOU CORRUPTED ME LIKE THIS."

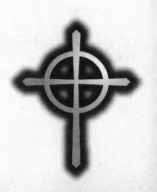

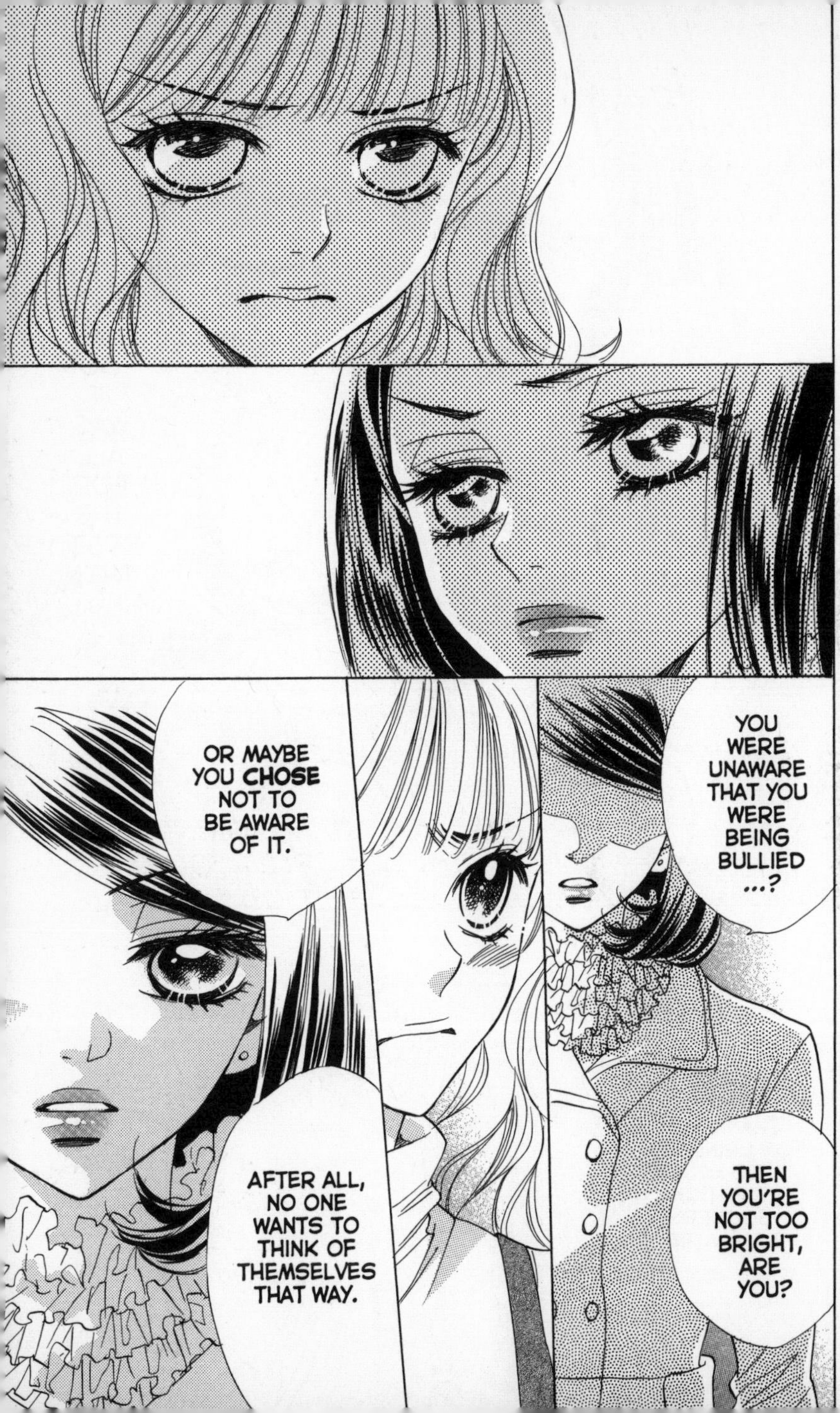
YOU WERE UNAWARE THAT YOU WERE BEING BULLIED ...?
THEN YOU'RE NOT TOO BRIGHT, ARE YOU?
OR MAYBE YOU **CHOSE** NOT TO BE AWARE OF IT.
AFTER ALL, NO ONE WANTS TO THINK OF THEMSELVES THAT WAY.

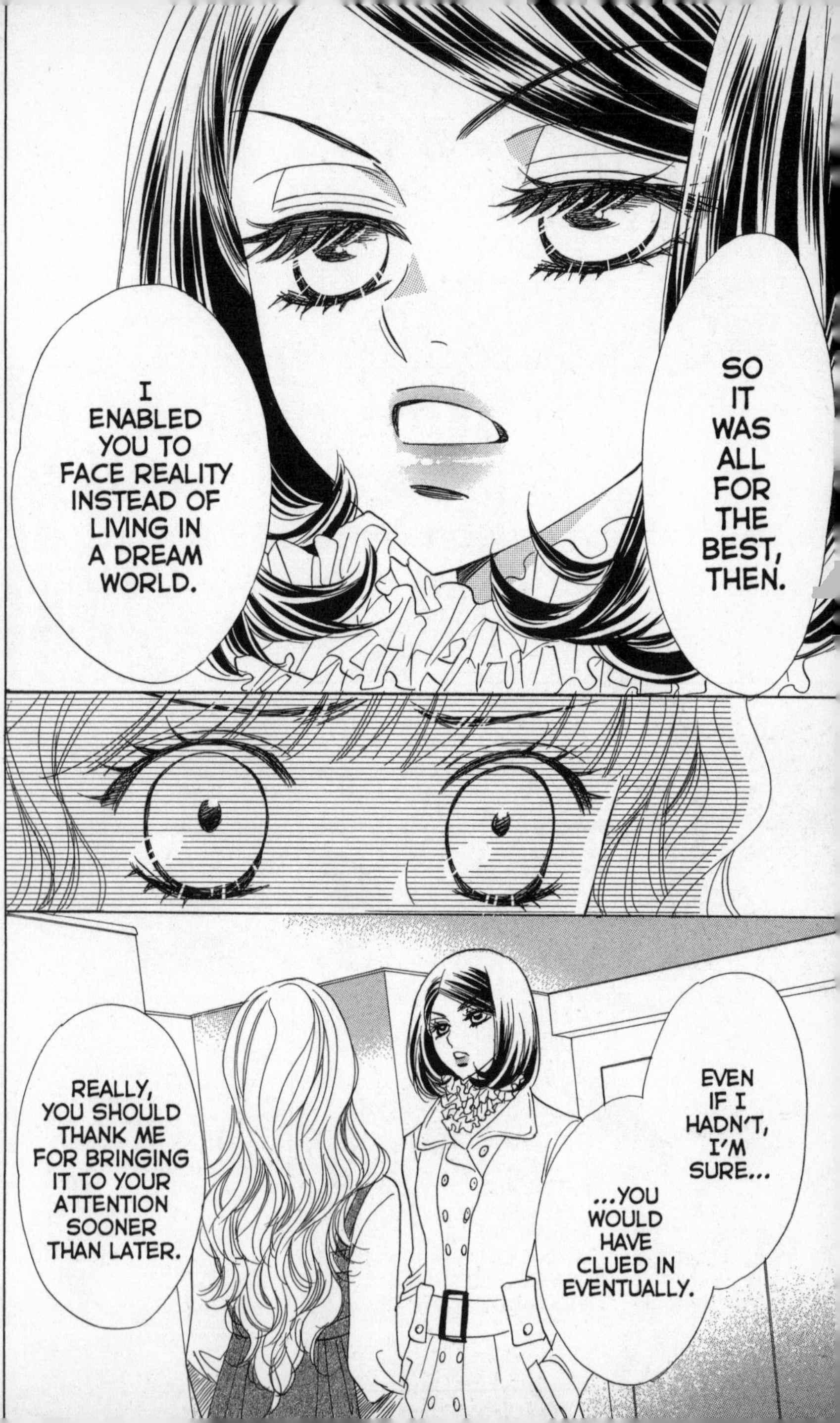
SO IT WAS ALL FOR THE BEST, THEN.
I ENABLED YOU TO FACE REALITY INSTEAD OF LIVING IN A DREAM WORLD.
EVEN IF I HADN'T, I'M SURE...
...YOU WOULD HAVE CLUED IN EVENTUALLY.
REALLY, YOU SHOULD THANK ME FOR BRINGING IT TO YOUR ATTENTION SOONER THAN LATER.

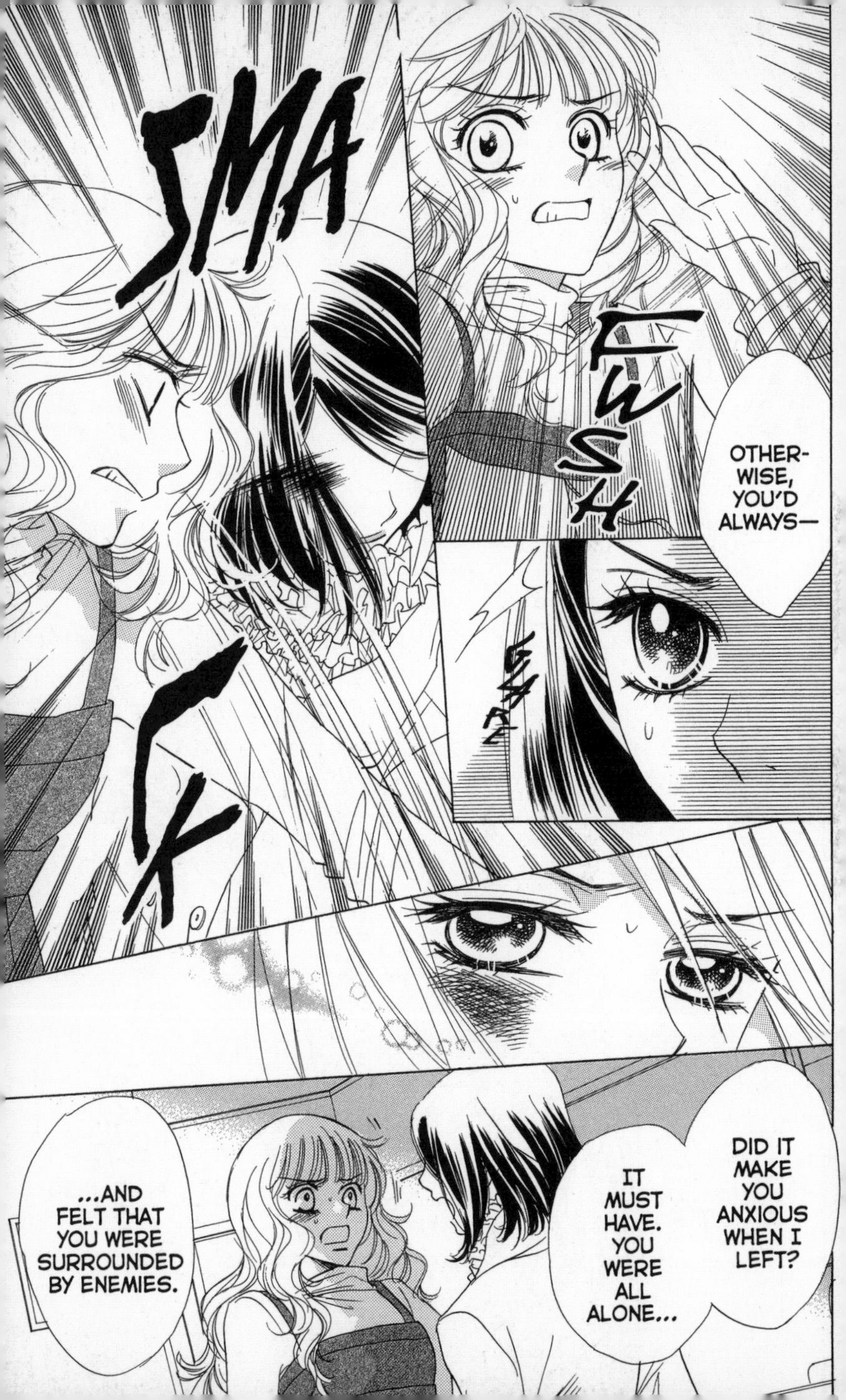
OTHER-WISE, YOU'D ALWAYS—
FWSH
SMACK
DID IT MAKE YOU ANXIOUS WHEN I LEFT?
IT MUST HAVE. YOU WERE ALL ALONE...
...AND FELT THAT YOU WERE SURROUNDED BY ENEMIES.

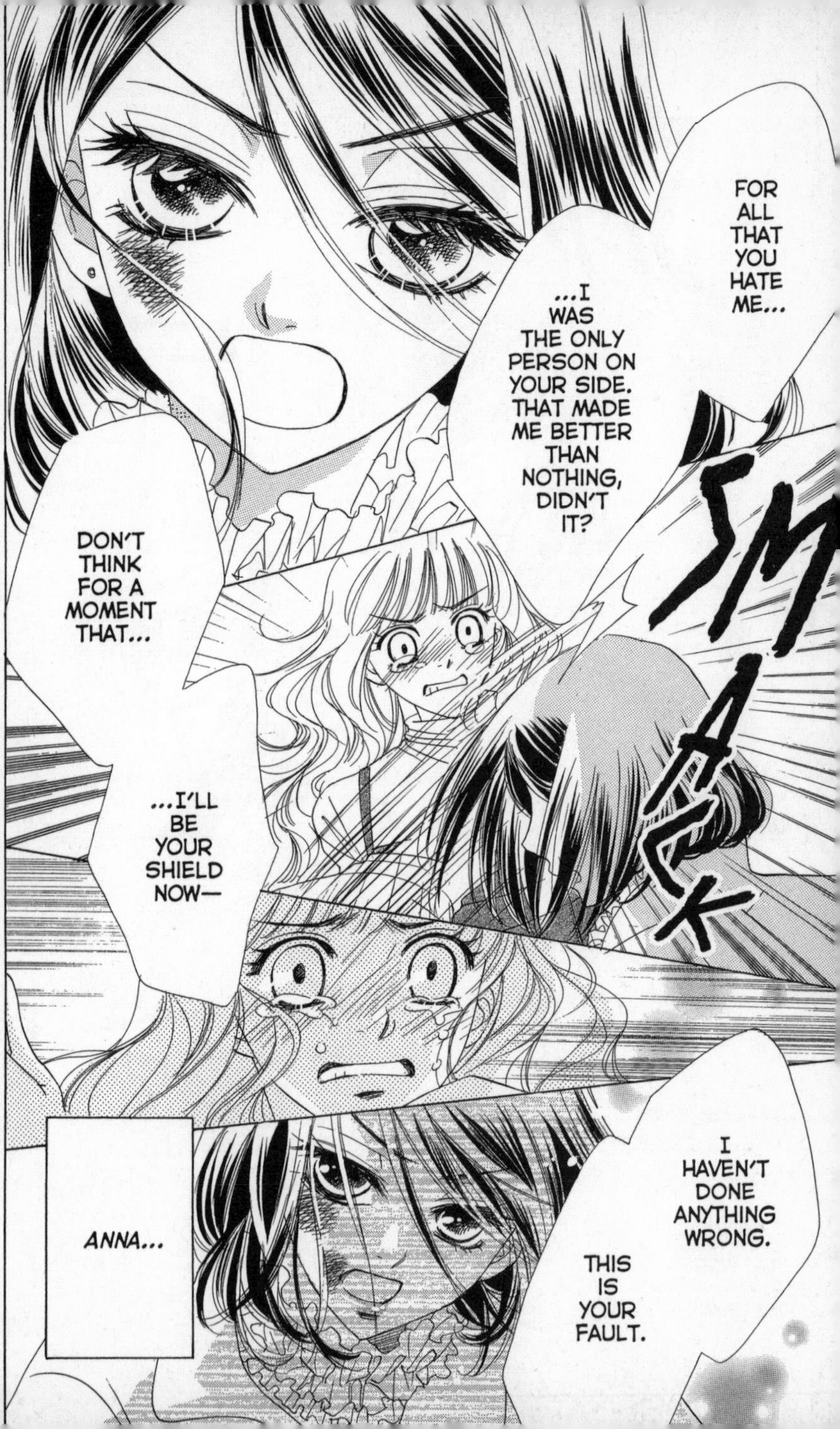
FOR ALL THAT YOU HATE ME...
...I WAS THE ONLY PERSON ON YOUR SIDE. THAT MADE ME BETTER THAN NOTHING, DIDN'T IT?
DON'T THINK FOR A MOMENT THAT...
SMACK
...I'LL BE YOUR SHIELD NOW—
I HAVEN'T DONE ANYTHING WRONG.
THIS IS YOUR FAULT.
ANNA...

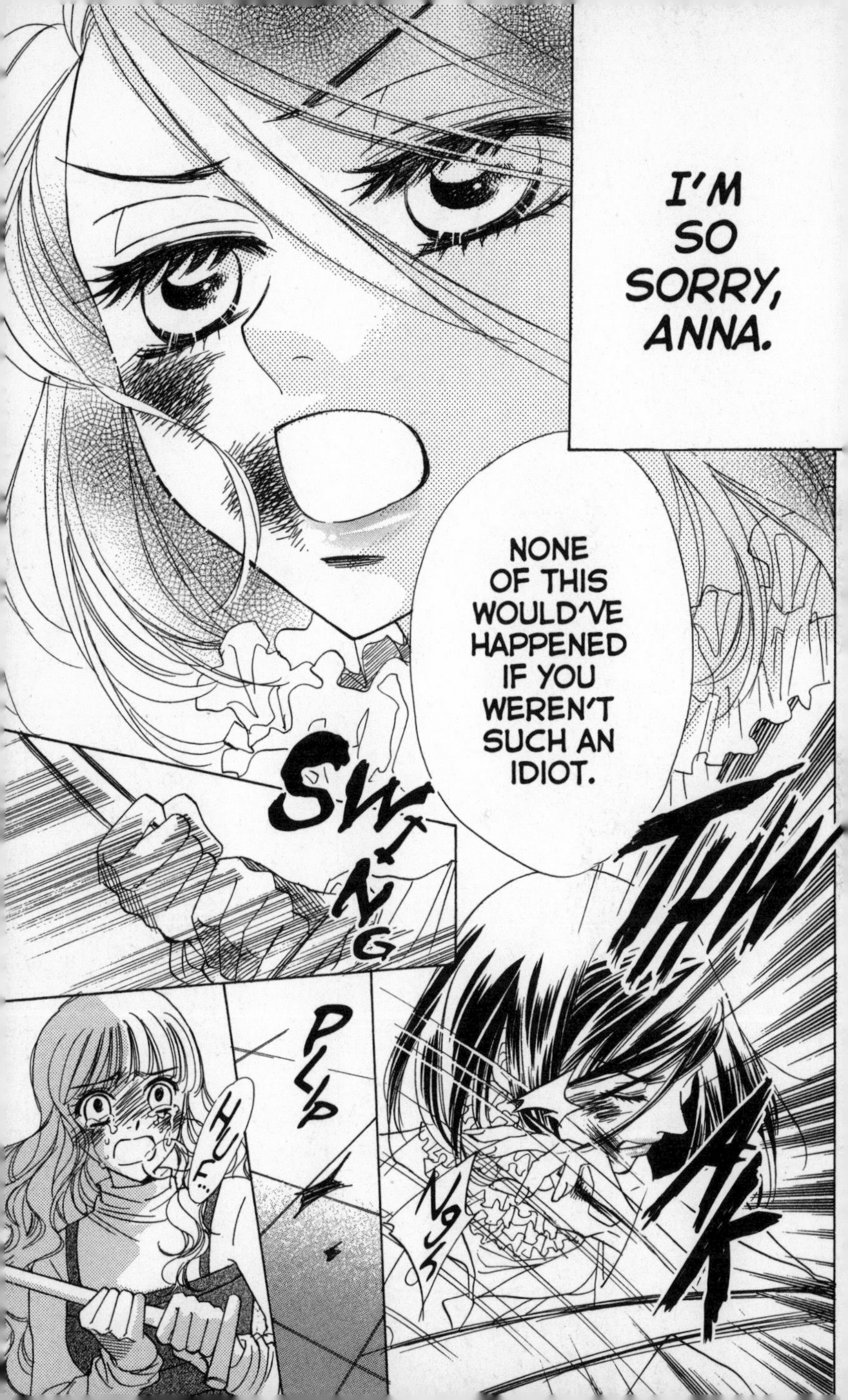
I'M SO SORRY, ANNA.
NONE OF THIS WOULD'VE HAPPENED IF YOU WEREN'T SUCH AN IDIOT.
SWING
THWAK
Ngh
PLIP
HUH...

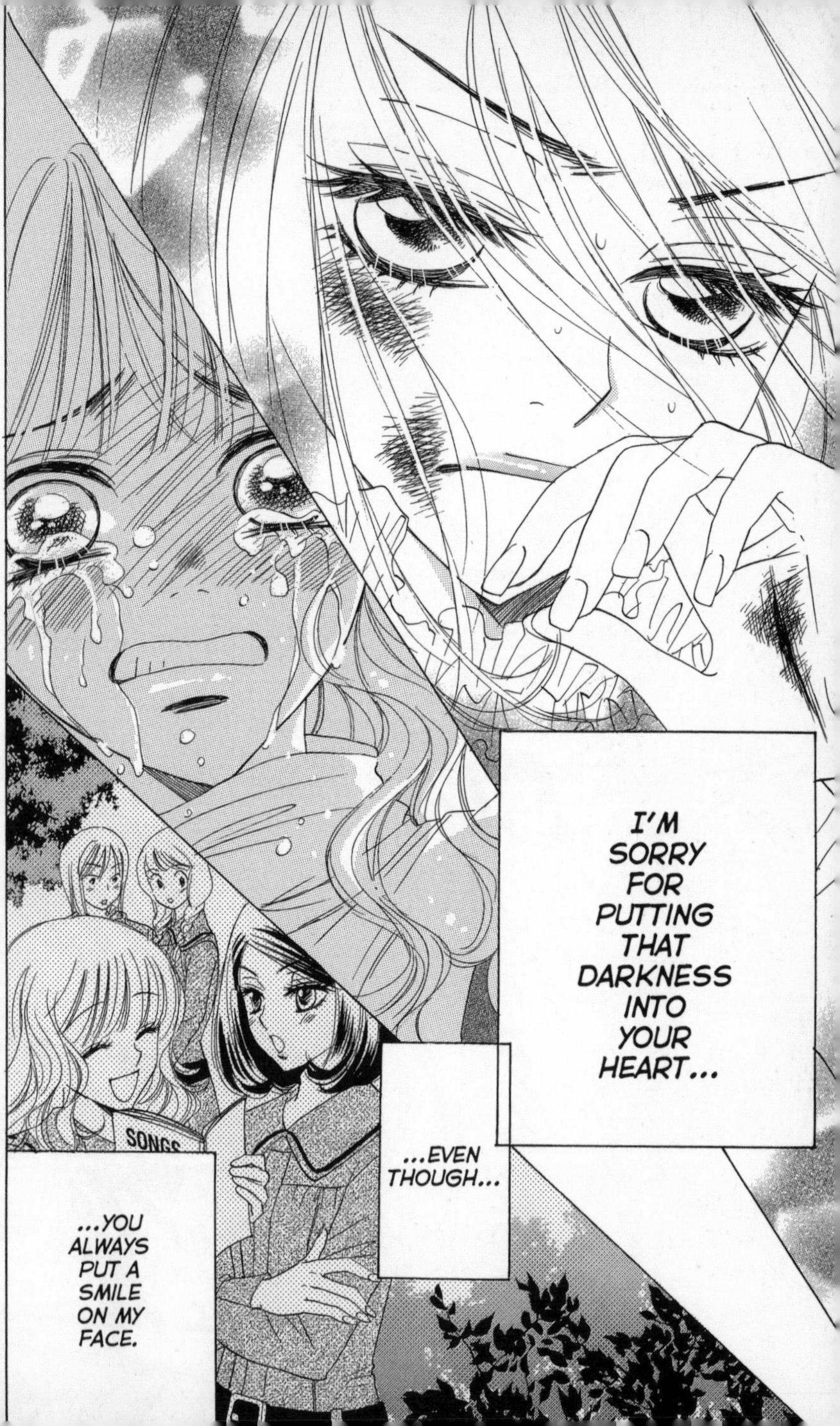
I'M SORRY FOR PUTTING THAT DARKNESS INTO YOUR HEART...
...EVEN THOUGH...
SONGS
...YOU ALWAYS PUT A SMILE ON MY FACE.

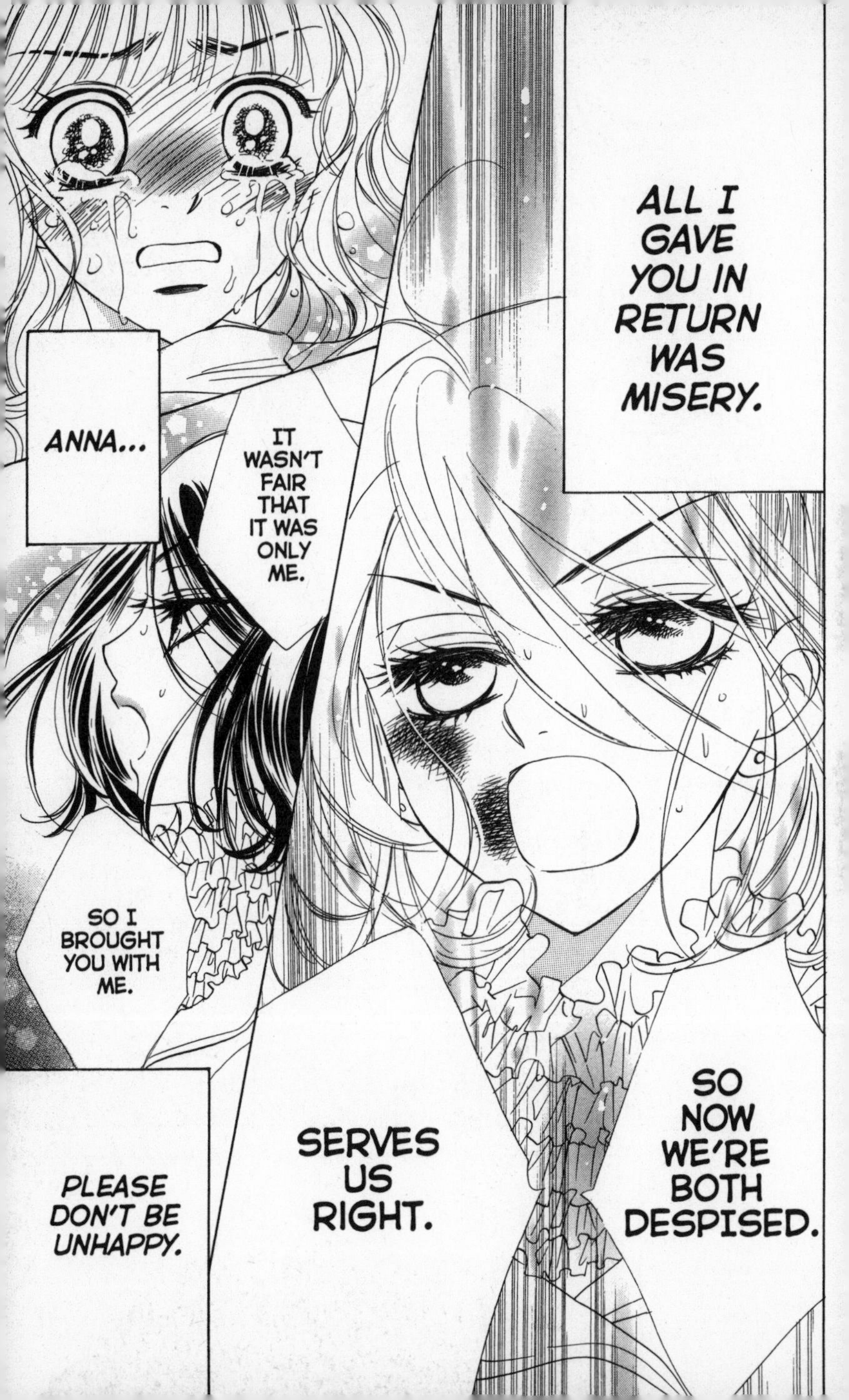

ALL I GAVE YOU IN RETURN WAS MISERY.
ANNA...
IT WASN'T FAIR THAT IT WAS ONLY ME.
SO I BROUGHT YOU WITH ME.
SO NOW WE'RE BOTH DESPISED.
SERVES US RIGHT.
PLEASE DON'T BE UNHAPPY.

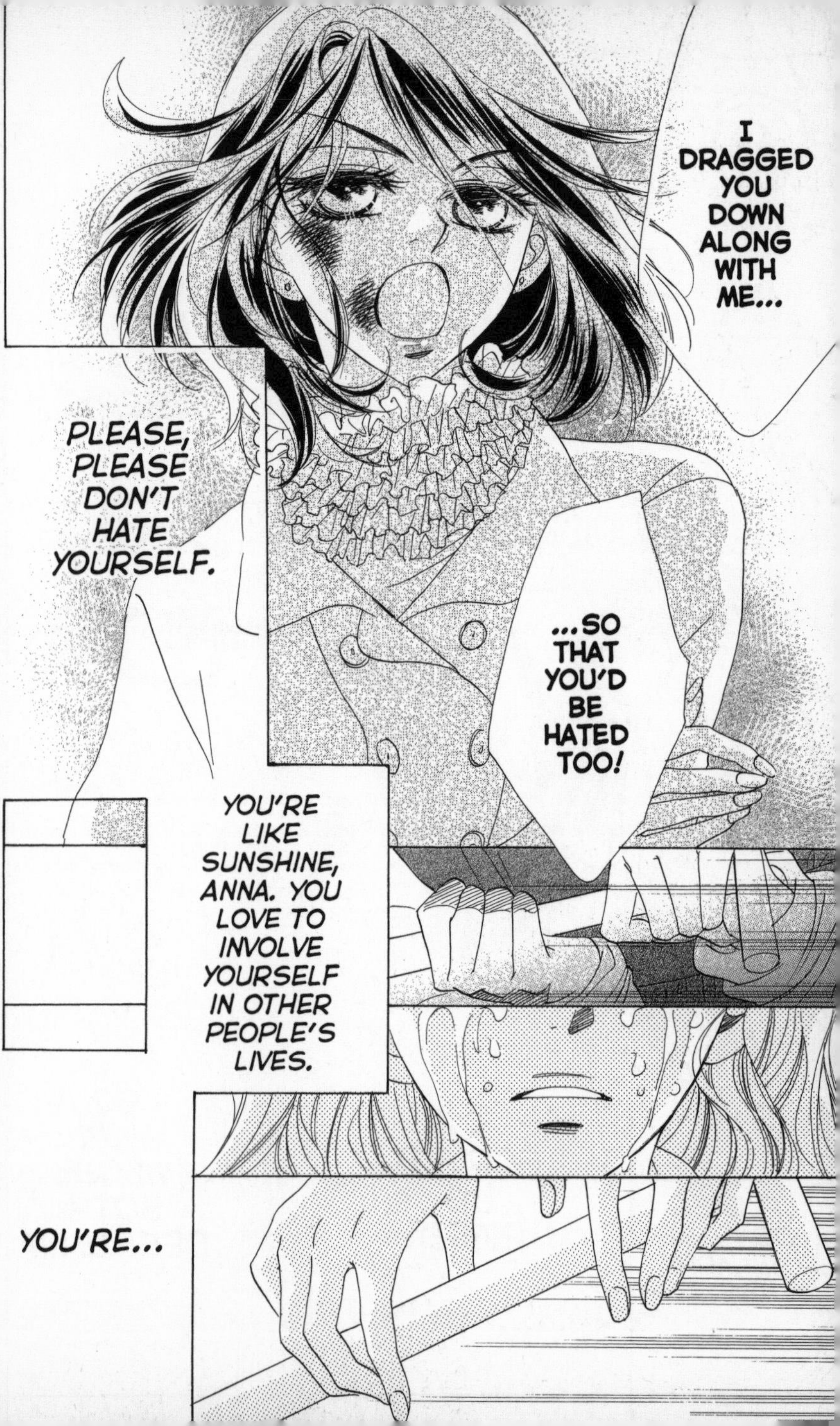
I DRAGGED YOU DOWN ALONG WITH ME...
PLEASE, PLEASE DON'T HATE YOURSELF.
...SO THAT YOU'D BE HATED TOO!
YOU'RE LIKE SUNSHINE, ANNA. YOU LOVE TO INVOLVE YOURSELF IN OTHER PEOPLE'S LIVES.
YOU'RE...

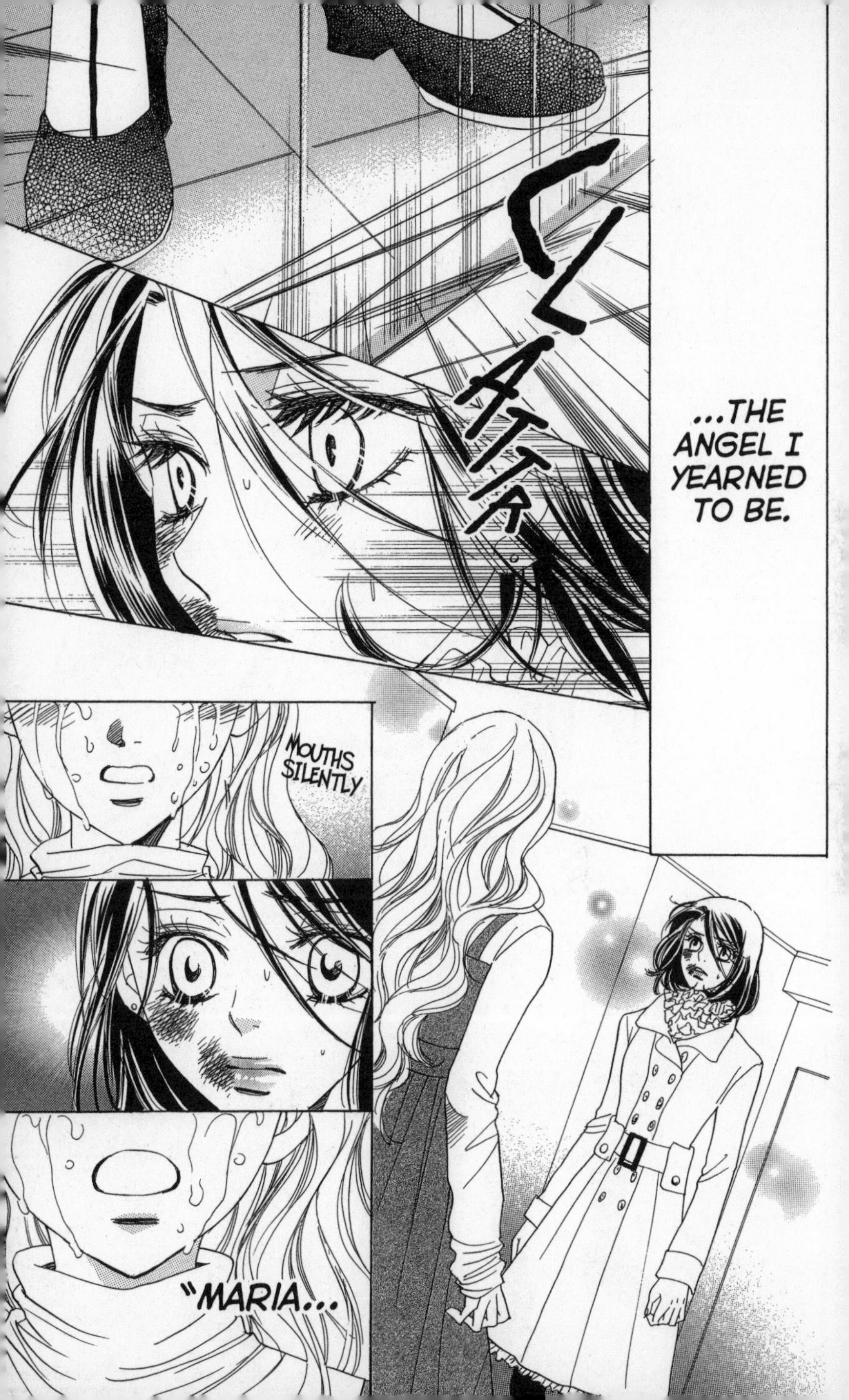
...THE ANGEL I YEARNED TO BE.
CLATTA
MOUTHS SILENTLY
"MARIA...

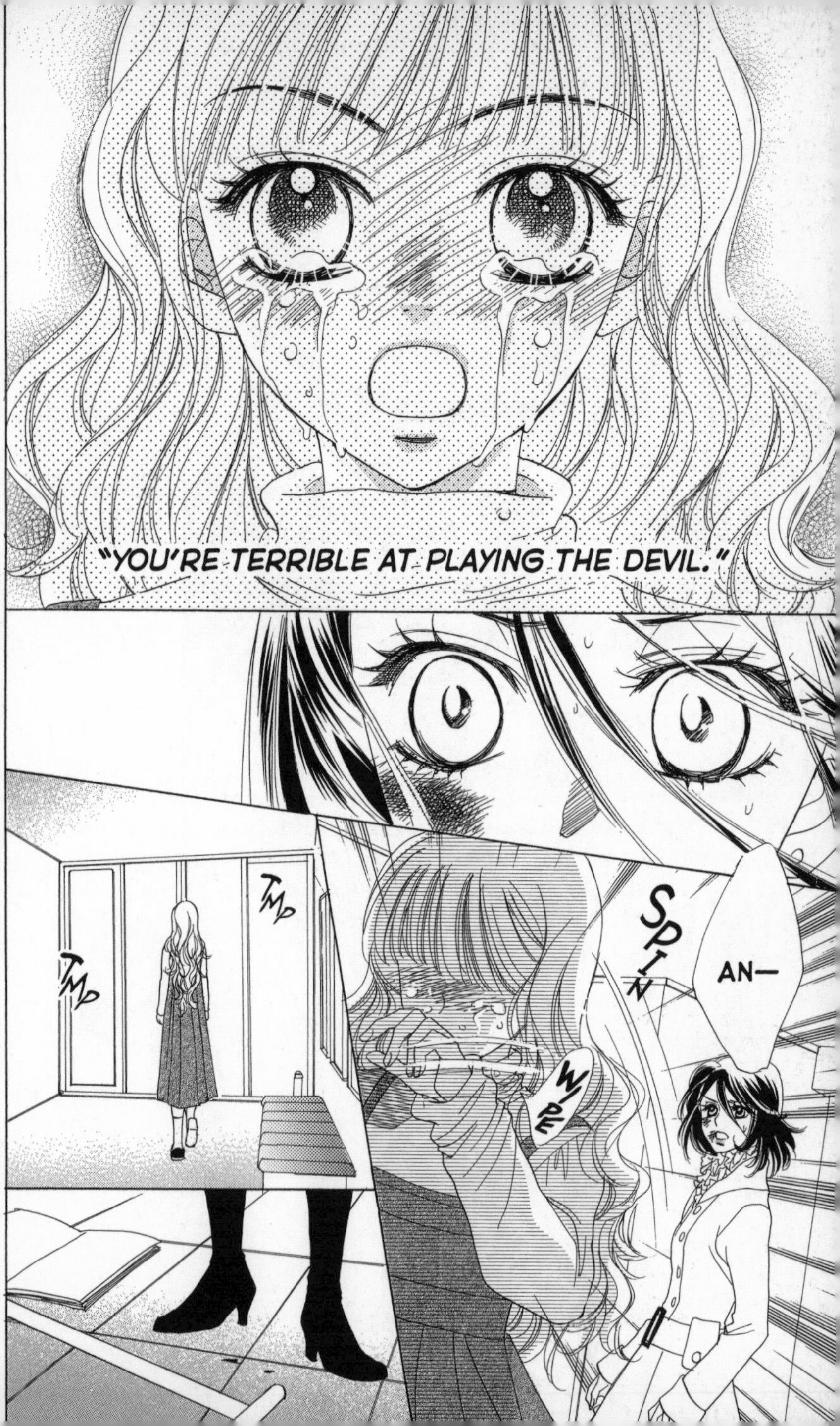
"YOU'RE TERRIBLE AT PLAYING THE DEVIL."
SPIN
AN—
WIPE
TMP
TMP

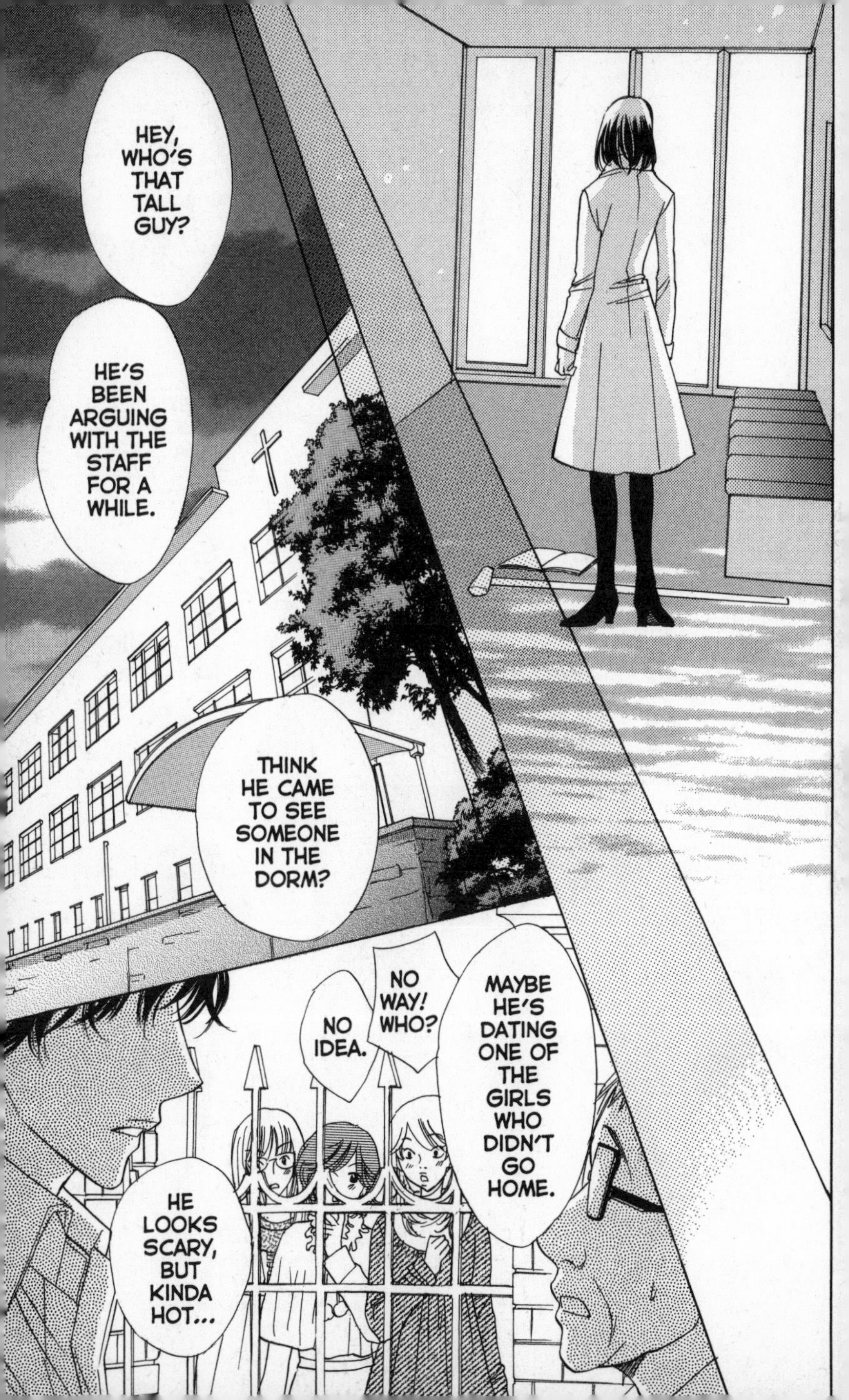
HEY, WHO'S THAT TALL GUY?
HE'S BEEN ARGUING WITH THE STAFF FOR A WHILE.
THINK HE CAME TO SEE SOMEONE IN THE DORM?
MAYBE HE'S DATING ONE OF THE GIRLS WHO DIDN'T GO HOME.
NO WAY! WHO?
NO IDEA.
HE LOOKS SCARY, BUT KINDA HOT...

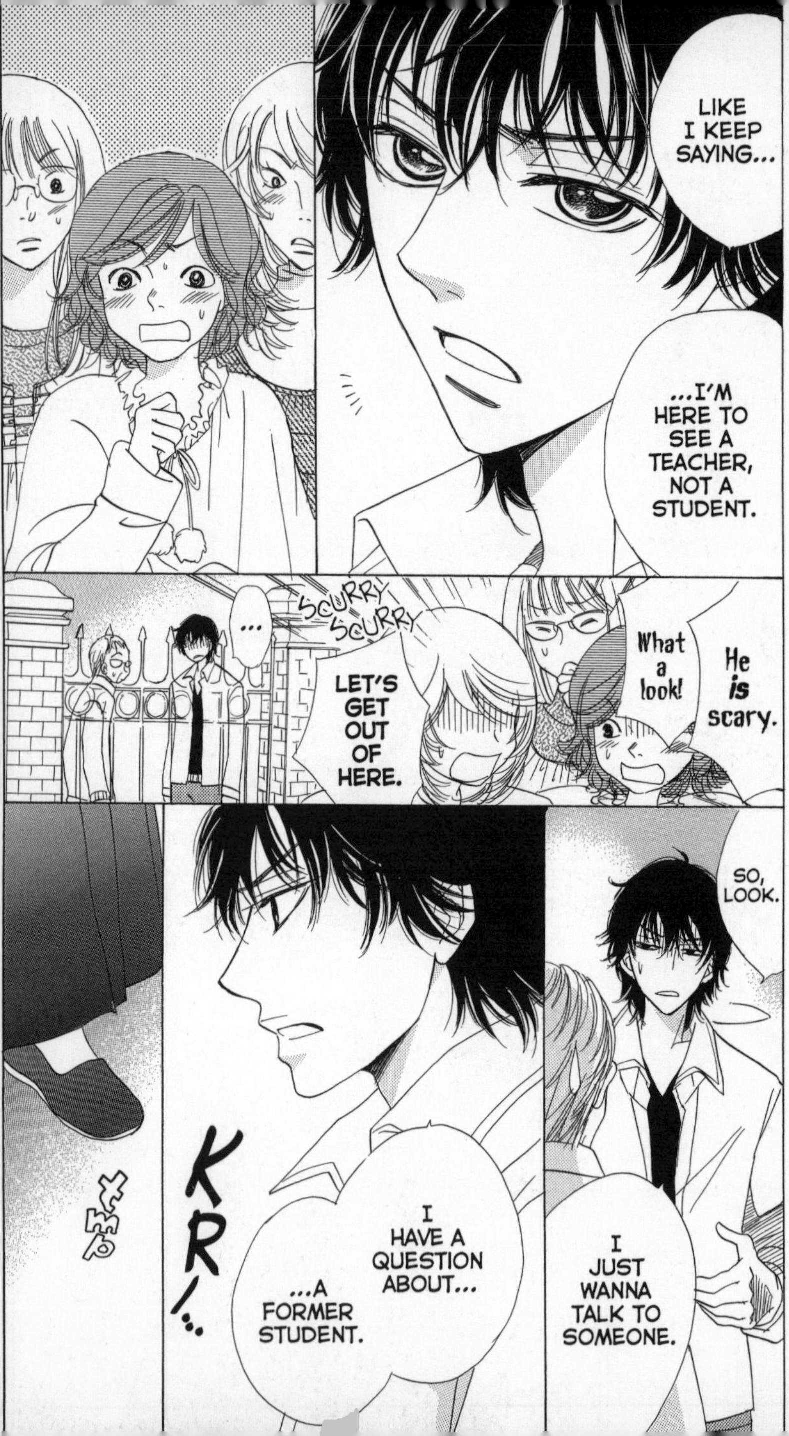
LIKE I KEEP SAYING...
...I'M HERE TO SEE A TEACHER, NOT A STUDENT.
He is scary.
What a look!
SCURRY SCURRY
LET'S GET OUT OF HERE.
...
SO, LOOK.
I JUST WANNA TALK TO SOMEONE.
I HAVE A QUESTION ABOUT...
...A FORMER STUDENT.
KRI...
tmp

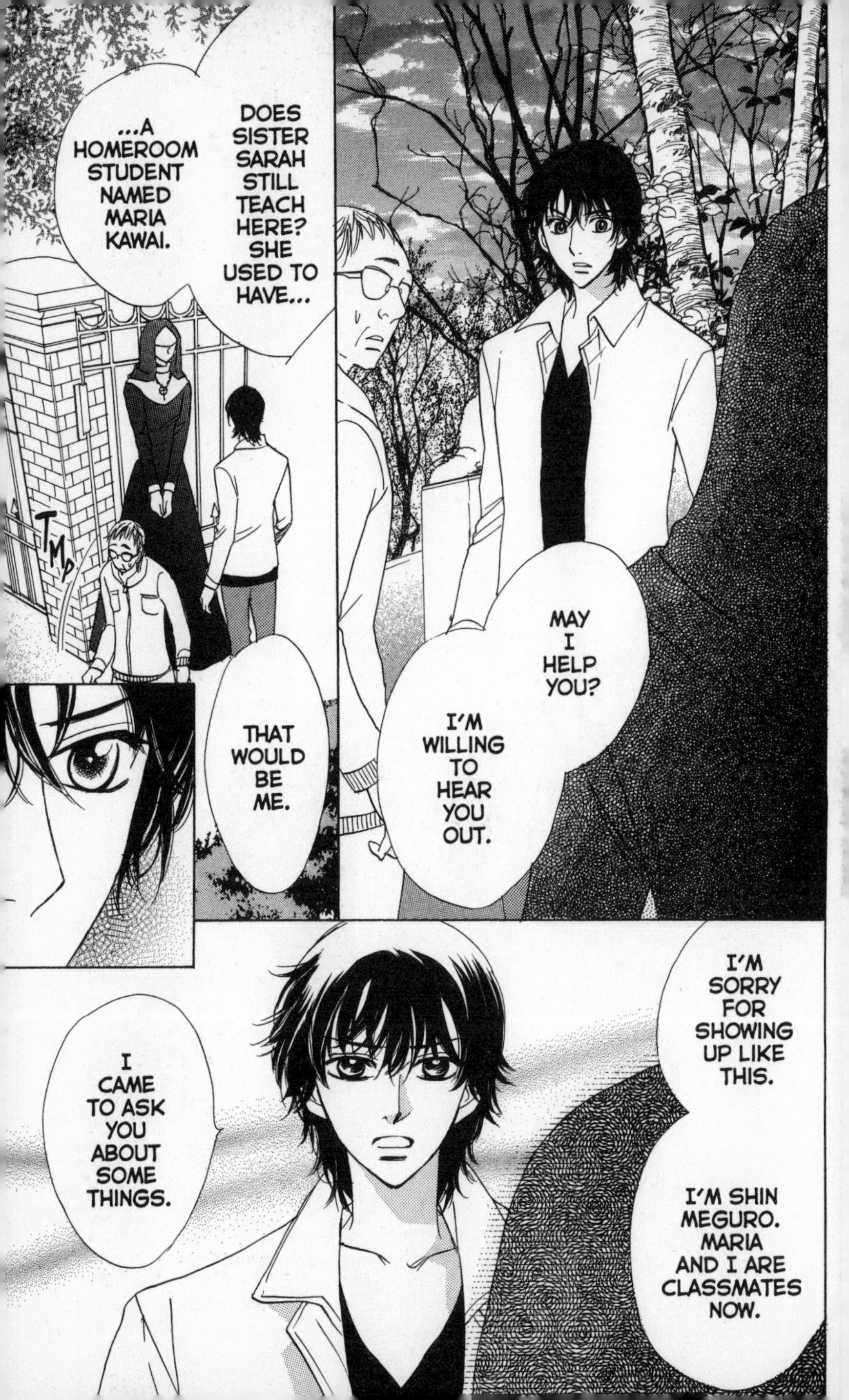
MAY I HELP YOU?
DOES SISTER SARAH STILL TEACH HERE? SHE USED TO HAVE...
...A HOMEROOM STUDENT NAMED MARIA KAWAI.
TMP
THAT WOULD BE ME.
I'M WILLING TO HEAR YOU OUT.
I'M SORRY FOR SHOWING UP LIKE THIS.
I'M SHIN MEGURO. MARIA AND I ARE CLASSMATES NOW.
I CAME TO ASK YOU ABOUT SOME THINGS.

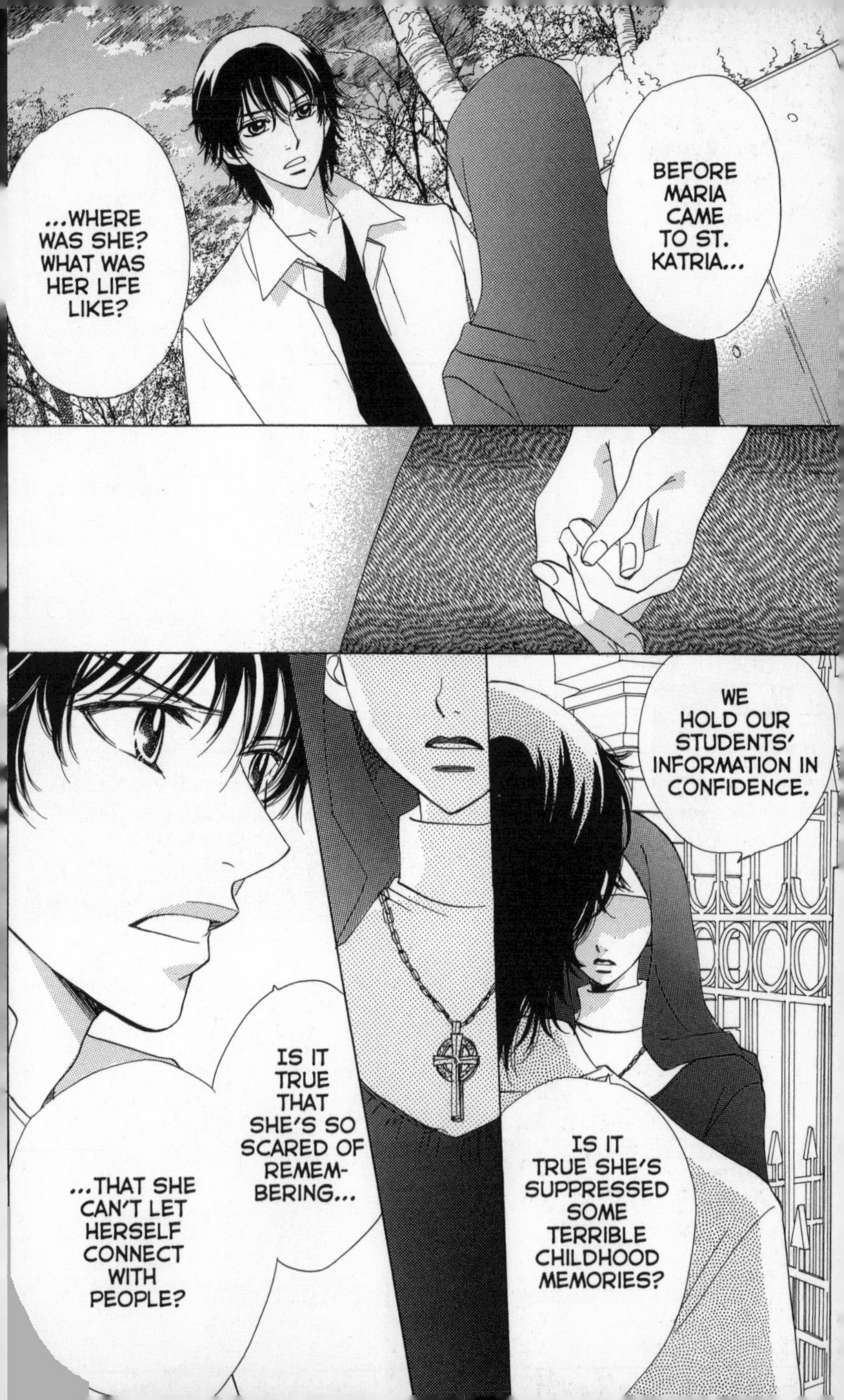
BEFORE MARIA CAME TO ST. KATRIA...
...WHERE WAS SHE? WHAT WAS HER LIFE LIKE?
WE HOLD OUR STUDENTS' INFORMATION IN CONFIDENCE.
IS IT TRUE SHE'S SUPPRESSED SOME TERRIBLE CHILDHOOD MEMORIES?
IS IT TRUE THAT SHE'S SO SCARED OF REMEMBERING...
...THAT SHE CAN'T LET HERSELF CONNECT WITH PEOPLE?

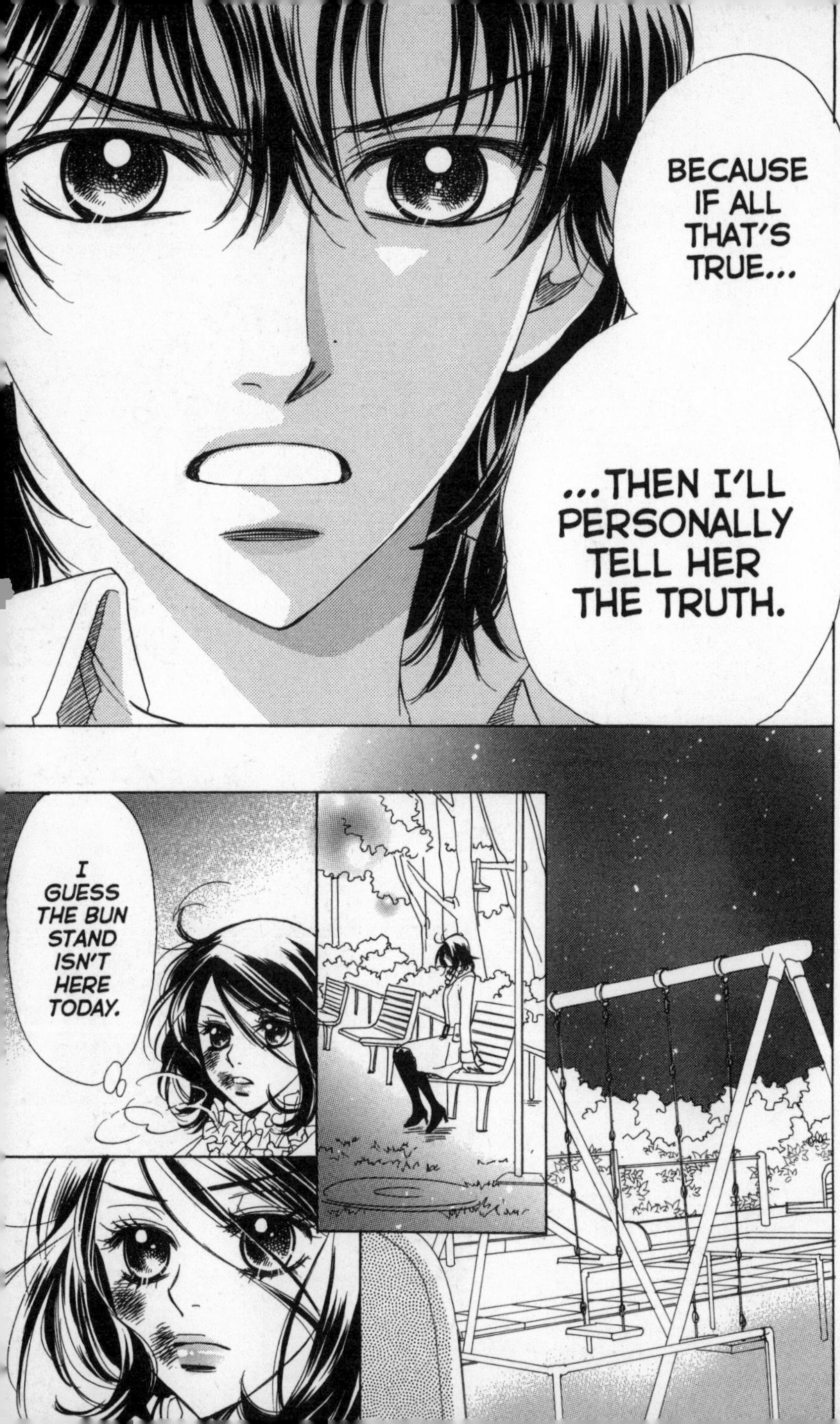
BECAUSE IF ALL THAT'S TRUE...
...THEN I'LL PERSONALLY TELL HER THE TRUTH.
I GUESS THE BUN STAND ISN'T HERE TODAY.

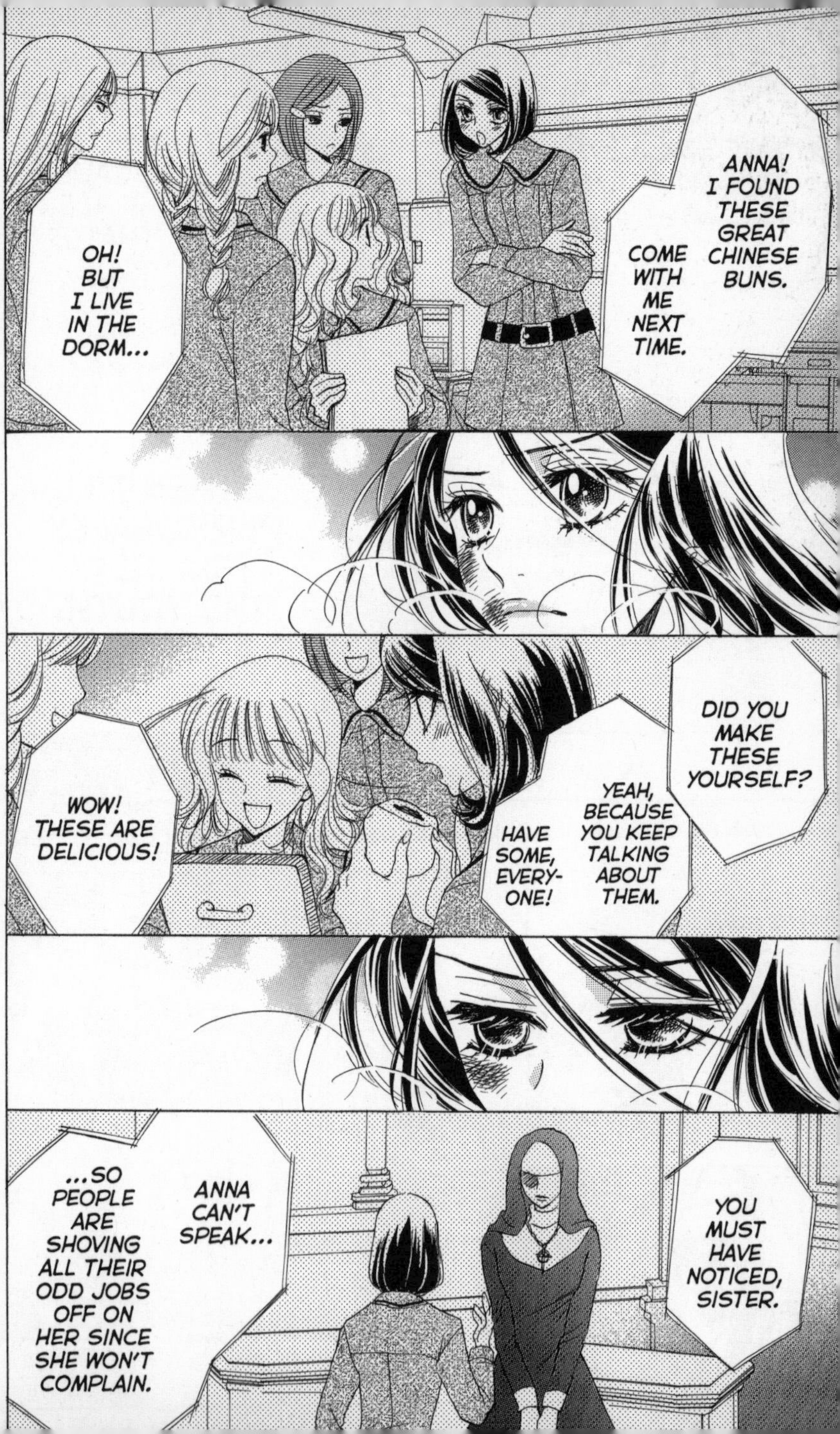
ANNA! I FOUND THESE GREAT CHINESE BUNS.
COME WITH ME NEXT TIME.
OH! BUT I LIVE IN THE DORM...
DID YOU MAKE THESE YOURSELF?
YEAH, BECAUSE YOU KEEP TALKING ABOUT THEM.
HAVE SOME, EVERY-ONE!
WOW! THESE ARE DELICIOUS!
YOU MUST HAVE NOTICED, SISTER.
ANNA CAN'T SPEAK...
...SO PEOPLE ARE SHOVING ALL THEIR ODD JOBS OFF ON HER SINCE SHE WON'T COMPLAIN.

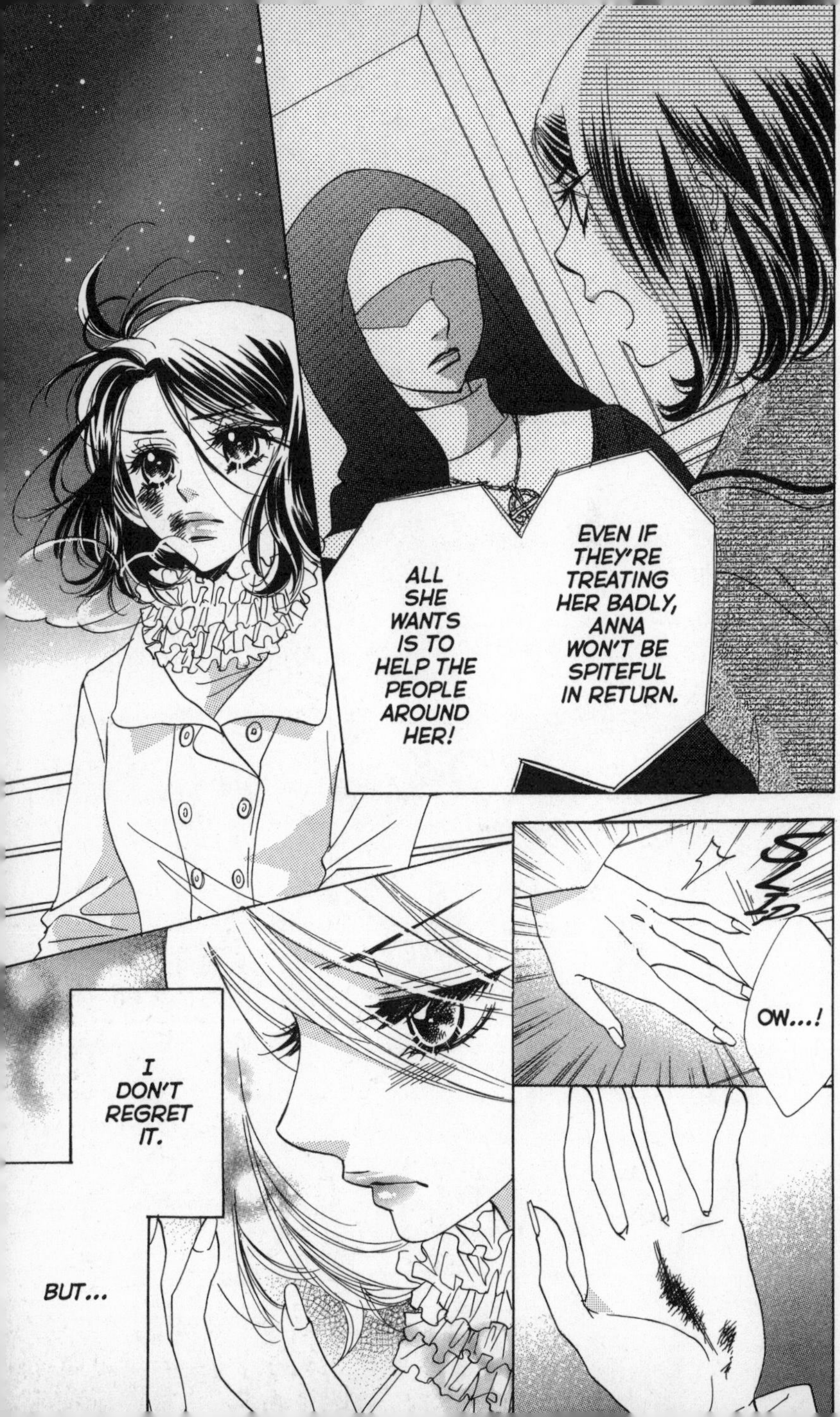

EVEN IF THEY'RE TREATING HER BADLY, ANNA WON'T BE SPITEFUL IN RETURN.
ALL SHE WANTS IS TO HELP THE PEOPLE AROUND HER!
SLIP
OW...!
I DON'T REGRET IT.
BUT...

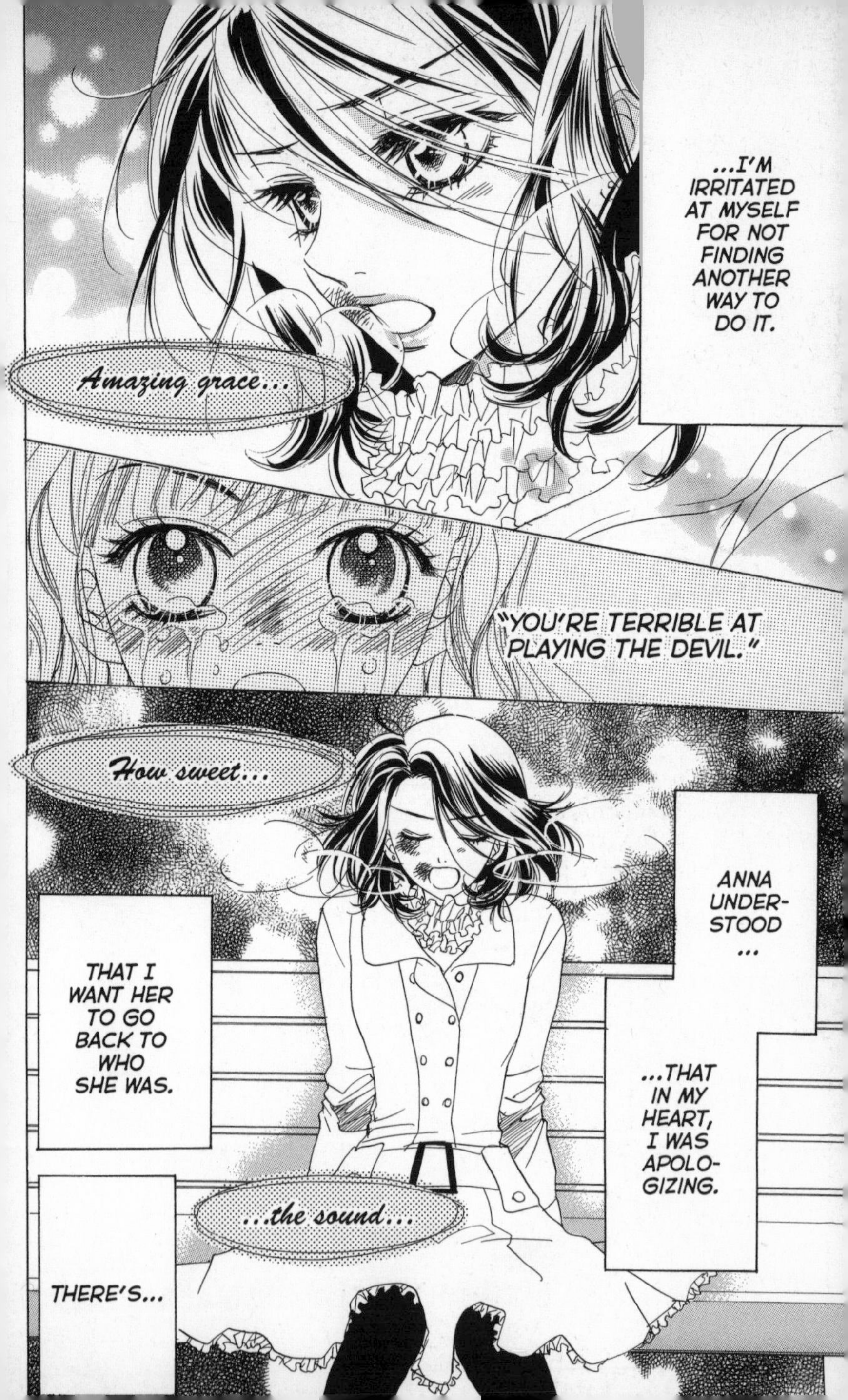
...I'M IRRITATED AT MYSELF FOR NOT FINDING ANOTHER WAY TO DO IT.
Amazing grace...
"YOU'RE TERRIBLE AT PLAYING THE DEVIL."
How sweet...
ANNA UNDER-STOOD...
...THAT IN MY HEART, I WAS APOLO-GIZING.
THAT I WANT HER TO GO BACK TO WHO SHE WAS.
...the sound...
THERE'S...

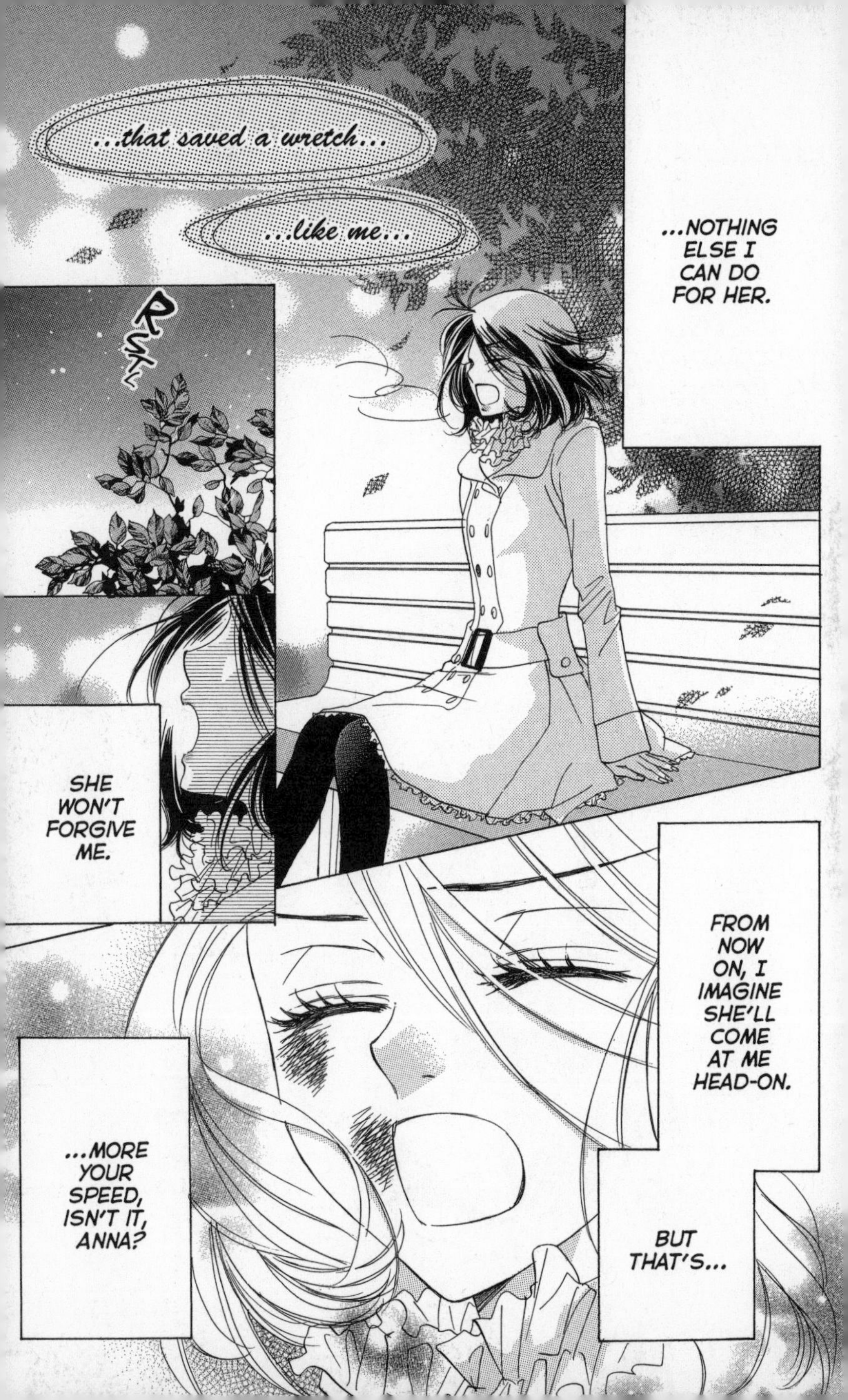
...that saved a wretch...
...like me...
...NOTHING ELSE I CAN DO FOR HER.
RSTL
SHE WON'T FORGIVE ME.
FROM NOW ON, I IMAGINE SHE'LL COME AT ME HEAD-ON.
BUT THAT'S...
...MORE YOUR SPEED, ISN'T IT, ANNA?

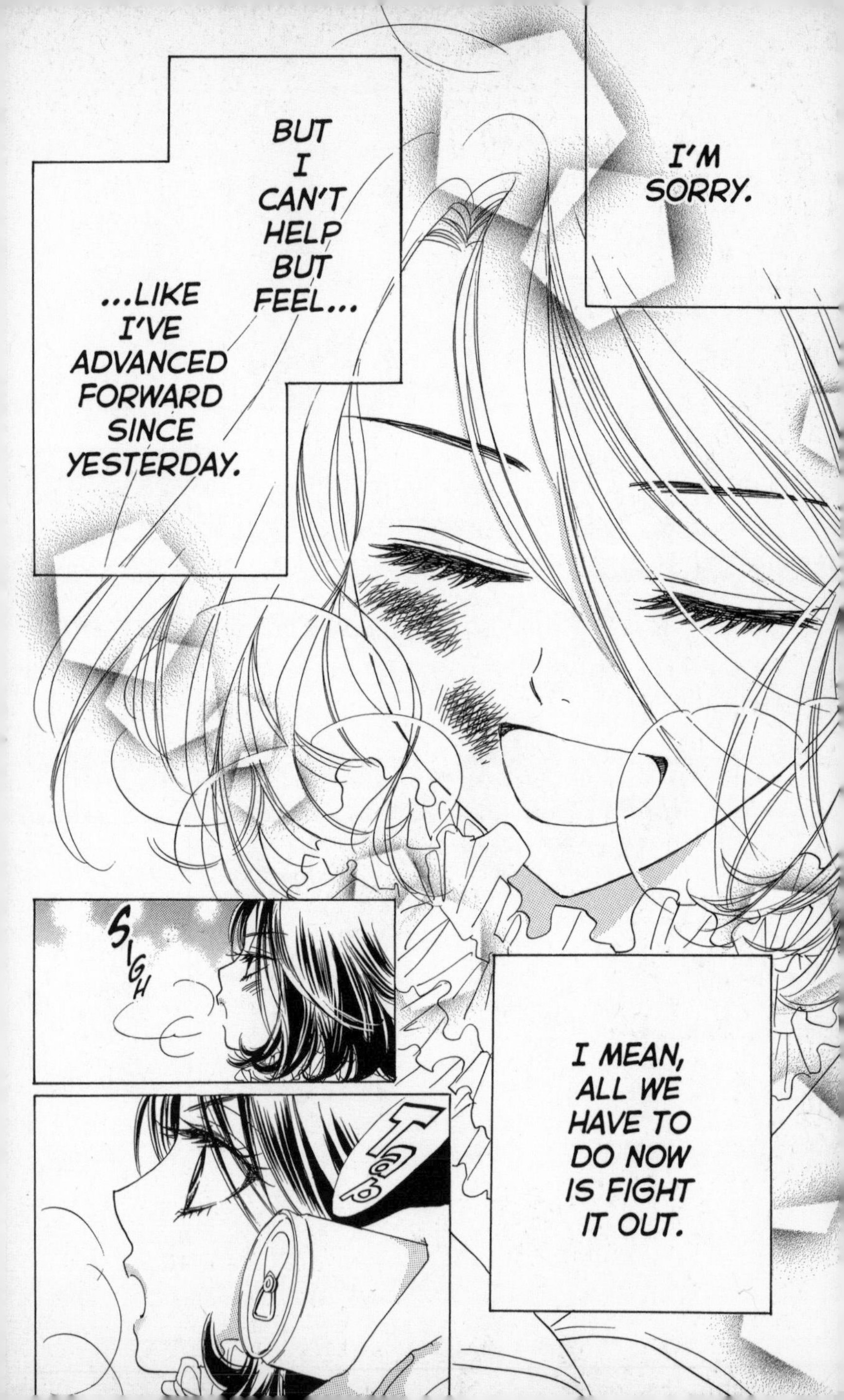
I'M SORRY.
BUT I CAN'T HELP BUT FEEL...
...LIKE I'VE ADVANCED FORWARD SINCE YESTERDAY.
I MEAN, ALL WE HAVE TO DO NOW IS FIGHT IT OUT.
SIGH
Tap

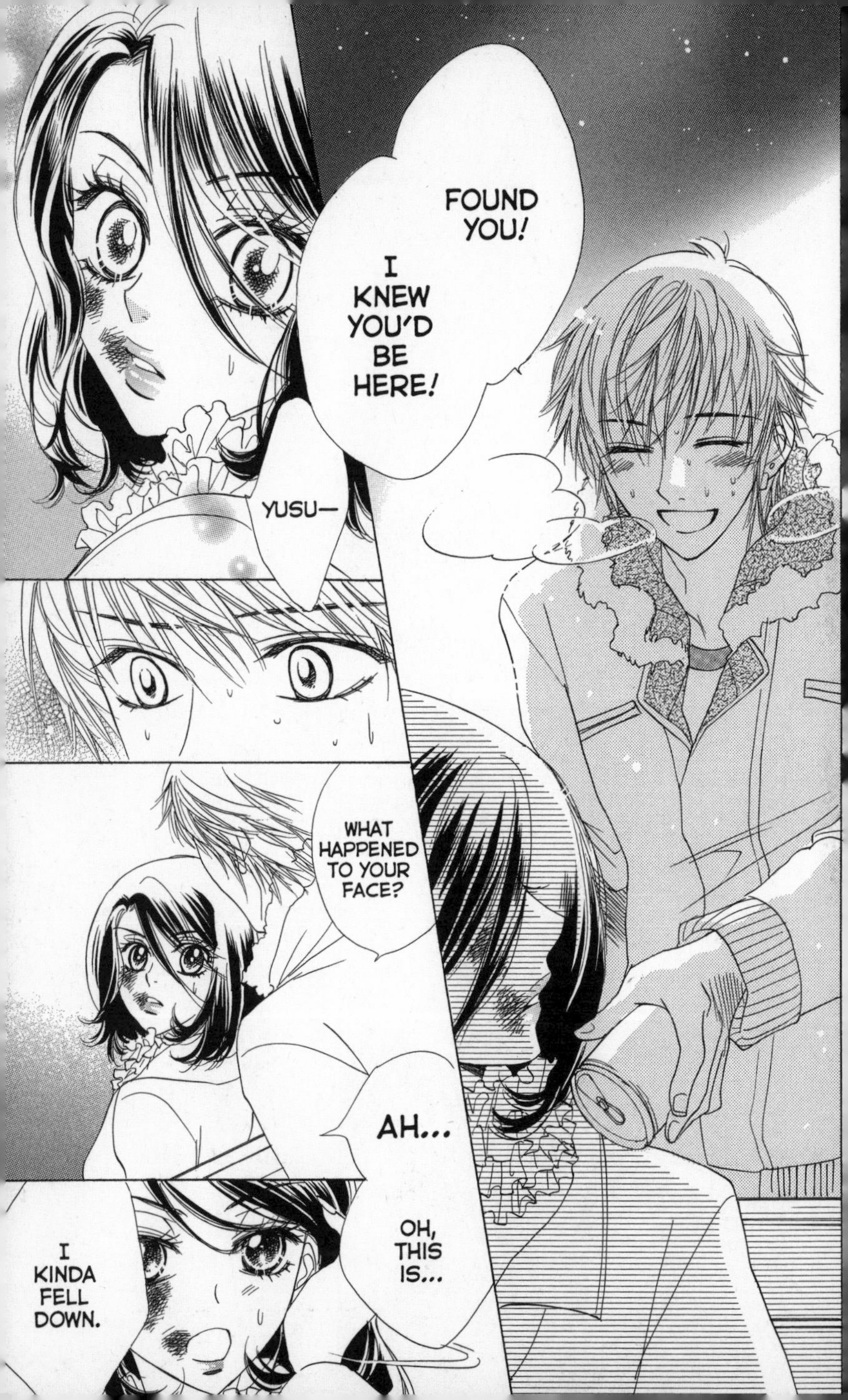
FOUND YOU!
I KNEW YOU'D BE HERE!
YUSU—
WHAT HAPPENED TO YOUR FACE?
AH...
OH, THIS IS...
I KINDA FELL DOWN.

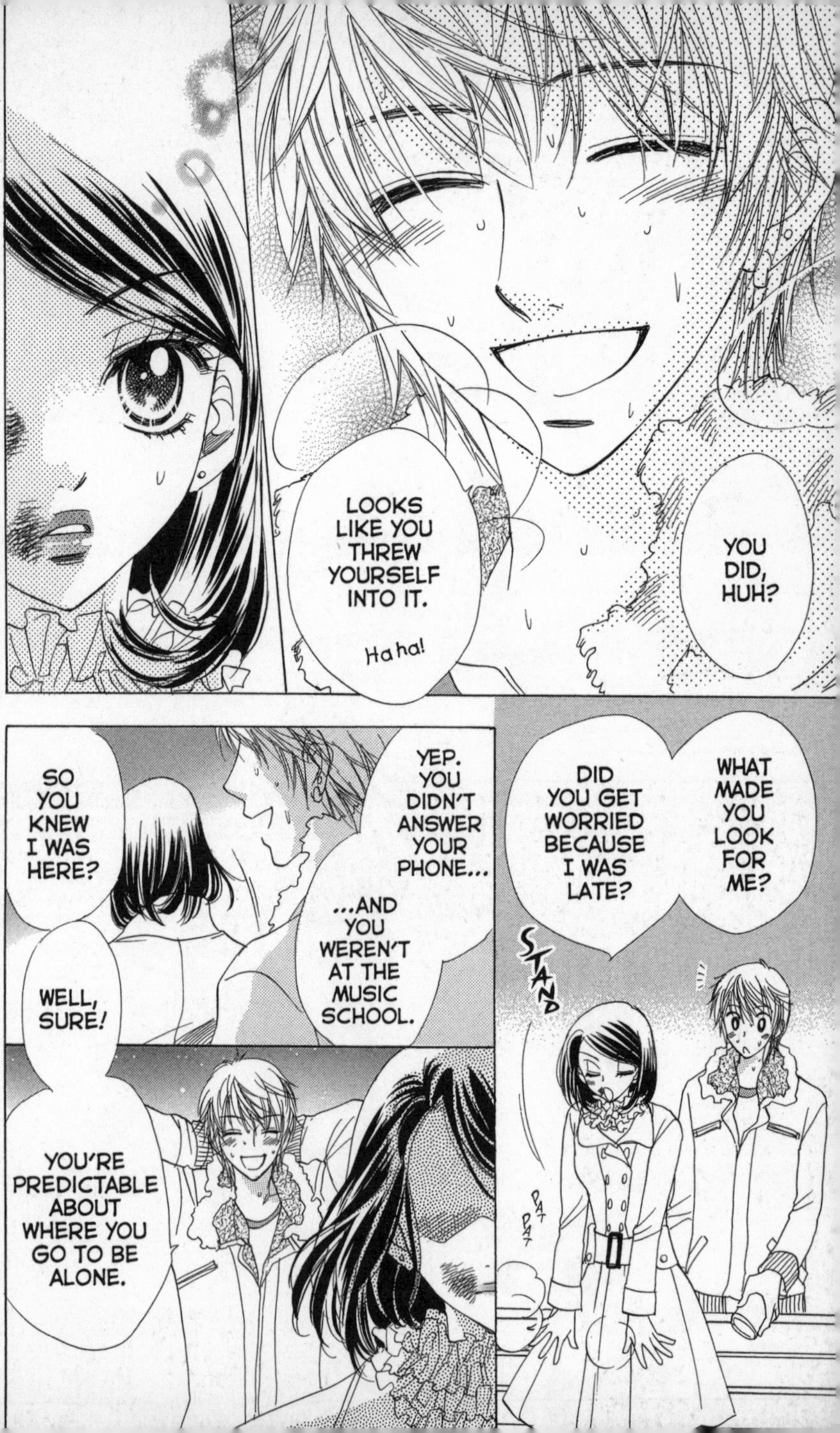
YOU DID, HUH?
LOOKS LIKE YOU THREW YOURSELF INTO IT.
Ha ha!
WHAT MADE YOU LOOK FOR ME?
DID YOU GET WORRIED BECAUSE I WAS LATE?
STAND
PAT PAT
YEP. YOU DIDN'T ANSWER YOUR PHONE...
...AND YOU WEREN'T AT THE MUSIC SCHOOL.
SO YOU KNEW I WAS HERE?
WELL, SURE!
YOU'RE PREDICTABLE ABOUT WHERE YOU GO TO BE ALONE.

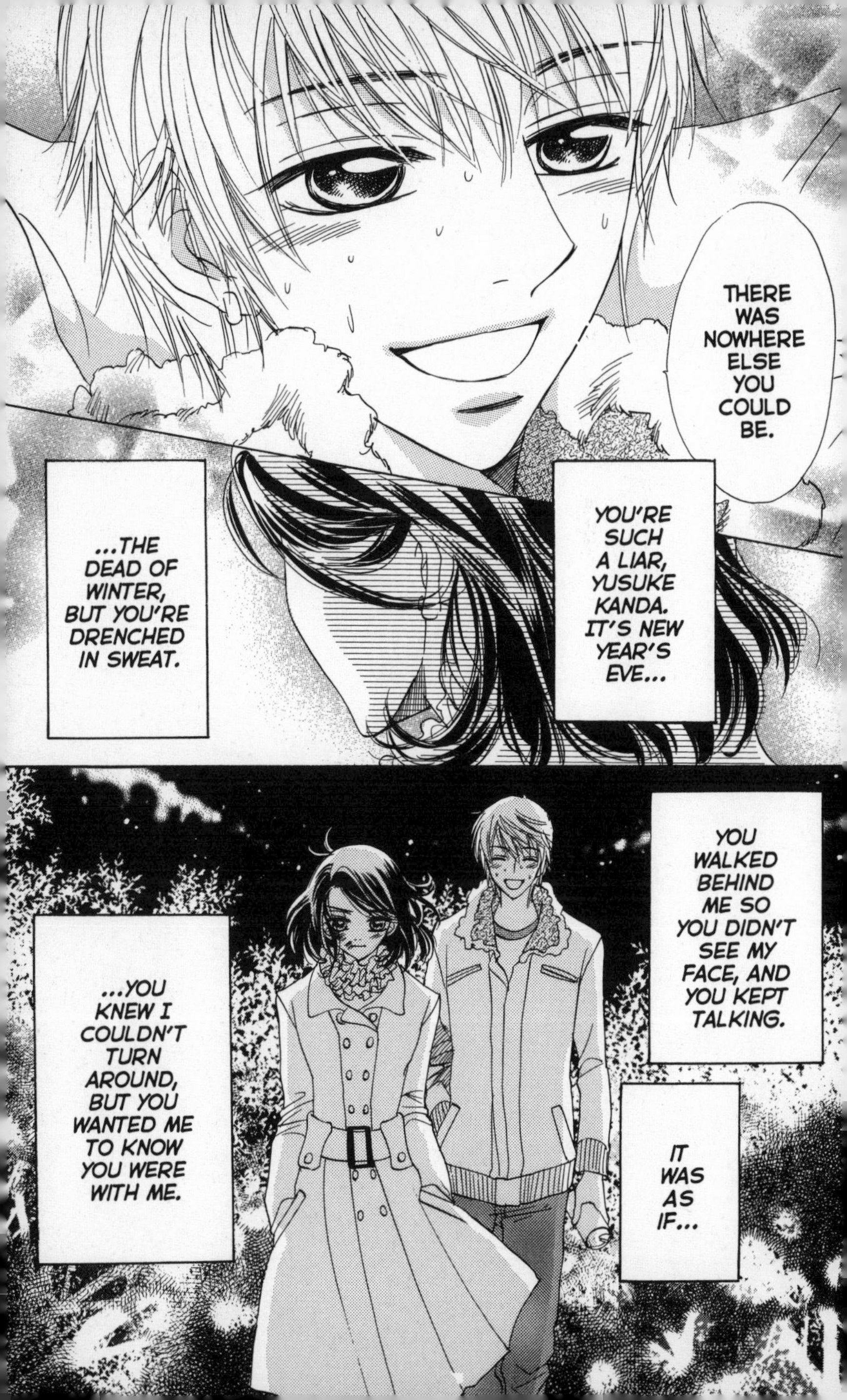
THERE WAS NOWHERE ELSE YOU COULD BE.
YOU'RE SUCH A LIAR, YUSUKE KANDA. IT'S NEW YEAR'S EVE...
...THE DEAD OF WINTER, BUT YOU'RE DRENCHED IN SWEAT.
YOU WALKED BEHIND ME SO YOU DIDN'T SEE MY FACE, AND YOU KEPT TALKING.
IT WAS AS IF...
...YOU KNEW I COULDN'T TURN AROUND, BUT YOU WANTED ME TO KNOW YOU WERE WITH ME.

Continued in volume 7

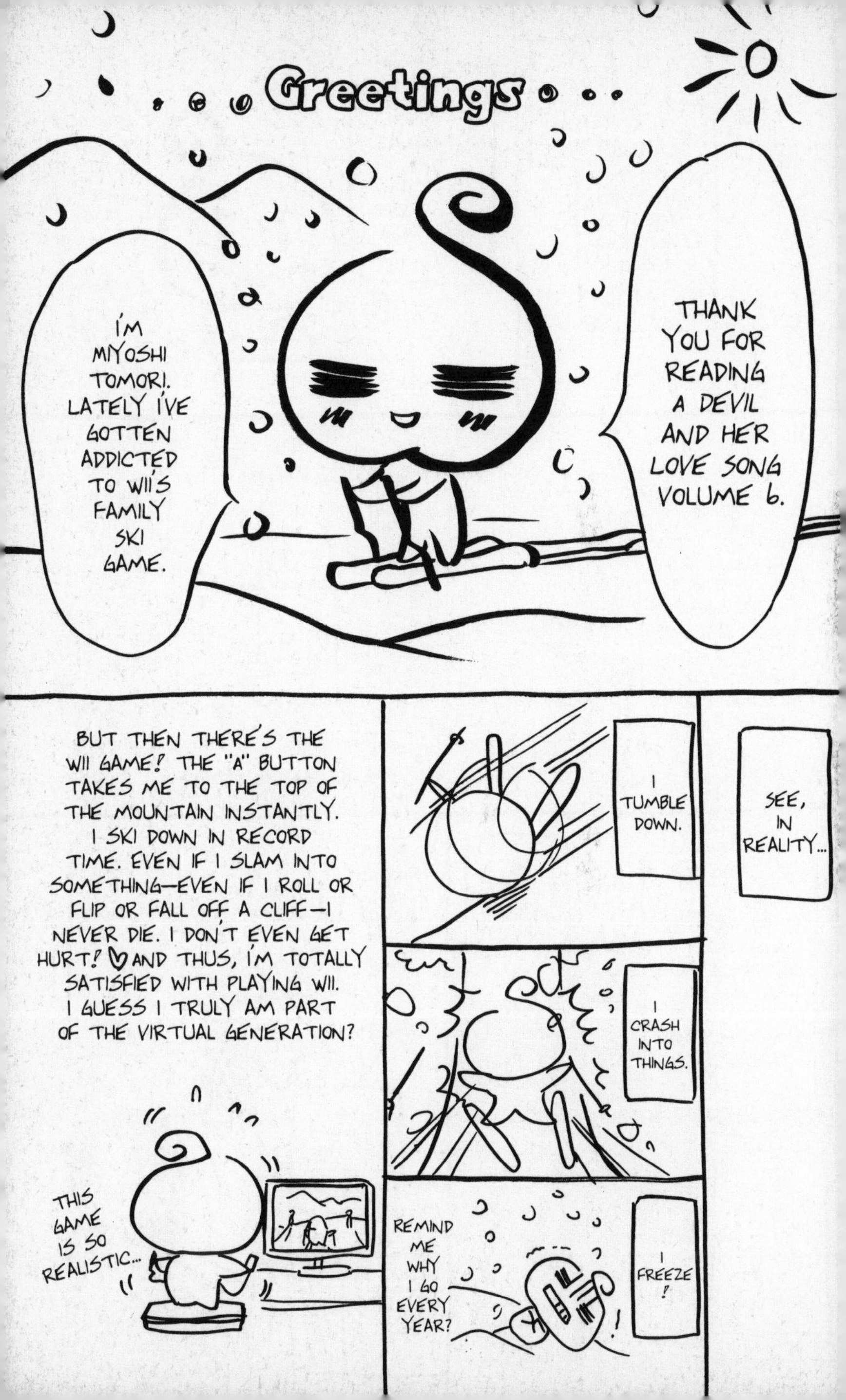
Greetings
THANK YOU FOR READING A DEVIL AND HER LOVE SONG VOLUME 6.
I'M MIYOSHI TOMORI. LATELY I'VE GOTTEN ADDICTED TO WII'S FAMILY SKI GAME.
SEE, IN REALITY...
I TUMBLE DOWN.
I CRASH INTO THINGS.
I FREEZE!
REMIND ME WHY I GO EVERY YEAR?
BUT THEN THERE'S THE WII GAME! THE "A" BUTTON TAKES ME TO THE TOP OF THE MOUNTAIN INSTANTLY. I SKI DOWN IN RECORD TIME. EVEN IF I SLAM INTO SOMETHING—EVEN IF I ROLL OR FLIP OR FALL OFF A CLIFF—I NEVER DIE. I DON'T EVEN GET HURT! ♡ AND THUS, I'M TOTALLY SATISFIED WITH PLAYING WII. I GUESS I TRULY AM PART OF THE VIRTUAL GENERATION?
THIS GAME IS SO REALISTIC...

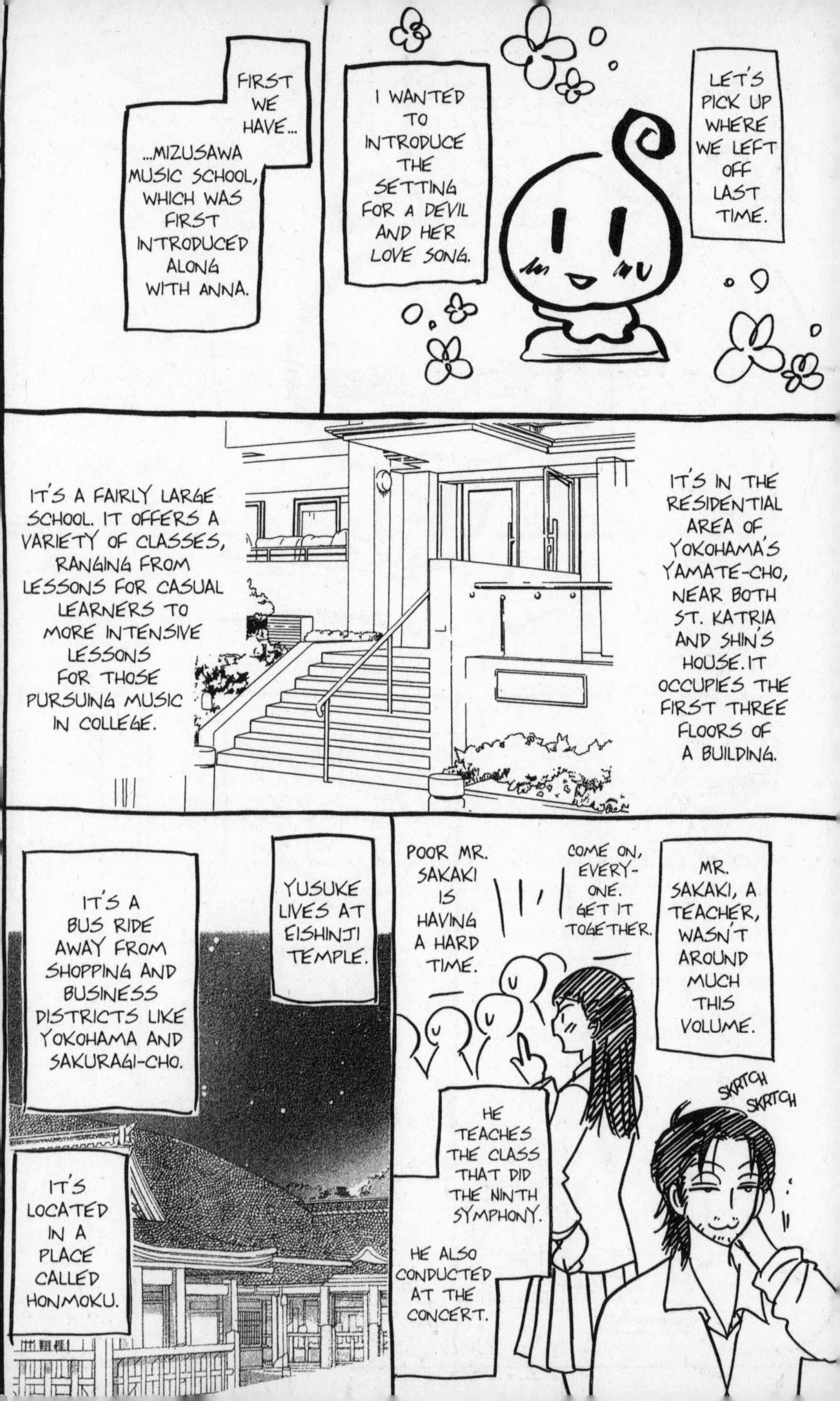
LET'S PICK UP WHERE WE LEFT OFF LAST TIME.
I WANTED TO INTRODUCE THE SETTING FOR A DEVIL AND HER LOVE SONG.
FIRST WE HAVE...
...MIZUSAWA MUSIC SCHOOL, WHICH WAS FIRST INTRODUCED ALONG WITH ANNA.
IT'S IN THE RESIDENTIAL AREA OF YOKOHAMA'S YAMATE-CHO, NEAR BOTH ST. KATRIA AND SHIN'S HOUSE. IT OCCUPIES THE FIRST THREE FLOORS OF A BUILDING.
IT'S A FAIRLY LARGE SCHOOL. IT OFFERS A VARIETY OF CLASSES, RANGING FROM LESSONS FOR CASUAL LEARNERS TO MORE INTENSIVE LESSONS FOR THOSE PURSUING MUSIC IN COLLEGE.
MR. SAKAKI, A TEACHER, WASN'T AROUND MUCH THIS VOLUME.
COME ON, EVERYONE. GET IT TOGETHER.
POOR MR. SAKAKI IS HAVING A HARD TIME.
SKRTCH SKRTCH
HE TEACHES THE CLASS THAT DID THE NINTH SYMPHONY.
HE ALSO CONDUCTED AT THE CONCERT.
YUSUKE LIVES AT EISHINJI TEMPLE.
IT'S A BUS RIDE AWAY FROM SHOPPING AND BUSINESS DISTRICTS LIKE YOKOHAMA AND SAKURAGI-CHO.
IT'S LOCATED IN A PLACE CALLED HONMOKU.

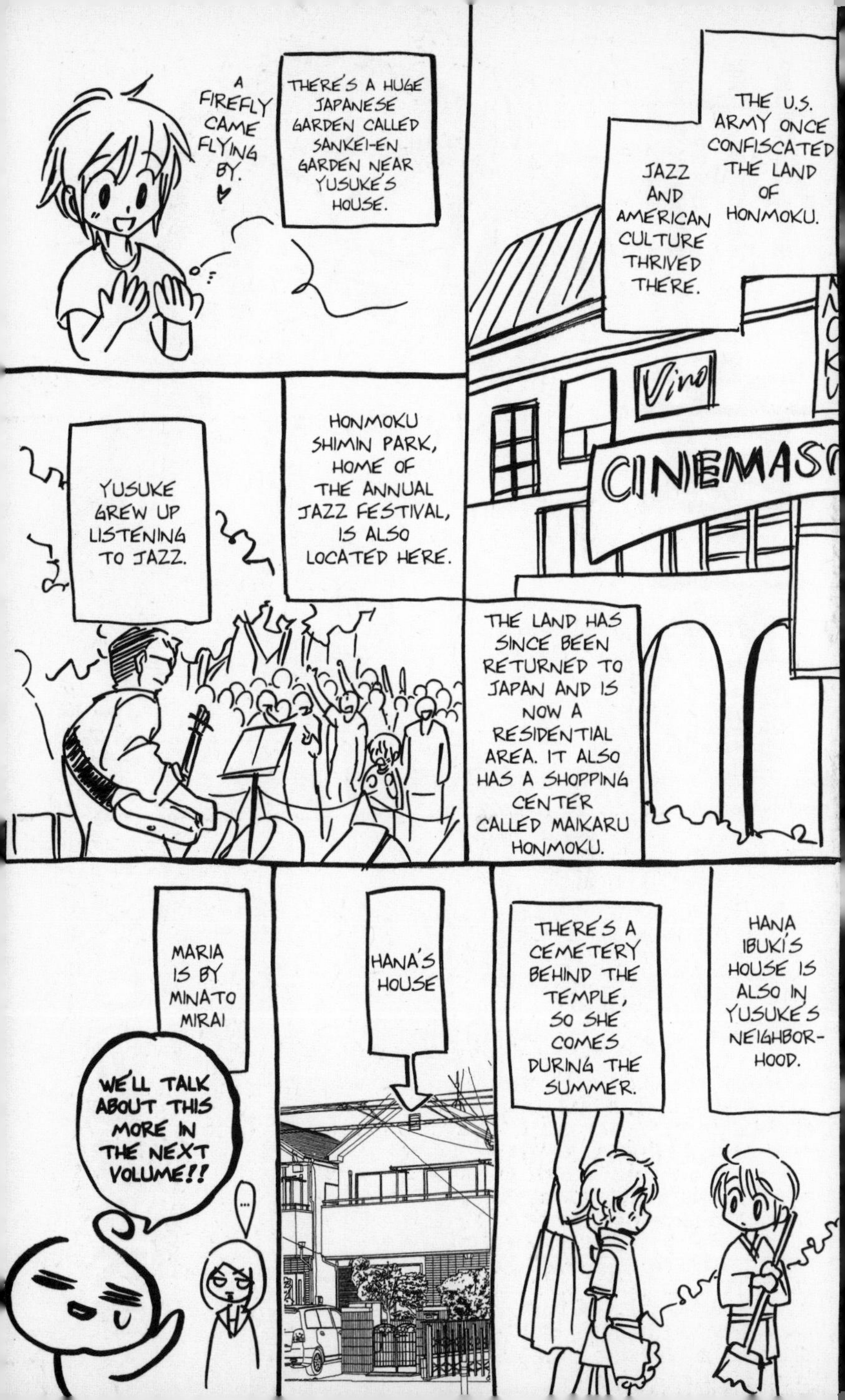
THE U.S. ARMY ONCE CONFISCATED THE LAND OF HONMOKU.
JAZZ AND AMERICAN CULTURE THRIVED THERE.
Vino
THE LAND HAS SINCE BEEN RETURNED TO JAPAN AND IS NOW A RESIDENTIAL AREA. IT ALSO HAS A SHOPPING CENTER CALLED MAIKARU HONMOKU.
THERE'S A HUGE JAPANESE GARDEN CALLED SANKEI-EN GARDEN NEAR YUSUKE'S HOUSE.
A FIREFLY CAME FLYING BY. ♥
HONMOKU SHIMIN PARK, HOME OF THE ANNUAL JAZZ FESTIVAL, IS ALSO LOCATED HERE.
YUSUKE GREW UP LISTENING TO JAZZ.
HANA IBUKI'S HOUSE IS ALSO IN YUSUKE'S NEIGHBOR-HOOD.
THERE'S A CEMETERY BEHIND THE TEMPLE, SO SHE COMES DURING THE SUMMER.
HANA'S HOUSE
MARIA IS BY MINATO MIRAI
WE'LL TALK ABOUT THIS MORE IN THE NEXT VOLUME!!
...

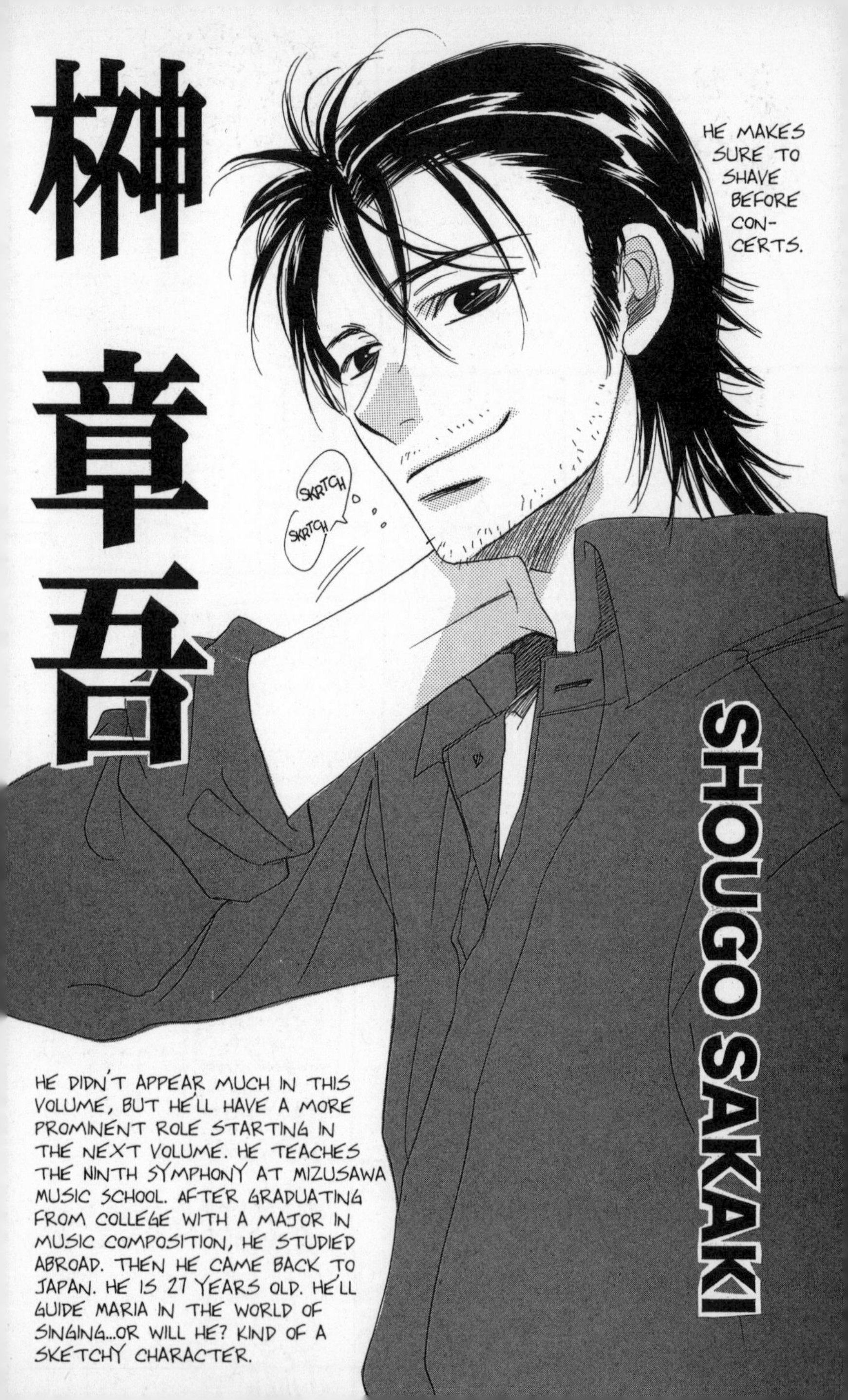
HE MAKES SURE TO SHAVE BEFORE CON-CERTS.
SHOUGO SAKAKI
SKRTCH
SKRTCH
榊章吾
HE DIDN'T APPEAR MUCH IN THIS VOLUME, BUT HE'LL HAVE A MORE PROMINENT ROLE STARTING IN THE NEXT VOLUME. HE TEACHES THE NINTH SYMPHONY AT MIZUSAWA MUSIC SCHOOL. AFTER GRADUATING FROM COLLEGE WITH A MAJOR IN MUSIC COMPOSITION, HE STUDIED ABROAD. THEN HE CAME BACK TO JAPAN. HE IS 27 YEARS OLD. HE'LL GUIDE MARIA IN THE WORLD OF SINGING...OR WILL HE? KIND OF A SKETCHY CHARACTER.

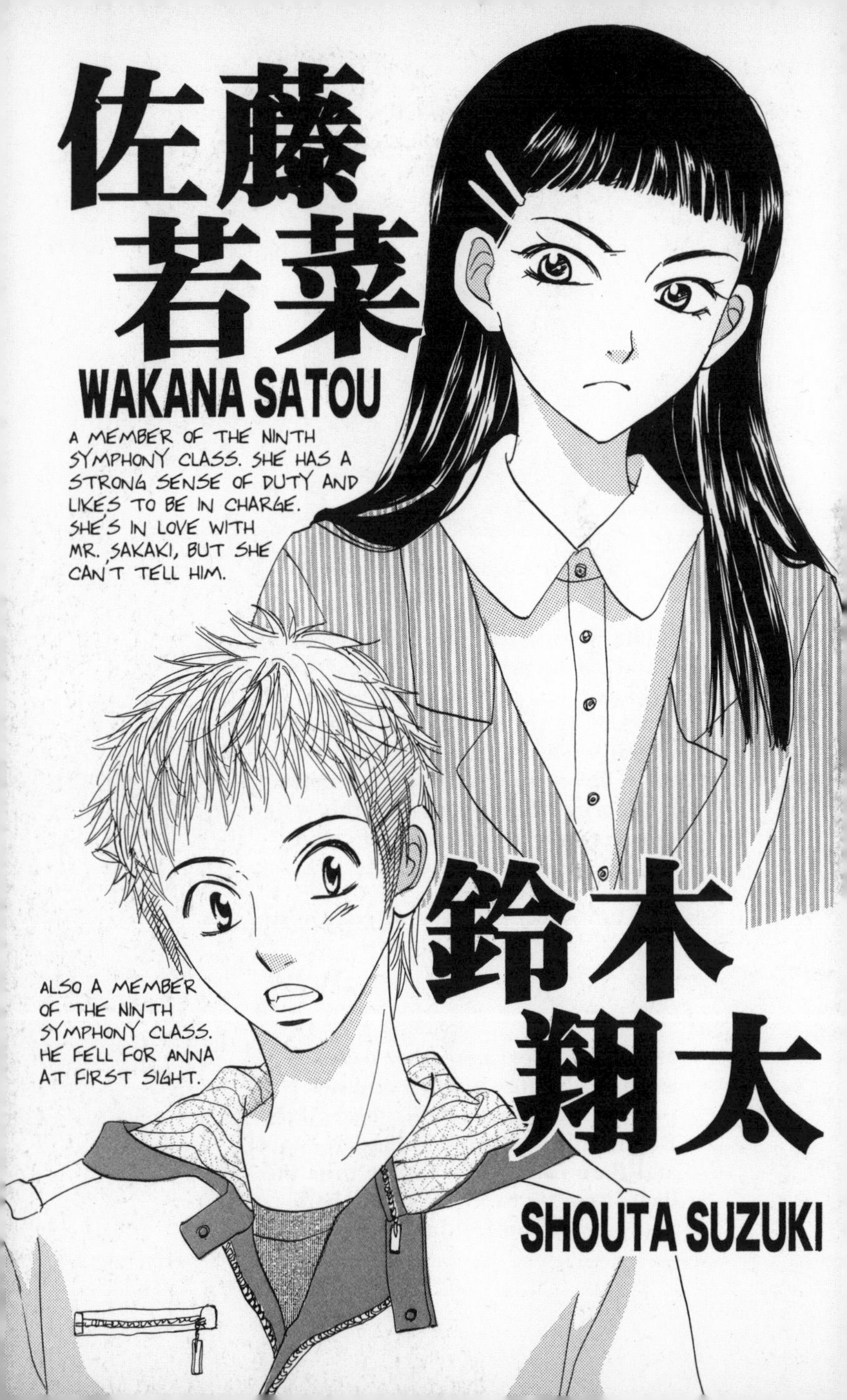
佐藤若菜
WAKANA SATOU
A MEMBER OF THE NINTH SYMPHONY CLASS. SHE HAS A STRONG SENSE OF DUTY AND LIKES TO BE IN CHARGE. SHE'S IN LOVE WITH MR. SAKAKI, BUT SHE CAN'T TELL HIM.
鈴木翔太
SHOUTA SUZUKI
ALSO A MEMBER OF THE NINTH SYMPHONY CLASS. HE FELL FOR ANNA AT FIRST SIGHT.

While writing this story, I accidentally sliced my finger with a paper cutter, requiring ten stitches. I was more shocked by the sight of the gaping wound than the pain and fainted dead away, like some European aristocrat in a period film. Because of this incident, my friends enjoyed calling me "Elizabeth" for a while...

-Miyoshi Tomori

Miyoshi Tomori made her debut as a manga creator in 2001, and her previous titles include *Hatsukare* (First Boyfriend), *Tongari Root* (Square Root), and *Brass Love!!* In her spare time she likes listening to music in the bath and playing musical instruments.

A DEVIL AND HER LOVE SONG
Volume 6
Shojo Beat Edition

STORY AND ART BY
MIYOSHI TOMORI

English Adaptation/Ysabet MacFarlane
Translation/JN Productions
Touch-up Art & Lettering/Monalisa de Asis
Design/Courtney Utt
Editor/Amy Yu

AKUMA TO LOVE SONG © 2006 by Miyoshi Tomori
All rights reserved. First published in Japan in 2006
by SHUEISHA Inc., Tokyo.
English translation rights arranged
by SHUEISHA Inc.

Printed in the U.S.A.

Published by VIZ Media, LLC
P.O. Box 77010
San Francisco, CA 94107

10 9 8 7 6 5 4 3 2 1
First printing, December 2012

www.viz.com   www.shojobeat.com

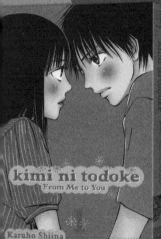

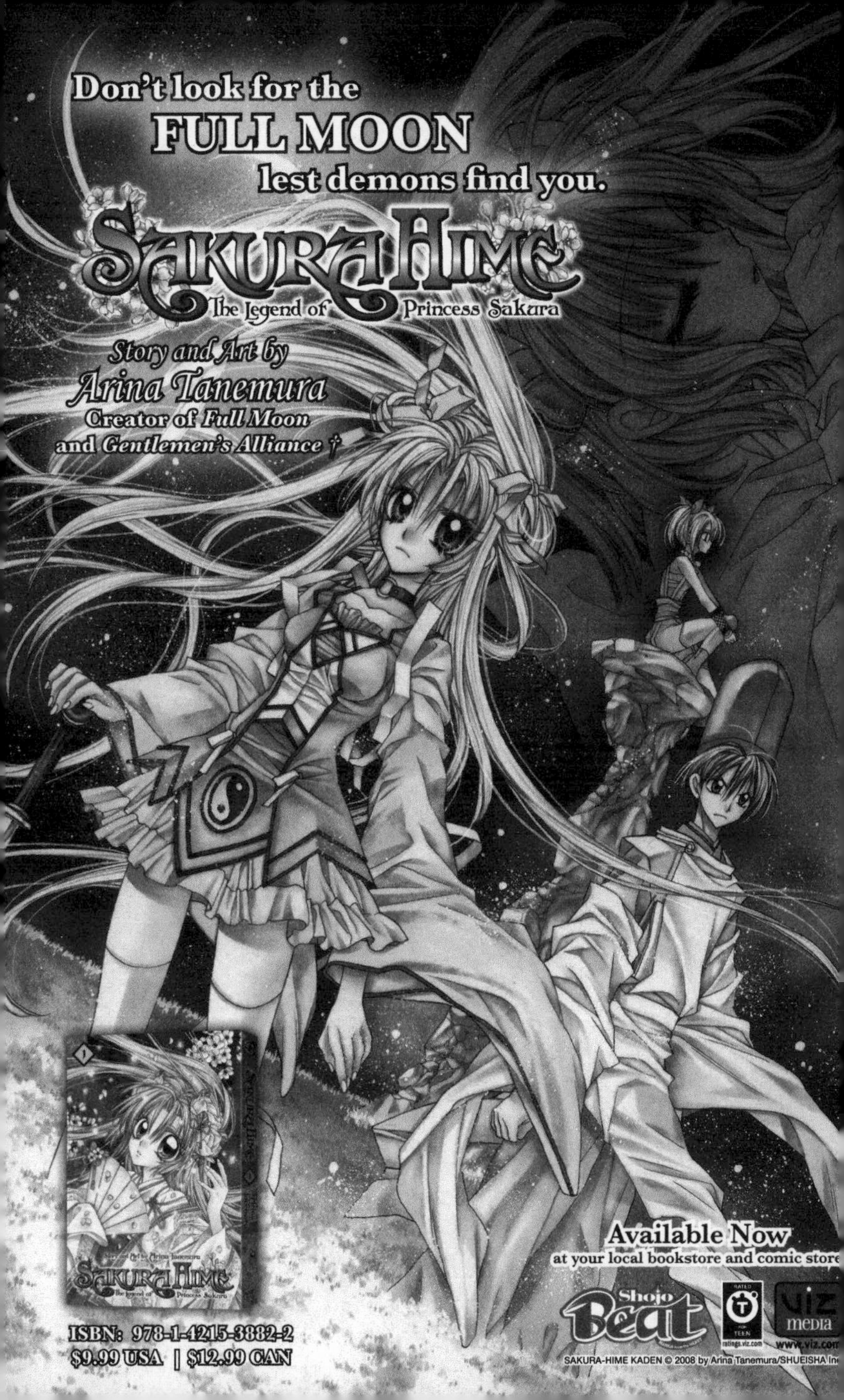

Don't look for the
FULL MOON
lest demons find you.
SAKURA HIME
The Legend of Princess Sakura
Story and Art by
Arina Tanemura
Creator of Full Moon
and Gentlemen's Alliance †
ISBN: 978-1-4215-3882-2
$9.99 USA | $12.99 CAN
Available Now
at your local bookstore and comic store
Shojo Beat
RATED T TEEN
VIZ media
www.viz.com
SAKURA-HIME KADEN © 2008 by Arina Tanemura/SHUEISHA Inc.

Surprise!

You may be reading the wrong way!

It's true: In keeping with the original Japanese comic format, this book reads from right to left—so action, sound effects, and word balloons are completely reversed. This preserves the orientation of the original artwork—plus, it's fun! Check out the diagram shown here to get the hang of things, and then turn to the other side of the book to get started!

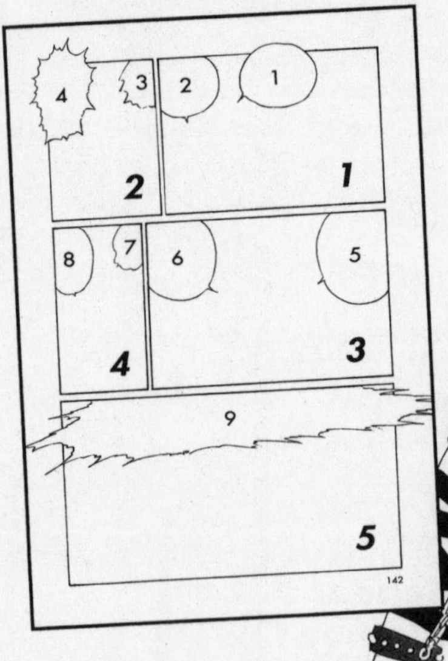
1
2
1
3
4
2
5
6
3
7
8
4
9
5
142

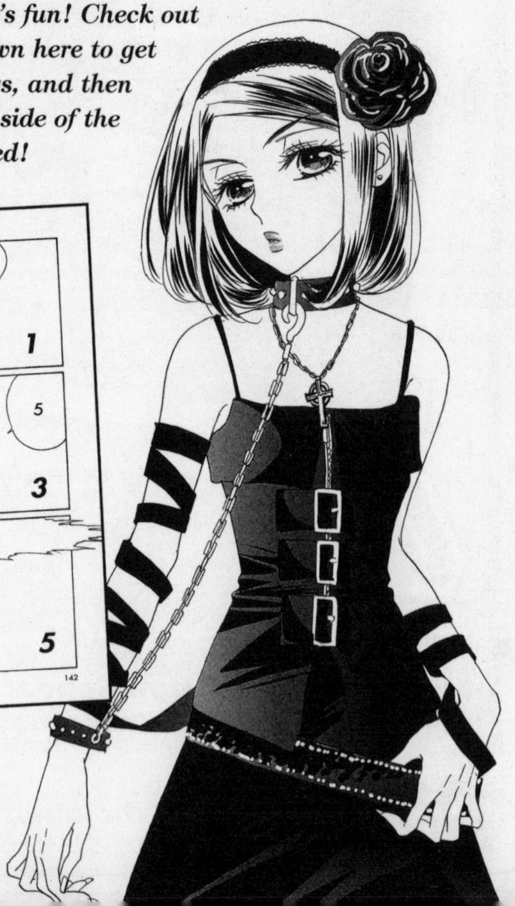